THE
DREAMWEAVERS

ALSO BY THE AUTHORS
*Science Fiction Filmmaking in the 1980: Interviews
with Actors, Directors, Producers and Writers*

THE DREAMWEAVERS

INTERVIEWS WITH FANTASY
FILMMAKERS OF THE 1980S

LEE GOLDBERG, RANDY LOFFICIER,
JEAN-MARC LOFFICIER,
WILLIAM RABKIN

Copyright © 1995 Lee Goldberg, Randy & Jean-Marc Lofficier, William Rabkin.
All Rights Reserved

No part of this book may be reproduced, or stored in a retrieval system, or transmitted in any form or by any means, electronic, mechanical, photocopying, recording, or otherwise, without express written permission of the publisher

ISBN-13: 978-1-954840-88-1

Published by
Cutting Edge Books
PO Box 8212
Calabasas, CA 91372
www.cuttingedgebooks.com

TABLE OF CONTENTS

ACKNOWLEDGMENTS	ix
PREFACE	xiii
FOREWORD: *Moving Pictures* by Marv Wolfman	xv
The Adventures of Buckaroo Banzai (1984)	1
Back to the Future (1985)	26
Big Trouble in Little China (1986)	51
Conan the Destroyer (1984)	61
The Dead Zone (1983) / *Videodrome* (1983)	76
Ghostbusters (1984)	100
The Golden Child (1986)	145
The Goonies (1985)	156
Gremlins (1984)	163
Highlander (1986)	195
Howard the Duck (1986)	205
The James Bond Films (1980–1989)	226
Ladyhawke (1985)	267
The Lost Boys (1987)	297
A Nightmare on Elm Street (1984)	313
Something Wicked This Way Comes (1983)	337

ACKNOWLEDGMENTS

The chapters in this book are culled from articles written by the authors in various publications, as follows.

The Adventures of Buckaroo Banzai   Interview with Earl Mac Rauch: Goldberg, Lee, *Starlog* #84, July 1984. Interview with W.D. Richter: Goldberg, Lee, *Starlog* #89, December 1984. Interview with Peter Weller: Goldberg, Lee, *Starlog* #86, September 1984.

Back to the Future   On the set of *Back to the Future:* Goldberg, Lee, *Starlog* #97, August 1985. Interview with Robert Zemeckis: Goldberg, Lee, *Starlog* #85, August 1984; Goldberg, Lee, *Starlog* #97, August 1985; Goldberg, Lee, *Starlog* #99, October 1985. Interview with Michael J. Fox: Goldberg, Lee, *Starlog* #98, September 1985.

Big Trouble in Little China   On the set of *Big Trouble in Little China* : Goldberg, Lee, *Starlog* #106, May 1986.

Conan the Destroyer   Interview with Arnold Schwarzenegger: Lofficier, Randy & Jean-Marc, *L'Ecran Fantastique* #48, September 1984. Lofficier, Randy & Jean-Marc, *Best of Starlog* #7, 1986.

The Dead Zone   Interview with David Cronenberg: Lofficier, Randy & Jean-Marc, *L'Ecran Fantastique* #35, June 1983; Lofficier, Randy & Jean-Marc, *L'Ecran Fantastique* #39, November 1983; Lofficier, Randy & Jean-Marc, *Bloody Best of Fangoria*, Vol. 5, 1986.

Ghostbusters Interview with Ivan Reitman: Lofficier, Randy & Jean-Marc, *Enterprise Incidents* #21, September 1984; Lofficier, Randy & Jean-Marc, *L'Ecran Fantastique* #50, November 1984. Interview with Richard Edlund, Laszlo Kovacs: Lofficier, Randy & Jean-Marc, *American Cinematographer*, Vol. 65, No. 6, June 1984; Lofficier, Randy & Jean-Marc, *L'Ecran Fantastique* #51, December 1984. Interview with Michael Gross: Lofficier, Randy & Jean-Marc, *Enterprise Incidents* #23, November 1984; Lofficier, Randy & Jean-Marc, *L'Ecran Fantastique* #50, November 1984. Interview with John Bruno: Lofficier, Randy & Jean-Marc, *L'Ecran Fantastique* #50, November 1984.

The Golden Child Interview with Michael Ritchie: Rabkin, William, *Starlog* #114, January 1984.

The Goonies Interview with Richard Donner: Goldberg, Lee, *Starlog* #93, April 1985; Goldberg, Lee, *Starlog* #94, May 1985; Goldberg, Lee, *Starlog* #97, August 1985.

Gremlins Interview with Joe Dante: Lofficier, Randy & Jean-Marc, *Twilight Zone Magazine*, Vol, 3, No. 4, October 1983; Lofficier, Randy & Jean-Marc, *L'Ecran Fantastique* #41, January 1984; Lofficier, Randy & Jean-Marc, *Twilight Zone Magazine*, Vol. 4, No. 4, October 1984; Lofficier, Randy & Jean-Marc, *L'Ecran Fantastique* #51, December 1984.

Highlander Interview with Greg Widen: Rabkin, William, *Starlog* #107, June 1986.

Howard the Duck Interview with Steve Gerber: Lofficier, Randy & Jean-Marc, *Starlog* #111, October 1986; Lofficier, Randy & Jean-Marc, *L'Ecran Fantastique* #75, December 1986. Interview with Gloria Katz: Rabkin, William, *Starlog*.

The James Bond Films James Bond Overview: Goldberg, Lee, *UCLA Daily Bruin*, March 1982; Goldberg, Lee, *Los Angeles Times Syndicate*, July 1987. On the set of *A View to *a Kill:* Goldberg, Lee, *Starlog* #92, March 1985; Goldberg, Lee, *A View to a Kill Magazine*, 1985. Interview with Timothy Dalton: Goldberg, Lee, *Starlog* #123, October 1987. Interview with George Lazenby: Goldberg, Lee, *UCLA Daily Bruin*, March 1982; Goldberg, Lee, *Starlog* #68, March 1983. Interview with Barry Nelson: Goldberg, Lee, *UCLA Daily Bruin*, March 1982; Goldberg, Lee, *Starlog* #68, March 1983. Interview with Richard Maibaum: Goldberg, Lee, *UCLA Daily Bruin*, March 1982; Goldberg, Lee, *Starlog* #68, March 1983; Goldberg, Lee, *A View to a Kill Magazine*, 1985; Goldberg, Lee, *Starlog* #120, July 1987. Interview with Tom Mankiewicz: Goldberg, Lee, *UCLA Daily Bruin*, March 1982; Goldberg, Lee, *Starlog* #68, March 1983. Interview with Roger Moore: Goldberg, Lee, *Starlog* #93, April 1985. Interview with Lorenzo Semple, Jr.: Goldberg, Lee, *Cinefantastique*, April/May 1983. Interview with Michael Wilson: Goldberg, Lee, *UCLA Daily Bruin*, March 1982; Goldberg, Lee, *A View to a Kill Magazine* 1985; Goldberg, Lee, *Starlog* #122, September 1987; Goldberg, Lee, *Starlog* #146, September 1989.

Ladyhawke Interview with Richard Donner: Goldberg, Lee, *Starlog* #93, April 1985. Interview with Michelle Pfeiffer: Goldberg, Lee, *Starlog* #94, May 1985. Interview with Rutger Hauer: Goldberg, Lee, *Starlog* #95, June 1985.

The Lost Boys On the set of *Lost Boys:* Rabkin, William, *Fangoria* #65, November 1987. Interview with Jamie Gertz: Rabkin, William, *Starlog* #124, November 1987. Interview with Corey Feldman: Rabkin, William, *Fangoria* #64, September 1987.

A Nightmare on Elm Street Interview with Wes Craven: Lofficier, Randy & Jean-Marc, *L'Ecran Fantastique* #24, June 1982; Lofficier, Randy & Jean-Marc, *Fangoria* #56, August 1986; Lofficier, Randy & Jean-Marc, *L'Ecran Fantastique* #74,

November 1986; Goldberg, Lee, *Fangoria* #51, January 1986; Goldberg, Lee, *Fangoria* #57, July 1986; Goldberg, Lee, *Starlog* #109, August 1986. On the set of *Nightmare on Elm Street*: Goldberg, Lee, *UCLA Daily Bruin*, October 24, 1984; Goldberg, Lee, *Fangoria* #40, December 1984; Goldberg, Lee, *Los Angeles Times Syndicate*, December 1984.

Something Wicked This Way Comes Interview with Ray Bradbury: Lofficier, Randy & Jean-Marc, *L'Ecran Fantastique* #42, February 1984; Lofficier, Randy & Jean-Marc, *Starlog* #72, July 1984. Interview with Jack Clayton: Lofficier, Randy & Jean-Marc, *L'Ecran Fantastique* #42, February 1984; Lofficier, Randy & Jean-Marc, *Starlog* #71, June 1984.

PREFACE

As soon as a movie goes into production, a unit publicist is hired to get the hype rolling. Reporters are wooed to the set, sometimes with the promise of a plane ticket and accommodations, to interview everybody and write glowing pieces for newspapers and movie magazines.

During production, the stars are challenged by their roles, the directors are in complete control of their "artistic vision," and even the screenwriters are satisfied. The studio praises the cast and crew, the execs declare their undying faith in the movie, and pundits predict enormous success.

Of course, that's before the actors battle for screen time, the producers lock the director out of the editing room, the screenwriters wrestle for writing credit, the studio pushes back the release date, the reviews come in and the box-office receipts are tallied. But by that time, the reporters are off to another set, quizzing another hopeful cast, the previous movie forgotten.

We know, because for a good part of the eighties, we belonged to that reportorial pack that lives off press kits, junkets, and crew catering. We visited sets here and abroad, transcribed countless interview tapes, weeded through thousands of canned quotes, and shaped it all into hundreds of punchy feature articles.

Rarely were the pieces we wrote, and the things our subjects said, ever revisited in light of what eventually happened to the movies they were hyping.

Until now.

We've compiled some of our most interesting and provocative articles so that you, armed with knowledge of what became of the films, the people, and the genres we examined, can explore the chasm between what was intended and what occurred, between the dreams the filmmakers had and the often harsh reality they faced.

Each chapter is dedicated to a film that was, in some way or another, a milestone, a defining moment in fantasy filmmaking during the decade. Each film is tackled from several angles, and preceded by an introduction that puts the articles in historical perspective.

We hope that this book, combined with its companion volume *Science Fiction Filmmaking in the 1980s*, offers a comprehensive and informative overview of an important decade in genre filmmaking.

LEE GOLDBERG / RANDY & JEAN-MARC LOFFICIER /
WILLIAM RABKIN
Los Angeles, May 1995

FOREWORD: *MOVING PICTURES*
(by Marv Wolfman)

When broken down to its basics, film is simply a series of single pictures which, when put together, create a narrative which, one hopes, tells a story. When we watch movies we obviously don't see each individual frame. Instead, we see a man walking across the street, a woman driving a car, a murderer squeezing the trigger of a gun, two people making love, etc. ad infinitum.

We can layer in special effects. We can make the viewer believe they're on another world, in another dimension, time or any place between. We no longer have to build intricate models of spaceships when they can be designed, created and animated solely on the computer. Actors can be filmed against blue screens then composited along with other filmed or created pieces on a computer to create effects Willis O'Brien could never have dreamed possible.

Movies have obviously changed, but one thing remains the same. By the time a film is shown in the movie theater, it is still presented one frame at a time. One fraction of a second put next to an action that will last another fraction of a second, put next to another and another and another. Movies tell stories, affect the emotions and play on the heart …

One picture at a time …

When I'm not going to the movies, I can usually be found writing comic books. I do other forms of writing, but for the past twenty-plus years most of my work has been done in the comics. In fact, Lee and Bill once wrote a film adaptation of "Blade, the Vampire Hunter," a comic book character I created back in the seventies. That version was never filmed, but now, several years later, a new script has been written and is supposed to go before the cameras probably by the time this book is published. "The Tomb of Dracula," another comic I wrote for almost a decade was turned into a movie in Japan. These two adaptations may be of my horror stories but I've also written fantasy comics, science fiction comics, adventure comics, funny animal comics, superhero comics, satiric comics, detective comics, and more. I've written everything from Superman to Mickey Mouse to Dracula, and, in fact, I once wrote a story where the Mouse meets the Vampire Lord. Okay, so Dracula was played by Goofy, but you get the idea.

One picture at a time ...

Comics are movies—printed on paper rather than shot on film. A comic panel is simply one frame taken out of a movie then put on a page. Because we don't have sound on the page we put the words in "balloons" which float over the characters' heads. By the way, the soundless comics page may soon change— the science necessary to transmit sound imbedded in printers' ink already exists.

Certainly there are differences between comics and film, but not as many as people may think. We are both story-telling mediums. We are both the handlers of words and pictures. There is also very little in the context of a movie that can't be done in a comic, and vice versa. Comic book stories can be as superficial as a superhero slugfest (though few are quite as dumb as, ummm, *Dumb and Dumber*) or as thoughtful as "Our Cancer Year," an illustrated story about a couple facing the disease together. If someone has a story to tell they can choose to tell that same story in prose or in comics or on film, and they can make an equally valid statement using any of those medium.

Comics and film have long affected the other. Orson Welles' *Citizen Kane* used camera angles straight out of the early comics while comic book artists have been known to mimic film shots, experimenting in Sam Peckinpah slow-motion shots, or the fast-paced frenetic action of the Hong Kong cinema. Many film directors have been or still are dyed-in-the-wool comics fans. I've gone to many directors' offices only to see comic book figurines on desks, pictures on walls, or comics sitting in the waiting room. I've gone to pitch scripts to more than one director I've greatly admired only to discover he wanted to talk to me about my comics.

Directors today are influenced by what comic book writers do and sometimes what's done in a comic completely changes a film; a writer friend of mine was hired to do a comic book adaptation of a big budget, very successful horror film. To make the final scene work for comics, the writer and artist altered it somewhat. The director saw what they did, then refilmed the end scene to conform to the comic.

Film, in fact, is told in comic form long before it is ever shot. Alfred Hitchcock was the first director to extensively use storyboards to design his film. A storyboard is a picture by picture comic version of the film with every shot indicated. Hitchcock used to say once the storyboards were done his job was done. The actual filming of the movie was boring.

It's also obvious comics and film are related in another way; since the late 1930s comics have been regularly adapted into film, although mostly in the old weekly serials. Since the 1970s, when the first Christopher Reeve *Superman* movie became a hit, there's been a deluge of comic book adaptations into full-length, high-budget movies. In the past year alone (I'm writing this in 1995) we've already seen five comic book movies (*The Mask, Time Cop, Tank Girl, Batman Forever* and *Judge Dredd*) and there are many more to come.

Although comics and film can handle any variety of subjects, it's obvious the greatest similarity is in horror, fantasy and science fiction. Fantasy films tend to cost a small fortune because of special effects, wardrobe and sets, but there are no additional costs involved in doing a fantasy or science fiction comic. Fantasy, science fiction and horror are comic book mainstays because a writer can ask an artist to draw anything the imagination can conceive. And unlike movies we can do it on a monthly schedule.

Once a year I watch the *Back to the Future* trilogy. The films may be considered comedies, but I believe the series is one of the best and most consistent fantasy/science fiction trilogies ever made. One of the reasons I keep watching them is to study and marvel at how clear the story telling is even when dealing with mind-exploding time-travel paradoxes. Too often fantasy and science fiction gets bogged down with meaningless "technobabble." This trilogy removes the babble; you don't have to be an SF aficionado or have a degree in quantum physics to understand and enjoy these films.

Buckaroo Banzai, on the other hand, delights in assailing the senses. You can't possibly understand what's going on the first time you see it. Or the fifth. You have to keep watching it as, like an onion, the layers are slowly removed exposing the sheer wackiness of the film. *Banzai*, like *Big Trouble in Little China, Golden Child, Little Shop of Horrors, Goonies* and *Gremlins*, are comedies which use fantasy or SF ideas to tell exciting and fun stories.

Ghostbusters is much more than just a comedy because, like *Star Wars*, it brings in myth, horror, and adventure. *Ghostbusters* is one of those fantasy films you can watch time and time again because it is so richly textured.

Mythology and horror also play their role with films like *Conan, Golden Child, Highlander, Something Wicked This Way Comes, Ladyhawke, Lost Boys, Dead Zone* and *Videodrome*. All of these are films that we comic book writers watch and learn from.

Though not obviously fantasy or science fiction, the James Bond films connect with the superhero adventure we comic book writers play with. There isn't a single comic writer today who hasn't "borrowed" one of the patented Bond massive finale scenes or chases. The use of Bond-like science and gimmicks has probably influenced all comic book series.

And as for *Howard the Duck*, perhaps the comic book/film connection does break down from time to time. We apologize. It *was* a good comic.

Go through these interviews in any order. You'll learn a lot about how fantasy and SF films are put together. The interviews, like the best fantasy movies, are fun to read.

Enjoy!

May 1995
Los Angeles, CA

THE ADVENTURES OF BUCKAROO BANZAI (1984)

All filmmakers set out to make a successful movie, few set out to intentionally create a "cult classic." From the beginning, director W.D. Richter and writer Earl Mac Rauch attempted to generate in the real world the same mystique that surrounded their fictional hero Buckaroo Banzai in the make-believe world on screen.

Perhaps they should have concentrated more on just making a good movie. In trying so hard to generate a "franchise" and spark a popular following for their manufactured cult hero, they created a film that felt forced at every turn.

Rauch actually wrote enough Buckaroo Banzai material for a book, and perhaps that's where the character should have begun, rather than on celluloid. Unintentionally, the movie became a bad adaptation of a book that hadn't even been written yet. An entire backstory, which featured Jamie Lee Curtis as Buckaroo's mother, was shot for a lengthy prologue but was ultimately deleted. But most of the details and background which would have given this movie some context never even made it into the shooting script. The movie ended up feeling like the third chapter in a continuing series—unfortunately, the audience wasn't let in on the first two installments.

The movie-makers were so sure of their success, they even ended the film by promising *Buckaroo Banzai* would return—taking an undeservedly self-confident cue from the venerable James Bond series. The same, misguided ploy was tried a few years earlier with the similar (but far campier) *Doc Savage: Man of Bronze*—ironically, a film Richter and his team watched in order to avoid its mistakes. Apparently, they didn't watch it closely enough.

There was a lot to like about the movie—including some inventive casting and production design—but not enough to generate interest at the box office. In desperation, the studio booked the movie into the midnight runs usually reserved for genuine cult classics, like *Rocky Horror Picture Show* and *Eraserhead*, where it did actually attract a handful of genuine groupies, but a real following never emerged.

SCREENWRITER EARL MAC RAUCH

When audiences see *The Adventures of Buckaroo Banzai* this summer, they will be glimpsing just a small part of the myth writer Earl Mac Rauch has been constructing, off and on, for the last nine years.

Nevertheless, Rauch "can't wait to see the movie with the music and all the special effects. I'm still surprised it was even made!"

Buckaroo Banzai (Peter Weller) is a neurosurgeon/rockstar/philosopher/scientist/entrepreneur/adventurer and confidant of the president who journeys into the 8th Dimension in a jetcar of his own design, accomplishing the impossible and bringing back an alien organism to prove it.

He makes headlines and creates a new field of scientific endeavor. Beyond that, and on a more personal level, he has successfully replicated a similar, disastrous, pre–World War II attempt to enter the 8th Dimension that killed his father.

What Buckaroo doesn't know is that an evil alien being (John Lithgow), one of thousands from Planet 10 banished to the 8th Dimension for their crimes, escaped decades ago by possessing the body of a scientist who tried to duplicate his father's experiment and managed to enter the 8th Dimension for a moment.

The possessed scientist, imprisoned in an insane asylum, reads of Buckaroo Banzai's successful excursion into the 8th Dimension and plots to use him to free his comrades, take over the earth, and destroy Planet 10.

The fate of the universe lies with Buckaroo Banzai and his team of scientists-turned-rock musicians, the Hong Kong Cavaliers.

"It's basically a B-movie plot," Rauch concedes. "What's so complicated is the backstory and all the little nuances and wisecrack ideas. It's not as crazy as it sounds."

But it *does* sound crazy.

"I know. Any doubts I have about the movie lie with me," he says, shifting the blame for any weaknesses the movie may have from first-time director W.D. Richter to himself. "Rick has done a wonderful job. I have no doubts about the actors hired, the jobs they've done, the style of the movie or the art direction. It's all going to be really good. But as a writer, I have to wonder, is the structure of this movie good? Will it hold up with an audience? Is the story strong enough? Are there too many things going on in this movie? Is Buckaroo Banzai too diffuse a character to ask an audience to swallow?"

It is that last question which concerns him the most. If audiences can't accept Buckaroo Banzai, then the whole film falls apart.

"He's many sided and in many ways larger than life. Is there anyway this guy can find acceptance? I think there is," he says. "The thing is, he isn't *so* unusual. People who really accomplish something in the world are very multi-faceted. Whether it's a brain surgeon who likes to race cars or a scientist who enjoys writing spy novels, these people aren't hard to find in the real world. There are people similar to Buckaroo."

Buckaroo Banzai was inspired by "all those out and out, press-the-accelerator-to-the-floor, nonstop *Kung Fu* movies that came out in the early seventies. But it didn't evolve in a direction fashion. It picked up a lot along the way until it became a big, tangled ball of string."

A ball of string which Rauch, a decade ago, dropped into Richter's lap over dinner.

"I had just come to Hollywood and he was making a nice living writing. I was struggling. I used to go over to his house three or four nights a week and one night I said to him I'd like to write a script about this unusual guy and it's called *Find the Jetcar, Said the President—A Buckaroo Banzai Thriller,*" Mac Rauch recalls. "So Rick laughed, said 'Okay, great, why don't Susan (Richter's wife) and me and our corporation give you some money to do it?'

"I hadn't been out here very long and I wasn't exactly working for Writer's Guild scale, you know. I was just trying to get a few bucks here and there writing. So I said sure, it'll pay the rent for a few months," he continues. "I went off to write it and never really finished it. I got eighty or ninety pages into it and just quit for some reason. Over the years, though, I would start other *Buckaroo* scripts."

Mac Rauch laughs. "It's so easy to start something and then since you're really, in the back of your mind, not as serious about it as you should be, you end up writing half of it and convincing yourself it stinks. You shove the hundred pages in your drawer and forget it."

So Rauch's drawers began to overflow with *Buckaroo Banzai* stories.

"Each time I'd start from scratch, do something completely different. One of them was called *The Strange Case of Mr. Cigars*, and it was about a big, huge, King Kong–size robot and there was also this bit about Hitler's cigars and some big secrets and some exotic locales. It was crazy."

Buckaroo Banzai remained largely forgotten, a fanciful notion that stayed in the back of Rauch's mind as he wrote *New York, New York* for director Martin Scorsese and several unproduced screenplays for various folks.

Then, three years ago, Richter and producer Neal Canton formed a partnership and started looking for projects for their company to produce. Richter remembered *Buckaroo Banzai*.

"Yeah, *now* we're getting into the modern era of *Buckaroo Banzai*. Rick was looking around for projects and, by this time, had a phone book–size file of *Buckaroo Banzai* stuff," Rauch says. "Somewhere along the line I had given him all the scripts. Rick's kind of like a script archive. His room is full of scripts that people have given him or that he has picked up."

Rauch smiles and leans forward. "In fact, he has more of my scripts than I do. If I don't have a script I wrote five years ago, I'll call him up and ask 'Do you have such-and-such script?' And he'll say 'Oh sure, right here.'"

Richter felt they could convince a studio to finance a *Buckaroo Banzai* film. All they needed was a usable, *completed* story. Rauch sat down at the typewriter and drafted a whole new adventure he entitled *Lepers from Saturn*.

Richter presented the script to MGM head David Begelman shortly before the writer's strike. "The deal," Rauch recalls, "was made in a week."

And then *Buckaroo Banzai* languished again. The strike dragged on, Begelman was ousted from MGM for embezzlement, and Richter took on several writing assignments (*Brubaker, Invasion of the Body Snatchers*).

Then Begelman, who still had the option *Buckaroo Banzai*, formed Sherwood Productions and offered the project to 20th

Century-Fox. Three drafts and several months later, *Buckaroo Banzai* was finally in front of the cameras.

"But *Buckaroo* isn't behind me by any means," Rauch says. "I'm going to write the novel now and use a lot of stuff I never had a chance to use in the movie. Some stuff from the old screenplays, some new stuff, some new characters I want to play with. What I hate are those quicky novelizations based on a screenplay. The characters are undefined and you have no insight into what is going on in his head. I'd like to make the book seem as though it preceded the movie."

By writing the novel, Rauch will be going back to his roots. He wrote his first novel while in high school, stuck the manuscript in a box and took it with him when he went to Dartmouth.

"The book was something in the *Catcher in the Rye* vein. The kind of thing every teenage writer does at first. Unfortunately for me, it ended up being published," he says. "I didn't know what I wanted to do. I felt something exciting would come along that I would do next. I mean, college was exciting, not that I was too active. I kept to myself, sent off my book, and started on another."

In 1969, *Dirty Pictures from the Prom*, his first novel, was published. No one was more surprised than Rauch.

"Suddenly I thought, 'Ah-ha! I'm a *serious* writer!' I started taking myself very seriously. Who needs college? I'm *a writer*. But, I was stuck there for four years," Rauch says. "I would enroll in a course, stay home and work on my novel. A week before finals I would cram. College, in a way, was a wasted experience. I took a few courses, made a few friends. I enrolled in law school at the University of Texas, not knowing what else to do. It was either go to school or look for a job. I didn't really want a job. I felt someone should support me while I write. In this case, it was my parents by way of law school."

His second novel came out the summer he entered law school and was read by a Dartmouth graduate in California named W.D. Richter.

"He was three years ahead of me, going to film school at USC. He read a review of my book in the Dartmouth Alumni magazine and wrote me a letter asking if he could do a screenplay from it. At the bottom of the letter he wrote 'If you are ever out this way, give me a call,'" he recalls. "I took him up on it. I met his agent and through him I got started. Rick has been my mentor."

Novel writing was forgotten.

"A seduction took place. Novel writing is such a lonely pursuit. Then the book comes out and there is no support behind it. It disappears in a matter of months and you wonder why you worked so hard," Rauch explains. "If you can live off the ego trip of having a novel published and getting good reviews, I guess it's a good way to stay alive. It's a pure way, you have integrity, it's wonderful, it's artistic and blah, blah, blah. I couldn't see that for me, especially with the kind of novels I was writing that didn't have a prayer of ever becoming bestsellers. It became simply an ego thing.

"The day to day thing of screenplays allows you to get by. There are story meetings; you interact with people, and you get well paid for it. It may never get made, but at least you are adequately compensated."

Rauch is already toying with the idea of a *Buckaroo Banzai* sequel and a possible series of books. "I have an idea what I'd like to do with the sequel. Rick and I have talked about it. I'd be happy if we could do more. Frankly, I wouldn't mind *Buckaroo Banzai* having the kind of instant recognition that Sherlock Holmes and James Bond have. But, I don't think *Buckaroo Banzai* will provide me with a retirement cushion. It would be great, though if it could!"

If *Buckaroo Banzai* becomes a series of movies, Rauch isn't sure he'd like to write the scripts. However, he'd enjoy writing the books. "It would be a nice sideline. I feel that I know the characters and I could write the books without as much effort as a screenplay."

He smiles "I didn't think *Buckaroo Banzai* would ever get made. *Now* listen to me!"

INTERVIEW WITH W.D. "RICK" RICHTER

W.D. Richter is happy with the way his premiere directorial effort, the off-beat *Adventures of Buckaroo Banzai—Across the Eighth Dimension*, turned out. But you've got to wonder if he thinks maybe it could make more money in the 8th Dimension than it has in theaters across the nation.

The critics like it. He likes it. His friends like it. The public, by and large, doesn't. By all rights, though, they should.

It is top-name stars like John Lithgow (as evil Dr. Lizardo) and Jeff Goldblum (as good-guy New Jersey). It is nasty weirdness from Christopher Lloyd, a new-wave sex symbol in Lewis Smith, a scantily clad and beautiful Ellen Barkin, and a charismatic hero in Peter Weller. It also has a nifty, pulpy adventure plot, bizarre alien creatures and spaceships that look like clumps of rotted fruit.

Added up, that makes this movie the strangest projection to hit the screen in ages. So what's wrong? Just that. Nobody knows how to promote the film and a good percentage of moviegoers leave the theaters with their faces wrinkled with confusion.

"When people don't get it, they really don't get it," says W.D. "Rick" Richter, the prolific screenwriter who brought his buddy Earl Mac Rauch's manic screenplay to life. "When people *do* get it, they seem to love it and forgive the faults we all know it has.

John Lithgow is the evil Dr. Emilio Lizardo, who spends his days in the nuthouse reading thrillers and plotting revenge in *The Adventures of Buckaroo Banzai*.

"I know that the plot is hard to follow, but what I suspect is that it's much more than the plot or too many characters or whatever that turns people off," he continues. "It's that they hate the whole sensibility and humor and the whole concept of *Buckaroo Banzai*."

And that's exactly the way W.D. Richter, his cast, and his production personnel wanted it.

"I think you have to be really naive to assume it will instantly be grasped by everyone," he says. "We are meeting a lot of people who say 'what the hell is that?' Some people get it immediately. That's inherent to any entertainment that takes risks and *this does*. I don't think you should spoon-feed people so they instantly grasp things. The whole central idea of *Buckaroo Banzai* is an enquiring mind."

"One of the most difficult questions people ask me is 'what is *Buckaroo Banzai* about?' If I could answer that in a paragraph, I wouldn't have spend two years making it," he adds. "I deliberately didn't want to make a straight, genre film. You can get confused trying to peg *Buckaroo Banzai*."

Twentieth Century-Fox, the distributors of the film certainly did. They were stuck trying to sell a film that rebelliously defied categorization and weren't sure what to do with it.

"They saw the spaceships and characterized it as pure science-fiction," Richter says. "The poster tells you that. It says there's aliens among us and shows a conventional spaceship blasting out of a wall. Studios like to peg films."

The poster showed Peter Weller in the forefront, wearing a trendy sport jacket with his tie loose around his collar, carrying a briefcase under his arm and sporting a TEAM BANZAI button on his lapel. Behind him, a staple-shaped spaceship crashed through a brick wall. The tagline "Beings from another dimension have invaded your world. You can't see them … but they can see you. Your only hope is Buckaroo Banzai" was written atop the scene.

The poster didn't seem representative of a film one observer once described as a "new wave thing, a kung-fu science fiction film with a country flavor."

"When it opened in small towns, the feedback was that audiences went in thinking it was a straight ahead, science fiction movie and it wasn't," Richter says. "Fortunately, it didn't open all over the country."

Instead, the film was released to a dozen key markets so 20th Century-Fox executives could closely gauge the audience reaction and retool their ad campaign before going into wide, national release. It also gave them a chance to test the critical reaction to the film. Critics loved it, describing it as "a wild bronco ride," "a hero for the rest of us," and "the oddest good movie in many a full moon." *Newsweek* even went so far as to "bless its demented little heart."

"The critics saw that it was an odd-ball, eccentric film," Richter says. The studio apparently didn't.

"*Buckaroo Banzai* didn't call for a real safe ad campaign. It needed a real bold approach up front and we didn't get that," Richter says. "You can't sell a film like this with a sort of half-baked campaign. You have to look at it hard and say 'this is different.' You can't sell it as science fiction; it's not about science fiction. But the poster tells you 'aliens are among us' and shows a conventional spaceship blasting through a wall. You can't sell it as heroism; it's not about heroism. Good God, there isn't any image that is less like the movie than a picture of a guy in a sport jacket looking at you."

To Richter, the most upsetting aspect of the poster art was the spaceship depicted bursting through the brick wall.

"It's a source of enormous annoyance to me," Richter says. "The absolute difference between this film and others is the organic quality of the ships. I don't know where that ship in the poster came from."

He is also miffed that there will be no *Buckaroo Banzai* soundtrack album even though they had some offers.

"It's a tragedy. Several labels wanted it but the powers that be kept upping the ante," he says. "We got a $150,000 advance on the table at one point, which was very, very, very fair and generous advance for a film that has no rock groups to promote. Then it simply became too late. We lost a major source of publicity."

In September, 20th Century–Fox was gearing up for wide release and a new publicity effort Richter hoped would "stress the oddness and not just a rocketship and clue people in that this is a comedy."

He's confident that, despite the off-target publicity, the audience he made the film for is seeing it.

"The people we made this for like adventuresome story techniques and eccentric, high energy movies," he says. "If this is an inarticulate response, I'm sorry. But it's hard for people who love it to describe it. It has so much going on in it that is exciting. We need a movie like that. If we went too far, we can challenge the complacent American films they are making now. They have reckoned with *Buckaroo Banzai*."

Although *Buckaroo Banzai* underwent some extensive editing, including the cutting of a prologue featuring Jamie Lee Curtis, Richter is satisfied with the finished product.

"Very much so," he says. "This represents the version of the movie that I want. It represents the sensibilities of the people who made it. I don't want to *ever* create the impression that there is another movie on the cutting room floor that I wish was on the screen."

And there are no scenes left unshot in the soundstage because of objections from Richter's bosses.

"Everyone was very supportive," he says. "If you undertake a very eccentric project you will have less interference because the traditional critisms don't apply. If they let you make the film at all, they will put fewer obstacles in your path."

The Jamie Lee Curtis scene depicted the fatal attempt Buckaroo's parents made to enter the 8th Dimension. Curtis played Buckaroo's mother. The scene explained how Buckaroo got his name and made clear his obsession with breaking through to the 8th Dimension himself.

"It didn't work. I think maybe it would satisfy those people hungry for more information about Buckaroo but it would have been a detriment to the rest of the movie," he says. "It worked internally but it was a source of enormous information and too many people were on screen to start a movie like that. It set up too much information to assimilate."

In preview screenings carried out while Richter was cutting the film, he learned some valuable lessons that helped him make the decision to snip the Curtis prologue. "We learned in previews that while I might know everything about the scene, the audiences found it hard to meet all those characters," he explains. "That was an interesting lesson. You have to be careful how you dole out information because it's less important to belabor Buckaroo Banzai's background than it was to let it go.

"Mac's screenplay was very rich but that doesn't mean you have to put it all out there," Richter continues. "It doesn't benefit the film to refer to two villains, Lizardo and Hanoi Xan, and only ask the audience to learn about one of them. The world of *Buckaroo Banzai* can be sampled in a lot of different ways: the movie, the book, and the comic book. If the film finds its audience, they will see they haven't exhausted the ways to get involved in *Buckaroo Banzai*. An invitation like that was welcome when I was a kid. There's a chance to find other nooks and crannies of his world. There's privileged information lurking around the world of *Buckaroo Banzai* if you're interested in seeking it out."

The information-laden prologue was substituted with a title scrawl similar to that in *Star Wars*.

"I did it because I really felt we needed to tell people something about what might be going on and perhaps provoke a smile and a sense of whimsy," Richter explains.

Also missing from the film is a conversation in a van between evil Lectroid John Bigboote (Lloyd) and one of his underlings. Bigboote is driving and the underling beside him offers him a dry-cell battery.

"No thanks," Bigboote says, "I'm trying to cut down."

The underling shrugs and sucks on the battery, his body shaking with electric current.

"That's the single, most-missed moment in the movie," Richter concedes. "There was concern on the production company part that we weren't making our Lectroids ominous enough. A moment like that makes you enjoy them too much and divested them of some of their threat.

"We were consistently trading things off. You don't want to absolutely lose control of the movie by taking a pig-headed position opposed to the man who ultimately has the final cut," Richter says. "You are constantly negotiating when you are shooting, writing and editing a film. You have to deal with the needs of the distributors, exhibitors, the advertising people; it goes on and on."

Richter picked an unusually arduous project as his first directing effort. That, too, was a planned difficulty. What surprised Richter was the lack of opposition to the idea of him directing the film.

"It wasn't hard to place myself as director and that did surprise me. The people who were *not* interested in making *Buckaroo Banzai* had no trouble with me wanting to direct. They just didn't like it," he says. "If I had given them a script they liked, they would have said go ahead. Me directing it had nothing to do with it. I guess if you're around long enough, they figure 'hey, why not?' By all formulas, I shouldn't have been handed it. It needed to be a script everyone wanted and I had to strong-arm my way and say 'if you want it, I have to be the director.' But, as Buckaroo says, expect the unexpected."

Richter has certainly earned the opportunity. He studied English Literature at Dartmouth University, graduating three years ahead of *Buckaroo* originator Earl Mac Rauch (who he didn't know), then went to study film at USC in 1968. While in school, he toiled as a script analyst for Warner Bros.

Shortly after graduating, his first post-scholastic script, *Slither*, was bought right away and became a hit comedy/thriller, launching a screenwriting career that has included *Brubaker, Invasion of the Body Snatchers, Dracula*, the flop Gene Hackman/Barbra Streisand comedy *All Night Long*, and a number of unproduced scripts—among them the film version of *The Ninja*.

Getting much more than that out of Richter about his background isn't easy. "I try as much as I can to stay away from the personal side of the ledger. I know some people are interested but I think the movies are the thing."

Not only does he write screenplays but he rewrites troubled stories penned by other scribes.

"I find rewriting fun," he says. "It gets you into someone else's head, you learn why things don't work. It's not because you're rewriting a bad writer but a writer who was involved in a project so long that he lost sight of it. It's also a way for me not to commit extraordinary energies. I'm in and out of the project in a short time it doesn't end up obsessing me for two years."

David Odell's script for *Supergirl* was his latest polishing job, a task for which he will receive no screen credit.

"Yes, I almost rewrote *Supergirl* from scratch but it doesn't bother me that I'm not getting a credit," Richter says. "I wanted it that way. I made it conditional that I wouldn't get a credit because I didn't know what the movie would turn out like. I wasn't close enough to the project. I didn't want to risk having my name in it and then find out later the film didn't represent my way of thinking."

He really enjoyed the experience, though.

Dr. Lizardo (John Lithgow) straps Buckaroo Banzai (Peter Weller) into the terrifying shock tower.

"I had a ball. Without ever having met them, I knew I was writing lines for Peter O'Toole and Peter Cooke," he says. "When they presented the script to me, I said what's missing here is the madness. It needs a possessed energy. They agreed. It was an amazing amount of license to be handed. There's a real trick to that. My God, the sets were built and the movie was cast. What an interesting challenge it was to weave eccentricity into something that's eighty percent formed. I had fun writing it but I have no idea what they did with it. The whole business is crazy."

The craziness of *Buckaroo Banzai* had its beginnings over a decade ago. While Richter was still at USC, he read a book by Rauch called *Arkansas Adios* and asked if he could adapt it as a screenplay. Rauch said yes. Grateful, Richter told Rauch to look him up if he was ever in Los Angeles.

Rauch eventually did.

"My wife Susan and I were living near MacArthur park and I convinced him to stay in Los Angeles and be a screenwriter," Richter recalls. "He had an apartment across the street and he would come over and play his guitar and shoot ideas at us. It was real easy for me.

"One day, he came up with this idea for *Buckaroo Banzai*. Then, at random intervals, he would come over with a hysterically funny forty pages or so," he adds. "I didn't take it seriously because I didn't want to pressure him for fear he would abandon it. I just encouraged him. I said it's still great, why don't you write this all into a story front to back? I kept them all in a big pile and eventually I showed them to my partner, Neil Canton, when we formed our own production company. He thought they were funny too."

Finally, Richter convinced Rauch to finish a *Buckaroo Banzai* story that could be pitched as the first film under the Canton/Richter banner. "It took some time, but in the seven years since he first came up with the idea he had gotten some experience as a screenwriter and had learned the structure. And, once a studio calls your agent and says 'we'll pay you,' a sense of responsibility comes down on you real fast. You take it more seriously than you would just writing it for your friend Richter."

Early on, Richter rejected the idea of producing one of his own screenplays as his first directorial job.

"Directing is very hard work, it divides you enough. The script always needs attention. I believe that movies take on a life of their own once filming begins and scripts tend to evolve during production," Richter says. "During a first film, it wouldn't hurt if someone else could translate that evolution to the page. It's a full time job directing and there's less chance that I would be flexible if it was my script. Besides, Mac writes with a sense of humor I find very similar to my own."

During the production of *Buckaroo Banzai*, Richter never had the inclination to do any rewriting of Rauch's work.

"It would have been unthinkable," he says. "It's all Mac's idea."

What did Richter learn about himself under the pressure of directing his first film? He doesn't know.

"You don't have much time to learn about yourself when you're directing. It's hardly an introspective process making something as complex and full of things as *Buckaroo Banzai* is. You just keep going and try to get it all in and stay in touch. The last thing you think of is yourself."

And now, the work behind him, he's thinking about *Buckaroo Banzai*. A little wistfully, perhaps.

"I'm feeling very good about it right now," Richter says. "I think it will find its audience and make its impression. I've made enough films, in a funny way, to know you never know what you've made until people tell you."

INTERVIEW WITH PETER WELLER

Buckaroo Banzai is Peter Weller, only better at it. At least, that's what Peter Weller thinks.

"I have a lot of Buckaroo's talents," Weller sheepishly contends, clad in his blue rugby shirt, dark sunglasses and sporty, navy blue "Team Banzai" flight jacket. "But, to a less extravagant degree. It's an amazing enlightenment to me to play this guy. He's the best person that I can be."

Or that anybody could be, for that matter. Buckaroo Banzai is a hero's hero, a man who excels at everything he does. He is a world-famous brain surgeon, a hot rock singer, a sensuous lover, a death-defying daredevil, a dashing adventurer, a wealthy entrepreneur and a wise philosopher. Banzai even finds time in his hectic heroic schedule to save the world from the evil clutches of ghastly aliens Emilio Lizardo (John Lithgow) and John Bigboote (Christopher Lloyd).

The only heroic qualities Buckaroo Banzai lacks are a license to kill and an aversion to Kryptonite.

Okay, so what does this fellow Weller, a New York actor whose previous big screen exposure is limited to a supporting role in *Shoot the Moon* and the lead in the box office dud *Of Unknown Origin*, have in common with a myth-maker like Buckaroo Banzai?

"I have senses for the stuff Buckaroo does," Weller says. "Because I grew up in a military family, I moved around quite a bit. Consequently, I've been exposed to so many different things; I have the kind of metropolitan nature about me that Buckaroo is about."

That's just the kind of guy *Buckaroo Banzai* director W.D. Richter was looking for to bring screenwriter Earl Mac Rauch's "renaissance hero" to life.

"It blew Rick's mind," Weller recalls. "He didn't know a guy like me who was a musician and also knew about guns, or a guy who could race motorcycles and could also race cars."

Still, Weller spent two and a half months preparing for the role, riding motorcycles and brushing up on his singing with voice lessons. Once production began, Weller's days began at 5 a.m. "I'd get to the studio by 5:40, work out until 6:30, show up on the set at 7:00, rehearse until 8:00, then shoot until 7:00 at night."

Rather than trudge into his dressing room and collapse, Weller would run four to five miles and return to the studio by 8:00, where he would spend an hour or so reviewing dailies and munching down dinner and a handful of vitamins. Weller rarely got home before 10:30.

And he didn't spend his days off lazing around the house, either. "When you create that kind of energy, you really want to swing, not lie around," Weller says. "You want to go out and drink beer with your high school buddies. And God, we did too.

Buckaroo Banzai (Peter Weller) prepares to drive his jet car into the 8th Dimension in *The Adventures of Buckaroo Banzai*.

"I threw a party about two weeks before the movie wrapped," he adds. "We went through $1,000 worth of champagne and then about eight of us, including Chris Lloyd, Rosalind Cash, Ellen Barkin and production designer Michael Riva, went down to a Mexican restaurant around the corner from MGM and sat there drinking pitcher after pitcher of margaritas until they tossed us out at four a.m."

Fun—that was the watchword for the cast and crew before, during, and after the filming of *Buckaroo Banzai*. It is what got Weller interested in the role, kept him going during the rigorous schedule, and it's the feeling that lingers with him now that the experience is over.

"It was the most fun I've ever had. The rock 'n' roll was a blast and I did all the stunts except one. I do everything. This isn't lip synching or stand-ins, *Eddie and the Cruisers* or *Flashdance*," he says, adding with a grin, "The arrogance of that stuff would be insulting to my training anyway."

It would also be insulting to accuse Weller of portraying a cartoon character, a one-dimensional superhero.

"There is a lot of depth to this guy," Weller maintains. "He has a lot of unique idiosyncrasies. He has a dilemna with women because his wife was killed, a fear of romance. He has his parents' shadow hanging over his head. They were physicists who failed miserably (at trying to get into the 8th dimension) and died. And, if you look deeper at him, you'll see that Buckaroo has a real basic lack of trust in bureaucracy."

To back up that last point, Weller looks to Banzai's Hong Kong Cavaliers, a collection scientists which included Jeff Goldblum (*Invasion of the Body Snatchers*) that double as his back-up musicians and his team of adventurers.

"They are all self-armed, they are a real elitist bunch of people set up solely to exist for the vision of Buckaroo Banzai," he explains. "It's like Jacques Cousteau and the crew of the *Calypso*. Yeah, that's Buckaroo Banzai, a Jacques Cousteau-type. Actually, he's more like a cross between Albert Einstein, Leonardo da Vinci and Adam Ant!"

The *Buckaroo Banzai* role, obviously, presents big problems for an actor. How do you make a character like that seem realistic? It isn't easy. Overcoming the problem begins with the writer, is aided by the director's choice of perspective and tone, and, ultimately, rests with the actor chosen to bring the character off.

"My handle on Buckaroo was simple," Weller says. "For him, there are simply not enough hours in the day. He works under the sincere belief, not just the intellectual notion, that he will die and when and where he doesn't know. So he pushes the possibilities every day. He's not a guy who says 'I can't wait to go home.' Sleeping and eating are just potions to support his going out and finding out more things. He's always searching and always teaching.

"The other thing that turned me on to Buckaroo is Zen. I like to dabble in Zen," he continues. "Buckaroo's whole notion of living is Zen. His whole vision and philosophy is Zen. His whole purpose in life is to watch the people around him get off. It's to learn something and then give it away. It's the basic Andrew Carnegie philosophy of economics and the Zen philosophy of living. I mean, in one lifetime, how many Ferraris can you own? How many dinners can you eat? The only thing anybody can do eight hours a day is work and soon that's a bore."

Weller doesn't claim to be like his Banzai character in this respect. "My purposes are driven, but I'm not as selfless as Buckaroo. I like Ferraris."

Buckaroo Banzai, in the movie, is a man of great fame and notoriety. Weller scoffs at the notion that his character might be a spotlight-hungry egotist. "Buckaroo doesn't buy his own hype, he doesn't get caught up in it. That's his salvation. His purposes are clear and defined. He doesn't stop to revel in his own b.s.; he's much more curious about things outside himself."

As for Weller, that's a different story. "I'm like most actors," he laughs, "a sucker for vanity and nubile nymphs."

"Hey, look," Weller warns, "the movie isn't as verbal and intellectual and not so abstract as I'm making it sound. It's a simple movie; it's very easy to see what makes this realist and adventurer tick. It's going to appeal to audiences, even if it sounds like a story about a Japanese cowboy, a short guy with a big horse. They are going to see a guy with a funky Eastern bent and old-Western charm."

Weller says he had strong input into the genesis of the Banzai character, an evolution independent of screenwriter Earl Mac Rauch's intricate scenarios and scuttled storylines.

"Writers get paranoid about things like that," he says. "They write something and they have their particular image of it and then along comes an actor and, if he's really good and really does his work, he starts doing things that are above and beyond or wilder or crazier than what the writer ever imagined. Sometimes these are things the writer falls in love with. Many times, though, they are not because the writer feels threatened because what's happening is this actor has come along and ripped off the writer's alter ego."

"I love Mac. He's got this army haircut, these old baggy wrangler jeans and wears these thick glasses," Weller grins. "A great guy. But Mac doesn't know shit anymore. We've really removed it from Mac's original conception. All those things Mac was spewing out about Buckaroo in the beginning of the thing, bless his heart because I love him badly, have nothing in the world to do with Buckaroo now. It's Rick's thing now."

Weller has nothing but praise for W.D. Richter's maiden effort at directing. "He became a millionaire writing movie scripts before becoming a director. He took *Buckaroo Banzai* out of the cartoon syndrome and almost put it into the film noir class. It has a bleak reality like *Blade Runner* and *Alien*. Bleek, oily and gritty. Not as clean and crisp as Mac's version. Rick gave it a form of vulgarity."

Richter, Weller says, was also adept at getting the best out of his actors. "He has a truly inspired sense. The best directors used to be actors. They knew exactly what they wanted and they know they'll get something magical if they let you do what you want too. They are never threatened by an actor's process. Others are, so they make actors do exactly what they tell them to. Richter, who has never been a professional actor, has this uncanny, precise feel for exactly what he wants all the time and gives the actors free rein to give their input."

Weller's contribution to shaping the Buckaroo Banzai character was in "taking Buckaroo out of the superhero element and putting him into the reality of the Leonardo da Vinci kind of guy who is trained and gifted and works at it."

If *Buckaroo Banzai* clicks, Weller is eager to do a sequel and says he and Richter are "sort of working on an outline now. We're tossing around ideas. Because indeed, soon, Buckaroo must confront the man who killed his wife, the incorrigible, the indomitable Hanoi Xan."

Weller isn't worried about being typecast, a nightmarish possibility that curdles the blood of actors like Christopher Reeve and Sean Connery.

"I don't have that fear because in the two cities that make movies, New York and Los Angeles, my reputation was fairly pat before *Buckaroo* came along." Weller says, "I'm not a *Flashdance* find. I wasn't a face picked out of a crowd. *Buckaroo Banzai* is just a part of my future, not my future. No matter how many millions *Buckaroo Banzai* makes, people who make the decisions know what I've done. The public might accept Harrison Ford as Hamlet but Hollywood will never cast him as Hamlet because he was known as nothing until he was in *Star Wars*. He had no track record. My point is, I have a history, a stage history. Certain actors before they get pinned have a track record. My opportunities to discuss doing Hamlet is five steps up the ladder of possibilities than anyone else who has been pinned as a popular hero only because of my body of work before *Buckaroo Banzai*."

So, he won't run away from new *Buckaroo Banzai* adventures.

"I have these two wonderful, ex-girlfriends and they're both nuts. They see me as a total compulsive. One of them, who lives out here, said 'what are you going to get off on after this movie? This one is sort of *it* for you. It's like you get to do everything you like in real life and now you get to be brilliant at it because it's a movie.'" He pauses, smiling. "She asked 'what's going to hold any fascination for you after this?'"

Weller pauses, fixing his gaze on his interviewer. "You know, I thought about it. And I got a little depressed."

He shrugs. "I mean, yeah, what could be better than riding motorcycles, fighting aliens, having romance, driving fast cars, dodging bullets and knives, getting into some rock 'n' roll and spaceships and stuff?"

Nothing probably. But 20th Century-Fox is no doubt hoping audiences find the next best thing is watching someone else do it.

BACK TO THE FUTURE (1985)

Time travel tales are nothing new, a fact director Robert Zemeckis was acutely aware of as he toiled on *Back to the Future*. Is this idea stale? Has it all been done before? Those were just a couple of the questions he posed to the reporter who had come to interview *him*.

The answer to the questions was yes, the idea was stale and yes, it had been done before … but never with the roller coaster excitement and charm Zemeckis brought to his story, which he co-wrote with long-time partner Bob Gale. While the script went through extensive revisions (it originally ended in New Mexico in middle of a nuclear bomb test!) and reshooting (when Eric Stoltz was replaced by Michael J. Fox as teenager Marty McFly), the end result had the manic charm of a Warner Bros, cartoon and the rapid-fire humor of a sharply honed sitcom, all of which more than made up for the tried-and-true story.

The manic charm came from Zemeckis E-ticket directing style, while the slick sitcom sheen can be attributed to Michael J. Fox, who was starring in the hit "Family Ties" literally at the same time, and to Christopher Lloyd, who became famous as part of the classic "Taxi" ensemble.

The movie was a gigantic hit and, naturally, the door was intentionally left open for a sequel. But instead of just doing the obligatory follow-up, the troika of executive producer Steven Spielberg, director Zemeckis, and writer/producer Gale decided to do *two* of them at once, to be released just a few months apart. The gambit didn't quite pay off.

Back to the Future II was a disappointing follow-up that hurled the characters into the future—a particularly bleak future—where things have gone terribly wrong. The best part of the film was actually a replaying of the *first* movie's climax—where past, present, and future Marty McFlys all collide. As clever as the segment was, it was still a repeat of something we had seen before. The movie had little of the charm, or pace, of the first film and, in fact, was completely outshined by the short preview for *Back to the Future III* that followed it.

The third film, by contrast, was an exhilarating and funny joyride into the old west, casting Marty as a reluctant gunslinger … who calls himself "Clint Eastwood." It was also a quirky love story, with Christopher Lloyd's eccentric Doc Brown falling in love with a schoolmarm, played by Mary Steenburgen. Unlike *Back to the Future II*, this film managed to recapture the elements that made the first film so much fun.

While neither of the two follow-ups faired as well financially as *Back to the Future*, the three together were a box-office bonanza for Universal and further established Zemeckis' reputation as a hit-maker … a status immortalized in 1995 with his Oscar for the phenomenal *Forrest Gump*.

ON THE SET OF *BACK TO THE FUTURE*

The remake craze in Hollywood has reached insane proportions. *Brewster's Millions, Tall Blond Man with One Black Shoe, Out of the Past, Unfaithfully Yours, Man Who Loved Women, Tarzan* and *Mutiny on the Bounty* have all recently been reworked.

But Steven Spielberg has outdone them all. He's remaking his film before the original is even finished.

So, in a tranquil Pasadena neighborhood, director Robert Zemeckis is doing his first science fiction film—for the second time.

It is called *Back to the Future*, and it is the story of teenager Marty McFly, who drives an eccentric scientist's souped-up DeLorean back to the 1950s, where he meets his parents as teenagers and nearly splits them up—jeopardizing his own existence.

The movie, starring Eric Stoltz, Christopher Lloyd, Crispin Glover and Lea Thompson was nearly complete, with six weeks of footage in the can, when Zemeckis, his co-writer Bob Gale, producers Spielberg, Kathleen Kennedy, Frank Marshall and Neil Canton came to a devastating—and expensive—realization.

The film was bad. Eric Stoltz was all wrong.

"We realized there was a problem earlier on but we said to ourselves 'Let's deal with it and fix it' and we thought we were doing that. Well, dailies can be misleading," says Canton, who, like Frank Marshall, got his start as an assistant to director Peter Bogdanovich. "It wasn't until we put it together that we said the shots worked but the reason they were was because we're focusing on other persons in the scene and not our hero."

Why did it take so long to realize *Back to the Future* should go back to the drawing board?

"Because Eric is such a good actor," Zemeckis says. "He really didn't do anything that was bad. We didn't know until we started to assemble film that he wasn't creating the right character to tell the story."

The producers were aware of Stoltz's comedic limitations at the outset.

"Eric is a very talented actor, a very serious actor. We always thought his talent would sort of enable him to handle comedy even though he hadn't done comedy before," Canton says. "But ultimately he just wasn't the right person for the role. He felt uncomfortable with the character. I think he felt uncomfortable with the comedy, and I think he had second thoughts about it. We discovered looking at the footage that, although it was supposed to be Marty McFly's story, you aren't following Marty McFly. That made us very nervous and we just decided that it was a mistake."

Because, as Canton says, "everyone agreed, from Universal and Amblin to all of us making it, that it's a great project and will be a hugely successful movie," scrapping *Back to the Future* entirely was out of the question. Scrapping Stolz and starting over was not.

"We wanted to be as nice to Eric as we could be but, ultimately, there's no way around coming right out and saying 'you're going to have to be replaced.' We decided the best way to do it was for Bob Zemeckis to talk with him first,' Canton says. "I think a part of Eric was relieved that it happened and he took it well."

Faced with a July release date, and an unexpected six additional weeks of shooting, the producers had to look for a replacement fast.

"At that point, if we had our choice of anyone in world," Canton says, "everyone agreed it would be Michael J. Fox."

The 23-year-old star of NBC's situation comedy "Family Ties" had originally been considered for the role but wasn't approached because of his commitment to the series. Now, the producers didn't care if Fox had to divide his energies between "Family Ties" and *Back to the Future*. They wanted him.

"He's great. He's got a terrific comedy sense and timing," Canton says. "He's a real eighties kid and so much of what this story is is about an eighties kid uncomfortably trying to deal with being in the fifties."

Spielberg gave a copy of the script to his friend, "Family Ties" producer Gary David Goldberg, who is writing *Reel to Real*, a script for Spielberg based on Spielberg's life. "I went up to Gary's office and he gave me this script and said 'they're going to call you tomorrow,'" Fox says. "He had kind of set up with Steven that it would be copacetic with him if I did both the series and the movie. So it just worked out. It happened in a matter of a couple days."

Sets that were destroyed were rebuilt. The remaining cast and the entire crew were rehired. Millions of dollars more were spent. And, once again, the *Back to the Future* crew transformed a Pasadena street into Elmdale, USA, circa 1950.

"*Dr. Brown, listen! I'm from the year 1985. I came here in a time machine you will invent—and now I desperately need you to help me get back to the future.* "

"It's awful to be doing this over again but it's good because we have been able to improve everything. We haven't slipped. We have been smart enough to say 'Okay, we made a mistake, let's go back,'" Zemeckis says between shots. He watches while crew members search for the hidden wind chimes which ruined the shot. Fox and Crispin Glover, who plays both the young and the old George McFly, sneak away for an orange soda.

"It's nice, in a way, to get to do it over, which is what every filmmaker dreams about," he adds. "But, when you get there, its very hard on everybody psychologically."

"It was very depressing for everyone concerned. What we set out to do was make the scenes better," says Canton. "But obviously Michael brings something different to the scenes and we are feeling better about them now. Ultimately, though, we are still back on the same sets and locations we were before."

A street usually lined with Hondas, Mercedes and Datsuns was again cleared and cluttered with Packards, Studebakers and obese Chevys. Picnic tables were set up and caterers prepared

BBQ chicken and watermelon for lunch while Zemeckis shot in the backyard of a nearby house. It looked like a 1950s block picnic staged by a family that really gets in to shooting home movies.

And it was.

Time traveler Marty McFly (Michael J. Fox) performs an "oldie"—for him, that is—at a 1955 high school dance in *Back to the Future*.

"I think if you asked anyone on the crew I think they'd say we've become a real family because people have spent so much time together. We've gotten very used to being with one another," Canton says. "During this shoot, we've had a total of four appendectomies and four children. I had a daughter, the electrician had a little boy, the sound mixer had a little girl, and the stunt coordinator had a boy. Appendixes were removed from a wardrobe person, an electrician, the first AD, and a PA."

For Michael Fox, *Back to the Future* is all new. "I just look at it as a fresh job." Yet, Stoltz's presence is felt ("I kind of wince a little when they suggest where to put the camera and someone will say 'Last time we did this scene.'") and there's more than a passing familiarity between Marty and Alex Keaton.

"I think the similarities in the characters had a lot to do with me even being here. They wanted someone with Alex's kind of energy." Fox says. "I never read for them; they just watched 'Family Ties' and called me up. Alex has a quality they wanted, a guy who has a kind of a drive to get things done."

"I guess it's basically the same character as Alex," says Canton. "It's what Michael does best and that's why, after watching the show, we knew that was the actor we wanted. That's why we didn't want to really deviate too much from that character other than that this is a feature."

The producers had to devise a flexible and unorthodox shooting schedule to allow Fox time to do the series.

"He was doing 'Family Ties' during the day and shooting with us," Canton says. "We shot split days, shooting without Michael during the day and with him Mondays and Tuesdays after five and Fridays after ten because that's when they shoot the show."

They were concerned the strain would show in Fox's acting so that tried to schedule "our hardest work on Monday, Tuesday and Wednesday and consequently it took us longer than six weeks to make up our lost ground."

But it was worth it.

"Any time anyone ever wonders if we did the right thing all we have to do is put up two scenes—one with Eric and one with Michael—and its clear we did," Canton says. "There is so much more energy in these. Michael just has so much more life to him."

> MARTY: ... George was supposed to get hit by that car. That's how he met Lorraine, my mother. But I took his place. Which means that now—
>
> DR. BROWN: Your mother's amorous infatuation with your father has been transferred to you!
>
> MARTY: Doc, are you trying to tell me that my mother's got the hots for me?

No one could be happier that *Back to the Future* is back on track than Zemeckis and Gale. It has been their pet project for five years. They originally wrote it in 1980 for Columbia Pictures, "which turned it down after two drafts," Gale says. "We took it all over town and couldn't get anybody interested in it because it is so unique and different from the stuff everybody was used to making."

Is it really? Haven't audiences seen enough time travel movies to know just about every twist?

"It's tough to know. Hopefully, you won't think it's been done to death," Zemeckis says. "All time travel movies are real serious, there has never been one that's fun or full of adventure and humor."

> LORRAINE: You know, you sound just like my mother. When I have kids, I'm gonna let them do anything they want. Anything.
>
> MARTY: I'd sure like to have that in writing.

"This movie is jammed with all the great stuff you loved in the *Twilight Zones*, like the great Cliff Robertson *Zone* or the one when the plane goes into time warp. For me, that's what is most fun about time travel. I don't particularly find it fun when a character goes to a future that is alien to us because you can't identify with anything," Zemeckis says. *"Time After Time* was a clever time travel movie and *The Time Machine* was the greatest time travel movie ever done. What was the most fun about it was that, when he went into the future we didn't know it became a monster movie."

"We take some chances, which is what we like to do," says Gale. "We believe that a knowledge of any sort of history is totally unnecessary to enjoy time travel movies. All the history you need is contained within our story. If you see *The Final Countdown*, you have to know about World War II to understand it. Also, in most time movies, people accidentally go back in time and can't go home until it's convenient for the writer. Just at the point where you can't resolve the story, that's when they can go home. We don't do that. We set up the rules and then follow them."

When *Back to the Future* didn't generate any interest, Gale and Zemeckis abandoned it and wrote a gangster movie. "We were in pre-production with ABC Films," Gale says, "but when it was clear things weren't going forward Bob (Zemeckis) said I'm going to direct the next decent thing that comes along."

That was *Romancing the Stone*. It made $70 million.

Now Zemeckis could "pretty much call his own shots," Gale says. They had planned on doing *The Shadow* but then Universal "said we could do this movie," says Zemeckis, "and we couldn't turn that opportunity down. We've wanted to do it for years."

"*The Shadow* is something we are real excited about doing but it is, after all, someone else's characters," Gale says. "We preferred to do our own thing the way we wanted to."

Back to the Future isn't quite the same story they were pitching five years ago. Like any script, it has gone through several revisions. "It isn't wildly different now, but it's different," Zemeckis says. "The time machine wasn't mobile in the first draft. It was left in the future and he happened to coincidentally get back to when the time machine was actually built in the fifties. We didn't like that idea."

"It also has a brand new ending, so we had to change the beginning, because both are tied together," Canton says. "At one time, for monetary reasons, we decided to change the ending because it was too expensive and hard to do and accomplish and required a big optical effect."

In that draft, Marty had to drive his DeLorean-cum-time machine through a nuclear explosion at a New Mexico testing site in order to return to the future.

"The movie is about people and that was sort of too high tech," says Canton, who came onto the project shortly after the release of *Buckaroo Banzai*, the critically praised, financially disappointing science fiction spoof he produced last summer.

"When I first came on they were working on casting Dr. Brown, who creates the time machine," says Canton. "John Lithgow was the first to come to mind. He usually does for anything that wacky and offbeat. John wasn't available and I had such a great experience working with Christopher that I suggested him. There were twenty-five to thirty names on the list but as soon as Gale and Zemeckis met Chris they knew they had Dr. Brown. You only have to meet him once to know he's right for the part."

For the roles of Marty's parents, George and Lorraine McFly, the producers decided to go with two young actors, Glover and Thompson, and age them with make-up as opposed to hiring older actors to play the teenagers as adults.

"George and Lorraine have to age from twenty-one to forty-seven. It's probably the most difficult kind of make-up there is to do. To make that look real on the screen is very difficult. It's harder to make someone look fifty than it is to make them look one hundred and fifty," says Len Chase, the make-up designer. "When you make someone extremely old, you have advantage of being able to cover their whole face with foam latex. When you make a young girl look middle-aged, you can't cover the whole face, you have to just cover part of the face.

"If make-up isn't good, it's best not used at all. Bad make-up calls attention to itself," he adds. "Usually when there is that kind of an age change they will change actors. This is a very daring thing to do. To make it believable isn't easy."

To make *anything* relating to time travel believable isn't easy. But if "the public likes it and if they have a taste for time travel that is less than conventional, yes there will be a sequel," says Zemeckis, who has already charted the story with Gale. "Oh yeah, we have a continuation in mind. We can't tell you about it though. We've got a great bunch of characters in store and a lot of fun traveling around time."

And Fox would gladly tag along for the ride.

"Hey, I'm ready to do it again," he says. "I like the story so much and when I read the way it kind of wound up, I went 'All right! Okay! Let's go!'"

MICHAEL J. FOX INTERVIEW

When teenager Marty McFly took a wacko scientist's modified De Lorean on a drive, he traveled 30 years into the past. When Michael J. Fox did it, he went back just six weeks.

Back to the Future, the story of Marty's jaunt to the 1950s, had already been shot once—with Eric Stoltz starring. But six weeks into shooting, director Robert Zemeckis, producers Steven Spielberg, Frank Marshall, Kathleen Kennedy and Neil Canton, fired him.

And turned back the clock. They started the film again, from scratch.

"At that point, if we had our choice of anyone in the world to be Marty," Canton says, "everyone agreed it would be Michael J. Fox."

The 23-year-old had been considered for the part the first time around but was passed over because of his commitment to the NBC sitcom "Family Ties." The catch was still there.

This time, though, the producers didn't care if Fox had to divide his energies between "Family Ties" and *Back to the Future*. He was right for the role—and with a July release date looming ahead, they didn't have time to search for second-best.

Fox was excited, but was "really afraid" his work in the series and the film would suffer from the pressure of doing both at once. "But what could I do? Say, gee Steve, I'm bushed?" he says. "You don't turn a Steven Spielberg movie down."

It was a torturous schedule. He worked on the series during the day and *Back to the Future* at night "and I had a job at 7-11 in the valley," he jokes. "It was intense. Managing time just got insane. I got four hours sleep a night. I just toughed it through, I guess.

"The positive way to look at the challenge is to say I'll be very conscious of not letting the pressure affect my work. It may have, though," he says. "I *know* it didn't on 'Family Ties' because doing the show gets to be like tying your shoes after awhile. It's not that you don't care about what you're doing, it just becomes second nature."

Unlike the movie method of reading the script, memorizing the lines, and going before the camera, "it's real easy to get the lines down on 'Family Ties' because that's a rewrite process and you're doing it for four days until you shoot on Friday night," Fox says, "though on Saturday I probably couldn't tell you a line one. So, I just had to concentrate on giving everything I had to *Back to the Future*."

He didn't give any thought to replacing another actor and doing scenes everyone else on the set had lived through before. "I just looked at it as a fresh job," he says.

And it's no coincidence that Marty and "Family Ties" Alex Keaton share more than a passing resemblance.

"I think the similarities in the characters had a lot to do with me even being here. They wanted someone with Alex's kind of energy." Fox says. "I never read for them; they just watched 'Family Ties' and called me up. Alex has a quality they wanted."

He's right. Producer Canton admits Marty is "basically the same character as Alex. It's what Michael does best."

While Fox concedes *Back to the Future*'s premise may be a bit stale, "it's really fun, you know? I don't know who said it or in what context, but there are only ten stories. So, when you read a lot of scripts, you see the same themes all the time.

"What was interesting about this one was while some of the themes were familiar, I had never seen them put together in quite the same way," he adds. "There were things happening that I'd seen before but never juxtaposed like that."

Fox wasn't aching for a movie career and scouring Hollywood for feature roles when *Back to the Future* came his way. "Hey, I'm working, I'm not looking to make some breakthrough. What's to break through to and what's to break away from? I'm working and real happy with what I'm doing.

"I was very comfortable with 'Family Ties,' it's my job, you know? I never thought of a movie. But when something like this comes along you don't ignore it," he says. "The only other film that I've starred in is a little one, a werewolf movie, which I did, not for any other reason except to be a werewolf. I think they're calling it now, much to my chagrin, *Teen Wolf*, which really upsets me because the movie is better than that."

Why do a low-budget werewolf movie when riding the crest of something as successful as "Family Ties"?

"Most people advised me not to do the movie but that's why I did it, you know?" Fox says. "I had five weeks off from 'Family Ties' and along comes this low budget werewolf film and it gave me a chance to see how films were made."

Besides, most of the movie scripts that come his way are about "two guys go to Tijuana to get laid, or about guy and girl go to New York and they screw all the way, scripts like that," he says. "This was a movie about a really lousy basketball player who turns into a werewolf and I thought what a really weird movie."

So Fox gave the producers a call and arranged a meeting. "They were really earnest and really pitched it so I said what the hell, let's do it. I liked it, it has its moments."

"By the time *Teen Wolf* comes out," he adds, *"Back to the Future* will be smoking along, I hope."

Michael J. Fox doesn't seem to have much to worry about. He's got a series and two feature films to his credit. But in his short, albeit meteoric, career, he has had his lean days.

Fox, one of five children of an army officer and a payroll clerk, dropped out of high school to play a ten-year-old in the Canadian television series "Leo and Me." A small role in *Letter from Frank*, a TV movie shot in Vancouver starring Art Carney, led to queries from Hollywood agents. He moved to Hollywood when he was 18 and landed roles in Walt Disney's movie *Midnight Madness* and guest shots on "Palmerstown, USA"; "Lou Grant"; and "Family." Between guest shots, however, Fox sold his furniture to keep the cash flowing and ate a lot of macaroni and cheese. But then he was cast as conservative high school student

Alex Keaton in "Family Ties," a dramatic series concept for CBS that mutated into a gimmicky NBC situation comedy about liberal parents raising not-so-liberal kids.

They have since scuttled the concept and relied on the comedic elements inherent in any family with teenage kids.

"We grew from that concept. That concept was something to tell the network boys when the producers sat down at the table to talk about the series," Fox says. "Once a series gets into its second and third year if it doesn't move beyond what that original pitch concept was it's in a lot of trouble."

After a rocky start, the series gained momentum and now, with the help of the blockbuster "Bill Cosby Show" that precedes it, "Family Ties" is a bona fide success and going into its fourth year.

"Survival is a mute point now," Fox brags. And he has every reason to brag. He is in a large part reponsible for the series' holding power.

And, although "Family Ties" is three years old and covers much of the same ground other sitcoms tread, he says the quality is holding up.

"It's real tough. A lot of people don't realize the effort involved for four writers and five actors to be entirely consistent," Fox says. "We have our A shows, and these, I'll put up against any other show on TV, and then, there are times when we just have bad shows. But for the most part, I think we're an over 500 club show, which is what I want."

Although Fox plays just one of the three TV children of Meredith Baxter Birney and Michael Gross, he has shaped his supporting role into what is now the focal point of the show.

"It started to happen towards the end of the first season, mostly because we always seemed to be after 'Facts of Life' or something like that, he says. Alex is the most well-defined of all of them and they wrote to their strength which was that character, who was rounded in a way that they created. They did a good thing. I was fortunate enough to be the guy who was playing that character. I enjoy that but I still think the strength of the show lies in the family."

Nevertheless, he is now the teen idol of giggly girls everywhere. But he shrugs it off because "it's kind of beside the point, you know? It's not an accomplishment or an achievement; it's nothing," he says. "What you do when you're working is an accomplishment and you can hold it up. How white your teeth are and how blue your eyes are you have absolutely nothing to do with it."

It isn't hard dealing with the fan adulation. He knows, though, if "I put on a tie, comb my hair real nice, put on a little and trounce to the Sherman Oaks Galleria at three o'clock on a Saturday afternoon, yeah, I'm gonna get bugged. I'd be a real asshole, too, so I don't do that.

"It's not Beatles time, I don't get chased down streets. I think a lot of that is hype," he adds. "If you *do* run into that kind of response, you just sit and talk to the kids and pretty soon they figure out you're just a person and if they still think you're neat, that's great."

Fox tries to "just live my life like I always did" but being a teen idol does have its benefits. "I can go to cities I've never been to before and I've got friends there."

The bad side is that every movie he makes is closely watched by fan magazines and scandal sheets. And when they aren't exaggerating the truth, they make it up.

"I just read in the *National Enquirer* that I saved a dolly grip's life. It said MICHAEL FOX ADMINISTERS CPR ON A CREW MEMBER. I mean, what are you going to do?" Fox says. "I called them up and said that's not true. They said yes it is. I said I was supposedly there and I think I'd know. They said they'd print it anyway. So what are you going to do? You can't get excited about it. I mean, they could have said I raped and plundered a junior high in El Monte."

His popularity hasn't created friction between Fox and his family in Canada. He says they are "really gassed" about his stardom because they are "so far removed from it that it's still magical."

"The things I might take as everyday and average to them are still really exciting," he says. "They still find it unbelievable that I'm working with Meredith Baxter Birney. They can't relate to it. So it's a lot of fun and I'm real glad it works out that way."

At 23, Fox has attained the kind of success many actors toil a lifetime for. Still, he has his dreams, though "right now it's strange to talk about dreams because everything is so great," he says. "But, someday, I think I'd like to produce television, direct films, and act in theater. And if I could do all those things, it would be great."

But he will stick with "Family Ties" "as long as it goes. I'm not tired of it at all. It's my bread and butter, it's the most fun I've ever had working, and it's an accomplishment for all of us. I'm real proud of it. I wouldn't leave 'Family Ties' for anything. No way."

INTERVIEW WITH ROBERT ZEMECKIS

Back to the Future looked like a guaranteed loser. It was a science fiction tale co-written by a director with a typo for a last name and two box-office duds to his credit. It was also about time travel. And time travel doesn't sell.

Nobody would touch it.

But five years later director Robert Zemeckis did a movie that raked in the bucks (*Romancing the Stone*). He also had an influential buddy named Steve who thought time travel movies sounded like a good idea.

Back to the Future suddenly looked like a guaranteed winner.

Universal Studios believes it could rival *E.T.* at the box office and industry insiders predict it will make Zemeckis a "seven figure" talent to be reckoned with. The wave of hype crashed through the gates of Universal Plaza, raged down Lankershim Boulevard, and swept over the offices of *Variety, The Hollywood Reporter,* and *The Los Angeles Times.* It raged through the city's swank clubs and eateries and didn't ebb out until hitting Wall Street, where the tide brought Universal's stock up to a year-long high.

The publicity had Zemeckis excited—and very worried. Interviewed on the eve of a nationwide press tour and just a few days before *Back to the Future*'s release, the 34-year-old Chicago native was understandably jittery. It's important to Zemeckis that *Back to the Future* succeed—there's a symbolic importance to it, a career imperative.

"It's the movie I always wanted to make," he says, "it's the dream, it's what I expected movie-making to be.

"I got into movies to tell this kind of story. I always knew this was a movie that would work."

While the hype is nice, it could also be suicide. Can *Back to the Future* possibly live up to its glorious fanfare? Or would the fanfare be its funeral dirge?

"I really don't want people comparing us to *E.T.*," Zemeckis said. "What he said was that it has the same *commercial* potential as *E.T.* Suddenly it was a headline. It's an awful big claim and I would never have done that. In the *Hollywood Reporter*, he compared it to the *Wizard of Oz*."

Zemeckis laughs self-consciously. "I respect his enthusiasm, and I love the fact he is a big fan of the movie but, well, it's a lot to live up to."

But it sure beats being a project nobody wanted—and it beats being a film that six weeks into shooting had to be tossed in the garbage.

His tale of a teenager, then played by Eric Stoltz, who drives a time machine into 1955 and almost prevents his parents from meeting "just wasn't working," Zemeckis concedes. "He wasn't creating the right character to tell the story."

The film might have died right there, stillborn after a four and a half year gestation and six weeks of shooting. But the most important man in movie-making, Zemeckis' college chum Steven Spielberg, never lost faith. They fired the star, Eric Stoltz, and simply did it again.

"It was a drastic, drastic thing that had to be done and it was my feeling that the movie hung in the balance," Zemeckis says. "It wasn't hard to admit it wasn't working; it was hard to realize what lied ahead."

They cast Michael J. Fox, a 23-year-old actor with a sharp sense of comic timing he polished during three years on NBC's sitcom "Family Ties." It was that very sitcom that both worked for and against him in assuming Stoltz's part.

Fox had to work two jobs which meant Zemeckis had to work around him—and still meet a July release date. But that wasn't the hardest part of the re-shoot. It was the lingering feeling that they had already failed.

"It was very psychologically debilitating. The pressure came when we did something we were happy with the first time and then did it again and did it exactly the same," he says. "That made us felt depressed because we didn't improve anything. Even though there was nothing wrong with it, you put all this pressure on to improve even when there's nothing that needed improving. Even if we did just as well as we had before, we walked away feeling we didn't do as well as we could."

Michael J. Fox and Christopher Lloyd in *Back to the Future*.

But Zemeckis is certain "we didn't slip." The movie is better. "We all worked very hard to maintain everything that we originally had that was good and to improve everywhere else," he says. Christopher Lloyd carried the biggest acting burden. As the co-star, he had to redo things he had already done to everyone's satisfaction again—this time with a different Marty and sometimes, due to Fox's schedule, with no Marty at all.

"Chris understood completely. As a matter of fact, a lot the stuff we did on the forty feet tall clock tower was salvageable from the Eric shoot and the stuff we did on the stage only six feet off ground was shot during the second shoot while we were waiting for Michael. Chris never got a chance to see the actor he was playing with throughout the entire sequence."

The bottom line, though, is "it's always rough to go back and do something over again." But there are no regrets.

Firing Stoltz saved the film.

"Michael is the absolute anchor of the movie. What is to his credit and to the credit of the film is that it's subtle," Zemeckis says. "You enjoy the other performances and all this wild stuff that is going on but the fact is you are not being pummeled by it because you're totally identifying and relating to Michael J. Fox. His performance is a perfectly measured one and the most difficult anyone could do."

The difficulty is that Marty McFly, an eighties kid caught in the fifties, is "a reactor, his mission is to react to all this. And he just does a wonderful job and that's absolutely crucial to the movie. He has to make the unbelievable part of movie believable and that is what he pulled off."

And Stoltz didn't.

"You completely believe that Chris Lloyd built this time machine. There was a real chemistry between him and Mike on and off the set and that really works for the movie," Zemeckis says. "Eric had a chemistry in a different way that would have worked for a different movie. It wasn't right for our movie. His movie was more mature. It had a main character who had less of a sense of wonder and vulnerability. It wasn't the film Bob Gale and me had in mind."

The film they wanted to make had been on their minds for a long time. They wrote *1941* for Spielberg, then, with some of Steve's spare change, made *I Wanna Hold Your Hand* and later *Used Cars*. Then they began crafting what would become *Back to the Future*.

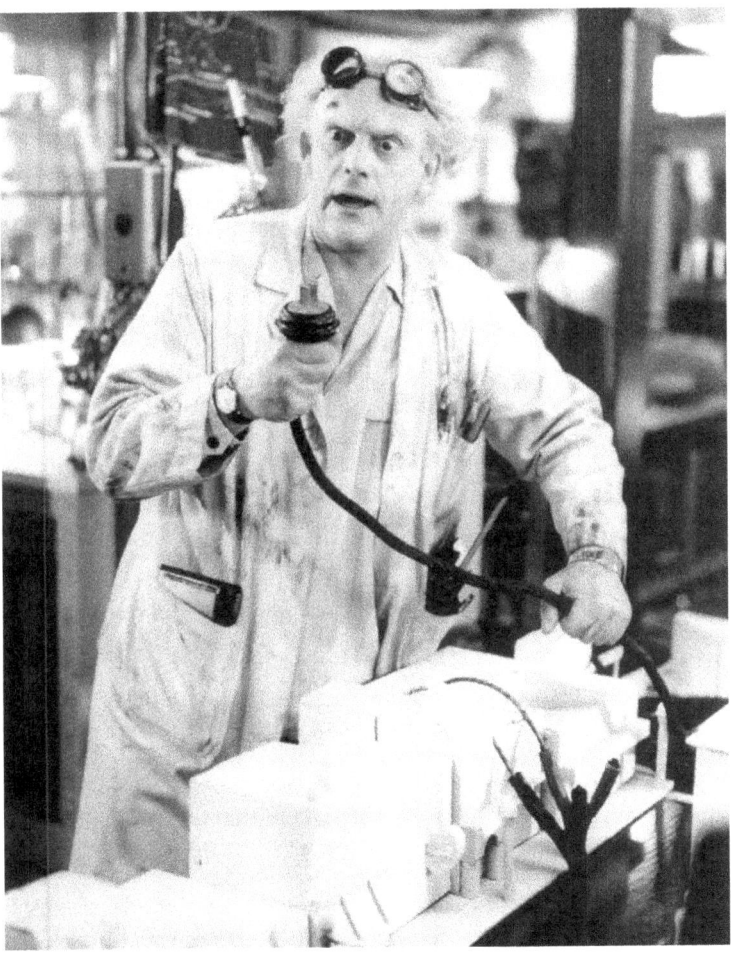

Back to the Future benefited from the sitcom experience of Christopher Lloyd, as the eccentric Doc Brown, fresh from his role in the classic series "Taxi."

They shopped the script around but "absolutely nobody wanted to do it," Zemeckis says. "The biggest concern was that time travel movies never make a lot of money."

They were tinkering around with a "gangster movie" for ABC Circle Films when Zemeckis got offered *Romancing the Stone*.

It was a film suspiciously like buddy Steven's *Raiders of the Lost Ark* and did surprisingly well. Zemeckis was set to segue right into *Cocoon* when, just prior to the release of *Romancing the Stone*, "I showed the finished movie and they fired me from *Cocoon*. And I don't understand why.

"I truly don't know why," he says. "It's the great mystery of my career. It made me feel awful, terrible, it made me feel like they were reacting to shoddy work on *Romancing the Stone*."

(Although he had yet to see *Cocoon*, he had heard that "the first two-thirds are great and the last third sags" because of a *Close Encounters*-like ending. "That was the problem I was working on when I was fired. There were also no real villains in the movie, no real antagonists." His only regret about not doing the movie is "that I worked on it so long and molded so much of the story and I didn't get to see it through.")

He and Gale were writing a movie version of *The Shadow* when Universal expressed interest in *Back to the Future*.

So was Steve, and when that happens, a dormant project can suddenly become Hollywood's hottest ticket.

"Steven was a big fan of the movie and Steven was a perfect executive producer," Zemeckis says. "He was there for ideas and casting. The most important thing he does is create an atmosphere for you to comfortably create a movie. He says it's your movie, if you need me I'm here. He respects the filmmakers vision. He lets you do the movie the way you see it.

"It's the perfect movie for Amblin," Zemeckis says. "It's full of all the stuff people associate with his name—the science fiction and fantasy and adventure and the very uplifting type story."

Still, it was a time travel movie and they have been done to death. Haven't audiences seen all the wrinkles? Will they want to see them again?

"I must say, I was concerned. It was most pointed and scary when *Starlog* expressed concern. You are representative of the subculture of SF aficionados," he says. "What I thought you were saying was 'all of us guys who are into science fiction will, once we see the first five minutes of your movie, know everything.'

"I knew we weren't going to have any spectacular special effects. In fact, it's a very unscience fiction science fiction movie," he continues. "The original design was never to make it a serious science fiction speculation movie. It was a movie inspired by *The Christmas Carol* and *It's a Wonderful Life*, which are all science fiction movies but not considered science fiction movies but in fact are *and* are time travel movies. That's what we rooted our movie in and, though it's tough to know, I hope people will want to see it and won't feel that they have before."

The movie is finally complete and Zemeckis is satisfied.

"I'm extremely happy that this movie got off the ground the way it did," he says. "It's very much the movie I wanted to make for so many years."

And he has a sequel in mind already.

"We're kicking around a lot of ideas. The sequel to this movie could really be great. We laid down the some really good stuff. It could be a wonderful, wonderful adventure," Zemeckis says excitedly. "I talked with Chris Lloyd and if there's a sequel, he wants to play two parts, the villain and the hero. He would have to travel to the future and stop himself, who has become some kind of diabolical villain."

He could open the sequel with the one scene he wasn't able to fit into the ending of *Back to the Future*. Dr. Brown returns from the future in his time machine and implores Marty to join him.

Marty looks at Dr. Brown incredulously. "I can't go driving off into future!"

"Don't worry, you'll be back in a minute."

BIG TROUBLE IN LITTLE CHINA (1986)

Long before John Carpenter broke into major league filmmaking, he wrote and directed a low-budget film called *Escape from New York*, which seemed to exist primarily to give Kurt Russell a chance to impersonate Clint Eastwood. And somehow, it worked.

Ten years later, and with at least $10 million more to spend, Carpenter helmed a movie called *Big Trouble in Little China*, which seemed to exist primarily to give Kurt Russell a chance to impersonate John Wayne.

Actually, it was closer to a cross between John Wayne and Inspector Clouseau. If that seems like an odd concept to grasp, then you've isolated the central flaw with the movie—and why for all its pedal-to-the-metal action, it never seemed to get out of park.

Was it a comedy? An adventure? A spoof? A martial arts movie? What?

It seemed as if even John Carpenter wasn't sure. When he began the project, it was envisioned as an off-beat western—by the time he was finished with it, it was a little bit of everything.

In many ways, this unfocused, excessively over-produced film symbolized the wayward career of this once-promising director, who seemed to turn out much more controlled, and much more entertaining movies, when he had less money to spend and a smaller studio to contend with.

Big Trouble in Little China was not the hip, wise, funny movie Carpenter clearly wanted it to be, instead he turned out a confusing, in-your-face onslaught of images, genres and ideas—a movie and a director in search of themselves.

ON THE SET OF *BIG TROUBLE IN LITTLE CHINA*

Not long ago an "underground movie" was what you called something shot quietly for a $1.98, shown by accident in a theater everybody thought had shut down years ago, and then raved about by a critic who usually hates cheapo little films nobody has every heard of.

Now an underground movie is something else entirely. Now it is films like *Indiana Jones and the Temple of Doom, Goonies, A View to a Kill, Young Sherlock Holmes, Return to Oz,* and the recently completed remake of *Invaders from Mars.* Now it stands for big-budget fantasy flicks set in elaborate subterranean worlds that exist under our biggest cities and smallest towns. Now it means production design gone wild.

It also means that *Big Trouble in Little China,* a $25 million investment for flop-plagued 20th Century–Fox, isn't nearly as unique as it might have been had it been shot five or six years ago. It means that the film, which director John Carpenter (*The Thing*) describes as a "an action-adventure-comedy-kung-fu-ghost-story-monster-movie," is in for a rough time etching out its own identity when it is released during the summer's cinematic slugfest.

"I can only say that people go to see a movie because they hear it's good," says Big *Trouble* screenwriter W.D. Richter, who directed *Buckaroo Banzai.* "If it's a stinker it isn't going to make any difference if it's above ground. Nobody is going to say, 'it's underground so don't see it.'"

Besides, the underground sets are well worth seeing. Production designer John Lloyd, a veteran of 1500 projects including Carpenter's *The Thing* and the original *Alfred Hitchcock Presents* series, had the mouth-watering assignment of creating such outlandish locales as the ornate Hall of the Infernal Judge, the fiery cave that is the Mansion of the Disloyal, the rotting corpse-filled Room of Upside-Down Hell, the treacherous Hell of the River of Ashes and, in a soundstage all its own, the awesome Great Hall.

The center of attention in the cavernous Great Hall, made to look as if its carved out of stone, is a massive skull with fangs ringed with neon and, flowing from its mouth, a staircase. Opposite the skull, across the Great Hall, is a giant, glaring Buddha, also ringed with neon.

The Spirit Path, which leads away from the Great Hall (but actually is constructed in a different soundstage) is seemingly endless and lined with evil statues. This effect is simply achieved in two ways—first off, only the guards in foreground are real statues, the rest, cardboard cutouts; and secondly, as the hallway recedes, it grows narrower giving the illusion of distance. Similar illusions are used in the numerous sewers, tunnels and pipes that Lloyd had designed for the characters to be imperiled in.

The special effects that will give the sets their supernatural dimension are being handled by Oscar-winner Richard Edlund (2010). "I can't say enough about Richard Edlund," says Carpenter. "He's very straightforward, very direct, and he's not flexing his ego all over the soundstage when you're trying to do a shot."

Beyond designing the subterranean world, Lloyd also oversaw the recreation of Chinatown itself, complete with two- and three-story buildings, roads, streetlights, sewers and phone lines, clouds and sunlight inside the confines of a soundstage. Only a tiny portion of the 20th Century–Fox backlot has been redressed from its 1940s facades (for *Johnny Dangerously*) for use in *Big Trouble in Little China*.

The sets cost a good chunk of that $25 million, but Carpenter believes that was the only way to go. "You can't do fantasy sequences that are stylized on the street," says Carpenter. "The types of action this film calls for—very elaborate stuff with lots of special effects, kung fu fighting, people riding around the streets on lightning bolts—if we went to San Francisco to do it, it would have been impossible."

Even seasoned pros like actor Kurt Russell are taken aback by the creativity and detail of Lloyd's elaborate sets.

"These are the nicest sets I've ever worked on, they are really beautiful," says Russell, who is reteaming with Carpenter for the third time in this film. "I really think as the sets go, 20th Century-Fox really came in strong for us. The look of this picture should be really exciting."

Kurt Russell fights for his life against a Chinese swordsman in *Big Trouble in Little China*.

Big Trouble in Little China must have looked great to 20th Century-Fox executives long before any sets were built. It is a bizarre hybrid of *Romancing the Stone*, one of the studio's few recent hits (along with its sequel), and *Buckaroo Banzai*, the studio's fiscal flop that wowed the critics and begat a loyal cult following. Like *Romancing the Stone*, it is a romantic action adventure with a likeable couple, assayed by Kurt Russell and Kim Cattrall, thrust into an extraordinary situation. Like *Buckaroo Banzai*, it's a stylish, offbeat film that is an inventive combination of many genres and looks at its heroes with a sly sense of humor.

"The characters are offbeat, nutty, they remind me of the characters in *Bringing Up Baby* or *His Girl Friday*," says Carpenter. "These are very 1930s, Howard Hawkes people." But, he says, "there has never been a movie like this, ever."

The hero is Jack Burton, a truck driver carrying a load of pigs to the San Francisco wholesale market. There, he wins a bet with restaurateur Wang Chi (Dennis Dun, *Year of the Dragon*), who can't pay his debt. So Burton follows him and, when Wang Chi's green-eyed bride-to-be is kidnapped by Ninjas, finds himself unwillingly thrust into the center of a centuries-old conflict between good and evil that's being waged on the streets of San Francisco's Chinatown and in a subterranean world of unimaginable, otherworldly dangers. The dangers include sewer monsters, flying eyeballs, living thunder and a drooling, fang-toothed monster called the Wild Man.

Jack Burton gets plenty of help and aggravation from attorney Gracie Law (Kim Cattrall, *Police Academy*), bus-driver-cum-wizard Egg Shen (Victor Wong, *Year of the Dragon*) and irritatingly eager reporter Margo Litzenberger, played by newcomer Kate Burton, daughter of actor Richard Burton.

The story is steeped in Chinese mysticism and ancient lore which the filmmakers say is more real than imaginary. "It's the first-time Hollywood has tried a Chinese fable," says James Hong, who plays Lo-Pan, the immortal villain. "It's a magical fantasy with lots of folklore but it's not meant to be a documentary portrayal of China." Still, the Chinese characters are not likely to be the brunt of anger from minority groups.

"I don't know of a better role for an Asian actor," says Dun. "I'm seeing Chinese actors getting to do stuff American movies usually don't let them do. I've never seen this type of role for an Asian in an American film. It's written that I'm Chinese but the way it's written I could be anybody. The humor is regular, good old American humor and doesn't come from me being a dumb chink."

"Jack is not portrayed as a God-like white man walking among them telling them what to do," says Richter. "It's a universe of characters in the same boat."

Kim Cattrall was an odd choice for that universe. Cattrall toiled in virtual obscurity on dramatic episodic television before breaking into feature films with Otto Preminger's bomb *Rosebud* (as politician-turned-actor John Lindsay's daughter). 20th Century–Fox noticed her after watching her in a string of Bob Clark films—*Tribute*, *Porky's* and *Turk 182*—and in Warner Bros.' low-brow hit *Police Academy*. Nothing she's done is anything like the heroics and fantasy of Big *Trouble in Little China*.

"I needed someone with a comedic sense and Kim was right," says Carpenter. "There's a lot of strange dialogue and I needed someone who could play it seriously, too."

"She's got a real tough role to play," says Russell, "because it's all fine-line stuff. You're over the top most of the time but you also have to believe what you're seeing."

James Hong as the villain in John Carpenter's *Big Trouble in Little China*.

Perhaps her big-screen comedy experience and her strong background in episodic television—a background she shares in many ways with Russell, who began in wacky Disney comedies before doing TV series fare like *The Quest* and *The New Land*—may be just the right preparation for the difficult role.

For Cattrall, it was the right role at the right time. After being typecast as a dramatic TV actress, and trying to avoid being pigeon-holed as "the girl from *Porky's* and *Police Academy*," she was looking for something that would synthesize the two perceptions and show her off in a brand new way. It is a part that requires her to do something she has never done before: "scream as many times as I can," she laughs. "Actually, I'm a very serious character in this. I'm not screaming for help the whole time. I think the humor comes out of the situations and my relationship with Jack Burton, I'm the brains and and he's brawn."

And he was almost played by somebody besides Kurt Russell. "It's a funny thing, but I didn't see Kurt as the lead," says Carpenter. Neither did Kurt Russell. But they were anxious to work together again. Russell read the script, liked it, but had troubles with the character. "It wasn't clear to me how to play it," Russell recalls. But Russell and Carpenter talked it out and were able to convince each other that Russell was right for the part. What finally swayed Russell was that *Big Trouble in Little China* seemed like "an out and out chance to have a good time and do something I had never done before.

"I've never played a hero like this who has so many faults," Russell says. "Jack is and he isn't the hero. He falls on his ass as much as he comes through. This guy is a real blow hard. He's a lot of hot air, very self assured, a screw up. He thinks he knows how to handle situations and then gets into situations he can't handle and somehow blunders his way through."

Richter sees his creation a bit more charitably.

"He's an average guy, not a guy whose daily life throws him into jeopardy. He is not an adventurer. Indiana Jones is an adventurer. Jack Burton is a truck driver who likes nothing more than to drive a truck. This experience is a real fluke or aberration."

The experience Jack Burton faces wasn't always a contemporary fantasy. It began as a western written as a sample script by two unknown screenwriters. Veteran producer Paul Monash (*Salem's Lot*) bought the project, realized it needed work, and hired W.D. Richter to give it an overhaul while still retaining its uniqueness.

"It was set in the 1880s and instead of a truck driver, there was a cowboy who rides into town," says Carpenter. "The problem was, first you had to believe Chinatown in the old west, then you had to believe mythical demons and heroes and villains. And Rick said, 'look, that's too much to believe.' He was right. Fantasy and westerns don't mix. He said 'let's make it modern day and he went off to do the rewrite.'"

Although most of the original script was junked, some elements have a carried through to the current draft. "The story of the villain remains almost intact," says Carpenter. "He's 2000 some odd years old and he was in the Court of the First Emperor of China and he was given a curse of being a ghost forever until he marries a girl with green eyes, then he can become a man again."

Personifying this immortal evil is James Hong, best known to SF fans as, he says, the "old guy in the refrigerator making eyeballs" in *Blade Runner*. He's played a lot of villains, but this one "is sympathetic in a way," he says. "He's 2000 years old and still waiting for the right girl to come along."

It's not likely, with a villain like that (and forgetting the underground setting for a moment), that there is any other film coming out soon that is even remotely similar. That's not what Paramount Pictures thinks. They believe their new Eddie Murphy project *Golden Child*, which they *did* offer to John Carpenter, is enough like Big *Trouble in Little China* to merit some heated phone calls. Murphy plays a private detective specializing in finding lost children hired to search for the mystical "golden child" kidnapped by the Forces of Evil (literally) from a temple in Tibet. The baddies hold the kid in Chinatown and try to entice him into evil.

"What I know is hearsay," says Richter. "I heard that the two guys who wrote the original version of this knew the guy who wrote *Golden Child*. They were sort of talking to each other while writing their spec scripts. Lo and behold, both scripts sold."

"Strange as it may seem, I got offered these two movies at the same time," says Carpenter. "They aren't really similar. Originally *Golden Child* was a serious, Chinese, mystical, very sweet, very nice film. But they don't know whether to make it funny or serious."

"What I've heard is that *Golden Child* is a straight-ahead, non-comedy, action-adventure thing with demonology," says Richter. "But it's all academic. We're coming out first."

But that doesn't mean they will be a hit. Marketing a film as quirky and unusual as Big *Trouble in Little China* is either a breeze or an insurmountable task. "*Buckaroo Banzai* is a good example," says Richter. "They didn't know what to do with it."

Russell isn't worried. "If the picture, overall, is fun to watch, and you care about the characters, I don't think the film is going to be difficult to market. If it lacks that and is just a great looking, action-adventure film, then it might be difficult."

CONAN THE DESTROYER (1984)

When Arnold Schwarzenegger decided to become an actor, no one took him seriously. With his heavy accent and weight-lifter's body, he hardly seemed cut out as a leading man in anything but the sword-and-sorcery movies like *Conan* and its sequel, *Conan the Destroyer*.

But Schwarzenegger had unwavering faith in himself and proved all the skeptic wrongs—in a big way. Although the *Conan* series of films he foresaw never came about, a small film he had just completed at the time of this interview, James Cameron's *The Terminator*, would prove to be the breakout hit that would catapult him into the forefront of action film stars ... a situation he was not only prepared for, but fully expected to face.

INTERVIEW WITH ARNOLD SCHWARZENEGGER

Arnold Schwarzenegger's company is located in an old Gas Company building in trendy Venice, California. It has huge, high ceilings with lots of windows. The walls are covered with photographs and paintings of Schwarzenegger as bodybuilder, actor and as *Conan the Barbarian*.

When Schwarzenegger appeared for the interview, greatly apologetic because traffic has caused him to be late, he was dressed in shorts and a green T-shirt. With his short, light brown hair that is just starting to grey in the front, and his open friendly face, he looked anything but barbaric.

He sat in his office behind a massive desk, smoking a pipe and drinking coffee. The walls of this room are also lined with photos of Schwarzenegger, but more personal ones, including a charming shot of him with his dog. Next to it is a photo from Schwarzenegger's last completed film, *The Terminator*.

Q: When you finished with the first *Conan* film, did you know at that time that there was going to be a second one?

ARNOLD SCHWARZENEGGER: Well, I have a contract for five *Conan* movies. But, in the end, it always has to do with how successful was the last one you made. I think that we pretty much knew that the first *Conan* was going to make enough money so that we would make a second one. We knew that there were a lot of *Conan* fans, fantasy movie fans, bodybuilding fans, martial arts fans, etc .… With that kind of combination, we knew that we had more than the normal audience that you usually have when a movie comes out. Then it was just a question of how much further could we go with that. The movie ended up doing enough business .… As a matter of fact, it did so well that Dino De Laurentiis and Universal both decided that they would go on and do a second one right away.

Now, we have just had sneak previews of *Conan the Destroyer*, and we have gotten the most positive reaction. So, now we know that there will most likely be a third one. In fact, Dino is already negotiating for that. So, the way it looks right now, I think there will be at least five *Conan* movies. I believe that the audience is growing. Universal is putting more commitment behind it. They've built this multi-million dollar *Conan* live show at the Universal Studio Tour, which every week gains another 50,000 or 100,000 new *Conan* fans. It's the most watched show that they've ever had. With all those elements, I think we will go on and do many *Conan* films, probably until I have a grey beard. Then, the last movie, we will call it *Conan Dies!* [laughter]

Q: A lot of the Robert E. Howard fans were disappointed with the first film, because they didn't feel it was faithful to the *Conan* books that they had read. How do you feel about that?

AS: It couldn't have been totally faithful because Robert E. Howard had never explained how and where Conan was born, how and where he grew up, all those things. Just all of a sudden, there was Conan. So, John Milius felt—and I think he was totally right—that he should explain all this at the beginning. Now, there's a reason for Conan's behavior, for his philosophies in life, and for his way of going about things. For instance, why did he end up being this muscular guy, so unlike anybody else? Why did he become such a fighting machine and such an expert in the various different weaponries? Milius explained all that in the first movie because he felt it was very important. Now, we can go on and do the next movies like Robert E. Howard, very loose, very light, just Conan going from adventure to adventure. The titles will be accordingly similar to Howard's books, like this one, *Conan the Destroyer*, and so on, depending on what the story is.

Q: Had you read the script done by Roy Thomas and Gerry Conway and what were your feelings about it?

AS: [Schwarzenegger stops to light his pipe and weigh his words]: I thought it was half decent, but I didn't feel there was much motivation in there. It had to be rewritten. There were no two ways about it. There were some elements of it that were left in the script that we shot, which I think are good elements, and I think that they contributed to the story. But, when I read it, I called Dino right away and I said, "Listen, as far as I'm concerned, this will not make a movie."

Arnold Schwarzenegger in *Conan*.

What I think they didn't realize is that a movie is not a like a comic book, where the story just starts out of nowhere and ends up nowhere. That's fine with a comic book because you can continue next month to read on the story, and then the next month again. With a movie, it has to have a beginning, a middle and an end. There has to be a love story there, and it all has to make sense within this one and three quarters of an hour. I think that's what they missed in the script. This is why they had to have the script rewritten by somebody that is aware of how movies work. With that combination, I think we now have a great script and a great movie.

Q: Do you feel that there are certain things that *Conan* has to do to be true to *Conan* as he's been created for the screen?

AS: Absolutely. I think that, from the beginning to the end, he has to be based on Robert E. Howard's character. There are characteristics of *Conan* that are very obvious. For example, he's a man of action, he's a very impatient man. He is the kind of person that goes into action first, and then, maybe, he thinks about it! This is why he's ahead of everybody else. Other people think about going into action beforehand, and by that time, Conan has already attacked, conquered or destroyed the enemy. So, he's just a man of action all the way through. He's a brave guy. If you make Conan a less brave person, then he becomes not true to the character. He's a warrior, all the way through. Therefore, he can plan or fight big battles.

So, all of those things have to be taken from Robert E. Howard's character. The same holds true of his physical development. You could not make Conan, all of a sudden, a lean, skinny guy. He has to be a heroic heman, muscular and all of those things. His whole behavior was always portrayed as kind of animalistic. In a way, he is a human being who is like an animal. The way he moves, he jumps, he runs, he rides horses.... Everything about *Conan* is very much instinctive and animalistic. So, all of those things have to be like Robert E. Howard originally conceived them.

Q: What about his personality? I suppose you have to keep him almost two dimensional and not have him experience the "softer" emotions ....

AS: One of the things that works well in movies is when a person does show some emotions, and also exhibits a certain sense of humor. I think that, in the *Conan* books, you very rarely see *Conan* showing any real humor, like scenes where he'd look at things in a funny way, or would have fun with the adventure that he's going through. Yet, those things are important. Although that changes from year to year, right now, we know that in the movies people like to have some comic relief, besides fantasy and adventure.

So, the way you set it up is by not necessarily making Conan himself a funny guy, but by setting him up with somebody that is his sidekick and that creates that kind of humor and comic relief. I believe this is necessary to make everyone in the audience have a moment of laughs, especially after being tense during the fighting or the dramatic scenes. The up and down, is very important in order to have a successful movie. So, there are certain things that you have to do, even if it means going a little bit off, because you have to cater to the times that you're filming for, and to today's movie audience.

Q: Do you think that, at the end of five movies, you'll get tired of being associated with *Conan*?

AS: No. First of all, I'm very loyal to *Conan*, because it is he who has helped me in the first place. I think that portraying the *Conan* character has gotten me an extra amount of exposure worldwide, and it has enabled me to make a successful movie. Because of that, I feel that I have to give back the same support as I have received from this kind of character. So, I am very happy to portray *Conan* for five movies, or ten movies, or for the rest of my life!

Number two, I think it's a great pleasure to play a character like *Conan*. Every time I've done a *Conan* film, I had a tremendous fun time because it lends itself to fun and to joy. It's an adventurous character, and the movies themselves are comprised of horseback riding, being outdoors, sword fighting, jumping around, being with people like Grace Jones or Wilt Chamberlain, or Jerry Lopez in the first movie …. People like that are all athletic, all out-doorsy, and not the traditional actors' types. I've had a lot of fun doing the *Conan* pictures, and I'm always looking forward to the next one. I really don't think I will get tired of it and worry about it.

The question that a lot of people ask me, of course, is whether I'm worried about being typecast. Again, I always look at the upside and never the downside. I say that I'm very happy that I'm working, and playing a character that is interesting, rather than playing in some movie that has no interest to me, and that one would just do for a salary. *Conan* gave me all the exposure I have, and it's a natural vehicle for me. So why should I be worried? On the contrary, I'm very proud and very happy to portray this character and do this kind of films.

Besides, I always have a chance to do other movies in between. So I'm very happy to be in this situation, and not worried at all. Frankly, I would be a lot more worried if I had no job. That would really worry me!

Q: *The Terminator* is science fiction, isn't it?

AS: It's futuristic. It's fantasy. I play a robot that is more like an android. I mean, I am a mechanical person inside, but the outside looks like a human being. Like the name says, I'm a terminator. That means I terminate people's lives in order to change the future. I come back from the year 2035 to our time to kill certain people in order to change the future, by not having a certain child be born that will become the leader of the future.

Grace Jones does battle with a horde of soldiers in *Conan the Destroyer*.

Of course, I'm not always very successful, because you can't really change a future that has already happened! [laughter] Anyway, it was a good attempt! It left the movie kind of wide open. At the end, *Terminator* gets crushed by a machine that crushes cars, and a microchip falls out and is picked up by the head of the lab there, and with that, of course, you can produce another thousand *Terminators*.

Q: So there could be a second Arnold Schwarzenegger series?

AS: Exactly! Why should the guy from Indiana Jones be the only one to have several sequels!

Q: You've done the *Conan* films, *The Terminator*, that funny western *The Villain*. Do you think that such varied films are helping to take you away from the image of being "only a bodybuilder" and force people to see you as an actor?

AS: I think that people realize that, with the *Conan* movie, you have to have more than just a bodybuilding physique. Otherwise, why is it that I am the one doing *Conan*, and not the other five hundred thousand competitive bodybuilders that are out there. There are a lot of great looking bodybuilders, There are a lot of great looking Mr. Universe physiques out there. So, there's one element that sets me apart, I think, and this is the acting. And also the athletic abilities that are necessary for the film.

In *The Terminator*, for example, there's not one scene in the film where I am exposing my body. Therefore, I must have been hired for something else besides the body. It couldn't be the name recognition factor alone, because again, there are many other people out there with a big name. So, I like to think that again, it must be the acting. In the case of *Conan*, of course, I think it's a combination. However, more and more, I think I can use the *Conan* films to show that I can also act, and therefore be able to do other films, like *The Terminator*. I think what I'm going to do is maybe a *Conan* film and then, one or two other movies that are unlike it, and go on like that.

Q: Will you keep up your bodybuilding activities as well?

AS: I have no choice if I want to continue doing *Conan* movies! I have to be in shape. As a matter of fact, for *Conan the Destroyer*, I'm in better shape than I was for *Conan the Barbarian*. So, if I go on like that, I may be in even better shape for *Conan III*!

But, for myself also, I always need to train and be in shape. I need to be proud of myself when I look in the mirror and say, "Yeah, I'm still in shape." That's very important to me, the idea that I'm doing something everyday physically.

Q: Do you find it difficult sometimes to find time to do that?

AS: No. Because to me, training is like sleeping and eating. You never worry about where you find the time for sleeping, you just go to bed when you're tired. Well, the same is true with training for me. It's just part of my life. It's planned in as a necessary thing, without worrying about where I'd get the time.

I just get up at six in the morning and go to the gym before breakfast, then have breakfast. At that time, there's nobody that can stand in my way and say I can't do that. During the day, of course, it would be more difficult, because I have to run to interviews or business meetings, etc ….

Q: In a recent interview, you said some less than flattering things about Dino De Laurentiis that made it seem as if you didn't get along too well with him, or that you maybe had some problems with the first movie. Have those things straightened out?

Arnold Schwarzenegger fights almost insurmountable odds as *Conan the Destroyer.*

AS: Frankly, I don't remember what I said, because I don't read back all my interviews. But I admit that we did not start off in the best way. He had some kind of friction in our first meeting. Nothing intentional really. It's just that I said things that set him off in the wrong way, and he said things that set me off the wrong way. Then, we were kind of fighting without really knowing each other. At the time, he had something against me playing *Conan*, but Milius said that I was the only one that could play the part, so he just accepted that fact. After seeing the first three days of dailies, he came and said to me [imitating Dino], "Hey, you are *Conan*," Which was kind of his way of complimenting me and saying that I fit the character and that I was right.

Since then, of course, Dino has been very, very nice to me. He has invited me to parties and has included me in his family activities and things like that. So, all of that has straightened out in the end. I think it was just one of those funny beginnings where you just hang on top of each other, and say weird things and make each other mad and so on.

Q: You seem to get along very well with Raffaella.

AS: Raffaella is even much easier to get along with. You see, Dino has a problem. He has been involved with over four hundred movies, in one way or another. In a way, it's like me and bodybuilding, so I can relate to his position because I have no patience myself. When I run the world championships in bodybuilding, and somebody comes to me with a problem, I just brush him off, "Forget it, forget it. I have no time for that kind of crap." It's really because you have no patience, or tolerance, for this kind of thing. It has to be your way or nothing.

So, Dino is like that with the films. Many times, it somehow backfires, because you cannot be a person that knows it all. I'm aware of that, and maybe he's aware of it, but he can't help himself, because I can't help myself either! So, that's why it's sometimes harder to deal with him, whereas Raffaella is enthusiastic about doing films because she has not been involved with that many films, and you can reason with her and deal with her, and that makes it pleasant. She's the kind of woman that, when you explain something, saying, "I think we have to do it this way or this way," she says, "Arnold, I'll call you back. Let me work on it. I think you're totally right." Or when I say, "I just saw this in this script that you guys sent, and I think it's shit," she says, "I agree with you, but it's very hard with Dino," and blah, blah, blah. So, I can deal with her on this level, and we have had a good relationship.

When you work on films like *Conan*, big budget films, you can have all the comforts in the world. The contracts that I signed have so many pages that you don't even want to start counting them! But what is really important is that you have a certain kind of respect for one another, and are willing to help one another. That is never covered in a contract. For example, in the contract, it says that I have to have a first class trailer that is so many feet long. Well, we got into a situation where, all of a sudden, we ended up shooting on a mountain somewhere, where a trailer like that could not be brought. Now, if you stick to the letter of the contract, they in turn have to comply. But then, you get stuck, because they say, "Well, we can't shoot in that location, although it's a wonderful location, because we can't get the trailers up there the way those actors have requested it in the contract." So what happened in this case is that Raffaella came to me and told me that they had this problem. And I said, "Forget the trailer, we'll sleep in a tent up there. I know it's important to the film that we shoot at this location." And the other way around, if I need something different than it's written in the contract, then Rafaella comes through my way. So, when you do films like that, and when you want to do the next five films together, you then have to become kind of brother and sister, rather than being on opposite fences.

Q: So you don't see yourself as the "prima donna" style actor?

AS: No, not at all. To me, the bottom line is that, first, I get my money. Number two, that I get the attention, time-wise, that makes me look good on the film and makes me portray the character in the proper way, So, if I say to the director that I need another take, then he should do another take. If I say to Raffaella that we should redo a scene, then she should jump for the money to redo that scene, if it doesn't work. So, those are the important things. What matters is that you work well with people and become one unit, where one person always helps the other.

Q: You worked very well with John Milius in the first film. Were you disappointed at first when you found that he wasn't going to be directing the second one?

AS: Yes. I was very disappointed when Milius was not asked to do the second *Conan* picture. Well, actually, he was asked to do it, but he couldn't because he was already committed to *Red Dawn*, the movie that he's doing now, and which he already had promised MGM that he would deliver at a certain time. So, he put on certain stipulations on Dino, and Dino couldn't come through with that because he wanted to move on with *Conan the Destroyer* and not wait until John had time to write it and direct it. So, it was a two-sided situation where everybody was faced with the situation that, no, John just couldn't do it.

So, finally, I just accepted the fact that it was a problem in finding the right man to do it. In the beginning, when they hired Richard Fleischer, I was worried because when I met him, he looked like such a fragile, small guy. He was 67 or some years old, and I thought he didn't have the vigorous appearance that Milius had. John was always there, with an axe or with a sword, hacking away at people, saying, "This is the way you have to do it!" He always would talk about Ghengis Khan and all kinds of historic battles and he would create a certain excitement. Richard Fleischer just didn't give that kind of appearance. But, I think it became very apparent, rather quickly, that he brought a totally different kind of quality to the film that was, again, a great asset. Which was, having the total confidence of a director who has done over forty movies, and having the ability of delegating responsibilities.

If there was a big battle scene, for instance, he would have the stunt coordinator take over and let him choreograph it. He was always totally relaxed and at ease. It gave you a feeling that, yes, there is somebody in total control of the thing. He always appeared like that. He was always systematic in the way he moved forward with the shooting. It never went beyond the time that was required. He was a very good director because he's very much into rehearsals and so on. So, as we started shooting, after a few days, I felt very happy that Richard Fleischer was directing the movie. Now, after having gone through the experience and having seen the film, I have to say that I would do a movie with him anytime again because he was a real superb director, very sensitive to actors and very inspirational and powerful in his own quiet way.

Q: How do you think his direction has changed *Conan*?

AS: I think he made *Conan* less of a heavy movie, a philosophical movie, like Milius had made it, and made it more light and more like the comic books are. Also, he made it less violent. He made it a PG rating, and he put a little bit more humor in there.

Q: What would you like to do as projects in the future?

AS: Right now, my big wish, besides doing the *Conan* films, is to do a Viking movie and to have John direct it. We've been talking about it several times and I think that will become reality eventually.

But then also, eventually, I would like to do a comedy because I think I can do that well. And other types of movies, of course. That's every actor's dream, to kind of broaden out eventually. But you can't force the issue, or force it upon the people, because that's when you fall on your face. You have to kind of ease in when you do a new kind of movie, so people don't say, "I don't want to see Arnold in a comedy, I want to see him hacking away on people!"

THE DEAD ZONE (1983)
VIDEODROME (1983)

David Cronenberg is, without a doubt, one of the most original directors in the SF genre. The ideas that he has developed in his films are disturbing, grotesque and often without equivalent anywhere—the "New Flesh" of *Videodrome*, the "psychoplasmics" of *The Brood, The Scanners*—these are all frightening and (sometimes literally) mind-blowing concepts.

This is due in major part to the fact that, until *The Dead Zone*, Cronenberg did not limit himself to the role of director. He always had a hand in writing his stories, as well as supervising their production. *The Dead Zone* was a departure for Cronenberg, since it was a Dino De Laurentiis production, based on a novel by Stephen King. Yet, the theme of the book, which has to do with biological fantasy (the hero develops para-normal powers after a car accident) leads itself to Cronenberg's unique, darkly comic vision.

Of all the post–*Carrie* King adaptations, *The Dead Zone* proved to be (with the possible exception of *Stand by Me* some years later) the most artistically and stylistically successful. And, despite its mixed financial results, it marked the first in a long series of increasingly bad De Laurentiis adaptations of King's major and minor works. However, *The Dead Zone* established Cronenberg as a director capable of maintaining his unique vision while still delivering a crowd-pleasing film, a delicate balancing act that landed him 20th Century-Fox's big budget remake *The Fly*.

The success of *The Fly* yanked him out of genre niche, out of independant film obscurity, and into the big leagues. But unlike John Carpenter and Wes Craven, who, respectively, opted for the safer ground of *Starman* and the Disney Sunday movie, Cronenberg didn't water down his dark vision in favor of uplifting studio fare or a cuddly television series.

The Dead Zone may have led Cronenberg to Hollywood acceptability, but it didn't distract him from his vision. If anything, it secured him the backing and the following to refine it, his style growing darker and even more disturbing in such movies as *Dead Ringers* and *Naked Lunch*.

INTERVIEW WITH DAVID CRONENBERG

Cronenberg was in the final stages of sound mixing for *The Dead Zone* when we met for this interview in a small Hollywood restaurant. The tall, lean, bearded director was wearing a *Dead Zone* logoed sweatshirt and happily recalled, over lunch, the details of his first film based on another writer's work.

Q: How did you get involved with *The Dead Zone*?

DAVID CRONENBERG: I had met Raffaella De Laurentiis and went to talk to her. She said that she had liked *Scanners* very much and we started to talk about a few things. She asked me if I had ever read *The Dead Zone*, because Lorimar had the rights to the book. I hadn't but by the time I finished it she had to confess that, unbeknownst to her, Lorimar had already hired Stanley Donen to direct it, and Sydney Pollack was going to produce it. So, I just forgot about it.

Then, a little more than a year ago I was in John Landis' office and Debra Hill came in and said, "By the way, what would you think if I said, *The Dead Zone?*" I said I thought it would make a very good movie. She said she was producing it for Dino De Laurentiis and she wanted me to talk to him because she thought I should direct it.

So, it was strange to have it come full circle after all that time. In the meantime, there had been some other people approached to direct the picture, and there had been several scripts written. One of them was done by Stephen King and one was by Jeffrey Boam, who was eventually the writer that we chose to write our version of the script.

We were not happy with any of the scripts that had been written, and I said that we really just had to re-adapt the book for the screen and forget about what had been written before. Jeffrey's script, that he had written for Stanley Donen back at Lorimar, had something that we thought would make him the right person to write the final script, and he's the one that did. It was really Debra, Jeffrey and I who locked ourselves in a hotel room in Toronto for three days, and just started to restructure the whole idea. Of course, there were many problems to solve, in translating the book to the screen, as there always are.

Q: The Stephen King script didn't work, as far as you were concerned?

DC: One of the problems that we had to try to solve, was that, in the book, there are three parallel stories going all the way through, but I didn't think it was possible to do it properly that way in the screenplay. Stephen did try to do it that way; I didn't think it worked. He started with Stillson in the past. I thought that we had to start with Johnny and have a triptych, a three-part film instead. The first part is Johnny and Sarah and what happens to him, then there is the Frank Dodd thing in the middle, and then the Stillson thing is the last third. Rather than pile them on top of each other.

Also, I thought that Stephen's script gave more emphasis to the Frank Dodd murders than I wanted to give in the version of the film that I wanted to do. His script was very different from the book. Very different in tone. I think that, ironically I suppose, our version of the film is closer in tone to the book than Stephen's script was.

Stephen has seen the film, and he really liked it. He said that there were some things that are in the movie that he wished he'd done in the book. Which I thought was high praise.

Q: Other than trying to separate the stories, what changes have you made?

DC: Many, many. In the movie there is no period of coma suggested. There is a crash, he [Johnny] wakes up in the hospital. He can't understand why he doesn't have any scars, bandages or even scratches. He thinks it's the next day. His parents come in and they tell him that he's been in a coma for five years. In the book there's a whole long feel of him being in a coma and Sarah's life going on. It would have been very difficult to do that on screen.

In fact, I thought that given the kind of compressing that you have to do in a film, that it would be a completely different kind of thing to have the audience wake up with Johnny and not know that either one of them has been away for five years. Of course, in the book, there's no attempt to do that kind of surprise thing at all. It does something quite different, which is to give you a sense of what consciousness might be like over a period of five years in a coma. So, in this case, it's not an improvement, it's just different because I think the difference in the two media demands it.

I couldn't see scenes of Johnny lying in bed with a voiceover radio broadcasting elections, etc. There are many ways you could have done it, and maybe it could have been done successfully, but I just didn't think it would work, and I didn't try to do it.

Another difference is that in the book, Sarah disappears about two-thirds of the way through the book, except by letter. I didn't feel that would work in a film. I really felt that she had to be woven through the last third of the film. How we did that was to have her working on Stillson's campaign, and having her be at the last rally, when Johnny tries to shoot Stillson. That way she is there to see it and there to be with him when he dies.

We didn't change the ending though, and strangely enough, most of the other scripts did. I can't remember, but I think Stephen's script also was different at the end. I liked the ending of the book, so we kept that. The difference is that Sarah is there with him at the end.

Q: It must have been an interesting experience for you, since it's the first film where you're working on someone else's material.

DC: No, it's actually the second. I did a drag racing film called *Fast Company*, for which I didn't write the original script. But on that film I did take a writing credit because I did do a lot of rewriting. On this film I didn't do any. Well, there's one scene that Debra and I wrote because the writer was not there and we needed it fast. But, that was it.

It is different, because certainly it's the first time when I've ever had such a substantial, preexisting story to work on. But, because I felt a lot of empathy for the story and the situation, and because none of the changes any of us did were to make it more like us than Stephen King .... I think that we're very faithful to Stephen. The tone of the characters is very different from what I normally do. My characters are usually urban, sophisticated and a little perverse. Stephen's characters tend to be rural, simple and accessible. I didn't want to change that. That's one of the things that attracted me to it. I would never have named the character John Smith, ever! And, I didn't change that.

THE DREAMWEAVERS

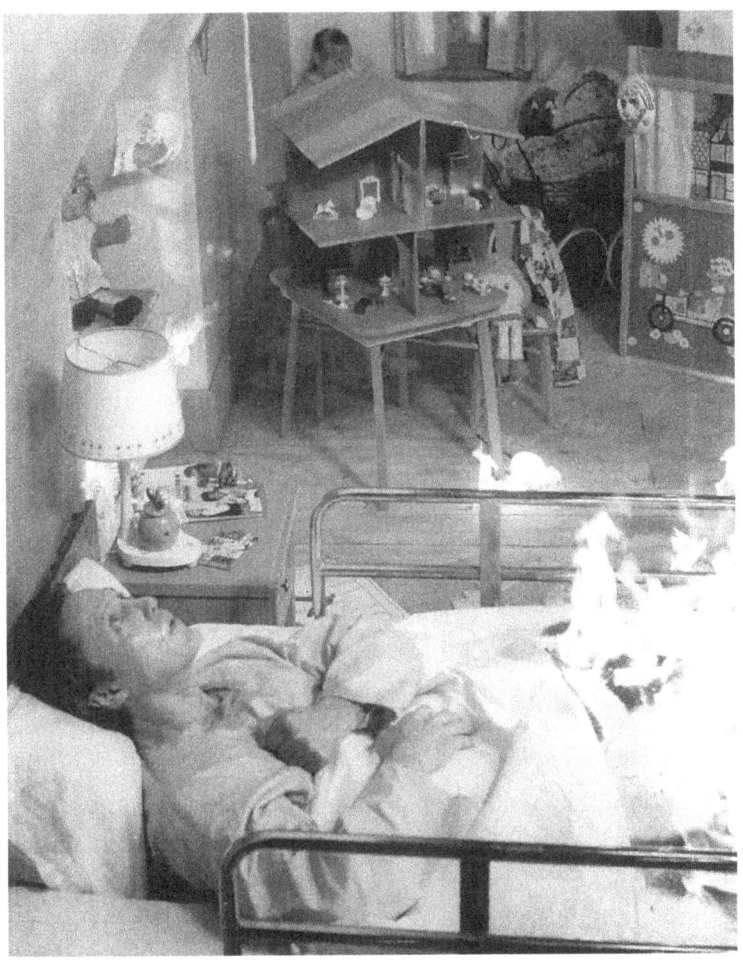

Christopher Walken explores *The Dead Zone*.

So, all the changes had to do with compressing and feeling what was necessary to translate all the emotions in the thing to the screen. Also, the way that Johnny had his visions in the book would not translate directly to what happens on the screen. I had to actually end some of his visions physically, which Stephen happened to like quite a bit. In the film, he's watching; he's present but he's watching. It's not a traditional psychic's experience of a vision; it's a little different.

Two other changes were the kid that Johnny teaches and whose life he eventually saves. Instead of being an eighteen-year-old "Jock" with a corvette, named Chuck, I named him Chris and made him about ten or eleven and shy. He also belongs to a very wealthy family, but he's very shy and sort of brow-beaten by his father. I didn't think that anybody would have much sympathy for Chuck if they saw him on the street. I didn't have much sympathy for him in the book, as a matter of fact. He was a jerk who just happened to have a learning disability, but otherwise he had everything in the world and he seemed quite strong. I wanted Johnny to see himself as a sensitive young boy, in this kid. That was one change that Stephen King really thought worked better than what he had done in the book.

Q: Does the film feel at all like a "step-child" because you didn't write the script?

DC: No. It never felt like that. Really not. In fact, some people that have seen it see many, many links with all the other films that I've done. It's not anything that I've imposed on it, but it deals with the pain and difficulty of dealing with a gift that is not completely understood. And that is difficult to handle, which, in *Scanners*, was very much my metaphor for art and creativity. It could also work in *Dead Zone* in the same way. Johnny was a very unspecial person to begin with, and becomes a very special person and an extraordinarily sensitive person afterwards. And it's obviously not all a bed of roses either, mostly thorns.

Q: How was working with Dino De Laurentiis?

DC: I loved working with him. It's always difficult because there are so many things to decide and choose from. But, I found that he was accessible. I wouldn't say that we ever really had arguments. We had discussions; we gave each other veto power. We could both say no to something and we'd both have to convince each other to say yes to some things. Whether it would be actors or any other thing. Dino had said to me that he would never impose anything on a director that he didn't believe in, and that's proven to be the case. There were cases where he'd disagree and say something wasn't going to work, and I'd say, "Yes it would, let me try. If it doesn't, we won't do it." It's worked out very well actually.

Q: Did you find any problem with the fact that the script had to be translated into Italian and back?

DC: Sometimes you get into funny situations, especially when the page numbers start to be different, and you realize that you're both talking about different pages. That slows things down a little, and yes, it's a bit of a problem because Debra and I are both fairly articulate, and Dino is too. It's just that there is this problem. You have to fight simplifying things when you speak to someone whose English isn't that quick. But, Dino is very aware of that, and it seemed to work.

There are other things I've had to deal with with other producers that were a lot harder to take. In general, I think you would be in trouble with Dino if you really were not in sync with what you thought the picture should be. That could be a problem. Perhaps Dino could be a lot tougher or more difficult if those kinds of differences came up. But, both Debra and I tried to be very up front about anything that was worrying us at the beginning.

What I found was that Dino would say he wants a scene that would do this. Then, he might suggest what the scene could be. He never seems to be totally married to his own idea. If you can say, "I don't like that particular idea because …. But, how about a scene where this happens instead and it will do the same sort of thing." If Dino feels that there's some step or beat missing in the film, you have to listen to him, because his instincts for those things seem to be very good. His suggestion as to what might be the solution might not be so good, but then I've not found that he would impose those things on us.

Q: How did the casting work?

DC: To me, one of the most important parts of preproduction is the casting, finding the locations. The director has to be the one to do that. Dino was also very involved. There was a "veto power" here as well. In other words, if I said, "This is the actor I think should play that role," and Dino said, "Absolutely not, I cannot see that person in the role," then I might be unhappy, but I know that he's not going to say, "You must have this person instead!" He might suggest somebody else. Once again, his instincts were good. Every once in a while he might veto someone for a reason that I could not fathom, or he wouldn't know someone that we wanted, and therefore he wouldn't get enthusiastic about that person. But, the end result speaks for itself, in that there's really nothing up on the screen that I wish weren't there, unless it's my own fault, in which case, it's my own fault. There's nothing I feel was imposed on me, from casting to anything else.

Q: Did you always have Christopher Walken in mind for Johnny?

DC: No. That was Dino's suggestion. Actually Dino wanted Chris very badly and I'd always admired Chris and wanted to work with him. But, I was worried that he was too old, and it wasn't until I could rationalize in my own mind the progress in the script with someone older than twenty or twenty-two that I then agreed that Chris would work.

I think Chris Walken is fantastically good in this role. Some people that have seen it say it's the best he's ever done, which would make it very good indeed. One of the other things I was concerned about with Chris, is that in most of his other films he's very aloof and cool, if not psychotic, depending on what the role is. I knew he could do the vision part of it, but I didn't know if he could do the warmth and the sadness and melancholy that is very intimate and passionate. He does it incredibly well. People will see things from Chris in this film that they will not have seen before. Even though I think he's done them before, but in films that are not that well known, like *Roseland* and *Who Am I This Time?* Once I saw those, I knew that he could do it. It's just that he's not been asked to do it in all the big films that he's done.

Chris Walken shakes hands with presidential candidate Martin Sheen.

Q: Did you just bump everyone's age up a little?

DC: Basically yes. There's a sticky moment in the script where …. There's a certain sexual innocence in the book which is important because you don't want Johnny and Sarah to have slept together before the accident. Well, this is the eighties and Chris does not look eighteen, even in the early parts when they both look younger, but not eighteen. There comes a point where she says, "Why don't you come in and stay overnight. It's raining." And he says, "No, some things are worth waiting for." Now, that could be hard to swallow or it could be funny, but we did it straight and very gently, and I would hope that people don't think this guy is a total jerk and unbelievable because of that. I think it's rather sweet myself, especially the way it's done.

He's from a small town, and it's not totally a sexual question either, which is explained in the film. There are other things. He's very disturbed at the time. And it's important because later they do make love once, after the accident, and I wanted to maintain all of that. So, rather than try to reinterpret it for his age, and also for the times, I tried to stay with that kind of naivete that Stephen is very good at, and I just played it straight. I was worried about it, you see.

Q: Did you move the whole time scale up? In the book it was around the late sixties through the seventies.

DC: The film is very atemporal, you might say. I don't use source music, I don't use rock music, I don't have Beatle posters on the walls, I don't mention Nixon. There are a lot of those things that are mentioned very specifically in the book. But, there is also a timelessness about the book. It's really more of a tone, somebody's idea of New England and the openness and naivete, rather than the actuality. That's what I wanted to do in the movie, so that you don't really get too many things that are specific about time.

But, in terms of what license plates we used, and so you would know what time we were talking about for clothes, hairstyles, what have you, yes, it's been updated somewhat. But only by a few years really. Only so it ends up being about now at the end of the film.

Q: Weren't you thinking of shooting overseas at one point during pre-production?

DC: There is a Poland vision, the invasion of Poland, and we were thinking about shooting that in Yugoslavia. But we ended up shooting it outside of Toronto, and it worked great.

We were all much happier doing it there because it was a challenge for everyone to do it. You don't do too many war scenes in Canadian movies, especially ones that are supposed to take place in Europe. But, it's also a vision and there are just flashes of it, so we set up a very elaborate day of shooting, which involved a lot of tanks, machine guns, explosions and all kinds of stuff. We did it in an abandoned brick works that's near a small town outside of Toronto.

In fact, there was a trailer park nearby, and I'm sure they didn't know what was going on! Suddenly at two o'clock in the morning these enormous explosions start, machine guns, mortars and everything. I assume that one of our people must have warned them of what was happening, but it still wouldn't help them to get any sleep. I'm sure of that!

Q: Did you do any storyboarding for the film?

DC: Debra wanted me to try to storyboard for some of the visions and some of the stunts. We did hire a storyboard artist to work on those. But, I felt it was not very profitable. It even tended to cause more confusion than not because I would update a storyboard and only half the crew would get the updates, so people were working on different assumptions.

Q: Did you have many special effects in the film? I would think that the visions would have used them the most.

DC: Yes, that's true. But they don't really overwhelm the film. It's not a special effects movie by any stretch of the imagination.

Actually, when I started to come up with the ideas of how the visions would be done, the writer of the film was very excited about them, but he also began to think that they would be a very dominating factor in the film, and he was surprised himself when he saw how it was still very much a movie of character and character interaction.

Q: How do you define the "dead zone"?

DC: It's defined very clearly in the film. I thought that it needed something much more precise in the film than in the book. It's that area in his future visions which is not immutable because he can change it. If he has a vision which has a "dead zone," it means it's a future vision about which he can do something. If he has a vision in the past, and it's something which has already happened, then there is nothing he can do to change it and it has no "dead zone." He only begins to become aware of it later in the film, when he starts to have future flashes as opposed to past ones.

Of course, that's very important to his actions, and the revelation comes at a very specific time, when he's deciding whether he should kill Stillson or not. Once he becomes assured that he can in fact affect the future, as seen in his visions, then he knows that he has to do that.

Q: How was working with Paramount?

DC: I've never had anything that I could call studio interference at all. *The Dead Zone* originally started as an independent Dino De Laurentiis production and, at a certain point, Paramount picked it up before it was finished. There were two things they wanted, one was a scene that would show Stillson to be a bad guy. Because in the book, of course, he's a terribly evil guy who not only kicks a dog, but kicks it to death. I don't have that scene in the movie and I don't start that far back in his career. They felt there still needed to be a scene where the audience could see that Stillson was a genuinely bad guy. That's the scene that Debra and I wrote without the writer because we needed it fast. This was not an imposition. I actually agreed that it was a good idea, so there was really no conflict there.

The second thing was, that I had written the vision that Johnny has about the boy that he's teaching being in danger, and Johnny convinces the boy not to do what is going to put him in danger, which is, once again, different than the book. In the book there was a fire at a dance, and in the film it had to do with kids playing hockey on a frozen pond. I had him never really knowing whether he would have been right. Because earlier in the film you've already had confirmation that his visions are correct. I didn't feel that this was a big deal. I thought this was more subtle. The studio felt that the audience was really going to want to see that Johnny was right.

I finally agreed, as long as I found the right way to do it. There was no way I was going to shoot a scene with kids falling through the ice and drowning. So we did something so that you know that he stays home and two other kids fall into the ice and drown. It was in a newspaper, a very traditional device. But there was one other thing that I did that I really liked, that made me very happy to have added it. I have Johnny seeing in the paper that the two kids have drowned. He knows that the father didn't listen to him. He phones and the little kid that he's been teaching answers the phone. Johnny doesn't say anything. He just wants to know that the boy is all right, but the kid knows it's him and whispers, "Johnny." Then Johnny hangs up. So, it was a very nice something that wasn't there before. So, in the end result, I have to thank Paramount for their insistence.

I actually think that at a certain point, those two scenes were things that they wanted or else they wouldn't pick the picture up. Although it was never put to me that way.

Q: What is your future? Do you want to go back to working on your own films? Or did you like working on someone else's material?

DC: I think it would be very frustrating if I were to think that I would never write again. That's very important to me. On the other hand, it's obvious that I can do a film based on someone else's work, enjoy it, and feel that the film was a terrific one at the end, as is the case here. So, I would never write that off as another possibility.

It's strange, because if I do a film that's not mine, I know that there's a film that would have been mine that I'll never know about. You only have so many years to work and each time I take on someone else's work, I'm going to have that much less time to explore my own.

I think that maybe just a healthy combination of the two. I was ready after *Videodrome*, which was certainly very intensely my own, to do something else. I also felt like getting into production quickly. After *Dead Zone*, when I finish, it's six months to a year of writing until I get into production, so you have to be prepared for that. It's a different kind of energy entirely that goes on in writing than that goes on in production.

Q: The story of *The Dead Zone* is as different for Stephen King, as this film is for you ....

DC: That's an interesting point. Yes, it is. It's not his normal kind of writing, that's quite true. As a result, the film is not what most people will come to expect from Stephen King. Which is a difficult marketing problem, I think. There are people who don't like the kind of movies that are made from Stephen's work, and I would hate to have those people not come to *The Dead Zone*, when in fact, they might very much like the film.

I think it has a different, and a broader, audience than people might expect. If they spell it as another "nightmare trip into terror with Stephen King" I think it would be a big mistake.

It's a very melancholy film in some ways. Although people do find it very tense and compelling, I'm happy to say. People who come into sound mixing and see a reel out of order, want to see the next reel, and are very frustrated when they realize that we have to go back and go over it a million times. So, that's a very good sign. So, it's not to say that the film is wimpy. It's very strong. It's compelling, tense, but it's not "jump out and scream at you" kind of scary. It's also not at all gory. There is one scene where you see a bit of blood, and of course Johnny gets shot at the end. But you can see that on television.

Q: Do you think that because it is a different kind of film for you, that people will go in expecting it to have a lot of graphic, gory sequences, and be disappointed?

DC: I think we all have a problem. Debra Hill has her fans; I have my fans, and Stephen King has more fans than all of us put together. I think all of those fans will expect something different from what the film actually is. I don't think they'll be disappointed. Certainly, there is an overlap between what they'll expect and what the film is. I think it's very important that it be sold properly, that people understand what it is when they go to see it.

In terms of whether audiences will like the film or not, I'm not worried. I really would be amazed if people don't like this film. Whereas, with some of my other films, I've known that they were so extreme in certain ways that I knew a lot of people weren't going to like them. This film should have a very broad audience that is crazy about it. I'll be very disappointed if that doesn't happen ….

Q: Are you convinced within yourself that this film will be a success?

DC: It's a total mystery to me what makes a film a success. I just know that people who see it will like it. It's very strong, and unlike many of my other films. It's also accessible. It just turned out that way. It's not something I tend to plan and not plan.

Q: All your films show a special feeling for their subjects. Do you think that being almost obsessed with a picture is necessary to your making it? And to which extent doesn't this feeling of obsession blind you to the film's possible faults?

DC: I would never work on a project which would be like a mechanic. It takes so much energy to do a film that I cannot imagine really carrying it through with style, unless you were obsessed with the subject. If you were doing something that you had contempt for, on any level, I don't really see how you could bring it off, in terms of not only shooting but also of all the work that goes into post-production, the editing, etc .... If you don't care for your film, you might as well be in the shoe-making business or something like that.

Of course, it's always hard to maintain a sense of balance when you feel that way, especially during the shooting because you're just immersed into the film so totally, so overwhelmingly, that you don't have much of a length between you and the picture. Your whole world becomes that of the film because you don't have time to read the newspapers or watch television. The film becomes the world to you.

So if something is going wrong, you may not catch it because it's very difficult to keep your sense of proportion. But you have to try to do it. Otherwise, minor things may become enormous and throw the entire project into jeopardy.

Q: When did you first get involved with *Videodrome?*

DC: I had an arrangement with Pierre David, who had also produced *Scanners* and *The Brood*, to do another film. At one point, when I was still finishing *Scanners*, we were talking about the possibility of doing a remake of *Frankenstein*. When I actually had time to consider it at more length, I thought, "I don't want to do that. Too much has already been done on the subject." So I said to him, "Why don't I present to you a couple of treatments, and you decide which one you want to do." And the one that Pierre chose was *Videodrome*.

It was in fact based on another treatment I wrote about eight years ago, about a cable TV network that shows snuff movies. I came across it again, and that's what became the basis of the movie. But, when I wrote the script, it started to go off in a different direction. I guess that's part of what makes the film so strange to people. With the basic premise, you could have made a very straightforward film, a thriller. I was surprised myself when I started to write the story that it took off in another direction entirely.

Q: Do you often make changes when you're doing your films?

DC: I usually hope that I do. What's exciting about filmmaking is when the project that you're working on starts taking on a sort of organic life of its own, which insists that it be made that way. That's when I usually feel that the film is going in the right direction. At that point, of course, you can't really start thinking about commercial considerations. You just have to let the film follow its own course, and hope that people will like it.

In the case of *Videodrome*, the script wasn't really finished when we started to shoot, at least not in the sense that we felt that everything was locked down. In fact the only film that I ever shot when it wasn't like that was *The Brood*. When you have a shoot that's ten weeks long, you have far better opportunities to move around in terms of rewriting, deciding on what's going to happen, alternate endings, etc ....

And then, of course, you have another chance to change it when you're editing. There you have the possibility of filling out the blanks according to what you feel, with footage that you shot but didn't expect that you'd need. I think that there are no films that don't get changed during their shooting. There are just so many things that happen, suggestions by actors on the set, or the weather, or something that goes wrong, or right .... You'd have to be a fool to ignore those things.

Q: Did you try to make the locations of *Videodrome* look futuristic?

DC: No, the cars are ordinary cars and things like this. There's really nothing futuristic about the film, except some kind of sensibility in it. We didn't have any trouble finding places to shoot that suited our purposes, because Toronto is still a very open city for filming.

Q: Did you use any storyboards?

DC: No, I didn't. For me, storyboards are really more for the benefit of other people to give them a feeling of security. It's a false sense of security, though, because as soon as you get out on the set, everything changes. I know that there are some directors who use them, but I suppose it's a matter of temperament. Whether you need to see what you're doing down on paper, or whether you don't.

I guess in my own way, I do my storyboarding in my head, except for some action sequences or stunts, that have to be planned meticulously. If you were doing a film like *Star Wars*, where there are so many optical effects, you do need to be very precise almost in a sort of mathematical way, then you would need storyboards.

With me, I come on the sets and I have my actors. The first thing I do is to rehearse the scene with them. I can't imagine storyboarding a scene before I even met my actors and gave them a chance to discuss it and make suggestions. Otherwise, you stick to the storyboard at the expense of letting your actors act. I can't imagine hiring actors like Chris Walken and Barbara Sheen and having worked out a scene before you even knew who they were, or before you even saw the set.

Q: But you need storyboards for planning the special effects sequences. Or did you leave Rick Baker the freedom to do what he wanted?

DC: Oh, no. I had very specific ideas. I know that a lot of kids today are enthusiastic about special effects, of the kind Rick Baker does. So you could say to him, "Okay, go crazy!" But then put yourself in his position. You have to hand a budget to the producer, and to make an estimate, you have to know what the script requires you to do. Everybody has to be very precise about what they want.

The imagery of *Videodrome* was all in the script, described in specific details. Rick Baker's task was to translate these into reality, given the budget, given the time and given the limits of technology. And, of course, to suggest ameliorations.

We had to change a few things, however, because they just could not be done given within our limits. For example, the way I had written the death of Barry Convex was different. Now, his body breaks up and tumors come out of it. Originally, he got shot with blobs of flesh which grew into tendrils that became tumors on the outside. Given our limitations, Rick felt that he couldn't do that, so we had to find another approach that would give you the same feel, but was more possible to make.

Q: Did the effects come out as you had intended?

DC: They're always better afterward when you see them for real. I'd say the effects came out even better than I had imagined. When I visualized some of them, I knew they were only just a possibility. I didn't know if we could make them become real. When I write a script, I try not to worry about how much it's going to cost, and how it could be done. And then, after I'm finished, I suddenly realize what I've done and I go through a phase of "Oh, my God, how are we going to do that!"

Q: Was Rick Baker always your first choice for the job?

DC: Actually, yes. I worked with Dick Smith on *Scanners*, but he wasn't available for *Videodrome*. Rick and I had some mutual friends, who always said that we would enjoy working together, which we did.

Rick did a lot of work in Los Angeles because he has his lab there, but ultimately we came to a point where he had to come up and set up another lab in Toronto.

Q: Did you have specific actors in mind when you cast *Videodrome*?

DC: You usually cast a couple of key characters based on the general look and the acting style that you want. In this case, Jimmy Woods' was the first part we cast. You could imagine casting other people for that role, but the whole feel of the picture would have been totally different. The rest of the film then accumulated around this character.

As regards casting Debbie Harry, she had been in *Roadie* and *Union City*. I quite liked the latter, and I thought she was pretty good in it, in a strange kind of way. So I met her, I liked her and I thought she certainly had the right look for the film. I believed that her combination with Jimmy Woods would be quite dynamic. She came up to Toronto for an audition, read for the part, and I was sure she could do it.

I was pleased with her and she was very easy to work with, very hardworking, aware that she was at a disadvantage in the sense that her film experience was limited. Woods was very helpful to her, because he's a superb technician in terms of acting. He gave her the benefits of his expertise, which was good, since Debbie is more famous on the street than Jimmy and there is always the potential of having some kind of strange resentment or something like that. But in this there was none and they worked very well together.

Q: How long did the shoot take?

DC: I think it was a nine week shoot. About the same as *Scanners*. *The Dead Zone* is longer, eleven or twelve weeks. I like having more time only up to a point. I think it is possible to have too much time. It dissipates the tension, and I mean by that the creative or artistic tension. It also makes it possible to lose the flow of the characters, or the continuity of the story.

Q: What role did you have in the scoring?

DC: Well, I'm not a composer, but I was a classical guitarist for a while when I was younger. So I may be able to discuss concepts, like I said on *The Brood* that I wanted it to be all strings. At one point, for *The Brood*, in order to have some screenings before there was any score, I used some other music which conveyed the mood I wanted. But I don't really like doing this because you then get locked into what you used as a temporary score, and after that anything else feels wrong.

Q: Unlike your other pictures, *Videodrome* was under the aegis of a major studio [Universal] from the beginning. How did this happen, and was it different for you?

DC: Pierre took the treatment I had written to Universal, to Bob Rehme. They were interested right from the very beginning, so they invested half of the film's budget, and agreed to distribute it.

In a strange way, it was not too different for me because I had worked with Bob Rehme on *Scanners* when he was at Avco-Embassy, and he had been at New World when *The Brood* was there. Then, suddenly, he moved to Universal and we were working together again! So, he was very familiar with me.

It took me a while to figure some of the ways in which the majors work. But there was almost no interference at all. On the contrary, they were very supportive when we had a test screening and decided at that stage that there were somethings wrong with the film.

Q: The majors usually prefer films that will appeal to a broad, middle-America–like audience, and all your films are marginal. Do you think that this is a problem?

DC: Yes, it is definitely a problem, in terms of having a major hit. It's the same kind of problem that Martin Scorsese has. He and middle-America don't exactly see eye-to-eye. There comes a time when I suppose you have to decide what you're making movies for. Of course, there's always the problem of being able to make movies at all because they're expensive and you're making them with other people's money.

Q: After you finished your first version of *Videodrome* and had that test screening, did it bother you to get negative reactions, and what kind of changes did you do?

DC: Yes, it did bother me, because you always psych yourself up to thinking that you may be closer to having the film finished than you really are. So it definitely hurts. But *Videodrome* was at a very unfinished stage at the time and had no music at all, which was very funny because someone wrote on a comments card that he hated the music!

I guess it says something about these types of previews. People usually can't spell on their cards, and their grammar is terrible. Yet, if you filter through all that, you find that there might be some kind of obscure truth, like something people really hated. But you get contradictory things, too, so you might have to ignore half of it anyway. You just have to be canny enough to know what to ignore. The other problem is that you might find yourself with some studio executives who are convinced that happy endings have to be tagged on to make everybody want to see the film.

Just sitting in the theater with people watching your film, people who don't owe you anything, who don't know your work, is an education in itself.

We were already set up for some additional shooting, some of which was for special effects. So it was relatively easy to change things. Originally, for example, I had Woods talking to himself on the TV set at the end of the film, saying the same lines that Debbie says now. One of the things that I realized from the screening was that people felt that she had disappeared too early out of the film and wanted to see more of her. I realized that it was better to have him talk to her because she was the ideal person to be the spokesman for the "New Flesh."

There were also one or two little things that we cut out. The ear-piercing scene was one that I had cut, more than I really wanted to. There was a dissolve in that scene with Jimmy and Debbie making love that was in fact one single long crane move. I hope I can put it back in the video cassette, if it comes out.

Q: What was the point you were trying to make in that film and what is the "New Flesh"?

DC: I guess it's the classic situation where I have to say that the film *is* the comment and it's not a simple one. I can't really say what I think the film says. It's an exploration of a lot of complex things, and it doesn't necessarily draw very specific conclusions.

The whole movie is real, in a sense that there is nothing real outside of your own perceptions of reality, in a philosophical way, if you wish. As regards the "New Flesh," I don't really want to discuss it specifically. When Max kills himself, he is not thinking that he's killing himself, but that he's going to evolve into something beyond what he is. The next stage is the "New Flesh," which might be flesh beyond flesh. We don't know whether we're talking about reincarnation or spiritual life beyond flesh.

GHOSTBUSTERS (1984)

Dan Aykroyd came up with the idea for *Ghostbusters*, which gave him a chance to work with a bunch of old friends—and to make hundreds of millions of dollars for Columbia Pictures at the same time.

Aykroyd wrote a first draft screenplay and showed it to longtime friend and fellow "Saturday Night Live" alumnus, Bill Murray, who loved it.

But gee, who could direct it?

Murray's two big blockbusters—*Meatballs* and *Stripes*—were both directed by Ivan Reitman. So why not ask Ivan?

Once aboard, it was Reitman who was instrumental in shifting the emphasis from the pure fantasy of Aykroyd's original concept, to broader and wilder comedy.

But gee, who could come in and help Aykroyd rewrite it?

Reitman suggested Harold Ramis, who had co-written *Meatballs, Stripes, National Lampoon's Animal House* and wrote and directed *Caddyshack*, which featured Murray in a hilarious co-starring role. He was also an old friend of Aykroyd's from their days together in the Second City improv group.

Once Ramis was involved in the project, the writers went off to Martha's Vineyard where, in the space of two months, a final draft of *Ghostbusters* was completed.

Reitman approached Columbia with the project in May of 1983. A month later, the film got the green light.

The script included a plethora of special effects, including ghosts, demons, ghouls, a refrigerator that's a portal to another dimension and a 112½ foot tall marshmallow man who stomps through Manhattan. Not your typical little movie. The budget kept inching upward. By the millions.

The only problem was that the studio wanted the film for an early summer 1984 release, in order to be in theaters well before the Olympic games.

The film was hurriedly put into production.

Richard Edlund's newly established BFC special effects facility was selected to handle the considerable work of putting together the almost two hundred effects shots required in the film.

The $30 million–plus that Columbia eventually pumped into the film turned out to be a good gamble—*Ghostbusters* eclipsed *Return of the Pink Panther* as the most successful comedy of all-time, sparking a merchandizing bonanza and inspiring *two* cartoon series, "The Real Ghostbusters" and "Slimer," (and, through a legal quirk, a rival cartoon series called "The Original Ghostbusters").

It was only a matter of time before a sequel, cleverly titled *Ghostbusters 2*, was mounted, with the original cast and with Ivan Reitman once more behind the camera.

Unfortunately, the sequel was merely a bland remake of the original, and *felt* like a bald attempt to make a fast buck. Although it was a hit, it didn't approach, creatively or financially, the success of the first film.

INTERVIEW WITH IVAN REITMAN, DIRECTOR

Ivan Reitman, a Czech native raised in Canada, first met with actor Dan Aykroyd when he produced a live television variety show, entitled *Greed*. Shortly thereafter, he produced *Spellbound* for the

Toronto stage, which evolved into *The Magic Show*, a five-year hit on Broadway.

After *The Magic Show*, Reitman produced another Broadway show, based on *National Lampoon* magazine. Its success eventually led to directing of *National Lampoon's Animal House* in 1978, starring John Belushi, which Reitman followed with *Meatballs* (1979) and *Stripes* (1981), both starring Bill Murray.

Then, in 1981, Reitman produced the animated SF fantasy picture, *Heavy Metal*, inspired by the magazine of the same name published by *National Lampoon*. In 1984, Reitman, Murray, Aykroyd and Ramis teamed up again to produce *Ghostbusters*, a zany SF epic which became the runaway hit of the year.

Q: When did you first get involved with *Ghostbusters*?

IVAN REITMAN: Dan Aykroyd had written a script called *Ghostbusters*, and he showed it to Bill Murray. They liked it and they decided that I would be the director for the movie. They sent the script to me, and I didn't like it at all. I sort of hemmed and hawed about it, then I sat down with Danny and started discussing what I thought we should do with it. He really liked the ideas. I also suggested that we get Harold Ramis involved as a writer and an actor in the film. That was last May. So, we started all over again, using his draft really for certain incidents and characterizations. We really redid it pretty well from scratch.

We worked all summer. Bill Murray came back from shooting *The Razor's Edge* in France, and we started shooting in October. It's not the fastest film I've ever been involved in, but considering the size of the film it's pretty remarkable.

Q: How much of the original script is still there?

IR: A lot of it is the kind of business that they're in. Two of the major incidents in the film were originally in that script, but reworked for the plot that we developed. His movie would have cost $200 million to make, it was more of a science fiction extravaganza than a comedy. I wanted to make a comedy that also had science fiction stuff and neat effects in it. But, I felt that the weight had to be on the characterizations and the comedy, rather than the other way around, which was his script. I made it much more realistic, also, in the process. I influenced its realism. They're the writers, and they did all the writing.

Q: Was there any resistance about changing it?

IR: No. Once Danny and I finally sat down face to face and talked about it, he was the most excited advocate. He couldn't wait and he seemed very appreciative of the whole development of it.

Q: After you got Harold Ramis in on the script, how long did it take from the time you started changing things around till you had a completed script ready to go?

IR: That first draft took about a month or five weeks. We went off to Martha's Vineyard, stayed there two weeks and did another draft. Then, we did another draft after that, that took two or three weeks. We did three drafts in the space of two months.

Q: Were there significant changes from one to the next?

IR: It was clearer where the movie was going with each draft and what the character differentiation was amongst the three of them, what the major plot incidents should be. That kept on shifting around. The science line became clearer.

Q: While you were doing the script, were you thinking in terms of what the special effects would entail?

IR: Yeah. But we knew that we were going to be in real trouble, time wise. Right away, the studio was saying, "We need this for next summer," and it was already less than a year away. Michael Gross contacted Richard Edlund, who we had heard was going to leave Industrial Light and Magic and set up a company here. I met him to find out what his plans were—I think this was already in June of last year—and he said it was true.

Decked out as cosmic crusaders and ready to do battle with New York City's vaporous villains are (left to right) Harold Ramis, Dan Aykroyd, Bill Murray and Ernie Hudson in *Ghostbusters*.

Q: Did you have any idea of what it would entail when you started out?

IR: I had a pretty good idea. I'd been through a little of this, so I had a pretty good sense of the scale to do it properly. It still ended up costing more than we expected.

Q: What were the problems involved shooting live action, to be printed together with effects? You had no previous experience with that sort of thing.

IR: Fortunately we had storyboards on everything, so I had a good sense of how it would be laid out. But we still didn't know how everything was going to actually look, until it was done.

I think it was harder for the actors because they didn't have anything specific to respond to. I always tried to give them as much visual information as I could, either from the storyboard or key development drawings that we had made. And, to cover myself, I would do a number of takes that had a range of emotion, from more subtle to more broad.

Q: What other tricks did you use?

IR: I tried to assault the actors and extras as much as I could with wind and cork stuff and paper. I feel that as much as their physical environment can change, the greater the effect and the more realistic the response of the actors.

Q: What about the trials and tribulations of closing off Central Park for a week?

IR: The New York people weren't happy about that at all. They felt we didn't have a good location manager. We should have been talked out of the location that we ended up choosing. It was right in the middle of three very important arteries. Quite apart from the Central Park West, which is a north-south flowing ... that was relatively easy to close. It was the east-west, crosstown traffic, flowing through 64th, 61st and 67th, right in the area where we were shooting. We had blocked those up, too, and one Friday night we apparently gridlocked Manhattan Island for about an hour.

Q: Didn't the Film Commission try to talk you out of shooting there?

IR: Yes, they did. But by then it was too late because we were deep into building the big set that matched the exterior, and there was a lot of other money spent, specifically for that building.

Q: Why did you decide to build such a massive set for the rooftop scene?

IR: John De Cuir, the production designer, is the last of the grand masters. It was appropriate to the story. For the confrontation, basically we needed .... I guess we could have built half of a rooftop, and sort of tried to play the action that way. But, it wasn't that great a savings, once you've built the scaffolding and everything, for the extra ten percent, you might as well go the rest of the way.

Q: What was shooting on such a big set like?

IR: Well, we couldn't shoot at any angle, but we had a fair amount of freedom. It was also so big that it took forever to light. I think there are only twelve Titans existing in the world, and we used ten of them on the stage. During certain key scenes, no other filming could take place on the Burbank lot! So, we tried to do it during the Christmas break time, and we scheduled carefully those days, so it would occur when there was no other filming. I think the last time this kind of power was used was for the big set on *Close Encounters*, when the spaceship landed.

Q: What kind of pressures were you under, in trying to do this so quickly?

IR: There was a lot of pressure. But, I'm a pretty quick study and having been so involved in the development of the screenplay, I had a pretty good idea of where I was going with it. I was lucky in that I had an extraordinary support staff.

Q: You were editing the film before the special effects were done. Was that a problem for you?

IR: Yeah! We had these sort of black and white slugs all over the place. They had just a plate or some crude line drawings in them. But one thing I learned from *Heavy Metal*, and from *Spacehunter* to a certain extent—the film better work without the special effects or you can forget it. Whatever inadequacies we felt in the work picture of both *Spacehunter* and *Heavy Metal* didn't disappear when the film was completed. Even though we always told ourselves that, "Well, *Spacehunter* will work better once we actually see it in 3D, and it's all together with the effects." Or for *Heavy Metal*, "Once all the color and effects are in it will work better." But, it didn't. It worked basically just the way it did, only it was more polished.

I screened *Ghostbusters* in its rough state, without any effects at all, except the mechanical ones that we did on set, to small audiences, just to see. I figured it was going to have to work as it is. It will only get better, but it better work right now. Fortunately it did. I found I'm no longer relying on the inclusion of everything to save me. My approach now was that it's got to work as a movie without anything, in its roughest form without special effects, audio effects, proper color balancing or music. If it works then, you know it's going to work. That's where we are now, I think. As I said at the beginning, my focus on this movie was that it work as a comedy about these three guys who go into business for themselves. That's what I think this story is about. These three very bright people who make a job change, and set up this very unique business. It's the problems of setting up a business, keeping their relationship together and the problems they run into in this particular business.

Q: Where did the idea for the Stay-Puft Man come from?

IR: I don't know where it came from, but that was one of the most important things that we kept from the original draft.

Q: How did it strike you, when you read that your major antagonist was going to be a giant marshmallow?

IR: It was what worried me because the film was very realistic until that point. As long as you accepted the theory as it developed, each thing led to the other quite naturally, and that's where it suddenly took a left turn and went way beyond. I kept on worrying that it might not work. And, going into filming I still thought that it might not work.

Q: What did you have as a contingency plan in case it didn't work?

IR: The reason it stayed was because we couldn't come up with anything that sounded as good, so we went with it. It's part of the risks of filmmaking.

Q: Do you think that having to be a part of setting up a new special effects facility made your job more difficult?

IR: I think it made Richard Edlund's job more difficult. He had to build a company and get it up to working speed. They've only hit their stride about a month ago, so it put them into a terrible crunch, getting this film ready. For us, it was a problem because it meant we were rushed in terms of getting some of the effects done. There are 195 effects shot in the film. And, it was more expensive as a result of a lot of it going into the physical set up, as opposed to into the movie itself.

Q: Other than giving yourself more time, are there things you would have done differently if you could have?

IR: No. This was the luckiest and happiest filming experience I've ever been involved in. It just came together quickly and smoothly, and the filming was generally a very happy experience. We weren't much over time and budget.

Q: Can you think of any funny incidents while you were filming?

IR: Well, I laughed every day, that's how I remember it. I was laughing on the set, even when I was the most annoyed. I found many opportunities to laugh. That would be the best way to characterize what the filming was like.

INTERVIEW WITH MICHAEL GROSS, ASSOCIATE PRODUCER

Q: Can you describe your job function, as you see it?

MG: Associate producer is a weird title, and it has caused me some problems. Because I interpret for Ivan a lot, it also means I'll be working with people, making creative decisions on a day to day basis. They'll present an idea and I'll say, no, we're not going to do that. They often feel, who the hell is the associate producer to sit here and make a creative decision? Or, "I'll take this up with the director. I'm not going to talk about it with you." As if my only job is to be sure that they're going to deliver and that the budget stays within certain limits. But, my job is more creative than that with Ivan.

Ivan knows what he likes when he sees it, his communication is very good, and I think he understands what's needed. However, I don't think he particularly wants to devote a lot of his waking hours to working with designers to try to solve problems. It's not that he isn't visually oriented, but he just doesn't have the time. He'd rather concentrate on script, story and comedy ... the things he should be concentrating on. But, since he can't ignore these things either, I've become his eyes, and somebody that can interpret for him, and go out and get this job done for him, and then bring it back to him, because he does finally arbitrate everything. There's nothing on film that he hasn't been a part of.

Q: What was the first thing that you did when you started on *Ghostbusters*?

MG: There are two associate producers on the picture, Joe Medjuck and myself, and we tend to separate our duties for Ivan. Mine are almost exclusively design and special effects.

Once an art director is on, he has the responsibility for sets and the look of the movie on a large scale. But, John De Cuir was a great man. He had no problems understanding that I would also have a lot of input on the design of the creatures—and what Ivan and I both call a kind of contemporary, science fiction, indoor humor sensibility that is very hard to find if you just plug into people already in the film business. There's a contemporary thing going on that was reflected in *Heavy Metal*. It was reflected in *Lampoon* and in other places, which doesn't involve an entire industry. It's a sensibility. Ivan and I share that sensibility, and he trusts me.

What I immediately did was put together a number of designers. We had some design work that had been done in Canada, for an earlier film that we were going to call *Big Trouble* and we just started putting concepts together. What do the ghosts look like? What does a terror dog look like? What is this creature we're talking about? And, of course the script was changing as fast as we could even work on it. But we had to try and conceptualize what all this would look like.

Then, we had to start storyboarding immediately. The biggest immediate problem, obviously, was that we knew that we had a huge amount of special effects, and such a short amount of time in which to do them. ILM couldn't take us. At that time, *Dune* was at Apogee, and not only that, but it looked like *Dune* was going to spread itself all over town. You could go to people like Dreamquest, who I have a great deal of respect for, but at that time they weren't really big enough to take on a project of this scale. And, they were the first to recognize that there were effects here that, although they could do them, it would have been the first time they were doing them, and we didn't know how much R&D there would have been and we just didn't have the time.

It was at that point that someone came to me and said I should talk to Richard Edlund because he was leaving ILM and setting up his own shop down here. So, that's what happened. I talked to him, gave him a script; it fell right into place. Then what happened is that the shop that's being set up is being financed by Columbia Pictures and MGM jointly, to do *Ghostbusters* and *2010*. But, if that hadn't happened, where would we have gone? There's a good chance that we would not have been able to make the film, at least on time.

Then we had the added benefit—that a lot of the people that work for Richard had worked for him in the past on other films, including *Poltergeist*. The advantage of having people who had literally handled ghosts before was a great benefit. Ironically, in the final cut of the picture, we removed most of the ghosts.

Then it went into the same kind of process as any production, really. Once that was assembled, we had to decide, while the script was metamorphosing, what these things would look like. It's easy to talk about a ghost, but then you say you want an original ghost ….

We have this thing called Onion Head (Slimer), which is not a guy running around with a big onion for a head, but what is he? The terror dogs, at one point, were dogs that were something running from the world on the other side. They were big, buffoon-like, silly, almost loveable animals. Not really loveable because they'd be monsters, but stupid, drooling, like a demented dog. Then, at another point they became something that were almost skeletal. And, it wasn't until we reached the point in the script, that we realized that they were coming here with a purpose, to devour these people, that the dog solidified. But, it solidified in the midst of a schedule that was so difficult that we were actually putting together the effects people to construct it as we were still trying to decide what it was. That kind of race was constant.

Q: What about the storyboards? That was obviously going on at that same time ….

MG: Yeah, we had to start storyboarding early, again, just to get the scenes locked down. We were storyboarding even before we got the effects people on, which is not a great thing to do. It helps the director and helps everybody to see just what the scene might be, but really the effects people have to do the storyboarding, because they know what they can produce.

Then, John Bruno came on. We had wanted him on early, but John was in France working on the Cheech and Chong film. By the time he got over here, we had half the film boarded. He had to go reboard ninety percent of that, as well as board original stuff that hadn't yet been done. He was given scenes which we liked the way they played, so it didn't have to be totally thought of from scratch. It was just a matter of fixing it to work. So, we didn't lose time by starting early, we gained some.

A lot of the special effects work that was in the first draft of the script remained unchanged in the last two drafts. Sequences would rearrange around, a character was added, characters changed, relationships changed, but the effects scenes, a lot of them, isolated as they were, remained in the film unchanged. So, a lot of that boarding, even with the changes, wasn't lost.

Q: Did all the first ideas for the various ghosts and terror dogs come from you?

MG: Yes. All the original concepts came from me and a team of five to eight illustrators, artists and sculptors implemented the stuff.

Q: Where did you draw your inspiration from for the terror dogs?

MG: I don't know. A lot of that thinking came out of *Heavy Metal* magazine, which represents a very different attitude about creatures, monsters, ghosts and stuff. Half of the artists I would bring in for this would give you just what you've seen on "Night on Bald Mountain" and every other cartoon. It was very hard to get somebody off center and say, "Come in from left field and give me ghosts like I've never seen before." I don't say that this is one we've never seen before, in its final configuration, but it's certainly right for the film.

So, what I'm constantly trying to do is to both identify the kind of talent that's able to do that, and then continually try and find ways to inspire them. After that, it's largely an editing, feedback process.

Q: What about reconciling the fact that the film is a funny/scary film? That's an odd combination of elements to have to deal with.

MG: That's a good question, because that is the single hardest problem of the whole film. Scary-silly, I can only think of twice having to deal with that in a film. As a genre, sometimes in the thirties and forties when you had *Hold That Ghost, Ghostbreakers* and all the rest of it, in which for the scary part, you relied on the horror movie cliche, and then you played the humor against it. That kind of thinking died away, certainly in the late fifties, and didn't exist at all in the sixties. Then, Landis brought it back with *American Werewolf* in an entirely different way, certainly a dryer, wryer, bizarre humor and horror that was truly scary, to the point where either it was brilliant and you loved it, or you were confused as to whether they should be laughing or screaming, and maybe that was his point as well.

We don't have that problem. We've clearly made up our mind with this. It's a comedy—broad, big, bold. This is much closer to the forties way of thinking about it, with contemporary sensibilities, humor, talents and a contemporary way of looking at horror. The only exception to that is that we don't do what a lot of contemporary horror films do, and that is we don't repulse you. It's more fun, like the forties. There's no blood, there's no people turning inside out. We don't want to put things on the screen that people can't look at.

When I was at *National Lampoon*, one of the problems you had, was that a writer would write a very dry piece of satire, and the graphic, visualization of it, would have to be very straightforward. It's like "Saturday Night Live," the strength of the parody lies in how accurately you present the reality of what you're watching, and then you put the jokes in. With *Lampoon*, the problem was, you'd call in some straight illustrator who would think it was his first chance to do a cartoon, so he gives you a cartoon back, which you didn't want. It had to be straight.

Well, this film had the same problem. I'd go to the guys and give them a picture and they'd give me their first funny ghost. Their first funny horror picture. I'd tell them, no, you can't do that. It's got to be straight, but don't go over the line where you create something so horrible that it's jolting people out of the film.

The Onion Head ghost is a clear exception because we decided to make him a funny ghost. And, even there we certainly didn't want to make him Casper. We had to make him something else. We think he works in the sensibility of the film.

Then, you deal with something like the Stay-Puft marshmallow man, God knows what line we're walking there! That concept was in Dan's original script. All the way along we kept asking people, "Do you think this is over the edge?" As we got closer and closer to it, I think it's brilliant. I think it's just the perfect touch to end the whole movie. It would have been so embarrassing to walk any kind of real monster up that street. You would have had Godzilla, which you can't take seriously anyway. But, at the same time, it walks a line because it has to be threatening, in a kind of ironic threat. You can't have a Thanksgiving day parade balloon come up the street. It just walks a very, strange, fine line. It does so conceptually in the script, and it does so visually in the film.

Q: What kind of problems were you faced with with having to build the top of the building set?

MG: We were very fortunate, because we had a genius of a production designer. John De Cuir is the kind of production designer who's not just an artistic talent. He worked on *Cleopatra, Hello, Dolly*, he can build anything. He's been working on films since the forties. He's just a wonderful man. He went in and put that thing up in, I think, ten weeks. He conceived it, he designed it. A lot of the concepts I had for the temple and what might be on top of the building were no good, they were not working at all. John could see that and did a beautiful job. He knew how he was going to build it. We were faced with an early decision making problem, in that John De Cuir believes that you should build everything, and Richard Edlund believes that you build nothing, and you put it all together in the effects shop. Ivan had to look at that whole ending sequence and decide if he should build the set, or if we were going to do it all with opticals, miniatures and paintings. But, when we examined the ways in which he really had to shoot, to have the freedom to shoot and make the shots work dramatically, and to be able to work with actors on a real stage, in real time in a very difficult sequence, we opted for a combination, which involved definitely the presence of a set, most of the time. The optical work there is to mostly add extra impact to the set, or to extend it either higher or lower than it exists, or to back it up to put it in New York City. So, we did decide that we needed that set, despite the fact that it cost over a million dollars.

When we were in New York, despite blowing up the streets and having three hundred extras and three hundred crew members running around, we got out of New York two and a half days ahead of schedule. We went right on to stage sixteen, and it immediately ground us to a halt. The record number of setups in New York was twenty-six. When we got onto stage sixteen the first day, we got one shot, that was it. The next day we got three shots. I don't think we ever got it to much better than eight. We figured that we were on the safety of a set and it would be simple, but the set was so big …. We had a 360 degree background that had to be lit from behind. There was so much power for that stage, 50,000 amps, that we actually had to shut down other stages when we shot. It presented heating problems, fire problems, tremendous lighting problems; we had steam and tremendous physical effects. Just the amount of people it took just to manage the set while we were shooting was more difficult to move around. That set put us behind about four or five days, and we never did manage to catch them up. Everything else, wherever else we went, went smoothly, in libraries, on location. Just that set was difficult.

Q: What were some of the problems encountered in shooting in New York?

MG: One of the more amazing feats accomplished in this film, is a stunt put together by Chuck Gaspari, who does the physical effects and John De Cuir, who designed it. They worked out something that's really spectacular. But, it made working in New York quite difficult. That was the scene dealing with the boys falling into a hole in the ground in front of the apartment building in New York City. We couldn't dig a hole in the streets of New York, although John De Cuir wanted to. So, for a couple hundred thousand dollars, we worked out a great stunt.

Ernie Hudson, Bill Murray, Dan Aykroyd, and Harold Ramis congratulate each other on a job well done in *Ghostbusters*.

When the guys rise up out of the hole, as well as when there are people screaming in the streets, you see tremendous rubble in front of the building, and the asphalt is torn up and at extreme angles. You see half a police car in a hole, steam pipes coming out of it, etc. Well, we couldn't dig into the street, so that's all built on top of it. The street is still there, and there are fake pieces, all cut at strategic angles to cover the fact that there is no hole. The automobile is cut in half and tilted at that angle.

At one point in the film, when you see the ground open up, and you see the hole, and you see the guys fall down in the hole, that was a recreation of the front of the building and the street built over here, on the Columbia Pictures Ranch, and which could only be shot in a limited number of ways. We dug a hole in the ground, and Chuck Gaspari rigged a street that was hydraulically controlled to collapse, and the pieces just split and collapsed, and everything fell right into it—stunt car, stunt men, the steam pipes popped up …. When you intercut it with the stuff in New York, you can't tell that it's not the same place.

Q: What about some of the other problems of shooting in New York, such as closing off Central Park West?

MG: Mostly traffic problems. New York is a city that is already congested to the limit, and when you take Central Park West and you close down everything but one lane, and it's 65th Street, which is a transversal street that runs through the park, and that's slowed down to a halt—you've tied up a third of Manhattan all the while you're shooting. We even shot through Friday rush hour once.

The hotel where we were staying was down the street from where we were shooting. I remember walking down at the end of one shooting day and hearing car horns beeping from as far away as the low fifties. I went into the bar of the hotel and sat down to have a beer, and I had a button on my coat which was one of our crew buttons, so we could be identified in the masses. This guy came in and said, "Jesus Christ! Two and a half hours to get from thirtieth street to here! What the hell is going on up there?" Some other guy jumps up at the bar and says, "A bunch of sons of bitches making a movie! They're screwing up half the town, making a goddamn movie!" I took the button off, stuck it in my pocket and hid it. Normally, you'd be in a place, kind of proud that you're making a film, but not us. I wasn't going to say a word! At one point, some guy asked me what I do, and I said I worked for a subsidiary of Coca Cola!

But, the press treated us very well, and most people had a really good time. People do like to see a movie shot, and the New York extras were fabulous. It was difficult only because we were on the streets the whole time. We only shot there about three and a half weeks. We had Central Park closed off for a week. There was a point, when we were coming to our last day, when we went to one of the cops who headed the group of patrolmen that we had on the film, and we said we may need to shoot another half day, a Saturday. He said, "No, you're not. It's over, you're wrapping at 11:30 tonight." They were great, but it was tough on everybody.

THE MAKING OF *GHOSTBUSTERS*' SPECIAL EFFECTS

Because of the large quantity of special effects required by the story—almost 2090 shots—and the pressure of a very short production schedule, *Ghostbusters* could have turned into what industry people sometimes refer to as a nightmare. Yet, the film was delivered on time, although not without its normal share of crisis and problems.

The story of the special effects of *Ghostbusters* is, coincidentally, also that of the first film made by Boss Film Corporation (BFC), a new special effects house set up by Academy Award winner, Richard Edlund. Very early on, a team of designers had started work, storyboarding the film. Meanwhile, the production had gone looking for a special effects house that could handle the sheer volume of work in the prescribed period of time. They were delighted to find that Richard Edlund had left George Lucas' Industrial Light & Magic in San Rafael, to form his own company in the Los Angeles area.

"We have to go back to *Star Wars*," says Edlund, whose credits also include *Raiders of the Lost Ark* and *Poltergeist*. "That show was my first big break in the business, or actually in features, because I'd been doing commercials. Shortly after *Star Wars* had begun, it became apparent that there were going to be sequels involved and it would be a trilogy. I had a goal of wanting to finish the first trilogy, even though I knew it would involve years of work. It was a new thing for me to be involved in a project that lasted two years long, and follow through on every aspect of it, so that it came out as close to what the director and we wanted to put in as possible.

"When I finished *Star Wars* I was a member of John Dykstra's Apogee group and, for a while, I even was a partner. But we had an understanding that, if Gary Kurtz were to call me to work on *The Empire Strikes Back*, that I would leave, and there should be no hard feelings. Which is what happened. When Gary called, he said that they wanted to move the effects facility up to Marin County. I balked at that because I felt that it would be more expensive in certain ways to do that kind of move. But, that's what was decided, and I agreed to go. So, I sold my house in Los Angeles and moved up to Marin to set up the effects facility.

"By the time I started working on *Return of the Jedi*, I felt that, by that time, I had spent a great deal of time under the Lucasfilm umbrella, and I wanted to go out and get wet myself. I felt that once I had finished *Jedi*, my job was essentially done.

Some opportunities began to present themselves down in L.A., and L.A. is the land of opportunity.

"There were a number of close friends and working associates who also felt the need to change situations, so I was able to talk a lot of those people into following me. It wasn't just myself coming down here. It was a group of people who were very talented. I feel extremely lucky to have this kind of camaraderie and enthusiasm and experience and talent to work with. We can all work together as a group, and people have an opportunity, with the way that we've set up the company, to go off on their own and contribute freely, without the need to be closely supervised, because they're all so talented."

Throughout his stint at ILM, Edlund had maintained ongoing communication with Douglas Trumbull. Aware that Trumbull wanted to direct (as evidenced by the later *Brainstorm*), and that Trumbull's partner, Richard Yuricich, wanted to become a director of photography in features, Edlund went into partnership with the two men. He and his friends moved into the premises of Trumbull and Yuricich's Venice-based EEG. "We're partners in this operation now, from the standpoint of the facility and the equipment," Edlund explains. "But the people who are working with me here are an intact group." They renamed the company BFC.

Early on, Edlund decided that BFC would do most of its work in the 65mm format. He explains, "I sort of resurrected Vistavision on *Star Wars*. Vistavision is a good format, in that you can use spherical lenses and work with a reduction when you composite. When you do that, you always have a generation loss. By reducing in composite, you minimize that generation loss. Since there was a great deal of 65mm equipment here, and that really is the ultimate format that's available, I was looking forward to working in it. Because the image is being reduced two to one, the quality of the dupes are the best that I've every seen."

One of the first things that Edlund and his team did when they took over EEG was to either build new equipment or modify that which was already in place. "I'm not the type of person that has to have all of the equipment in hand in order to do anything," explains Edlund. "I can build up the equipment and do it again if necessary, and get it all ready to go and get a project together. That is what we did here. We have different ways of working than Douglas and Richard. We had to build an aerial head optical printer, which was a first priority. We built a magnificent printer, and I think it's the best one yet. It's the third one that I've built, basically from scratch. That enabled us to have a lot of facility to reposition mattes, to fit things very carefully and crucially, to diffuse and modify, etc. We built that with a huge casting of ductal iron, so that it's solid as a rock, we can have an earthquake and not miss a frame. We also put optics on the other two printers that were here.

"I brought my 35mm printer in, so that we have 35mm capability as well. The other main achievement is the high-speed, 65mm reflex camera built by Gene Whiteman." (Whiteman was equipment supervising engineer on *The Empire Strikes Back*, *Raiders of the Lost Ark* and *Return of the Jedi*. He also designed the optical printer used on *E.T.*) "It's the only spinning mirror reflex 65mm camera that I know of, and the only one that will run over a hundred frames a second. We'll have it up to 120 pretty quick.

"Our field is so rarified, that almost everything has to be hotrodded to some degree, because it always has to do something extra. You can't buy anything off the shelf that plugs directly into our system without modifying it someway. It is a production camera for example, like the Mitchell BFC. We may need to be able to put a line-up clip in the viewfinder, so we modified it to do that. They also have to be absolutely rock-steady. We have to do movement work which has to be accurate to a tenth of a hundredth or less. The problem being that, if you have one image weaving against the other, it gives away the illusion. Also, it had to have special lenses that were all calibrated, going from a very wide angle, to a relatively long telephoto, and that were all tricked out in one way or another. For example, we have lenses that we can tilt on a ball joint, so that we can extend depth of field. There's every manner of trick item being made up all the time, and we never seem to have enough. The machine shop is always busy with several guys working all day, every day, constantly modifying and adding to our quiver of arrows." BFC's start-up was financed jointly by Columbia and MGM/UA to handle the effects on both *Ghostbusters* and *2010*. "The theory here," Edlund continues, "is to have two projects in here all the time. One of which releases at about a six month interval after the other one. That would be the ideal working situation for us as a group because I find that to have more than one project scheduled for the same date, in the same house, really creates pandemonium. That way, too, the different departments can segue away from project to project, and maintain a continuity of effort over a period of time. I would not want, all of a sudden, to run out of things to do around here, because then you have the prospect of losing this marvelous chemistry of personality and talent."

This blending of people is, to Edlund, the most important aspect of a top quality effects facility. He feels that the enthusiasm generated by his team has added to their creativity. "I have a 'hunting band' theory," he says. "There is a core group of twenty or so people here that all have a good inner relationship. Some of them came with me and others, whom I've known for years, were already here. When you have that kind of situation, then you have control of the whole project, because everyone in the 'hunting band' is going after the same goal. What I try to do is shield these people from outside things that are going to bother them and make things more difficult for them. I try to get them what they need when they need it.

"I guess my main function is to go through and talk to all these people, make sure that everything is all right, see what people are doing, maybe make suggestions or listen to suggestions from others. Then, when we all get together in the screening room, everyone gets to understand and come up with a suggestion for something that doesn't have to do with their specialty. The screening room is a real important catharsis for everyone because everyone goes off and works in his own area and gets really involved in that. Then, when we run a piece of film that another guy was working on, everyone starts getting a sense of the big picture."

Richard Kerrigan, production supervisor, whose credits include effects production associate on *The Right Stuff*, feels that this "team spirit" is what makes BFC different from other companies. "Someone once told me that filmmaking wasn't a democracy," he says, "but at BFC, it is more of a democracy. Richard Edlund is the fountainhead, but people relate more directly to him than in other organizations. Normally, you come to the production manager, who assumes more of a stronger political position. But it doesn't work that way here. My job function is more to make sure that everybody is talking to everybody else, that the shots are getting done correctly, and generally taking a 'can I help you?' posture."

In addition to the considerable expertise and teamwork that Edlund and his crew brought to *Ghostbusters*, there was an added benefit: most had worked on *Poltergeist*, giving them prior experience in handling ghosts! Visual Effects Art Director John Bruno, for example, was visual effects animation supervisor on the Steven Spielberg / Tobe Hooper film. He had also worked with Director Ivan Reitman on the *Heavy Metal* animated feature as special effects director.

Bruno was in France, working as production designer on Cheech and Chong's *Corsican Brothers* movie, when he was contacted to work on *Ghostbusters*. "During that time, I kept getting calls telling me that this project was going, and that they needed me to come back and start designing the effects shots. I was really swamped over there, and started on this six weeks late. When I came back, a lot of the film had been boarded. The only thing that I originally boarded was all the terror dog scenes, because there wasn't anything done on that earlier. Otherwise, it was all basically redone. I came in with a more direct approach as to how the effects would be done. I would design a shot that I believed could be done. I always approach boarding by trying to see the best way, the most spectacular way in which a scene can be done, within the context of the story. But I don't do completed, clean drawings because I get upset when they get thrown out."

Bruno would rough out the boards and show them to Reitman for approval. Then, they would be cleaned up and sent again for final approval, where it would sometimes be decided if more or less action was needed, or if any other changes should be made. The final stage was to have a meeting of cameraman Bill Neil, Richard Edlund, Terry Windell and Garry Waller of the Animation Department, and Matte Camera Supervisor Neil Krepela. They would look over the shots and decide what effects elements were required to bring the scene to life. Their decisions were then written into the notes on the storyboard.

"We decided early on," explains Bruno, "that we didn't have the luxury for research and development, although there was some. We didn't have a situation where we had three different methods among which we could choose. If we could have had six to eight more months to finish the film, we could have experimented with and saw what produced the best results. In this particular case, it's been: 'I feel that this is going to work, and I've done it enough before that I know it will. Therefore, it's better to go this way rather than than trying to develop another method.'"

Bruno sums up his philosophy. "Basically, effects are impression. You're supposed to show just enough so that audiences know what the scene is all about. You don't really want to go back and hold on so that you can see the effect. *Star Wars* is a whole series of two second shots. Most good effects films are. We have been pushed to another maximum on *Ghostbusters*, in that some of our shots are fairly long. At this point, we're trying to trim them down a little, because there isn't a shot in the world that you can get away with for twenty seconds."

Because *Ghostbusters* was shot partly on location in New York, and partly on stage 16 at the Burbank Studios, where John De Cuir had built his giant "Gozer Temple" set, a number of mattes were required to enhance the picture. This job fell to Neil Krepela, who came with Edlund from ILM, and Matthew Yuricich, who did the matte paintings for the film. Yuricich, one of the most respected artists in the industry, has worked on such classics as *The Day the Earth Stood Still, Forbidden Planet, Ben-Hur, Mutiny on the Bounty, Close Encounters of the Third Kind, Star Trek I* and *Blade Runner.*

"There are about fifty mattes I did for this picture," says Yuricich, "and they're mostly architectural. To match with the temple top created by John De Cuir, I added about thirty stories onto the building that we actually used in New York. It's a weird design, but it really fits. It's actually kind of an old fashioned kind of matte work, because you must respect realism, and yet take license with it. You have to make it look like real buildings, even though you cheat a little, as opposed to a film like *Blade*

Runner where they were buildings of the future. People never question the miniatures in these futuristic pictures because, deep inside, they know it's not real, so they accept it. But if you're painting a building or a tree or something that's got to look like the real thing, then it's harder because what you're painting is really out there. For instance, there were many real buildings, two, three or four times shorter than this one building. We had to cut those other buildings down shorter, so that the temple top looks like it's up alone. We wanted this to be the building that you see. That, in itself, was difficult because it makes the building look different. Whenever you see the Empire State Building in the New York skyline, you buy it, because you're familiar with it. The Gozer building, on the other hand, looks real, but people are going to wonder where it came from.

"The panoramic view of New York posed a problem, because it was like having two paintings on one. We were painting a building on top of an existing building, and the two had to fit together. Now, whatever camera trick they use to bring that together will change my painting of the whole city panorama. So, I have to get the centerpiece tied together well enough that I know how to go on from there."

"We also did a lot of what I call 'band-aid' shots," adds Krepela. "They're not matte paintings in the truest sense, but more like fix-its. It might be just taking one building down. Or, if you're going to shoot one little scene, and you want to change one area to make an effect work better, or because somebody forgot something that's going to cause a problem, we can paint it out or put something else in there. For example, in one scene we painted out some street lights that really cluttered up the frame. It's not the greatest use of a matte painting, but it's certainly cheaper than going back with a cast and crew and reshoot the whole scene all over again."

Edlund and his crew took their 65mm cameras down to stage 16 of the Burbank Studios and on location in New York. "All of the plates were shot with a 65mm camera," he recalls. "Actually, we had two cameras. The high speed one, which we used when we needed reflex viewing, and a Mitchell BFC camera that was all decked out for location shooting. It's perfectly steady and it's hotrodded for effects work."

Neil Krepela worked with D.P. Laszlo Kovacs, A.S.C., to ensure that the 65mm footage would match that of the 35mm live action photography. "We used the 65mm cameras to shoot simultaneously with the 35mm cameras," he explains. "We would pick a different angle, or we would have a different shot than the first unit. We shot a lot of the temple sequence using the 65mm in a wide shot, with a bluescreen behind it, while the 35mm was getting the same actions right next to us on a tight close up on one of the characters. On many occasions, there were four cameras running, two 65mms and two 35mms. We did that because the director wanted to cover all the angles on scenes that were difficult to restage. For example, the scenes in the hotel, when the *Ghostbusters* are chasing a ghost, blowing huge holes in the wall, blowing up tables full of food, knocking chandeliers off the ceilings, etc. You only want to do that once.

"We pretty much told Laszlo our needs for exposing our negative. We overexpose, as compared to what he's doing with his negative. We rate our film a little different, more towards the normal of what Kodak specifies, to get a heavier negative. We find that, as we add effects, the heavier negative dupes better in the optical printer than the thinner negative that you can get away with in normal live action production. Laszlo knew that, and he always had enough light for us, and told us what our stop was. It was always the correct one, and he would actually stop the 35mms down from that. He's got a great eye too. We would have storyboards of our shots. We'd line up and he would check the cameras. If he ever moved the cameras around, it was always for the better. You can't fight that."

Krepela also explains that a good depth of field is required for matching the live action plates. "For matte painting and effects work in general, if you're going to put something into the scene, such as a monster running towards you, you don't want to have a short depth of field. If you did, it would be mushy back there and then, when you start shooting your miniature, you've got to match that mush. It just adds a lot of complexity to the thing, and it doesn't always look good, because what you want the public to look at will often be lost."

Ectoplasmic exterminators Bill Murray (left) and Dan Aykroyd (center) have just removed some uninvited guests—rather, ghosts—from a fancy hotel in *Ghostbusters*.

Because the 65mm cameras were always used on the set, there was very little chance that any effects would have to be matched to a 35mm live action plate. Says Edlund, "The only time that really happens is if there may be one or two shots that are needed almost as an afterthought, and we can do that by running the elements in bi-pack in the composite camera. Or, if we need to shoot at 350 frames per second, with a special camera that will go that fast, since there is no 65mm camera that will. Occasionally, we'll shoot an element at 300 frames a second, and then we'll take the negative from that, blow that up to a 65mm interpositive, then fit it back into our process."

While the live action work was being filmed in New York, and later at the Burbank Studios, the special effects team at BFC were busy trying to meet its deadline. Under the direction of Stuart Ziff, a special "ghost room" was put together to handle the final design and construction of the fantasy creatures appearing in the film. These include a ghost dubbed "Onion Head" (later known as Slimer), the terror dogs, dog-shaped agents of Gozer, and finally, the "Stay-Puft Man," the giant marshmallow creature used by Gozer in his final confrontation with the *Ghostbusters*.

John Bruno explains how the ghosts were created. "We had a number of concepts of how many types of ghosts there were. I just took the approach that a ghost is anything dead. You could have weird, prehistoric things, strange amoebic blobs, animal ghosts, etc. You could have anything possible as far as what was a ghost, and that's what comes back in this film. In the 'ghost geyser' scene, there's just everything that was ever alive, or ever lived for an instant, such as mosquitoes!"

In keeping with the spirit of the film, some of the ghosts were conceived to be scary, and others funny. "Slimer, for instance, is a funny ghost," explains Bruno, who traces its evolution to

John Belushi! Slimer, conceived by Dan Aykroyd, and originally designed by Associate Producer Michael Gross, was finally sculpted by Steve Johnson, who worked on *Greystoke, An American Werewolf in London* and *The Howling*. "Slimer's such a lunatic," says Bruno. "As originally boarded, he reacts and can do a lot more, which is a blessing. He has a personality, and basically we've been working off that. The first thing we heard was that he was based on John Belushi. Danny Aykroyd wanted him to be treated as a silly guy. So, we studied *Animal House*. We studied the expressions that John Belushi did in that. But, in some cases, John Belushi would be too broad for the action that's asked for. So, it evolved and just acquired its own personality, also because of the actor that's in there. Now, if it doesn't get a laugh in the film, I won't understand."

To find the right balance between scary and funny was a big struggle. "Ivan would hate some scenes and like others," explains Bruno. "The same with Michael and everybody else. Slimer is funny, but everything else is played straight. The humor is in the way the film is written and acted. At no time are the terror dogs considered not dangerous. They're scary. What happens in Dana's apartment is scary too. The set up is funny, but not what goes on. The humor comes out of the situation. So, Slimer is just going on in his own plane of existence. Bill Murray and Dan Aykroyd never treat him as funny. They're frightened of him; he's a ghost. It's played straight. The marshmallow man is not funny either. He is ridiculous, but we never approach him as a joke. You never forget that he is a giant demon, a huge devil god."

To bring these ghosts to life (half-life?), Stuart Ziff hired about forty artists and technicians. Ziff previously worked on *Star Wars, The China Syndrome, Star Trek I, The Empire Strikes Back, Dragonslayer* (for which he won a technical Academy Award for designing the Go-Motion Figure mover that was used in the film), *Amityville 3D* and *Return of the Jedi.* "I wanted a really dynamic and creative group," he explains. "But, more than that, I didn't want one look. If I were to just hire people for one genre, everything would have looked the same. So, I made a point of bringing in different groups of people, which has really meant a lot more turmoil on my part in the various personalities. Initially, I hoped to have one person per ghost, and have five or six different things to do. But it didn't exactly work out that way. Some guys got more, some were group efforts, some were one man shows. The sculptures take the personality of the person working on them. For example, Linda Frobos, who is just delightful and bubbly, designed the Stay-Puft Man's head, and it has her personality in it. We have another guy who is sort of sinister, and everything he does is pre-Neanderthal and scary."

John Berg, who is credited as an effects consultant on *Ghostbusters*, agrees with Ziff. "It's always difficult to find people who have that unique gift of being able to synthesize a personality. It's even more difficult on a project like this, because you have several people associated with one creature. So you hope to get a really good group of people able to do that, and that they have to have enough time and enough good, clear direction to pull it together, so that the entity can start to personify."

Deciding when to use a full-size costume or a stop-motion puppet was a constant problem for the production. John Bruno says, "We constantly needed to figure out if there's something we should do live, to maybe take the weight off the animation department, or stop motion." For Slimer, Terry Windell and Garry Waller, the two animation department supervisors and former ILM employees, used a two-inch miniature, which they shot on the Oxberry motion control camera. Windell explains, "We're using the miniature, because the actual acrobatics that it does can't be done by the large puppet. With this, Garry has the capability to tumble it and sweep it up out of frame, etc. Annick Terrien and Peggy Regan are two of our technical animators. They are doing a lot of the rotoscoping to meld the characters, such as Slimer, into the actual live action scene."

Steve Johnson, who sculpted Slimer, explains, "The thing that I wanted to do with Slimer, and I think I pretty much succeeded, was to make a two-dimensional cartoon, like a Tex Avery character, or an old Looney Tune, three-dimensional. Because he was a ghost, we could go real broad with the mechanism, which we couldn't have done on a thing that was supposed to be alive.

"Slimer was the one character that everyone was concerned about the most, so there was really the most amount of group effort on its design. Michael Gross had worked with some studio sculptors before I came on the project and had come up with a design that he was really in love with, and which everybody really liked. When I came on, I ended up sculpting about seven variations on that design, until one was finally accepted. Then, I worked it out and refined it."

However, in other cases, the original designs had to be modified to fit the effects work. Ziff explains, "For example, the terror dog design we got looked good, but Randy Cook, who was going to ultimately stop-motion animate it, noticed that, if the mouth closed, the lower teeth were going to puncture through the jaw, and also that one of the legs wouldn't be able to turn. For each terror dog, we had one person half-way inside, and ten people operating all the mechanisms. Just the logistics of moving all these people around, moving the mechanisms and keeping everything working, was a technical headache. It ultimately worked out good. We were saved because they shot it second unit. If we would have had to do that first unit, it would have been a disaster.

"The terror dogs start off as creatures of stone and transform. We made this rubber claw that had to break through the plaster.

But it was very delicate and couldn't push through anything. So, Chuck Gaspar had his guys make push rods to break the plaster. But, for whatever reason, the day of shooting, it didn't work. We pushed the lever so hard that the cable in the mechanism broke. It was seven p.m. at night. Ivan Reitman turned towards me and said, 'Stuart, I want that fixed by seven a.m. tomorrow!' and walked out. Ultimately, Gaspar got his guys to fix the problem. In the scene where the terror dog's arms break through the chair, I decided that we had to treat the cloth to rip through. Our first idea was to treat it with acid to weaken the cloth, then the arms would break through. Three days before shooting, it just didn't work, and we'd been working on it a month. So, over the weekend, I worked with a few other people, and we ended up slicing it by hand and gluing tissue paper on it. This is one business where people get paid double time to correct their own mistakes!

"Another thing to touch on is, that while we were building all the creatures, we had to be shooting live action. We had to continue to build them at BFC, at the same time as we had to deal with production schedules that were just changing constantly. For example, some days we'd go to the soundstage and they wouldn't even use us, and they were the same people that I needed back here to build things. We worked continuously, seven days a week, to complete the terror dogs."

Linda Frobos, whose previous jobs include sculpting on *Spacehunter* and *Buckaroo Banzai*, sculpted three Stay-Puft Man heads, one happy, one frowning, and a third one with two major expressions: a grimace, and suprise. "I did sculpt a fourth head, a very angry face, affected by the fire, starting to melt," she explains. "His mouth is getting real gooey. But they did not use it. They gave us several cartoon drawings of the Stay-Puft Man in different poses and angles. We talked a lot about the feeling that he was supposed to have. I saw it as just a very simple, smooth form, with enough indication on the shape to distinguish the features. It had to be subtle. When I'm working on a character, I try to develop a feel for it, which I then try to impart to the work.

"What I did was to sculpt a maquette of each expression, so that I could look for shapes that could be moved in a certain way, so that they could form either expression. On the face where we needed two very different expressions, I started out with the maquettes and I sculpted a face that was in-between the two expressions required. So, the sculpture itself looks bland. The expressions are achieved with articulations. Because the Stay-Puft Man's face is very smooth, there's a real difficulty and challenge in trying to articulate it. Something wrinkled, hairy, or that has very distinguishing lines, is very forgiving because it hides a lot. On something very smooth, if there are little bumps or irregularities, or some of the cables are sticking out, everything is going to show. I did use some indications of form, like rolls of flesh or something, but I tried to keep it all very smooth.

"I worked with the men who articulated it, and they had to understand how far to move things. There's a real limit to how much it can move because you have to consider the strength of the rubber. When we make the core for the sculpture, we have to have the thickness thin enough that it can move, but not thin enough so it will tear."

Bill Bryan, who built the Stay-Puft Man costume, and acted the part (except in the stunt scenes portraying the destruction of the monster by fire!) describes it as a combination of a sauna suit and a universal gym. "I was handed the design and was told, 'This is what we got approved and it's probably what we want.' So, I played with making the shapes a little more marshmallowy and cylindrical. But Stuart decided he preferred the smoother outline, basically cigar-shaped, narrow at the bottom and top and wide in the middle. The body was made from foam sheet. We just had to get the seams around to the back where you didn't see them. We built front view suits, back view suits and side view suits. There was also a top view suit, which was a back view suit that had been split and widened by about a foot. Each shot really had its own problems. There were four burning shots, and each of those required two suits. We also built one suit that had extra long arms and oversize hands to force the perspective. The head had to have a skirt for the neck, because there would have been a vulnerable spot at the connection. Especially, since that's where all the flame would happen.

"To wear the costume, you have to be able to translate just how fast he would walk. I spent some time just figuring out what the walk was going to be. Would it be a fat man waddling, leg and hand moving at the same time, or would it be more a Godzilla swing. We ended up with the swing. Actually, it's almost a regular walk, but with a little bit of extra up and down. Since we're shooting at seventy-two frames per second, I had to translate it into one third speed movement."

The major problem with the Stay-Puft Man costume was to enable it to burn, and at the same time, make it safe for the stuntman wearing it. "Originally, I thought we'd be faking the flame by airbrushing some browning and blackening while on camera," continues Bryan, "and maybe some chemical mixture to get a little bubbling action and some bladders under the surface to get a larger bubbling action, and then animate in the flames, or stick them in optically. But, Richard didn't want that, and the word came down that it did have to be fire, and it did have to look like he'd been doused with gasoline and lit. That's when it really started getting scary. We were already pretty far into the project. They had been saying it, but when they say something like that, they tend to chuckle, so you take it with a grain of salt, depending how much you want not to believe it! We were lucky in that the method that we had been using to construct the suit lent itself to including a layer of nonburning foam. Also, we were lucky that the type of foam that looked right also burned right!

"We started with inch-thick foam. Then, we decided that in order not to get as much pollutants in the air, a half-inch thick would be sufficient. Also, that way it doesn't eat as close to the stuntman. On the body, there's a half-inch of flammable foam, then a half-inch of the best non-flammable foam, which has forty-two percent fire-retardant additives. We glued it down to a more rigid foam, then smeared another fire retardant into it. It's a leathery texture foam, which has no air bubbles in it, and which keeps the other foam from absorbing air. Another relatively lucky thing was that, once we burnt the first back view suit, Ivan decided that he wanted less flames. We had flames that were reaching almost to the top of the building, and they let it burn for thirty seconds. That's a pretty long burn, especially when there's somebody in it and you're responsible for his life. We found where the flaws were and improved it."

Supervising the destruction of the Stay-Puft Man was the job of Thaine Morris, mechanical effects supervisor, who is another ILM alumnus. "We were going to use an air mortar to blow his head away," he explains, "but because it was so heavy, it actually ended up being jerked out of frame with a string. As regards the actual burning, we came up with a foam that would retard the fire and would not burn through and get to the stuntman. Then, we had to find some kind of flame that would conform to the scale of the Stay-Puft Man, which is one-twelfth scale. We ended up using something called Krackle Kolor which is a flammable liquid that burns with just a little bit of sparks, and it seems to keep the flame down. We've taken some liberty with the Stay-Puft concept, in that we used red sparks instead of blue ones, when everybody knows that marshmallows burn blue!"

Terry Windell explains how the marshmallow man was integrated into the live action footage of New York City. "When the Stay-Puft Man walks down Columbus Circle in New York, he's scaled at 115 feet tall, and there are literally hundreds of people running away from him. To incorporate him into live action, you have to literally hand draw each of the characters that pass in front of him. Rather, you create the illusion that they pass in front of him by animating the cars and people to eliminate portions of his feet and put him into the background."

Mark Stetson, supervisor of BFC's model shop, was responsible for all the miniature New York buildings in the film. Stetson's previous miniature work includes *Blade Runner, The Right Stuff* and *Close Encounters of the Third Kind*. "The biggest thing that we did was Dana's apartment building with the Gozer temple on top," he explains. "The miniature we built for that started at the eighth floor level. From there up, it's about a fifteen foot miniature. We stuck it up on a five foot platform to indicate the bottom eight floors, and that gives us a twenty foot model to shoot out in the parking lot. There are several shots on it, mostly involving physical gags. When the building doesn't have something physical happening around it, generally it's a matte painting. When the marshmallow man is on it, generally it's a miniature, although there are shots of the existing building, with plates of the marshmallow man composited to it.

"The Gozer temple is blasted apart at the end of the film, and that was all done as a pyrotechnical gag on the model," continues Stetson. "Thaine Morris has had five shots at blowing the top off. We quickly rebuild it each time he does it." Morris explains, "The miniature explosion has sort of fallen into a state where there's two or three of us in the industry that seem to be able to get away with it and make it look reasonably well designed. What you have to do is blow it up slow. That sounds like a contradiction in terms. You have to use a bunch of smaller explosives and actually push whatever it is apart. You time it so it's stretched out, so you get what looks like a very large explosion that's actually a whole bunch of little ones. I have a timer so that I can control them to .001 seconds."

The model was built with strong construction plywood and meticulously put together. "There's no stage we have here that's tall enough to accommodate the whole building," comments Stetson, "so we had to build it in such a way that it was open enough inside to be able to light up rooms as required, strong enough to be able to withstand people climbing on it, including the marshmallow man as well as the people working on it. It had to be able to come apart in three sections, and finally be able to withstand the pyrotechnic blasts. Most of it was a matter of careful construction to begin with. But in the pyrotechnic area, we had a bomb chamber. The temple floor is quarter-inch steel, and has big, square, tubular steel upright columns welded onto the bottom plate, and also welded onto a top cover plate, so that the entire blast is actually contained in welded steel. To the upright columns, we added aluminum fixtures and cast urethane paneling. In the first test, the aluminum braces were actually riveted to the steel, and the rivets were blown out.

"The facade is all in either vacuum form brick paneling or ornamental cast urethane to simulate ornamental plaster. Some areas on it that are break away are cast in lighter urethane or plaster. The top fountainlike ornament is in fiberglass. The scale of the building was determined based on the size of the marshmallow man. Since it had been decided that that would be a man in a suit, and since we knew he was supposed to be 112 ½ feet, we scaled the building to that. It came out to be an eighteenth scale building. Which is an awkward scale to build in because there's nothing available in that scale that you can buy stock components of. It was about a ten week job and we've been maintaining and modifying it for the last two or three weeks."

Another weird concept that was created in the film was the weapon used by the *Ghostbusters* to deal with the various creatures they encounter. These "Neutrino Wands" are used to actually entrap the ghosts. "We wanted something different," says Bruno. "We didn't want lasers. We didn't want lightning bolts at the ends. When the beam is aiming at something, when you pull the trigger, it starts from that point—there's a flash on the wall—it goes into the gun, then the energy that causes this little electrical net that's suppposedly to catch ghosts, forces itself back out, automatically charged. You can dial it up and down. What it's doing is pulling atoms out of the wall. When you move it, it moves like a hose of water and is stuck to a point and dragging all the time." The Neutrino Wands effects were animated by Garry Waller and Terry Windell's department. "At first, we designed them to be a straight, black and white high-con element," explains Waller. "In other words, we produce black and white artwork, shoot a negative which then becomes the optical printing element, which they print in color. It's designed in such a way that there are actually three separate pieces of artwork per frame on black and white. The wand is thus animated, inked, and separated into three levels shot and sent to opticals.

"Since then, it's now multiplied up to five elements. Several new color elements that are compounded with multiple moves, such as the guntips now flare as if they have a muzzle flash. There's a spectoral light like two lines of a starburst. It's a magenta flair bisected by blue, horizontal light. The center is like a laser, only rubberized. It's as if the gun is shooting out energy and sucking in molecules at the same time. It's very hard to do convincing animation, because they have to be more than a slick laser. The first time they come on, they get a laugh just because of the reaction. But, at the same time you have to give them enough polish so that it merits the laugh.

Waller and Windell also developed a tunnel effect to portray the door into Gozer's dimension that is located inside Dana's refrigerator. "It's basically like a Hitchcock effect," says Waller. "Something's coming at you, but you zoom away from it." "What that is, at this point in the film, is a glimpse into the future," explains Bruno. "We want everybody to see it, and not know what they saw. Technically, we took a plate that we already shot of the pyramid and the stairway. We did a painting that was basically a typical hell setting, with flames, orange colors and lots of heat. In there are the clouds that you will see at the end of the film, but everything will be orange. As we move into the refrigerator, there will be flames and images of the terror dog. You'll be able to see it if you know what it is, but at that point, you probably won't know. In the long shot, we don't want the audience to quite be able to see it. The close up will have a dog rise right up into the frame, and there will be a flare coming out of its mouth that will obscure anything that you think you saw, and which will scare Dana enough to make her close the door. We needed dry ice smoke at floor level for the effect. The problem was that we couldn't have flames come up through it because it puts fire out. So, Thaine Morris came up with some other solution—yellow smoke, a light lemon color, with flames coming out of that, and the dog rises up and jumps out."

For this sequence, as well as others, Platek designed and executed various laser-generated effects. Platek worked previously on *Star Trek I*, *Poltergeist*, *The Right Stuff* and *Gremlins*. He explains, "The laser system is a five watt argon laser, which gives me about nine different shades of greens and blues and ultraviolet light. Then, I also have a dial laser which gives me continuous shading control over yellow, orange and red. The outputs of those are aimed at an X-Yy galvanometer, which are little electromagnets with mirrors on top. One moves vertically and one moves horizontally. Combine those two and you can draw a circle. Combine them even faster and you can write a name or draw a picture. The galvanometers are hooked up to an Apple computer. That computer has a Gibson light pen and a program that was written by a man named Gary Leo. We started this little system on *Poltergeist*. With the light pen, I can draw on the computer screen whatever shape I want the laser to draw. I can draw up to sixteen shapes, and then I can pick what order I want those shapes to appear in. For example, it has the capability to draw a little man that runs around and changes size and shape.

"In the end sequence, in the temple, there's a pyramid. At the top of that pyramid is a golden, yellow light. That's a laser effect. What I did was, draw a pyramid shape with no bottom and aim it at a piece of mylar, then aimed that right at the camera. So, you have a pyramid shaped piece of light coming at you, but you can't see it. So, I have to introduce something into the air that will let you see it. For that, I have a fifty gallon drum of water that I heat, then I put dry ice in there and blow the dry ice towards the camera for about three feet. That way, we get this sort of light fingers effect.

"Another place where I used the laser is with Slimer. He's going to go crashing into a wall in one scene. They wanted an 'ectosplat' effect. All I did that time was draw a straight line with the laser in a parallel to a table, with the camera above it looking down to match the angle of the camera looking at the wall in the scene. Then, I took a beaker of hot water with dry ice in it, and then just let a little wad of smoke go down to hit the table, and all you see when it hits the laser light is that shock wave."

Bill Neill, the cameraman, was in charge of photographing the special effects plate and the miniatures. "My contribution hopefully doesn't stand out," he says. "I hope that it all blends in and becomes a part of the story. Part of what I do is to try to understand what the first unit director of photography is doing and why he's doing it, so that the material that we're either inserting into his imagery or, in some cases, that we are generating will cut in smoothly with his material. What he does is a guide to what we do here, in terms of lighting and the feel of it, even in terms of composition.

"We often have to have much more light on the set because we have much less depth of field. So, where the first unit 35mm unit can shoot at 3.5, we have to use 4 or 4.5. We have to be at least a stop, and sometimes two stops, hotter than they are to hold the field. We also expose for a denser negative, so that we can manipulate the film. First unit film is not going through the generations that we're going through. We can't work on the edge, we have to have a very well exposed negative.

"We don't have scaled down lights. I was able to do that on one picture, and it worked out pretty well. With this one, we're working pretty much with stage lights, the same kind of lights we use in the studio. We just have to cut them and play with them to fake the scale. We're often running not at twenty-four frames, but some elevated or lowered frame rate, and that changes the way the light appears too. I may be using a 10K to light a very small building, and it's a huge light source, so I have to squeeze it down in some way to get the levels I need. Wherever there's reference material from the first unit, I try to use that as a guide to try to get this material to blend in and disappear and not look like it was done at another time and another place and scale."

The Stay-Puft Man, because it was made of foam, and had a white, reflective surface, posed its own set of problems. "When you have a miniature building that is in darker earthtones, and you have this pristine, white marshmallow creature that's supposed to be dimly lit, then you have a problem. So, the building takes much more light than the Stay-Puft Man, so you play around and keep the light off the Stay-Puft. When you have the Stay-Puft right against the building, it's a real problem to light the building at one level and the Stay-Puft at another and try to keep it all looking like it's coming from the same sources. Fortunately, we had the luxury of doing some testing ahead of time.

"We tested out how the Stay-Puft behaved in different lighting situations. It also depended on how many days old the suit was, because reflectivity changes with time. If the suit was made a week ago, it would photograph differently than if it were made yesterday. The foam yellows in a mysterious sort of way. It's not that it changes color, it changes in apparent brightness. It either absorbs or reflects a substantially different amount of light in just a matter of a few days. The tests you might have done three days ago, are not entirely valid by the time you shoot. So we had to keep track of that. I've worked with a lot of creatures, and I've never had them change from day to day!"

The task of putting all these special effects together went to Conrad Buff, visual effects editor, whose credits include *E.T., Poltergeist* and *The Empire Strikes Back*. "My responsibilities are to take all the elements that are shot and try and compose them and synchronize them in such a way that they play well in the scene, based on what the live action editor has done. In the case of *Ghostbusters*, there were a lot of live action things which we were adding things to. A lot of the effects material is shot in wild form, such as the cloud tank and the Slimer material. There's a lot of footage there, and I have to edit out the pieces that I think will work best physically with the scene. There are problems in terms of pacing and timing elements, trying to give the effects shots life and make them physically look like they belong in the scene, that the characters are reacting and the ghost is reacting. All of that is a lot of designing on my part, along with the cameraman and the art director initially. So, I had a lot of input up front, as opposed to having things delivered to me and trying to make them work."

One of the intriguing things about *Ghostbusters* is that it was one of the first big budget, big special effects, comedies. At the limit, it could have been called a pastiche of *Poltergeist*. Edlund, who worked on both pictures, has the final word, "I am very proud of the work that everybody turned out on *Poltergeist*. I felt it was really a great film. What I felt was really interesting about *Ghostbusters* was taking those serious, frightening images from *Poltergeist*, and turning them into comedic ones. These two films were two ideal situations for us to set up a new company. A lot of the talent that worked on *Poltergeist* has worked on *Ghostbusters*. A lot of the ideas that we had that we didn't have time for on *Poltergeist*, or that we discovered after we were already so far into a shot that we didn't have time to change, have come into play in the making of *Ghostbusters*.

"Also, when you do this kind of work day in and day out, you're dealing with people who have to have a great sense of humor. What was interesting about *Ghostbusters* was that, in a conceptual sense, we could go further out, because it was such an outrageous comedy. In *Poltergeist*, it would have been difficult, because it took place in 'everyman's' home. It was like an anthropological time capsule. Because of that, the effects had to look more convincing. On *Ghostbusters*, on the other hand, we have an outrageous concept, where ghosts take over New York, fly throughout the city, come beating down hotel corridors, or in the case of the marshmallow man, marching down Central Park West. These are outrageous concepts, yet they still had to work visually. And you know, they did work!"

THE GOLDEN CHILD (1986)

In many ways, *The Golden Child* was just another typical eighties wannabe blockbuster—a huge budget, a big-name star, big-name special effects, all in service of a derivative, fantasy-adventure story. Like so many other post–*Star Wars* spectacles it was millions of dollars spent bringing to life a story that a decade before would have been considered barely adequate for an ultra-cheap B-movie.

But in one way, the film is special, because it epitomizes the mindless pursuit of the giant fantasy hit that drove the major studios throughout the decade. And because it epitomizes the vast waste of talent that went into that pursuit.

From the moment that *Star Wars* became the highest-grossing film in history—later to be eclipsed by *E.T.*—every studio tried to duplicate that success. And many writers and directors who years before might have been turning out the small, personal dramas and comedies that defined Hollywood's output in the early seventies, found themselves working as traffic cops on super-spectacular comic-book fantasies. Robert Altman, whose *Nashville* and *McCabe and Mrs. Miller* were two of the most critically acclaimed films of the previous decade, turned to adapting the comic strip and cartoon "Popeye." Peter Yates, famous for hard-bitten thrillers like *The Friends of Eddie Coyle* and *Bullitt*, turned his hands to Columbia's disastrous fantasy epic *Krull*.

And then there was Michael Ritchie and *The Golden Child*. Ritchie rose to fame as a young director in the early seventies on the strength of biting, cynical, clear-sighted movies: *The Candidate* was a documentarystyle portrait of a young, Jerry Brown-like politician (played by Robert Redford) who agrees to join the system to fight for his values, and loses his values to the system during the election; *Smile* was a remarkably tough-minded look at a small-town beauty pageant. Even Ritchie's biggest commercial hit of the decade, *The Bad News Bears* was far more insightful than its family-comedy image suggests.

But by the mid eighties, Ritchie's style of movie was out of date. Hollywood had little interest in biting irony, complex characters, or off-beat plotting. That Ritchie continued to get assignments had more to do with his reputation as one who could work with stars—based on his successful association with Redford, Walter Matthau, Chevy Chase, and Goldie Hawn, among others—than with the style or substance of the movies he made.

Eddie Murphy and Charlotte Lewis cross a Tibetan lake on their way to a monastery to get the sacred dagger in *The Golden Child*.

It was Ritchie's reputation as a star's director, more than anything else, that landed him the job on *The Golden Child*, which was intended to complete Eddie Murphy's transformation from comedian to wise-cracking action hero. Personal input was not required from the director, who was handed a formula script, a headstrong star, and a large special effects budget and put to work.

The result was predictable. *The Golden Child* was indistinguishable from many other big-budget fantasies and adventures of the time. Although the story featured a street-smart black private eye exiled to Tibet and confronting an ancient religion, the clash gave no insight into either culture beyond the predictable Murphy wisecracks; although there were stirrings of interracial romance between Murphy and co-star Charlotte Lewis, no comment was made on the subject anywhere in the movie.

MICHAEL RITCHIE INTERVIEW

Hundred of years ago the Ni'Ching oracle predicted a perfect child would be born that could save the world but that it would be abducted by the forces of evil and taken to Los Angeles. Only one man would be good and pure enough to save the child. Only one man would be chosen. That man is ... Eddie Murphy?

Dozens of months ago, the Paramount oracle predicted a perfect film would be developed for their favorite star, a fantasy film of epic proportion. Only one man could handle the herculean task of shepherding this monster production from development to completion. Only one man would be chosen to direct this colossal achievement. That man is ... Michael Ritchie?

It's true that Ritchie is a well-respected director with several major hits to his name. It's true that his early films like *The Candidate*, *The Bad News Bears* and *Smile* have recently been gaining critical respect. It's true that the directorial career that was seemingly floundering after a number of flops, had picked up with the big success of *Fletch*. But *The Golden Child*? A fantasy film? With special effects? And monsters? Even Ritchie admits that's hardly his style.

"The script is a contemporary supernatural sword and sorcery epic," Ritchie says. "It's something I might have had second thoughts about or just said 'why me?' to if I hadn't known that Eddie Murphy was committed."

A contemporary supernatural sword and sorcery epic is simply not a Michael Ritchie film. A contemporary sword and sorcery epic with Eddie Murphy is.

"Knowing that Eddie was committed gave the script a kind of perspective and humor in every scene," Ritchie explains. "What I like about the movie is the contrast of the street-smart, wiseacre disbeliever caught up in a world of believers and magic in which he must ultimately believe. It's an exciting prospect."

Not only an exciting prospect, Ritchie believes, but one that is extremely different from all the other fantasy adventures out there.

"We're not treading on Spielberg territory," Ritchie says. "Spielberg's films depend on the central character believing almost from the word go. Indiana Jones believes. The kids in *Goonies* believe. They never say 'Hey, wait a second—this underground cave is impossible.' They want to believe, and they believe. I am more of a skeptic, and the sardonic and ironic style of my films comes from that skepticism. The fun of having a character who is a skeptic become a believer gives the film an added tension beyond the normal adventure films."

The film may not be treading on Spielberg territory, but it is deep in the heart of Ritchie territory—in his films, characters regularly move from skepticism to belief, whether it's Walter

Matthau learning to believe in self-respect in *The Bad News Bears* or Burt Reynolds learning to believe in love in *Semi-Tough*.

What seems out of place in Ritchie territory is the size of the production. *The Golden Child* is his biggest film ever and the first to use extensive special effects.

Eddie Murphy wields the sacred dagger as he attempts to rescue J.L. Reate from the forces of evil in *The Golden Child*.

"This is the first time I've ever *wanted* to deal with special effects, because they've never been integral to the film I've been doing," Ritchie says. "The few times I've been involved in the past, it's been so irritating. People moved so slowly and seemed to be so uncertain."

That wasn't the case with Industrial Light and Magic, which handled *The Golden Child's* effects.

"ILM was always at my back door—I lived in Marin County until a month ago—but I only knew them from softball games at the Fourth of July Lucasfilm picnics," Ritchie says. "These guys are terrific. They know exactly what they're doing, and they are perfectionists that never let something go. It's the kind of perfectionism you haven't found since the thirties at Disney where they used to spend hours and hours on the opening credits of *Pinocchio* simply because that's what they loved doing. These guys are the same way. There's no impetus to get it out unless it's perfect."

Sometimes that perfectionism reached heights that seem like trivial pursuits.

"We've got a scene in the movie with a Pepsi can that breaks into a dancing figure. I said this is fine, this is great, and they said 'No, we have to add some shadows, this would have a shadow. This chicken bone that it picks up should have a shadow as it picks it up.'"

Other times, that perfectionism resulted in what Ritchie believes are truly spectacular effects.

"We have some great stuff, things that have never been seen before," Ritchie says. "There's a transformation into a hideous creature which is a state-of-the-art effect because it has a sort of documentary realism. For the first time ever, we have a hand-held-looking camera treating a stop-motion creature. That was never possible before they came up with the current high-speed computer camera which can match the movement on the background with the movement of the stop-motion scene. As a result, when we're trying to have the feeling that the whole earth is caving in, we could physically hit the camera with our hand to give that strobing high action effect and the computer would match the movement of the blue-screen and the stop-action figure perfectly with the movement on the plate. So you have with a stop-motion creature all the vitality you would have with a live-action human character."

This was all a little new to Ritchie and he wasn't particularly comfortable with it at first. But then, neither were the ILM technicians.

"The use of the apparent hand-held camera for the creature stuff is a first and they're still experimenting with it, but it is working. We were all nervous, and it wasn't until they did a few tests—and we protected ourselves by shooting cover footage."

But the special effects were the only part of the film that caused its director nervousness. While some directors might fear working with a star as powerful—and as reputedly difficult—as Eddie Murphy, Ritchie looked forward to it eagerly. He has worked with Robert Redford, Burt Reynolds, Robin Williams, Goldie Hawn, and Chevy Chase and survived. There was no reason to think this would be any different.

"A lot of directors shy away from working with stars," Ritchie says. "I would guess they feel they'll be limited in their own creativity by having to occasionally defer to the wishes of a star. I love working with stars because they bring such a magic to the screen it makes my job easier and more fun."

Ritchie insists he never had a major disagreement with a star, and the only minor disagreement they had, he says, was one in which Murphy was *right*.

Eddie Murphy holds the sacred dagger he plans to exchange for the release of a child with magical powers in *The Golden Child.*

"One moment when we were doing a fight scene he felt I was rushing," Ritchie recalls. "He wanted more time for his stunt coordinator to work out something, just so we would look good, have a good looking fight. I had felt that the energy was ready to go, and frequently with guys like Eddie if you wait too long, if you rehearse too much, you diminish that. But safety has always been one of my main concerns, and since there was an element of safety in his request for more rehearsal time, I was quick to grant it and there were no hard feelings. That was the only time I ever got complaints from him on any scene."

In fact, Murphy was easier to work with than many other stars.

"From the day we did the screen tests for the girl, Eddie actually welcomed direction, and I certainly was not sparing with it, or intimidated from giving it," Ritchie says. "Any good actor—and Eddie is a very good actor—welcomes that critical viewpoint. Eddie is probably the only comedy actor I've worked with—and I've worked with lot: Chevy, Robin Williams, Goldie, Burt Reynolds—he's the only one I've worked with that never said to me 'I'll be the judge of what's funny.' Usually at some point they pull rank on me and point out that they're the comedian and I'm not. That never happened with Eddie."

Not that Murphy didn't have a mind of his own when it came to certain decisions.

"Eddie didn't want to ride a yak in one scene, and I don't blame him," Ritchie says. "We were hoping to get his brother Charles who doubled him in a few shots and is a very game guy, but he tried the yak on a lawn out here and got thrown by it. Yaks are very difficult creatures for riding. They're basically beasts of burden, and even in Tibet they're not ridden very often. They're fairly low to the ground, they sink into the snow—there are all sorts of reason why it never would work. But it was an image that I would never give up, so we got a stuntman to ride."

People may go to *The Golden Child* to see Eddie Murphy cracking wise with supernatural beings, but Ritchie says the film has another star—one most people won't recognize.

"Michael Riva is the production designer and he's brilliantly talented," Ritchie says. "His work for *The Goonies* just scratched the surface. I just think he's the best. The people he employs are the best. As a result, the film was a piece of cake for me. We built a gigantic Tibetan temple for a minuscule amount of money. When you see it on film, it looks enormous. ILM did a matte painting for us that covered the roof and doubled the length. Then we had a stage that was large enough to pull back to the stage wall and instead of using wide lenses, we could use longer lenses in order to compress it, and the audience has the impression because of the matte shot that it's much bigger. As a result, we were able to create this enormous spectacle for very little money."

Of course, brilliant production design won't bring people into the theater—as was proved this summer by the disastrous failure of *Big Trouble in Little China*. Although there are some similarities between the two scripts, Ritchie isn't worried that *Big Trouble*'s failures presage troubles for his film.

"Their film does not begin with the skepticism. It begins with belief in the supernatural, and I think that's the only reason the film, which was quite wonderful, failed to reach an audience," Ritchie says. "All the things that happened that are fantastic, the hero sees right from the very beginning. So though he is a shit-kicker and gives a kind of 'aw shucks' reaction, he believes it. He can't not believe it—you can't not believe it if characters are flying through the air right in front of his truck. There's no naturalistic explanation possible that could be given for any of that. Therefore the base of the humor is a guy thrown into a wild and woolly jeopardy scene behaving as if he's not in jeopardy. That's quite a different type of milieu for storytelling than ours.

"Also it would be very hard to recount to anybody what the story of *Big Trouble* is. I mean, what is the one-liner on that story? Who knows? I think that's the director of *Buckaroo Banzai* having some more fun with conventional perceptions of narrative. I loved the film and my kids loved it, but if people say to me 'Are you worried about *Golden Child* being similar?' I say no, because ours begins with a fantastic opening but is nevertheless in the realm of reality."

Which doesn't mean that Ritchie is already counting the billions of dollars his *Golden Child* points are going to bring him. He's been around too long for that.

"When we previewed *Smile* at the Cinema One in New York, the audience went crazy," Ritchie recalls. "I went with my agent Sam Cohn to dinner, and because we were socializing, he didn't want to talk business, but he passed me a little card that said 'This is how much money you'll make from *Smile*.' Well, *Smile* didn't make a nickel. Its total domestic grosses are something like $242,000, which is just insane. Since then I gained a real perspective on prediction. What we do know is that *The Golden Child* will be in a tremendous number of theaters, that Paramount is extracting very good terms from exhibitors, and that, because of *Ishtar* dropping out of the Christmas scene, there are not many films for people to choose among at Christmas."

Which means that *The Golden Child* could do quite nicely. It had better—with Eddie Murphy's popularity at an all-time high, anything less than a $100 million gross will be seen as a disappointment. Ritchie isn't too worried. He's already got the good word from one important source.

"Let me put it this way," Ritchie says with a smile, "we ran it for Eddie and he said it was a 'bad motherfucker.' For him, that's the highest compliment."

THE GOONIES (1985)

In the 1980s and into the early nineties, Hollywood seemed intent on recreating its past—not all movie-makers, but certainly the prolific, new generation of creative talent which had been weaned on movie serials and television series.

They took what they liked watching as children and threw money at it. They would do it all again, only bigger, better and hipper. So Jungle Jim became Indiana Jones. Buck Rogers became *Star Wars*. The "Twilight Zone" became, well, *The Twilight Zone—The Movie*.

And *Our Gang* became *The Goonies*—a band of kids who get into trouble, only this time it's bigger, better and hipper trouble. But not necessarily more entertaining.

The trend mushroomed as the decade wore on—more *Indiana Jones*, more *Star Wars*, and more old TV shows turned into movies, but no more *Goonies*. Although the film raked in big bucks, the bucks weren't quite big enough to merit the risk.

INTERVIEW WITH RICHARD DONNER

The Goonies is a Steven Spielberg movie, all right. No doubt about it. The story is so cute and adorable, Warner Bros, could probably turn *The Goonies* scripts into stuffed pillows and make a fortune.

Seven kids from the proverbial "wrong side of the tracks," known as the Goondocks, find a pirate map and stumble into a secret labyrinth of booby-trapped tunnels and caves. If they evade the escaped convicts on their tail and unravel dozens of mysterious riddles, they will find a legendary, long-lost, sparkling treasure. It's pure Spielberg in every way but one: Spielberg isn't directing.

"I had just finished cutting *Ladyhawke* when Steven called and said 'Hey, I just finished this script I loved very much. I can't do it. Will you?'" says director Richard Donner. "Talk about a love affair, *Ladyhawke* was mine. It was a four-year labor of love and I was exhausted. But I loved *The Goonies* story. I thought it was charming, funny and very exciting. So I said sure."

In Richard Donner, Spielberg found his perfect surrogate, a director well-versed in Spielberg's brand of endearing, prepubescent-minded adventures. His mixed bag of credits include episodes of "Gilligan's Island" and "Twilight Zone," and movies like *The Omen, Superman, The Toy*, and the recent release *Ladyhawke*, all works kids have no problem relating to. Spielberg calls Donner "a big floppy kid," which is the trait which best recommends Donner for inclusion in the elite Amblin club.

Both Donner and Spielberg are unabashedly honest about what they are doing with *The Goonies*. They are dusting off the oldies-but-goodies and giving them an eighties gloss.

"It's a wonderful adventure that borrows from every adventure ever written and yet is totally unique," Donner says. "It's the *Hardy Boys* and *Nancy Drew* and it's also Mark Twain. We've got our own Tom Sawyer, Becky Thatcher, even an Indian Joe. It's that kind of story."

The Goonies in jeopardy.

Spielberg is sticking to his proven formula. Starting with a generous budget and an old, familiar story, he adds satirical jabs, homages and injokes about movie lore, cliffhangers and wild stunts, and heavy doses of sentimentality. And to that, Donner has added the "verisimilitude" he says he imbued his previous fantasy films with.

Donner, Spielberg and screenwriter Chris Columbus (*Gremlins*) brainstormed and redrafted the screenplay, which had been based on a story idea by Spielberg.

"We came together over a week, sat down and made it cuter, faster, funnier and more realistic," Donner says. "There were some things in it—funny, a little bigger than life and sometimes it went too far. We just pulled it back to verisimilitude. We eliminated some things and added some things. We basically sat around and laughed ourselves silly."

But it wasn't all fun and games. Coming right off *Ladyhawke* and going right into *The Goonies* was not the smoothest transition imaginable.

"I was a nut. I didn't take into consideration the problems. I thought everything would be a cinch but once I got into it I realized I had taken on total insanity. It was bananas," Donner says. "All of a sudden what I thought would be this simple little picture became the most difficult film I've ever done."

He had only 14 weeks to shoot the film, leaving him next to no time to prepare. And he didn't count on the difficulty of working with children—no matter how talented the children are.

"It was brutal. They've got to have school and rest periods and their attention span is about ten seconds. While you are concentrating on two in front of the camera the others in the background are looking in wrong direction or picking their nose or falling asleep," Donner says. "I felt like a harried camp counselor. I now know why I never got married and had kids. But, at the same time, I desperately loved all of them. The energy they gave to me was phenomenal."

When help was needed, Spielberg was at his side. Donner drafted him to do second unit work as did producer Harvey Bernhard (*The Omen*). "Even Michael Riva, the production designer, got a DGA card and shot a unit just so we could get the damn thing done."

Riva didn't do a bad job designing the film, either. Donner personally selected Riva to create *The Goonies*' elaborate pirate caves. The director was impressed by the detail and imagination of Riva's work on *Buckaroo Banzai* and felt "anybody with that kind of creativity had to be so far off the wall he would totally understand what the tunnels should look like and feel like."

The Goonies discover an underground world under Suburbia.

Rock, right?

"No, much more than that," Donner says. "Lo and behold, he saw what I saw and then improved on that. He's the most inventive designer I've ever worked with, with the possible exception of the late John Barry (*Superman*). He gave the tunnels and caves *suspense* by giving the cave an ambience, a character."

Once shooting was finished, Donner and his love, *Ladyhawke* producer Lauren Schuler, took the earliest flight they could get to Hawaii.

"I finished shooting on a Saturday. We had a wrap party and the kids were all kind of down. They were not as enthused as I thought they would be. I said good-bye, got on that plane, and when I got to Hawaii I slept the entire day," Donner says. "The next morning my next door neighbor woke me up and asked me to drive him to the market because his car had broken. When I got home all the *Goonies* were on the beach and in my house.

"It was Steven's idea of a surprise. It was wonderful ... to think they knew about it for a week and for them to keep a secret that long," he continues. "I was desperate to get away from them but it was such a great put on. There were lots of tears and laughter. But obviously they were on a plane *that night* for another island."

After recharging his batteries, Donner returned to Los Angeles and shot a *Goonies* video starring Cyndi Lauper. Donner insists the inclusion of Lauper tunes, along with music from REO Speedwagon and others, isn't evidence that Amblin bowed to studio pressure to package a hot soundtrack album.

"The studios would like to pressure you to work pop music into a film. Steven doesn't bow to it and I sure as shit don't. I can't stand it when they jam songs in for no reason."

Once again, this time on the video, Donner played surrogate Spielberg. "Right up to last minute Steven was going to do it but got real busy with *Amazing Stories*. He didn't have the time and energy to pull off this thing."

Donner gladly volunteered and is glad he did.

"It was incredible. I've never had such an experience in my life. When you shoot a picture, you shoot twelve to twenty-five setups a day, if you're lucky," he says. "The first day on this rock thing I shot sixty-six set ups with Cindy, the kids, and six world wrestlers. It was three wonderful insane days."

Now Donner and company are "down to the eleventh hour with *Goonies* and we're crazed," he says, "everyone is crazed." *Goonies*' release date is looming in May and *Ladyhawke* has just hit the theaters nationwide.

"I can't look at *Goonies* and say it will be a big hit. It doesn't have any gimmicks. I don't know what the hell it will do out there. *Ladyhawke* is a very special, very unusual, very difficult movie to sell and a very difficult movie to get critical acclaim from," says Donner. "But I'd be very disappointed if *Ladyhawke* didn't really pack them in. The test screenings at high schools and colleges have been marvelously successful."

Ladyhawke has opened to generally positive critical response but is hampered with a lackluster promotional campaign. The ads completely omit star Rutger Hauer and feature a bemused Matthew Broderick with a hawk landing on his head. Hidden in a murky gray haze, a shadowy overprint of Michelle Pfeiffer looks on.

"I'm not happy with it. We worked an awful long time together and I feel quite honestly that the PR department failed me on that. I think the goddamn studios and everybody are so involved in research that they forget all their instincts," Donner says. "I'm fed up with research to be honest. They have all these idiots researching it by talking with sixteen old ladies at the supermarket. It's bullshit."

If *Ladyhawke* proves successful, Donner has no doubt Warner Bros. will want a sequel but thinks it would be a lousy idea. He knows what sequels can be like—The *Omen* and *Superman* each begat two sequels.

"If a studio wants a sequel, they want to go instantly, to have it out before you turn around," he says. "To do that, the studio will put anybody on and knock it together. They don't get the original people because they want to save money and time and they end up turning out a piece of shit, usually."

Although Donner "sure as hell" isn't thinking about sequels right now, he's feels *"Goonies* lends itself to a sequel beautifully" and is sure "in Steven's head there's a sequel."

As soon as *Goonies* is finished, Donner will again escape to Hawaii before returning to do an *Amazing Stories* episode for Spielberg.

"I enjoy Steven and his operation," Donner says. "It's a real nice home to hang out in."

GREMLINS (1984)

Director Joe Dante's career is one of tremendous potential unrealized. Or an unfortunate example of really bad luck. But it wasn't always that way.

Dante graduated from the Roger Corman school of guerrilla filmmaking, where an abundance of talent and wit behind the camera have to make up for the inevitable shortage of production value on screen. He began by editing trailers for Corman's New World Pictures and persuaded him to let him and his friends Jon Davison (later producer of *Airplane*) and Allan Arkush (who would become a director himself) try their hand at filmmaking. The result was *Hollywood Boulevard*, a mixed-bag comedy which has become something of a cult classic.

Dante went on to direct *Piranha*, which became one of New World's most profitable films and brought him into contact with future special effects stars Rob Bottin, Chris Walas and Phil Tippett. The film's well-deserved success also enabled the young filmmaker to join the "majors," first toiling on Universal's aborted spoof *Jaws 3—People 0*, then shifting to Avco-Embassy, where he made *The Howling*, a remarkably inventive werewolf picture that earned kudos not only for him, but for Rob Bottin and screenwriter John Sayles.

Overnight, Dante was hurled into the Hollywood forefront, where he caught the attention of Steven Spielberg, who was looking for somebody with an off-beat sensibility to helm *Gremlins* and one of the segments of his *Twilight Zone* feature.

He followed the extraordinary success of *Gremlins*, and the acclaim for his *Twilight Zone* segment, with a succession of inventive bombs (*Explorers*, *Innerspace*, and *The 'burbs*) before mounting the inevitable *Gremlins 2*, which critics loved and audiences virtually ignored.

Dante shifted his attention, briefly, to television, where he helmed segments of "Police Squad," and later produced and directed the quirky NBC series "Eerie, Indiana," which captured the off-beat sensibility of his post–Gremlins films and, unfortunately, shared with them the same fate—commercial failure.

Nonetheless, Dante remained in the nineties one of Hollywood's most sought-after directors, one with a rare comic sensibility who, matched with the right project, could strike box-office lightning again.

INTERVIEW WITH JOE DANTE

Q: How did you get into movies?

JOE DANTE: I got into movies the way everyone who is lucky enough to get in does. I went to a lot of movies and decided that was what I wanted to do. It was 25 cents on Saturdays, and they let in the first boy and girl for free. Then you could spend all your quarter on jujy fruits, popcorn and turkish taffy! That was back when the kiddie matinees would have ten cartoons and two features. They usually played Disney films on Friday and Saturdays. Sometimes instead, they would show the science fiction films that had played on Wednesday and Thursday. That's how I got to see almost everything that was any good.

Q: Did you like science fiction pictures even then?

JD: Sure I did! What kid doesn't like science fiction pictures? I did my share of hiding behind seats, though. I remember when my father took me to see *Tarantula*. I was the cause of some amusement to the manager, who pointed me out to his assistant as I was worriedly pacing in the lobby. I was so scared that I couldn't go back and see the film! Every so often, I would go and peek, but it was just too horrible and I would have to leave again. This made my father very happy, as you might imagine, because he was not likely to have gone to see *Tarantula* unless he was taking me. So he was just sitting there, by himself, watching this giant spider movie!

Q: Jon Davison told me that he convinced you to come to Hollywood. Is this true?

JD: Yes, he did. I went to art school and was going to be a cartoonist. At the time, I was working on a movie trade magazine for exhibitors, *Film Bulletin*. It was a great job, because I got to do nothing but see movies all day. I would see them before they came out, and often before they were cut. I wasn't really happy, but I was happier than I thought I probably deserved to be.

Jon and I put together a film called *The Movie Orgy*, which was a seven hour compilation of scenes from 1950s movies. They were edited together to make a kind of story. We did things like edit together scenes of Morris Ankrum from different films of the period. He played an army general in a lot of them, and always wore the same uniform, no matter which studio made the picture. We found that if you cut all these movies that contained the same actors together, you could make it look like the same people were fighting giant spiders, giant gorillas, giant anything!

There was more to it than that, but in a nutshell, that was the basic idea. We took it to colleges, and people still come up to me and say that it was the greatest thing they ever saw in their lives.

It was designed, like life, to be able to be walked out on at any moment. When you came back, you hadn't really missed anything. In many ways it may have been the forerunner of today's TV movie!

Jon had come out here to work for Roger Corman in publicity, and he thought that perhaps I would be a good candidate for doing trailers. So I came out to help him on a trailer for a picture called *The Student Teachers*. Then, I went back to Philadelphia, thinking, "Oh well …." I guess it worked out OK because Jon called later saying, "They really want you to come and do trailers. We'll have a trailer department and, instead of having to go to a different editor on every picture, we'll have a person in-house, and they'll learn to do them the way Roger likes."

I came out and did a trailer for *Caged Heat*, which was Jonathan Demme's first picture. I had never actually cut in 35mm. Like everybody who comes out to work for Roger, I didn't know anything. So, I was going to work for almost nothing, which is why I was being hired! I somehow managed to learn how to cut in 35mm and to make a trailer. To this day, the embarrassment that I feel at remembering the first rough-cut that I showed Roger is tempered only by the fact that I have since come to realize, that he was used to seeing things even worse than that.

Things worked out, and I got a job in the newly formed trailer department, which was myself and Allan Arkush.

Q: Wasn't that boring?

JD: No, I love trailers. I'm one of the few people who can sit through a trailer marathon. There is a science to doing trailers, which has kind of been abandoned. If you look at old trailers from the forties and fifties, they have lots of wipes and hyperbole, like written things and titles that wipe on and off. They have a sort of pace and momentum all their own. Trailers today tend to be narrated scenes from the film.

We experiment with different things, because with many of the pictures, we didn't really want to show too much. In fact, the best approach was not to show anything at all. We learned that the more you showed people in the trailer, the less curious the were about the movie! I think that holds true for most movies, but particularly for movies that were made at New World in less than twenty days for no money!

We had favorite voice-over phrases like, "She Wanted Love, He Gave Her Terror and Death"! That was one that would find its way into almost every trailer!

Q: How was it to work for Roger Corman?

JD: Well, he would come in, look at our trailers and say "Make this shorter," or "Take five frames off here." That was his specialty, taking a number of frames off a scene. He's very good at that.

It was a lot of fun, because you could learn an incredible amount of things about movie-making, by just watching a picture over and over.... We did some reprehensible things too! We did trailers that got people to pay money to see *Tidal Wave*, and things we should probably be ashamed of! But it was actually kind of fun at the time. It was like putting something over. You really felt vindicated for all the work that you had done—even though you weren't paid very much—when you saw your spot on TV twenty-five times on Friday night. You knew that when people would go to the movie on Saturday, they would be disappointed. But, on Friday night, when they saw your spot, they were probably going to think that the film looked pretty good.

Q: How did you get to direct your first film?

JD: To make a long story short, at one time we were doing three trailers simultaneously, one for *Amarcord*, one for *Street Girls* and one for *T.N.T. Jackson*. We started to get footage all mixed up, and Fellini would be appearing amid this kung-fu footage. We finally said, "I bet we could make one of these pictures. Look at this, there are hardly five set-ups in the whole reel. We could do one of these."

So, Jon, Allan and I tried to get together and convince Roger to let us make a picture. This is something he contends with frequently. Everybody who works for him works there for one reason: they want to make a picture. Sooner or later, they come up to Roger and say, "We want to make a picture." And then he has to think of a reason why they *can't*! Because he doesn't want to let them make a picture! He's finally got them working to his satisfaction in the trailer department or whatever. The last thing he wants to do is to hire new people to replace them, while these guys go out and make some picture which is probably going to be a disaster because they don't know what they're doing.

But we were very persistent. Jon managed to get Roger to let us make a film if it was the cheapest one that New World had ever made—and this was no mean feat, let me tell you! In substance, Roger said, "OK, I'll let you make a picture, but you have to make it in ten days, and you have to make it for $60,000."

This is similar to what he told Peter Bogdanovich, which was "You have to make a picture for a certain amount of money, you have to use Boris Karloff because he owes me three days, and you have to use footage from *The Terror*. After that, I don't care what you do!" That ended up being *Targets*. We weren't lucky enough to have a picture that was as good as *Targets* come out of all this.

But we did use a lot of footage from a bunch of other pictures, and we made a picture about a movie studio that some have said seemed suspiciously like New World. It was called *Hollywood Boulevard*, a mistake I blame myself for, because it was not a good title. I insisted on it because I thought that it was classier than *Hollywood Hookers*, which was what Roger wanted to call it!

Q: Why wasn't *Hollywood Boulevard* more successful, in your opinion?

JD: We made a movie about itself, which was the cardinal sin of the century. With only ten days and $60,000, it was also not much to be about! It's big on hotel television now. They run it late at night, or whenever the slots are for pictures where girls take off their clothes a lot! That was a prerequisite, and not one of the most entertaining aspects of the film. That was because *Hollywood Boulevard* came at the end of a series of movies that Roger was making, which would be about nurses and teachers. The formula was, that there were three girls who would get in trouble and take their clothes off. That was pretty much it!

All things considered, we tried to make it as personal as possible. Allan likes rock 'n' roll, so he put all this rock 'n' roll stuff with *Commander Cody and the Lost Planet Airmen*. I like science fiction, so I had a guy in a Godzilla suit and Robby the Robot. We used Paul Bartel and Dick Miller, the actor that we liked the most from Roger's old pictures. Jon produced it and put the whole thing together for next to nothing, which was pretty remarkable. We saved a lot of money by being able to use our own cameras and lights as props, and the crew as extras.

Q: Did you enjoy making the picture?

JD: It was a very interesting experience. I don't remember much about it, but people tell me that I had a good time! We learned a lot. It wasn't a movie for everybody. In fact, it turned out to be a movie only for people who were B-picture fans! It was so esoteric as to defy credibility. Vincent Canby reviewed it in the *New York Times* and claimed that it was set in the 1930s. It wasn't. Anyway the picture did not set the world on fire, so we went back to doing trailers. They were much better after doing this picture.

Q: What happened next? *Piranha*?

JD: Well, a lot of other things came up, but none of them panned out. Roger was going to sell some pictures to TV and we were going to, maybe, shoot some extra scenes, which is one of his specialties. That didn't work out for some reason. Probably because, once they cut all the violence out, there was nothing left. He would have had to have shot a whole new picture, so he gave up on the idea.

Then, there were two pictures he wanted to do, one was *Rock 'n' Roll High School* and the other was *Piranha*. Roger let Allan and me choose which one we wanted. Allan got *Rock 'n' Roll High School*; I ended up with *Piranha*. That was Roger's *Jaws* rip-off, which he had the temerity to wait two and a half years after the original to do! Then, he was going to release it the same summer as *Jaws II*, which was the multi-million dollar rip-off. The budget was $600,000, and the only reason he made it was because United Artists put up half of the money.

For New World, it was a fairly big picture. As it turned out, even $600,000 wasn't much money at all to make a film on location, but it enabled us to get Pino Dinaggio, and to put a classy veneer on it.

We were lucky that *Avalanche* was being made at the same time, and Roger was off supervising that. So he left us alone, and we got to do pretty much whatever we wanted. We didn't have to show it to him until we thought it was in half-decent shape. Usually, he makes people show him the picture on the second cut, when they're still a mess. Then, he can step in and "save" the film.

Q: Why did he let you out of the trailer department to do it?

JD: I think that Roger always liked us because we had seen his movies. I don't know if everybody who came out of USC and went to work for him, understood or liked his movies. We did, and I think he sensed that. So, we always had a good relationship. I never had any of the troubles with Roger that a lot of people have had. I think that, at a certain point, he must have just trusted us.

One thing about Roger, is that he's doing all this because he knows that it's the cheapest and easiest way to get movies made. But, on the other hand, he does at some point have to say, "OK, I trust this person to be able to go out and make something that I can cut together and release." Sometimes he's right, and sometimes he's wrong. His problem has been that, every time he's right, the person has had higher ambitions and left him to go on somewhere else. Every time he's been wrong, the person has not gone any further than working for him. I don't know if he respects that.

Q: How did the making of *Piranha* go?

JD: It was one of those situations where, if I had known how impossible it was going to be to make the picture, I don't know if I would have. We had to shoot most of it underwater. I had to learn to scuba dive. Glug.

We also had a lot of special effects, but we had great people there. We had Jon Berg, Chris Walas, Phil Tippett and Rob Bottin. All of them were terrific, and some went on to do *Star Wars* immediately after. But none of us knew how to do the effects when we started. Nobody had really ever done convincing piranha effects. They had only photographed real ones. There was some 16mm footage of them eating a cow. Every other time, in a film, all that they would show would be people flailing in the water.

Basically, we primarily ended up using puppets that we could control. They were fish puppets with mouths that moved. They would go under water and eat into prosthetic limbs. We shot them at eight frames a second. They would move so fast that they actually did approximate the kind of movement that piranhas really do—which was remarkable and lucky for us! The one thing we couldn't do, because it was very difficult, was to have more than two or three of them in the shot.

Q: How was working with big-name actors for the first time?

JD: Great, especially Bradford Dillman. He's no slouch, the guy's been in a lot of pictures. The people who are very secure about what they're doing tend to be, if you let them, very creative and to give you ideas about things. They tell you what they think about their character, discuss it with you as opposed to just walking in and doing it.

Q: Were you happy with the film, in the end?

JD: I was never very happy with some of the compromises that we made, but it turned out much better than we had any right for it to. It was a real movie. I knew it was going to be distributed overseas by United Artists. It was not just going to play the drive-ins and leave.

Also, it was John Sayles' first screenplay. He was hired to rewrite a script that had us all very worried. John managed to make as much sense out of it as could be made. Then, in the editing, we were ruthless and cut out lots of footage and managed to make it work as well as it possibly could.

Q: The fact that *Piranha* was successful must have helped you to get out of New World.

JD: Yes, it made a lot of money for UA in Europe. That was good for me, because that meant I didn't have to do any more movies for $8,000, which is what I got paid for doing *Piranha*.

Of course, the truth is that I would have paid Roger $8,000 just to be able to do it! I would have done it for nothing! That's something people always forget when they say, "Boy, that Roger, he's really cheap! He doesn't pay anybody any money!" It just amazes me when people say those kinds of things. When I was there, I used to complain, "Roger doesn't understand my movie!" Then, later, you get older and you look back on it, and you say,

"But so what?" You assume that you're going to go beyond that stage.

The point is that you either want to make movies or you don't. If you just want to make money, then you might as well not work for Corman. But if you want to learn to make movies, he pays you some money, and you're not paying tuition to some film school. I think that you're very lucky to get a viable genre to work in, and some money to make a picture. Then, you have to use your own ingenuity and responsibility.

You're not shooting little short films that you're going to keep in your basement and never show anybody. You're shooting things that people are going to see. You're a part of the movie business, however small it may be. You can't help but learn things.

Piranha got me offers to make more fish movies, like *Orca II*, a giant alligator movie, and a giant turtle movie. I didn't do any of those, not because I don't like those kind of movies, but just because I didn't want to get into the water again! So, I stuck around at New World for a while. Roger offered me *Humanoids from the Deep*, then I left!

Q: What did you do then?

JD: I went to Universal. I got this offer to do *Jaws 3—People 0*. It was all very interesting because I learned how people live in Hollywood. They make deals for pictures that don't happen. I found that to be no fun. It's very frustrating and boring. At Universal, they sat around for months and months. We worked on the script. We scouted locations. We worked on the art. We talked to the cast. It was going to be Bo Derek's next picture, after *10*, which hadn't come out yet. They got to a point where they were almost ready to make the movie, and had already spent a considerable sum on it. I think it would have made money and been a pretty funny picture. They, however, didn't feel that way. So they didn't make the picture.

Q: How did you get started with *The Howling*?

JD: Well, luckily it turned out that, at the same time, Dan Blatt and Mike Finnell were going to make *The Howling*. I segued right over to that without having to wonder where my next meal was coming from.

Embassy originally wanted to make it a little more of a straight horror picture, probably a little gorier. Having funny things happen is my tendency. It was something I was able to get away with in *Piranha*, because Boger realized that there were the requisite amount of legs being eaten by fish and things, so he didn't care what else I put in! That was also true, to some extent, on *The Howling*. Although Dan Blatt, who was the executive producer, was a lot more quality-conscious in terms of wanting to make a good picture. So, he was very supportive and that was a big help.

Q: What were your feelings towards the finished film?

JD: I liked *The Howling*. I had some problems, but basically for what it is, it's fine. Frankly, if I had to do it all over again, I'd cut the film differently. So much of it was done at the last minute, before the picture was released, that we really didn't have time to step back and look at it properly.

It was not a very expensive film. We had a lot of people working for not a lot of money because they all wanted it to turn out well. It's something I hope to continue to get as I make movies.

I think Rob Bottin did a great job on the effects, which were very difficult to shoot and make believable.

Q: Hadn't you talked with Rick Baker about the film?

JD: Yes. The whole situation was that Rick Baker had wanted to make a werewolf picture for years with John Landis. He had a lot of ideas about what he wanted to do. We talked to Rick, who almost did the film, until he realized, "I'd better ask John if he's ever going to do his picture." Perhaps, John then may have decided to do his even more quickly because he said to Rick, "No, no, I'm doing mine, I'm doing mine!" So Rick didn't do our film and did John's instead. Rob Bottin was then put in charge, since he was always going to work on it from the beginning.

Q: I had heard that there was some stop-motion animation that was cut out of the final release print. Is this true, and why?

JD: Yes, we had more stop-motion animation. I think it's only one shot now, near the end. The werewolves are standing up and howling at the moon. It's very short and it's got a dissolve over it. It goes by so quickly that it's not really a problem. I didn't use the shots in the barn, for instance. You may have seen pictures of them in some magazines, but we cut them out of the film.

I love stop-motion. I always wanted to put some in the *The Howling*, but the movements just did not mesh with the live action. This was not "go-motion" where it's computerized with built-in blurs to make it seem real. This was classical stop-motion, and it tended to stick out a little bit, even though Dave Allen did a great job, and Roger Dicken designed some wonderful puppets and miniature sets, nicely lit and all.

We ran the rough cut and people would say, "What picture did you get that shot from? That's a neat shot." That wasn't exactly the reaction we wanted to get. We did a very complicated scene with Dee Wallace, where she's in the frame and there's a stop-motion werewolf behind her. It was very complicated to set up, and hard for Dave to do. We ended up just not using it.

I'm sure he wasn't thrilled about that. But we tried. We tried cutting it differently, we tried putting smoke over it, we tried everything we could do to save it. Then, we started to realize that it was an indulgence for us to leave it in, although it cost a lot of money. That happens a lot in the industry.

Q: How did the actors react to all the effects? And how was Patrick Macnee?

JD: On this kind of film, the actors will often have one of two attitudes. One is, that they're walking through the special effects and it's "Just give me the money." The other is, seeing that you care about the film, that they want to do a good job. I think much of that depends on how you yourself act during the first couple of days. If they can figure out whether you're really doing this movie because you care about it, or if it is just something that everybody's doing for a lot of money. In which case, why shouldn't they?

Patrick Macnee was always my first choice for the part because he's a slick, but likeable, and not really menacing guy. It was such a menacing role as written—the bad psychiatrist. I just didn't want to make it that obvious. Patrick had a lot of things on his mind at the time, but he was never less than totally professional.

Q: What did you do after *The Howling*?

JD: After *The Howling*, there was *The Philadelphia Experiment* at Embassy. Then, Embassy changed owners. I had felt secure with Embassy. But after that, all the executives left and the new people decided they didn't want to make this kind of picture anymore. So, I waited for this film to happen for about a year.

Q: How did you become involved in *The Twilight Zone*?

JD: Accidentally! One day I got a call from Steven Spielberg's office. They were interested in my possibly doing a different picture than *The Twilight Zone—Gremlins*. I had never met Spielberg. The first thing I did when I met him was apologize for ripping off *Jaws*. But he told me that one of the reasons he had called me in was that I had done the best *Jaws* rip-off, which was a nice thing to hear.

At the time, *The Twilight Zone* was in an embryonic stage of development. Steven and John Landis were working on exactly what they were going to do. How many directors there were going to be, who they were going to be etc ....

I think John put in a plug for me. There I was and, suddenly, I was a part of it! Which is even truer in George Miller's case. George happened to be at a meeting at the studio one day. Steven met him and said, "Well, why don't we have George do one?" It's the way things happen in Hollywood!

Q: Has the story of *Gremlins* changed much from the original script?

JD: Yes. Originally, it was written on spec by Chris Columbus, who was about twenty years old at the time. It was a little more of a standard horror movie. All the *Gremlins* turned into monsters, including Gizmo. In fact, there was no Gizmo. Basically, all they did was eat people. That was their main modus operandi. They were hungry all the time. There was a scene in a McDonald's where everyone is eaten, except the McDonald's burgers. There were people lying on the tables with pieces missing from them, but the burgers were untouched because the *Gremlins* wouldn't eat them. McDonald's wouldn't go for that! Also it was a little more gruesome than we wanted.

Q: Maybe McDonald's would have liked it if the hamburgers had been eaten as well ....

JD: They would have, probably, if the hamburgers had been eaten, but it was funnier if they didn't eat the hamburgers.

Yes, it was considerably more graphic, and we've tried to make it a little less of a gruesome picture and more of a fun picture. It's not a serious picture. It has things in it that are sort of interesting sub-texts. Also, it's not the world's most logical plot, so to treat it with any degree of gravity probably wouldn't have helped people watching it.

Q: Have you had any problems in trying to make it more logical?

JD: Well, for a while, we were seduced into trying to account for every odd little plot point. For instance, it used to bother me that the *Gremlins* could go out in the snow—the movie takes place at Christmas—and yet, not be affected by the water. So, we wrote in a plot point that they became affected only when the water was above a certain temperature, and we dutifully put that into the film. But, then, when we went to cut it, we realized that none of those things were really very important, as long as there was an internal logic that we were operating with.

Director Joe Dante, seen here directing his segment of *Twilight Zone—The Movie*.

It all would make a certain kind of sense, because the whole tone of the project is kind of like a fairy tale. So, we hedged on a number of things, such as the rules that the Chinese kid gives to the father. He says, "don't do this, this and this." We said, "That's kind of arbitrary isn't it? He just made these up and why does this guy believe this? Why does he take this seriously?" So, we did a lot of hedging voice overs, where the father would explain the rules to his family, and he would say, "Well, it sounds silly to me, but maybe we should listen to these people."

As we started to dub the picture, we looked at all this material, and we realized that the force of the movie comes from the fact that these are a certain set of givens that are like a fairy tale. You have to believe them in order for the story to make sense. We were robbing ourselves of the conviction of the story, by making fun of them, or even suggesting that there might be something odd about them. So, now the picture is just out there. It's take it or leave it. You either like this story or you don't. And, if you don't, then you can find a lot of things wrong with it. But, if you do, everything does make sense in its own, scatterbrained way.

Q: Are there many special effects other than the little creatures?

JD: The little creatures are the special effects, but they're in so many scenes, that it really ended up being a big deal. We shot them in two parts, one with the live action and one with just the effects, and the effects ended up taking as long, or longer, than the principle photography.

There was one stop motion shot. When I first read the script, I thought that the whole thing had to be done in stop-motion—in which case we would still be shooting two years from now, because there was so much of it. But, as it turned out, by planning it down to the wire, we found a way to do most of what was in the script without having to compromise too much. There were still some things that we just couldn't do. There's a limit to how clever you can be in hiding things. There were so many people on the set controlling cables from all these various special effects, that it was literally impossible to walk! It's a tribute to the movie that the actors aren't stumbling all over the place, because underneath every frame there's something like five people that they have to step over in order to get anywhere. It's the hardest picture I ever made.

Q: I imagine the *Gremlins* were too small to put people inside costumes?

JD: No, we couldn't. We originally "talked" to some monkeys about being in the picture. A guy came over and brought a tree monkey, and we thought that maybe we could put one in a suit. Anyway, this monkey proceeded to run about the office, leave little monkey deposits everywhere, and didn't look like the most controllable kind of actor. Also, Steven had told me a story about trying to use monkeys for aliens in *Close Encounters*, and all the monkeys did was to rip off their alien costumes, run all over the set and throw things at the crew. So, it just wouldn't have worked. Besides, the specifics of what they had to do were too complex. It was hard enough for people to do them, let alone asking some animal.

Q: What were some of the fun things with doing this picture?

JD: The cast was great. I had fun working with them. People have said that one of the best things about the picture is the casting, which was done by Susan Arnold.

Keye Luke is in the picture, and getting to meet him and hear his stories …. He's eighty years old and looks fifty. He remembers all the aphorisms from his old Charlie Chan movies, and will spout them at the drop of a hat. Things like, "May your shadow always fall in pleasant places." He's just a charming, wonderful guy, playing a role which will not exactly advance the Chinese race. But, it's a fairy tale. It's an affectionate stereotype, still, it is nonetheless the kind of portrayal of Chinese people that probably went out in 1940.

Inventor Rand Peltzer comes across a most unusual live pet for his son Billy, in *Gremlins*. Left to right: Keye Luke, Hoyt Axton, and John Louie.

But, it's all germane to the plot, because at the beginning of the picture, you really don't know where Chinatown is. You don't know if it's out of the country, in the country or what it is. It's sort of a state of mind, as opposed to a real place.

Q: You're one of the few people, if not the only one, that has ever had the opportunity to direct Steven Spielberg in a scene ....

JD: This is true. Steven worked on the same day as Robbie the Robot and Bob Burns who owns the original Time Machine. It takes place at an inventors' convention, and we used these as inventions that are going on in the background. Steven had broken his foot, which was in a cast, and which lent a properly odd tone to the thing. He drives around with his electric car, covering up the actor's dialog.

We did a joke in the background where we cut back to the Time Machine, which isn't there anymore. This guy who has been sitting in it has obviously been vaporized away somewhere.

Everytime I would shoot it over, Steven would say, "No, no! Have the guy who owns it be more upset!" It's a background joke, it's not supposed to be that obvious. Finally, I did a take where this guy that has lost the Time Machine is throwing his briefcase up in the air and pounding the floor. Steven said, "Well, maybe that one is too much."

That was the only time he visited the set really. He was there one other day and he tried to coax me into some other piece of outrageous directing, but I had none of it. No, directing Steven was fine. He didn't ask for any.

Q: You had Jerry Goldsmith as well ….

JD: Jerry Goldsmith is in that scene, and he complains that I didn't direct him much, and he's right. It didn't occur to me until the last time I looked at the scene, and I noticed that he's looking at the camera throughout. Nonetheless, it's his big moment.

Q: How long have you been working on the film?

JD: I've been working on this forever! I could have made twenty Roger Corman movies in the time it took to make this one. I was doing pre-production and storyboards on *Gremlins* while we were making *Twilight Zone*, which is something I'm never going to do again. Then, when *Twilight Zone* was almost finished, everyone left and went off to do their own things. Only Frank Marshall and I were left to put it together, shoot the new ending, etc …. All the while, Mike Fennell was saying, "What are you doing? We've got to work on *Gremlins*!" And, at that time, we didn't know whether we were going to shoot it on location or here, or even how we were going to do it. The whole thing stretched into an incredibly long period of time.

Q: Do you think you should have done it in six months?

JD: No. But I think it would have been a different picture if I had. We ended up with a three and a half hour rough cut. Which is an awful lot of film. That partly happens because you just spend so much time working on the picture. You sit around so much on a special effects picture, that you start to think, "We ought to be doing something with this scene. We ought to be embellishing it somehow." And by the time you're through embellishing it, you've got an hour of embellishments!

Q: Do you feel pleased with the film?

JD: I have no idea. I'm probably the worst person to ask. I'm pleased that certain problems I saw in it have been overcome. I'm not pleased that others haven't. I basically will be pleased if people like it, because it's probably the most .... I wouldn't say it's the least personal movie that I've ever made, although it started out to be true at the beginning. But, it didn't end up that way. It is, however, the most "commercial" movie I've ever made, and this is coming from someone that used to work for Roger Corman! Those movies were entirely commercial, and therefore, anything you did in between were entirely your own. With this picture it's a little different. There's a lot of money riding on it, and there is a pressure to try and make something that you think people will like. But, in the end, all I can do is try to make something that I think I'll like. Within the boundaries set for me by the project.

Q: You've been working on this film for such a long time, and have been so close to it, aren't you afraid that that may have affected the final outcome?

JD: I was afraid that was true until I started showing it to people. For instance, I showed it to Steven, who hadn't even looked at the dailies. He pronounced it my greatest work. I said, "But is it any good?" He seems to be pleased with it. I think one thing that pleases him, is that although this is the kind of picture that he likes, it's not made the way that he would make it. Therefore, I don't think he feels that he's going to be accused of repeating himself, in the sense that he's gone off and taken a bunch of commercial elements from his previous pictures and thrown them all together in a similar manner.

The thing that originally attracted him to this, I think, was the tone of the script, which, even in its most horrific early draft, was always sort of whimsical and eccentric. That's been preserved and even enlarged upon. It's also takes place in his favorite venue, a small town. It's got kids, it's got families, it's got dogs, it's got people who are not from earth. It's got everything that he likes.

Q: Speaking of people not being from Earth. Did you ever come up with an explanation of where the *Gremlins* came from?

JD: We have a lot of interesting ideas that we used ourselves, as to where they came from. George Gipe, who wrote the novelization, has invented an entire background on where these things come from and what they are. Although I don't totally subscribe to that, it's very clever and imaginative. The book has a lot of interior monologs on the parts of the special effects characters, which you can't do in a movie. It sort of gives it an extra dimension.

Q: Everybody has been going around saying that this is Steven Spielberg's *Gremlins*. Does that bug you at all?

JD: No. As a matter of fact, I specifically didn't take that credit that they like you to take, that says, "A so and so film." Not because it isn't my movie or anything, but it just isn't something that I'm comfortable with. But, it is Steven Spielberg's *Gremlins*. If it wasn't for him, I wouldn't be making it. It doesn't bother me, because I don't think anybody, once they see this movie, is going to confuse it with the way Steven would do it.

Q: Did you think *Gremlins* was going to be so controversial?

JD: I had no idea. I just thought that it was this little movie about these creatures.

A Gremlin discusses the joy of home improvement.

Q: Amanda told me that she walked out when they threw the darts at Gizmo ….

JD: It was still worth it because it was the most rewarding and satisfying scene to shoot in the movie.

Q: You mean he was too sweet even for you?

JD: No, no, no, no. Gizmo was a pain in the ass. It's like working with an actor who has some sort of a problem, like he goes in his trailer and comes out drunk or something. Gizmo just couldn't walk. There were many things he couldn't do and it was very hard to work with him … very neurotic!

Everybody was happy to do that scene. We must have done twenty-five takes!

Q: When you came in on *Twilight Zone*, had the stories been chosen?

JD: When I came in, the film was at the point where everybody seemed to know what they wanted to do. John knew what he wanted to do. Steven wanted to do the episode that I ended up doing, and then he changed his mind. So I inherited that episode, which didn't bother me because I had always liked the original.

Q: Why was Richard Matheson called in?

JD: The studio felt that since Rod Serling wasn't around anymore, they needed someone who knew the series first hand. Matheson had probably written more of them than anybody else. Charles Beaumont had done a lot but he wasn't around any more either. Ray Bradbury did a couple, but not really that many. Then, it was a descending order .... So Richard seemed to be the best choice for the job.

Q: Would the tone of the film have been the same without Matheson's collaboration?

JD: Possibly. Everything is a guess. You can guess what you think everything is going to be like. But you don't know what that actual tone is going to be until you see it. My episode, for example, might have seemed a little more horrific than it actually turned out to be. I think, in fact that the whole movie moved a little further away from being a horror movie per se than might possibly have been expected. In fact, it's a little more like the TV show really was, as opposed to perhaps what people's memories of the show might be.

The attempt was made to be as faithful as possible to the spirit of the program because during the years it was on, especially the first three, I think it was the best dramatic show on television.

Q: It was rumored that you would be using original voice-overs made by Serling. Is this true?

JD: No, if were having voice-overs, we're probably going to get Burgess Meredith. We hope to use Rod Serling's voice somewhere, but the idea of using existing narrations didn't work, because the stories have all changed. That's good because you can't give people the same stories they saw on TV, with no changes. They would all be ahead of us.

What we tried to do is to sort of reinterpret these stories for a present-day movie audience. There are spectacle values in a movie that you can't have in a TV show. The trick is to make sure that those values don't outweigh the drama. Like the show, it relies more on atmosphere than special effects. "The Twilight Zone," as contrasted to, say, "The Outer Limits," was not a special effects show. It was a show about people who would find themselves in fantastic situations. I think the attempt has been made here to make all these stories about people.

Q: Did you ever consider doing it in black-and-white?

JD: There were talks at one point of having one segment in black-and-white, but it seemed too much like an affectation. People expect color today and this is the movie, not the TV show. My episode, for example, might not have worked in black-and-white, although I love it and always wanted to work in it.

Q: How did you approach the retelling of the original TV episode?

JD: Richard and I worked on the script for a while. We originally went back to the Jerome Bixby short story. I hadn't read it in a long time, and I wondered what might have been left out. It was written in 1950. In it, the kid has awesome mental powers, origin unknown. He doesn't like technology so he does away with electricity, cars and modern conveniences in general, forcing everybody into a kind of pioneer existence. Once their remaining resources are used up, that's it, unless they can convince the kid that things can be different.

In 1950, this was a fascinating premise, but we figured that a modern kid would probably use such powers in a different way. So, our kid reshapes his world into more of a reflection of the like that a frightened, lonely kid of today might find appealing. H.G.

Wells' *The Man Who Could Work Miracles* operates on much the same premise—the person who can have anything he wishes for, except what he really needs.

One thing we dropped was the kid's ability to read minds. In the original, the characters always had to say and think nice things because of this. In our story, that was a needless complication. Also, we didn't want to tell the same story. There was something vaguely funny about the way people always said how nice everything was in the original TV episode. I think that, if you ran it in a theater today, you might get some bad laughs in the wrong places, because people might just find the reactions to the kid a bit too much.

One thing we kept, however, is that in the old story, the kid literally made television. There wasn't any electricity, but he would put images on it and the characters would all have to sit down and look at it. I found that to be an interesting piece of the story to develop a little more.

Q: What are the differences between your segment and the original "Twilight Zone" episode?

JD: I read Rod's script, and I watched the show again. It was as good as I remembered it. But it was kind of bleak and hopeless, ending where it started, with this child in control of all these people. In that, it's a rather atypical "Twilight Zone." Most of them have a moral, and some sort of redemption takes place within the individuals. In this particular story, no one changes. The characters just realize that there's no escape. In fact, Rod Serling's last comment in his narration of the episode is that he has no comment: "No comment here, no comment at all."

Our segment, on the other hand, is not just the slice of life that the original story was. It's a little more of a story, with a regular beginning, middle and an end.

The way that our story wound up developing was that we added a heroine to it. This was another "Twilight Zone" element that was not in the original. The original story took place in the "Twilight Zone," and nobody escaped, whereas most "Twilight Zone"s usually start with somebody from the outside going *into* the "Twilight Zone." Our story is not initially about the little boy at all. It's about a school teacher who encounters the kid and the world that he lives in. It enabled us to tell the story from a different viewpoint.

The kid finds this woman and takes her home with him. She goes inside his house, which is a little Victorian house, and there are these three people there who are the kid's ostensible uncle, mother and father etc .... In fact, they're actually people that he's brought in as surrogate parent figures and won't let leave. The thrall with which he holds these people in his power is sort of slowly demonstrated through the story so that, at the beginning, you don't know whether the adults are crazy and the kid is being held captive against his will in the house, or if it's the other way around.

In the house, everything is centered around the television. The kid makes everybody else watch cartoons, whether they want to or not. The inside of the house is, in fact, made to look like a cartoon! The result is somewhat like an Off Broadway cartoon designed by Chuck Jones.

I talked to Chuck about this, and asked his advice and invited him to visit the set. We used a lot of Warner Bros, cartoons throughout the picture. This makes it more personal for me, because I love cartoons. If I had my way, I wouldn't mind having a channel that had nothing but cartoons and no commercials. This is where my segment perhaps breaks tradition with other "Twilight Zone"s. In the middle of the story, it's maybe a little bit more about cartoons, than it is about people.

Q: Is the story funny, or scary?

JD: You mean, is it more funny than scary? I really don't know. People laugh, so it is funny. But it's also kind of weird. I have had people tell me that they haven't seen anything like it, which is a good compliment, because that was the idea.

At the end of the story, the kid makes cartoon characters come out of the television set. Rob Bottin built them for us. He built some things that are quite unusual to say the least. Then, it gets kind of scary, but it's also kind of funny.

In fact, the tone of the whole movie is escapistly scary, amusingly scary, as opposed to terrifyingly scary. It's not comic book scary like *Creepshow*. Because *Creepshow* has a lot of gory stuff in it and a lot of black humor. This has some black humor, but the movie is lighter than people may be expecting. I hope it has a somewhat broader appeal than these kind of movies usually have. The stories are very accessible for any age group. They're warm stories, and the people in them are mostly quite likeable.

Q: Was it different to do a short rather than a feature.

JD: It's wonderful to be doing a short. I could have never gotten away with anything as strange for an entire feature. But when it's bracketed with other things, then it seems that people have four times more chances of liking it than they normally would.

Q: In all your films, you put in some in-jokes or references. Did you do the same here?

JD: Yes, I tried to put in some "Twilight Zone" references. *The Howling* was full of werewolf movie references. Whatever I'm doing, I may as well acknowledge what has come before. It adds perspective, and it's something that I always appreciate in movies. But, it only works as long as it doesn't get in the way of the story.

Zack Galligan and Corey Feldman in *Gremlins*.

Anyway, there are a lot of references to old "Twilight Zone"s. There are a lot of actors from the show. Carol Serling, Rod Serling's widow, was supposed to be in mine but she had to go out of town, so she's in George's. But Buck Houghton, "Twilight Zone"'s original producer, is in mine, as are Billy Mumy, who starred in the original TV episode, Patricia Barry, William Schollert and Kevin McCarthy.

Q: How was the kid who played the original Billy Mumy part?

JD: It's hard finding a kid to do this kind of a part because he has to be likeable and kind of scary at the same time. We changed the focus a little bit so the kid is a little more of a real kid, and a little less of a monster than he was in the original show. He's also older.

His name is Jeremy Licht and he'd been in some other movies and TV shows. He is a real nice kid and a real hard worker. The hardest thing for him to do was to be mean and to get angry.

He'd always say, "You're not going to make me be mad again now in a scene, are you, because it gives me headaches! I always get headaches when I have to get mad!" He was such a nice kid that he actually found it hard to be mean.

Q: Did you use storyboards?

JD: Yes, we had lots of storyboards.

Q: How long did the shooting take?

JD: Maybe fourteen days. It's interesting that it was only a thirty minute episode and it took more time to shoot than my whole first feature. It would have taken less time if we had made it in the summer, but in the winter when you have a kid, you can only use him for so many hours. In the summer, he doesn't have to go to school. But I was very happy, I used every possible minute they gave me!

When you think that the original shows were done in three or four days, it's astounding! Admittedly, they had access to standing sets and things like that.

Q: Can you tell us some anecdotes that happened during the filming?

JD: I had a great time shooting this because the actors were lots of fun. For example, as part of the plot, the characters have to eat a lot of junk food and act like they love it. The kid makes all the junk food because that's what he likes. Of course, our heroine, Kathleen Quinlan, finds all this rather odd. These people are just digging into candied apples, potato chips, burgers …. Just horrible food! The kind I eat! I told you I identify with this kid!

We have so many takes of these people scarfing down this stuff. I'd call "Cut!" and Kevin McCarthy would keep eating! And I'd say "Stop!" and he'd mumble, "Oh, okay, okay …" and stop. Then, I'd look again and in-between shots, when I was setting something up, Kevin would be eating jelly beans, anything that was around. It was just astounding! It was like, "Kevin, come on, this stuff is cold now!" I don't know how he did it! I think we gave him some cold candied apples on his way out, just as a memento of *The Twilight Zone*!

Q: Jerry Goldsmith is scoring the film, isn't he?

JD: Yes, Jerry had done a lot of original "Twilight Zone"s in the sixties. He's very, very good. In fact, he just got nominated for an Academy Award for *Poltergeist* this year. He likes the project and is very enthused about it. The score is in stereo which is great. I never had a picture in stereo before!

Q: Did you tell him what kind of music you wanted?

JD: No, I can't tell him how to write a score, and a good thing too! But I know what I like and what I want. I often get it. I have a lot of faith in Jerry. One thing I did here, which I suppose was kind of rude, was that, when I showed him my episode, I put the old Bernard Herrmann "Twilight Zone" music on it! It was just because I wanted it to seem more like an old "Twilight Zone" episode .... I wanted to see how much of the old feeling it could evoke in me again. And it did! Jerry is obviously not going to do the same music, but he is going to be in that tradition. He's very good at ethereal and atmospheric stuff.

Q: Over the years that I've known you, you've always seemed disatisfied with your films while you're working on them. Do you think that lessens the disappointment that you might feel, or makes you more excited when it comes out beyond your expectations?

JD: I think that's probably true. But I think it's genuinely because nothing ever goes the way you want it to, and when you have to make the thousand compromises that you make to get something that is somewhat what you wanted but different, it takes you a little more time to trust it. It takes you a little more time to say, "Well, this isn't exactly what I wanted, but how much have I loused it up? Or have I made it better by all these changes and things I'm doing?"

As I look back, the only thing I've ever done that I'm completely happy with was the *Twilight Zone* segment. But I think that was partly because it didn't have to be a whole feature film, so it was able to be a little bit more eccentric within itself, than a feature film which has exposition. There are certain things you have to do in a feature film and you have to ride herd on all these different elements. It's harder over a period of 105 minutes than it is over a period of 28.

HIGHLANDER (1986)

By the mid-1980s, it seemed that everyone in America was working on a screenplay. All across the country, every pediatrician, priest, and parking valet had a script somewhere in a drawer that would bring at least a hundred grand as soon as it was finished. Screenwriting seminars and story structure classes replaced singles bars as the happening hot spots for hip people.

What caused this sudden mass desire to create the perfect script? People like Greg Widen.

To many people, Widen was proof that anyone could sell a script and make a fortune. A struggling film student, he wrote a script called *Highlander* for his class project—and sold it for several hundred thousand dollars. If this punk could do it, the thinking went, why can't I?

And the next few years seemed to bear out that kind of thinking, as Widen's friends Shane Black (*Lethal Weapon*), Fred Dekker (*If Looks Could Kill*), and Ethan Wiley (*House*) all went on to sell "spec" scripts for amounts ranging as high as $1.75 million.

Of course, what the plasterers and pump jockeys failed to realize as they cranked out their scripts was that Widen and the others didn't just sit down and whip something out—their screenplays were the result of the writers' discipline, talent, and dedication to their craft.

Which explains why Widen has gone on to a successful career as a Hollywood screenwriter, penning the thriller *Backdraft* (and even appearing in a cameo role in that film), as well as being paid for numerous scripts that have yet to be shot, and his script *Highlander* has since sparked two theatrical sequels and a television series. And why so many others are still working that day job.

GREG WIDEN INTERVIEW

In a fog-shrouded glen in Scotland, five hundred kilted warriors prepare for their final battle. At a cry from their leader, five hundred horses fly down into the thick of the fight.

Christopher Lambert fights for his immortal soul in *Highlander*.

And on the sidelines, smiling happily as he watches the assembled clans butcher each other, stands a young man in a UCLA T-shirt and dirty jeans. One thought goes through his head as the body count builds: "None of this would be happening if I hadn't had that silly thought in college."

Greg Widen's "silly thought" was the idea for his fantasy-adventure script *Highlander*, which will be released as a $15 million epic starring Sean Connery and Christopher Lambert. It was an idea he might never have bothered to follow through on if it weren't required for class. The 26-year-old UCLA graduate never planned to be a writer.

"I never really thought seriously about screenwriting until I was at UCLA film school," Widen says. "Even then, I took the class more because it was a requirement than because I was really interested."

The class requirement for Theater Arts 135: Beginning Screenwriting is a finished first draft screenplay. Widen's was "Highlander." It was not your typical film school script—it had no divorced women making it on their own; no frustrated lonely people finding each other at last in the cold, hard city; no righteous protestors finally proving to a doubting world that the U.S. government is really sponsoring animal research experiments in Third World countries. What it did have was *action*.

The story of an immortal Scotsman fleeing through the centuries from his immortal foe, *Highlander* was the first script Widen had ever written. It might well have been the last, if it hadn't been for a dedicated teacher.

"My screenwriting teacher Richard Walter was very excited about *Highlander*," Widen recalls. "He gave me a lot of support, critique, and mostly a lot of confidence. At that age a teacher's response to your work is very important because they're your first critics aside from your mom and dad. To have a teacher say 'this is terrible' and throw it in the trashcan can really hurt your development. Fortunately, Richard was very nurturing, and gave me the confidence to go out and submit it around town."

With his newfound confidence, Widen started looking for an agent. As he admits, he did everything wrong. He went to the wrong people. He didn't go through the proper channels. But, miraculously, it worked.

"It's a little difficult for me when people ask how they can break into the movie industry," says Widen, "because I did it the way you're not supposed to. I'd recommend to anyone who wants to get an agent the way to do it is to go through a personal introduction: give your script to somebody the agent has a personal relationship with, and it's guaranteed the agent will read it. Otherwise, who knows? They get scripts every day. But I didn't do that. I literally took the Writers' Guild list of approved agents, went 'eenie, meenie, mienie, mo' and mailed off scripts to six of them, just saying 'Hi, I'm Greg Widen, represent me.' One of them did. And they set up *Highlander*."

The producers Widen's agent set *Highlander* up with did something even better.

"When the script was sold it was conceived as a low budget film," Widen says. "I saw it as a personal film. But EMI got ahold of it and said 'Wait a minute—this is a $15 million movie!' As soon as that happened, the whole angle of the film changed. It became more adventurous."

Unfortunately for Widen, when the producers decided to change the film's angle, they also decided to change the writer.

"There was another writer brought in for some of the sequences," Widen says. "I'd done about a draft and a half before they asked some other writers to come in for a different angle. It's still basically the same script. People go in and out of the same doors and say roughly the same things. A few minor characters were created. A few scenes were injected to lighten it up a little bit because I had a very brooding, dark story and they wanted a much happier adventure."

Although being rewritten was unpleasant, Widen tried to stay philosophical about the ordeal.

"It was the first and only time I've been rewritten," Widen says. "It's painful, but, fortunately for me, it was my first film and I was ecstatic just to be fortunate enough to have it made. As my writing professor Richard Walter used to say: 'There's a line that would go from here to the moon that would *love* to have somebody ruin their material.' I think I was able to rise above it. Fortunately, I was having success with some other projects, and that kept my attention on something else."

Widen wasn't completely out of the project. Soon after the rewrite was turned in, the producers decided that *that* wasn't what they were looking for, either. They turned back to their original writer.

"After they had done their draft, I came back to do yet another draft and tried to smooth out some of the differences I had with the project. I was brought back in last September to redo it yet again."

With Widen's rewrite, the producers decided the script was ready. It was time to start looking for a director. A certain kind of director.

"The producers knew very much the movie they wanted to make," Widen says. "It was not definitely *not* going to be an auteur film where the director is brought in and changes everything to do it his way."

That meant most of the top directors were out of the running—no successful director would take on a film he couldn't make his own way. But they needed someone who had proven he could handle the logistics of a studio production, and who would hopefully bring a unique style to the film. They chose Russell Mulcahy, the former rock video director who had made his feature debut with *Razorback*, a horror movie about a giant pig.

"I ran out and saw *Razorback*," Widen says. "I thought it was fun, but a bit gory. The producers made a point of saying *Highlander* would *not* be gory. Even though it involves decapitations, they would be done without blood all over the walls. *Razorback* wallowed in blood. Even Russell said he thought that was a mistake."

Although Mulcahy was not allowed to change the story, Widen says he brought a lot of his own style to the film.

"Russell is a visualist," Widen says. "He has a lot of depth in visual ideas. There are a lot of scenes that revolve around visual ideas that were his."

With the script done, the director ready, and a cast including Christopher Lambert (*Greystoke*) as the hero, Sean Connery (*Five Days One Summer*) as his mentor, and Clancy Brown (*The Bride*) as the villain, the film started shooting in Scotland. For Widen, this was his dream come true—only better.

"I never thought they'd film on location in Scotland," Widen says. "Back when it was going to be a $5 million film, I thought we were talking styrofoam castles in Marin County. I never thought we'd actually take the thing to Scotland and stand out there in the moors. We shot in an actual castle, with an actual drawbridge and a moat. We built a medieval town around the castle. It was just stunning to be there and see all of it. Visually, it turned out better than I ever thought it would."

Widen got a chance to see his fantasy coming to life when the producers flew him to Scotland.

"Technically and on the books I was there for rewrites, but I think a lot of it was 'You wrote it, you get to go,'" Widen says. "That was nice of them. I had a really good time there."

Which shouldn't come as a surprise—the writer was seeing millions of dollars spent to see his notion put on film.

"The high point for me was one day when it was raining and pouring and muddy and horrible, and all the clansmen were out there stomping in fifteenth century costumes," Widen says. "I decided I wanted to get out of the rain, so I went down to this pub down the road which was about three hundred years old. I went in to get a beer and I was the only one in there when the film broke for lunch.

"The extras had a tent they could eat under if they wanted to, but a lot of them had the same idea: they wanted a beer and a warm fire. So about a hundred of them, still in their kilts and fifteenth century skins and long hair and swords, marched down to this pub. They were all crowding around going 'URRR.' And since I was the only one who was dressed twentieth century, somebody recognized me and a whisper sort of went through the crowd that I was the writer. One guy stands up and they all stick their swords in the air and went 'Three cheers for the author, lads! Rah! Rah!'"

Of course, not everybody cheered when Widen walked by. Some of them just couldn't figure out what the hell he was doing there.

"I always got a laugh out of people's reactions to me because I'm sort of young," Widen recalls. They had been shooting for some time, and I showed up in Levis and a UCLA sweatshirt and people asked 'Who are you?' I said 'I'm the writer.' They say 'You mean you ride the horses?' I said 'I'm the writ-*t*-ter' and they said 'Oh. Ten-hut!' It was so funny to see the look on their face when they found out because they thought I was some production assistant."

By the time *Highlander* was shooting, Widen was well established as an up-and-coming writer with several projects in development at studios, including a big budget fantasy called *Clan of One* for Warner Bros. But things weren't always so good for Widen. In between the time *Highlander* was optioned—for a fraction of what he would eventually be paid when shooting started—and his next sale, Widen found himself in financial trouble. To pay his bills, he did what many hungry young writers have done—and no established writer will do: he went to work for Empire International Pictures.

"Mr. Band very kindly offered me money to write a movie," Widen says. "I was given a remarkable amount of freedom. I was essentially given a two-sentence pitch and from there I was on my own. The pitch was: 'Take a machine that can read thoughts and turn it into a teenage sex comedy.' I tried to approach it from the most tasteful angle possible. I think it actually came out all right."

Some people think it came out better than all right.

"Ironically, a lot of my friends think it's my best script" Widen admits. "I suppose it's like school. When you're in writing class and they tell you to write something, your mind always goes in the same way. But if a teacher says 'You must write about a tree,' at first you bitch and you moan, but when you force yourself to do it, your mind works in ways it never would have before. Often from that comes talent or directions you never knew you had."

Although Empire is notorious for bad movies and even worse pay, Widen feels that they have their good points.

"There are pros and cons of everything, but I think the big pro of Empire is that they make movies," Widen says. "Whatever else you may have against that kind of from-the-hip filmmaking, the fact is his films get into theaters. If you are a young screenwriter looking to make a mark who believes in his own talent, if you're willing to work for a lot less than you would get anywhere else, and write a film for them, and come out with something half decent—sometimes even if you don't come up with something half decent—it's going to get made and you're going to get a screen credit. There's a whole dimension between writers being paid and earning a living, and writers who get things on the screen. They're a world apart. And Empire does work with young talent."

Not only is Empire willing to take a chance with an untested writer—mostly because they won't pay enough to get a tested one—they will also let a writer move up. If they stay around long enough.

"Empire is very good about letting you direct," Widen says. "If you're willing to sign away your life and write five zillion projects for them, they'll let you direct one. They're really open about that. I kid about it a lot, but the fact remains they're willing to let somebody play with a million bucks. It's like film school with a million dollars. There's something to be said for that."

Widen still owes Empire a script under a contract he signed when he was really hungry. He will probably be rewriting David Allen's *The Primevals*. But don't expect to see "from the author of *Highlander*" on the ads. If he has his way, Widen's name won't be anywhere on it.

"I'm not ashamed of working for Empire," Widen explains. "But this is a rewrite and I'm trying to establish a reputation as an idea person. I turned down a Ron Howard film that had already been written because I want to establish a reputation as someone who does his own ideas and doesn't work on other people's. Ideas are power. That's what makes Hollywood run. There are lots of good writers, but if you're the guy who comes up with the idea, you have the power. And I'd just rather do my own stuff."

Sticking to his own ideas is part of Widen's master plan. He didn't go to film school to be a writer, remember. He was there because he wanted to direct.

"Absolutely, I'm thinking about directing," Widen smiles. "Fred Dekker, who's an old roommate of mine did it the way you're supposed to do it: he wrote a story, and rather than try to set it up as a contract writing job, he just went off and wrote it on spec. Tri-Star liked it, and he said you can only have it if I direct.' They said okay. He just wrapped. It's called *Kreeps*."

In the three years since Widen's fateful first writing class, he's written three scripts for major studios, the fantasy *Clan of One*, one action comedy set in World War II, and one "dead serious action film." But underneath all the success, he feels he's still the college kid who reluctantly signed up for Theater Arts 135.

"I'm doing okay," he says. "But I still live in my college apartment with the same old roommates. You always think it's going to change you, but things are all pretty much the same."

HOWARD THE DUCK (1986)

Hollywood has long needed one spectacular disaster to measure their other failures by. In the fifties, it was *Mutiny on the Bounty*. In the sixties, it was *Cleopatra*, then *Star*. In the seventies, it was *Heaven's Gate*. In the eighties, it was *Howard the Duck*.

It wasn't just that *Howard* was expensive and unpopular—the decade saw plenty of other big-budget duds. It was that no one could figure out why the movie had been made in the first place.

Granted, there was one obvious reason the movie was made: executive producer George Lucas, whose last two improbable ideas had been *Star Wars* and *Raiders of the Lost Ark*. His name at the time was practically a guarantee of success—and after other studio executives had been pilloried for turning down the earlier Lucas projects, no one wanted to be the one who turned down the next box-office bonanza.

But George Lucas was not going to take creative control of the duck picture—that chore was going to Lucas' film-school friends, co-writers Willard Huyck, who would direct, and his wife Gloria Katz, who would produce. And while Huyck and Katz had written Lucas' first smash hit, *American Graffiti*, the pair's later efforts had failed to reap even a modest success: *French Postcards*, a mildly amusing comedy about American exchange students in Paris, was barely released, while *Best Defense*, a wild farce about military hardware starring Dudley Moore and reigning box-office champ Eddie Murphy, was an out-and-out disaster.

But even granting Universal executives a complete faith in George Lucas' aesthetic judgements and a complete lack of faith in their own, it's hard to figure out why they chose to make *Howard the Duck*. It is even harder to figure why, having made that decision, why they felt such a thin concept should shoulder such a large budget. Although Gloria Katz bragged to the press about how "different" her film would be, in fact, it was nothing if not a by-the-numbers fantasy-comedy. The story, the characters, the filmmaking style, the look, even the soundtrack of the film were all routine.

But even granting the essential wrongness of the project, the list of missteps on *Howard the Duck* is fairly astonishing. First, there was the script, which reduced Steve Gerber's smart, cynical, and thoughtful comic book series to a set of "fish-out-of-water" cliches familiar to anyone who had seen *Splash, Short Circuit*, or any number of similar films that were being made at the time. Then there was the approach to the story, which took the duck character and stuck him into a generic mad scientist-and-monster formula.

And then there was the duck itself. Although Katz spoke quite glowingly at the time of the technology available for creating the duck, the final result seemed to use none of it. Jim Henson had created a universe of fascinating, believable mutated muppets to populate his *The Dark Crystal*; Chris Walas had found a way to make Joe Dante's *Gremlins* look frighteningly lifelike. But Howard never looked like anything besides what he was—a short guy in a duck suit.

Since *Howard* came out, of course, there have been other notable disasters. But *Howard* still seems fresh in Hollywood's mind. Shortly before Tim Burton's *Batman* was released, there was speculation that it would be a disaster. Although the film turned out to be a smash, for several weeks wags in the industry insisted on calling it *Howard the Bat*. And when producer Joel Silver and star Bruce Willis came up with the first huge bomb of the nineties, *Hudson Hawk* was immediately nicknamed *Hudson the Duck*. *Howard the Duck* itself was forgotten minutes after it left the theater; the tinny quack of disaster echoes long after.

INTERVIEW WITH GLORIA KATZ

It's only the first week of August and your movie summer seems like it's dragged on forever. You've seen dozens of movies in the last three months—and there wasn't one that didn't leave you feeling like you'd seen it before. You sat through science fiction remakes disguised as sequels and science fiction remakes *not* disguised as sequels. You've seen another kid find another flying saucer, and one more "Saturday Night Live" comic peer down one more bimbo's blouse. You've seen the Stallone rip-off of Eastwood's last film, and you've seen the Schwarzenegger rip-off of Stallone's last film. And all you want is something different.

Well, now you have it. It's called *Howard the Duck* and it's the story of a normal duck-person from a duck-planet who is accidentally trapped in a human scientist's transporter beam and zapped to Earth, where he teams up with an all-girl rock band and defeats a mad monster from outer space that possesses the scientist who brought the duck to Earth.

"It sounds like an insane idea for a movie," says producer/co-writer Gloria Katz. "You think 'Oh, no, people will never take it seriously.'"

A lot of people are gambling that thought is wrong. Universal Pictures is plowing an estimated $20 million into the movie because MCA Chairman Frank Price liked the comic book it was based on. George Lucas is staking his credibility on it as Lucasfilm Ltd.'s first in-house production since the end of the *Star Wars* cycle. And the writing-directing-producing team of Willard Huyck and Gloria Katz are hoping *Howard the Duck* will prove they can make a hit after their flops *Best Defense* and *French Postcards*.

"Obviously, this is an enormous gamble," says Katz. "It's so off the wall, so not like any other picture."

Howard the Duck may be *too* off the wall. There's a chance that American audiences simply don't want to see a duck starring in anything besides a plate of orange sauce. Katz's solution to that is to play down the fact that this is a movie about a duck—this, she insists, is first and foremost a character comedy. It's not *that* different from the last Bill Murray comedy—it's just that in this version, Bill Murray wears feathers.

Jeffrey Jones in *Howard the Duck*.

"This is a comedy about a person with certain particular characteristics," says Katz. "From Howard's unique personality comes the story of the film. He has a wonderful quality of humor and toughness that makes him appealing. I don't think of him as a duck. I think of him as a person."

But Howard *is* a duck, and *Howard the Duck* is a movie about a talking duck, the first in the genre since the disastrous 1961 Mickey Rooney/Buddy Hackett farce *Everything's Ducky*. You have to wonder why the writers of *Indiana Jones and the Temple of Doom*, the creator of *Star Wars*, and the executive responsible for *Out of Africa* would all feel a strong desire to make audiences believe a duck can talk.

The answer lies in a comic book published by Marvel in the midseventies. That comic was, of course, *Howard the Duck*, and it featured the bizarre, satiric adventures of a sarcastic, flightless waterfowl who fought vampire cows and silly barbarians. The book didn't last long, but while it was alive, it was considered the best around, thanks to the sharp, funny writing of Steve Gerber.

"We first heard of Howard ten years ago, when the comic first appeared," Katz recalls. "I'm not a big fan of comics, but this was very different. The writing was very sophisticated. I liked the character."

Within reason, that is. She did not immediately run out and buy film rights to the comic book. In 1975, the world was not ready for a talkingduck movie and Hollywood certainly wasn't ready to make one.

"At that time, the technology didn't exist to do the movie unless you wanted to do an animated film," Katz says. "And you can't control animation unless you're an animator yourself. You have turn it over to animators. Even if you could, animation wouldn't work for *Howard the Duck*. Howard is real. The humor is his reality, how he relates to the real world around him."

But times change and technology improves. *E.T., Gremlins,* and other creature films proved audiences don't demand that characters be human—or even made of flesh and blood. A movie starring a grouchy duck doesn't seem quite so strange after you've seen films about lovable aliens, lovable robots, and lovable disgusting creatures that eat people.

"We began to take the idea of doing the duck seriously after we saw what Jim Henson did in *The Dark Crystal* and what Chris Walas did in *Gremlins*," says Katz. "They had created a viable, believable creature, which hadn't been done before except in animated movies."

Still … Howard is a *duck*. It's not the kind of gamble studio heads leap at. Katz says she believes they would have been thrown out of every executive suite in town—except that they knew of one studio head who shared their fascination with the character.

"*Howard* would have appeared to be a difficult project to set up," Katz explains. "We expected to be thrown out of executive offices. But Frank Price is a comic book fan. He knew about Howard, and had always been intrigued with it, but he never knew exactly how to do it."

With a go-ahead from Universal, Katz and Huyck started writing what the producer unabashedly calls "Howard's first adventure."

"Howard's first adventure had to deal with problems on earth," says Katz. "In the comic, he is stuck on earth and becomes a cab driver. Our story deals with how he gets here."

Aside from that, Katz says, the script remains true to the comic book. Perhaps the best proof of that is that they stayed on speaking terms with writer Steve Gerber, who created the character for Marvel Comics.

"Steve Gerber did not participate in the writing of the script, but we did ask his advice on specific things," Katz says. "Howard is his creation. We didn't meet Steve until after we owned the comic for about a year, then we called him and got together and talked about how he created Howard. Outside of that, we met for lunches every now and then to tell him where we stood on the project."

Once the script was fairly solid, Katz and Huyck began to realize what a mammoth project they were about to undertake. They turned to an old friend who had had a little experience of his own with mammoth projects—and whose first hit—*American Graffiti*—they had written.

"After we had done three or four drafts of the script, George Lucas became involved," Katz says. "We realized that the film was going to be technically very complicated and thought he would provide a stable, supportive, creative environment."

He did. He provided Industrial Light and Magic, which designed and operated the duck.

"The basis of all our shooting was that we had to be near ILM," says Katz. "The picture was so technical, we couldn't take all the massive amounts of technicians with us to a distant location."

With a picture that depends completely on the believability of a mechanical duck, you'd expect there to be a lot of problems with that creature. Katz insists that there were none.

"The duck has always been wonderful to work with," she says. "It's fantastically designed. I'm not allowed to say anything about how it was done, but we never had any problems with it. This was thanks to the effort of ILM. Even after we had designs that were acceptable, they went on further and further looking for the best possible Howard."

Or at least, the best possible half-Howard. ILM could only figure out how to make Howard walk like a duck and look like a duck. Katz and Huyck spent months trying to figure out who should make Howard *talk* like a duck. The proper voice is essential to make Howard believable—and tough to find. Less than three months before the film's release, the actor who would quack Howard's lines had still not been chosen. Such stars as Jeff Goldblum and Robin Williams had been ruled out.

"We're still looking for the right voice," Katz says. "Robin Williams was considered, but we didn't want a recognizable voice. Howard is his own unique person, and this type of film depends on the audience's ability to accept Howard totally as the individual creature that he is."

Other elements of the sound track have not been quite so hard to cast. Singer and synthesizer wizard Thomas Dolby was hired to write a score—his second, after *Fever Pitch*—and several original songs for the film's all-girl rock band.

"We chose Thomas Dolby because we wanted someone who could capture the spirit of the movie," Katz says. "We like his music a lot. He's been very involved with the actual making of the movie—usually the composer arrives at the last hour to do the score, but he's been here all the time."

The woman who will be singing Thomas Dolby's songs is Lea Thompson, who, after *Back to the Future*, *Space Camp*, and *Howard*, is rapidly becoming the reigning queen of big-budget science fiction movies. That was not the reason she was cast, says Katz.

"We looked at a lot of actresses," says the producer. "There's a lot of acting required of this part, and the bimbettes we saw didn't give us comic delivery. Lea is extremely capable. She softened Beverly and took her out of the bimbo syndrome."

And just in the nick of time. The Hollywood rumor mill was already spreading stories that Universal was nervous about a bedroom scene which hinted at a form of sexual perversity too weird even for Los Angeles. Katz insists there was never any truth to these rumors.

"There was no nervousness about the bedroom scene," she says. "It's a very funny comedy scene. Nobody's ever expressed nervousness about it. The entire adventure is humorous, a duck-out-of-water story. We deal with the story in essentially comedic terms."

Which is how Katz and Huyck dealt with the story in their last film, the Dudley Moore and Eddie Murphy-starring *Best Defense*. That film, however, did not turn out too well.

"I thought *Best Defense* had an interesting organizational device—the present and how it affects someone in the future," Katz says. "We wanted to cast an unknown in the Eddie Murphy part, but we let ourselves be talked into casting Murphy, and the film's perception got twisted by the Eddie Murphy phenomenon. We were caught in a sociopolitical backlash we didn't see coming."

Another reaction they didn't see coming was Eddie Murphy's. When the film came out, he trashed it publicly. Katz finds this behavior inexcusable.

"No one put a gun to Eddie's head to do the film," she says. "He took the money and knew exactly what was involved. It makes you mad that he works for ten days and dumps all over you, while other people have worked on the film for much longer for far less money."

Katz's experience with *Best Defense* was frustrating, but not nearly as frustrating as her experience with one of her pet projects, an unproduced Hyuck and Katz period thriller called *The Radioland Murders*. Although the project was announced years ago as a Universal production to be produced by Katz and directed by Willard Huyck, nothing has happened with the script since.

"We've always wanted to do *Radioland Murders*," Katz says. "But the script is tied up at Universal. They're just sitting on it. We'd love to get it back and do the movie, but they won't let it go."

Katz and Huyck are clearly hoping that *Howard the Duck* will bring in a lot of cash for Universal, persuading the studio to go ahead on *The Radioland Murders*. On the other hand, if *Howard* brings Universal that much money, there may be another project for Gloria Katz to do first.

"We're not exactly planning the sequel right now," she admits, "but Howard *is* a character that lends himself to further adventures."

Unless, of course, *Howard the Duck* lays an egg.

INTERVIEW WITH STEVE GERBER: CO-CREATOR OF *HOWARD THE DUCK*

Steve Gerber is known to comic-book fans as the writer who co-created the characters of "Howard the Duck" (with artist Val Mayerik) and "Stewart the Rat" (with artist Gene Colan). He also is the man who wrote the somewhat existentialist stories of the "Man-Thing," the strangest adventures of "The Defenders," and, more recently, the highly controversial "Void Indigo."

Today, Gerber lives in Hollywood, but unlike several of his fellow comic-book writers, does not aspire to writing movies. Instead, he masterminds (as the story editor) animated series such as "G.I. Joe" and "The Transformers" for syndicated television.

In the midst of preparation for a second season of "The Transformers," Gerber has also been serving as creative consultant on the Lucasfilm production of *Howard the Duck*. Gerber is as entertaining a speaker as he is a writer. While talking about his creation, whom he calls simply, "the Duck," he frequently laughs and uses his biting wit as punctuation.

Q: Would you tell us the story of the creation of *Howard the Duck*?

STEVE GERBER: My office was on the ground floor of the townhouse where we were living in Brooklyn. It faced out on a whole strip of backyards a block long. It was basically a sound trap. Some guy had just bought possibly the most expensive stereo on the face of the Earth. How do I know that it was the most expensive stereo on the face of the Earth? Because he could only afford one record. A 45 rpm Salsa record. It had to be. There was only one song on it, that he would play over, and over, and over and over again, while I was sitting there trying to work. The story that I was working on was the "Man-Thing" No. 19, with the barbarian jumping out of a jar of peanut butter, and Attila the Hun flying dirigibles, and stuff like that. I needed a visual to top those things, and in a Salsa trance, the Duck came walking out of the swamp, totally unbidden.

Q: Did you have trouble getting away with it? What was the reaction at Marvel when they saw the Duck?

SG: Well, I wrote the story that we just talked about and sent it off to the artist (Val Mayerik) to be drawn. You know how the Marvel system works: you write the plot, then the artist draws the pencils, then you dialogue it from the pencil art. The pencils came back. Nobody had seen them except John Verpooten, who was Marvel's production manager at that time. John was a friend of mine. He was very funny, about 6'7" or 8" and 400 pounds. I walked into his office the day the pages came in, and he was standing there, giving me the strangest look I've ever had in my life. You have to picture this; he's at least a foot taller than I was, and huge. He looked down at me and said, "Here are your pages." I looked at the pages and freaked out. There was the Duck. I immediately realized that I had a problem on my hands. I had just written a talking Duck into a horror comic!

Feeling really nervous, clutching the pages, I went into the associate editor's office, where Marv Wolfman and Don McGregor were working, and I sat down, trying to keep from laughing. I said, "I have a problem. I have something I have to tell Roy Thomas." They asked what I had done, and I said, "I put a Duck in 'Man-Thing.'" They looked at me and said, "The book takes place in a swamp. What's the matter with a duck being in 'Man-Thing'?" "Well," I said, "It's not that kind of a Duck." "What kind of duck is it?" they said. At that point, I couldn't even speak anymore, so I just handed them the pages. Marv started laughing, and passed them to Don, who started laughing too. The three of us just sat there with tears running down our faces. They said, "You know you're going to be fired!" And at the time, I thought that was the end. I really did.

Then, I took the pages to Roy. He also laughed, but he said, "Get rid of that Duck. I don't care how you do it, but it's a horror comic. It's going to spoil the atmosphere. Axe the Duck!" So I was given orders to kill him off in the next issue, which I did. But, it was a comic-book death. You didn't see the body. He just fell in the void. That's when all the silliness started. We got letters saying, "How can you murder this Duck!" We got one duck carcass sent in a box from Canada. The duck had been eaten for someone's dinner, but the bones were there and it was obvious what it was. I missed this because I was out of town at the time, but I heard about it later. Apparently, there was a note tacked to the carcass saying, "Murderers! Bring back the Duck!" The rest of the story, you know. First, there were a couple of "Howard" short stories in the "Man-Thing" book, and then, finally, he got his own magazine.

Q: What about the conflict with Disney, when Howard had to start wearing pants ....

SG: I don't know a great deal about what went on behind the scenes about that because that was right towards the end of my association with Marvel on Howard. I do know that I screamed bloody murder at the idea. Both at the pants and at the changes in the shape of his face.

Disney basically wanted us to redesign the character. By some strange coincidence, the design that they gave us looked more like a Volkswagen than a duck! I don't think that was an accident. If this thing had any commercial potential, they were going to take care of that!

I didn't think Howard was a rip-off of Donald. I don't believe it, not in the slightest. I just don't think that if you put the two of them side by side—for example a Gene Colan drawing of Howard, inked by Steve Leialoha, and a Carl Barks drawing of Donald Duck—there would be any resemblance.

Marvel is real good at fighting battles with people smaller than they are, but when the name "Disney" appeared on the horizon, they basically went, "How high do you want us to jump? How low do you want us to bow? What can we do for you? Pants on the Duck? No problem! Cuffs? No cuffs?" It was a lost cause because they weren't going to fight it. They weren't even going to attempt to fight it.

Q: What brought on your split with Marvel?

SG: That was in 1978. The big argument started over the "Howard the Duck" comic strip, which had appeared in newspapers for maybe a total of six or nine months all together. I wrote a handful of them, and Marv Wolfman wrote the rest.

There were two problems with it. One is that they expected it to be a huge success immediately, and it wasn't. It was the kind of strip that was going to have to grow on people. But nobody likes that anymore. The fast dollar is the only good dollar. The other problem is that we went through three or four artists on the strip, the reason being that Marvel refused to advance the artists any money. We were receiving a share of the profits for the strip, which was fine, but the artist needed something to live on in the meantime. I could wait for the money because I had other comic books to write, but for the artist, the strip was a full-time job. Marvel was never able to appreciate that. When push finally came to shove, the syndicate backed Marvel because there was this kind of unsuccessful strip about a Duck, but they were also doing the "Spider-Man" strip, which was being very successful, and a couple of other things. So there was a huge argument, then ultimately I was fired.

Q: After you left, they did a couple more of the color books, and then there were Bill Mantlo's black-and-white magazines. I know that you don't think that his universe had anything to do with the Howard universe as you see it.

SG: Not really. The god's honest truth is that I don't envy Bill Mantlo the job that he fell into. I sort of wish he had been smart enough to say no to it, because he would have saved himself a lot of embarrassment that way. But, I have to feel a certain amount of pity for him for having to deal with that character. The only way to have made it work, and I'm not sure that the editorial regime up there would have let it happen, because it would have been a repeat of the same situation I had before, would have been to totally remake the character in his own, personal way.

I don't know if that could have been done, but if anything could have saved the Duck, that would have been it. Essentially that's what Frank Miller eventually did to "Daredevil." He totally rebuilt that character from the ground up. That's what had to have been done to "Howard the Duck." But no one ever attempted it, and as a result, they were not able to really write about the character successfully.

Other people have taken over comic strips, but it's usually because the creator has died. And even then, could anybody other than Walt Kelly have written "Pogo"? Could anybody but Trudeau do "Doonesbury"? Or could anybody but Al Capp have done "Li'l Abner"? Next to impossible. And nobody would have presumed to.

It's only at a place like Marvel, where they are used to interchangeable artists and writers on any given character, that they could have thought that that would work with "Howard the Duck." If I had been them, I would have done one of two things: either drop the book entirely, forget about it, pretend that they had never published it; or else find some writer that was willing to put as much of himself into that character as I was. But they did neither.

Q: What did prompt you to sue for your rights?

SG: Yes, why did I sue? Had the "Howard" book died after I left it, I might never have. As it turned out though, the interest in doing the character as a movie started as far back as 1978. There was a group of guys out of Chicago that wanted to do it. They actually spoke to me about writing it, or consulting on it, or something like that. My feeling about that was that, if I could come to some kind of terms with Marvel, then okay, I'd be happy to work on it.

What we first tried to do then was to negotiate something with them. I tried first with a writer's agent, then through the lawyer who ultimately filed the suit. But we tried to negotiate something first. They absolutely refused to negotiate. When it became clear that they absolutely refused to negotiate anything, I had to make a decision. Either I was going to allow myself to be put into a position where I could be frozen out of, not only the movie, but the comic book and the character and everything forever, or I was going to take a real gamble and just say, "No. I created this. Your claim on it is at best arguable, possibly as much as specious, and I'm going to fight you tooth and nail and find out which one of us really owns it." And that's what happened.

Q: Hadn't you signed a contract?

SG: Virtually all of the issues of "Howard the Duck" were covered not by any contract, but by a statement that they literally stamped with a rubber stamp on the back of their checks. When you turned in your check, you turned in the "contract," so-called, if it was a contract, and I don't believe it was for an instant, and you never got a copy of it.

The interesting thing was that I had drawn large "X's" through half of those statements on the back. This, among other reasons, was why I thought I might have a very serious claim to the character. Even despite the fact that I'm not sure a contract signed by only one party, and of which that one party is not given a copy, is really a contract. I think it's doubtful. Let me say also that, in my particular case, there were other documents involved. But this is the way that most of the issues of "Howard" were covered, and those other documents did not bear on the matter very much. It was a very complicated case.

Q: Eventually, you decided to settle out of court?

SG: For any number of reasons. We were weeks, maybe months, maybe not even that, from actually going to trial. It had come right down to the wire. There was a chance we could win the case, but there was also a chance that we could lose it. The chances were comparable to somewhere in the neighborhood of fifty-fifty either way. A lot of it was going to depend upon who made the stronger arguments in the courtroom, because neither case was beyond a shadow of a doubt. I think it would all have been a matter of which side of the bed the jury got up on, and whether they felt regular that day. There was no way of predicting it. It could really have gone either way.

We decided to make one more attempt to negotiate with Marvel. We wanted to negotiate something very similar to what I had asked for in the first place. I was willing to settle for that a couple of years earlier, so why not now. Ultimately, that's what we did. That had two advantages. Number one, a decisive loss would have been a real blow to me. I spent about $130,000 on the law suit, and despite "Destroyer Duck" and the "F.O.O.G." (Friends of Old Gerber) portfolio, I still owe quite a bit of money. The other thing is, the precedent that could have been set by that case would have made it that much more difficult for anybody else, under similarly ambiguous circumstances, to come along and sue them on the same grounds.

The terms of the settlement are confidential, because Marvel wants them confidential. I would talk about them in the next split-second if Marvel would allow me to. But, I agreed to it, and I'm honoring it. But, essentially, I felt that we got a very good settlement. It was ultimately good for Marvel, and it was ultimately good for me.

Q: What made you think that you could go back and write "Howard" for them again?

SG: Blind, stupid, optimism! That's it! To tell the truth, in some ways, I didn't know that I could write "Howard" again, for them or anybody else. I was very surprised, when I sat down to actually write the script, at how quickly I found the character's voice and personality, and at how easily I was able to slip into it. Writing the character itself, after the first couple of pages, was almost effortless. It was frightening to me sometimes, because the guy is so real. I know that character. Really, when I'm writing him, I become that character. So, having cleared that hurdle, I figured it was worth a try. How was I going to live with myself if

I didn't try. Besides, my lawyer was badgering me to death. There was no way Henry Holmes was going to allow me not to try that comic book.

Well, I wrote the comic, and you know what happened. They edited the guts out of it essentially. So, I pulled the script and now I'm not writing the comic book anymore.

Q: When did you know that there was finally going to be a *Howard the Duck* movie?

SG: I found out about it in the very early stages of Willard Huyck and Gloria Katz's involvement with Universal. They were already working on the script at the time that I found out about it. I had a meeting with them, and we talked about their plans for it. I was stunned. It was real interesting. They were quoting me lines from the comic books that I had forgotten, story titles and things like this. I couldn't believe it. This was stuff that I hadn't looked at in several years, and they had obviously steeped themselves in it.

Listening to them talk about it, my feeling was that these were the people to do the movie. They know this character. They understand what it is that makes it work. When I read the script, that was all borne out. The tone of the film is lighter than the comic books. Actually, it's like some of the lighter stories that we did, "The Thief of Bagmom" and that kind of thing. No similarity to the plot, but the tone of it is very much like that. Yet, it has its moments, its dark moments, as well. But, they got the character of Howard better than any other writer that's ever tried it. I was thrilled to see it. That is the Duck.

Q: Were you sorry that you weren't given a chance to write the script yourself?

SG: No. I don't want to work in the movies. I have no ambition toward that at all.

Q: How do you feel about the way they have Howard come to Earth? Do you agree with that?

SG: Well, it's different from what I did, but again, it works with the spirit of what I did. My story was essentially that he was walking down the street, then suddenly vanished in full view of fifty people, or whatever. Their set-up is a little different, but it basically accomplishes the same thing. It's very funny. I think the opening scene of that picture is going to be a small cinematic classic, and something that's going to be remembered for years and years. I burst out laughing reading it.

I don't mind that they differ in the details. The spirit of it is what I was really concerned with, and boy, do they capture that! That is as absurd a sequence as any we ever did in the "Howard" book, and it's funny. It's really funny.

Q: What did your relationship as creative consultant entail?

SG: I hope Willard and Gloria are reading this and laughing, okay? I read the script. I made suggestions. They ignored them. No, it's not quite that bad! We actually talked out a couple of scenes. I gave them suggestions on a couple of lines of dialogue on the character and on things that he would and wouldn't do or say. Beverly would think this way but not that way. They made some more serious modifications to the character of Beverly, but again, I didn't mind. It's not the same character, but it works. So, I had no problem with it. I was less likely to tread on their concept of Beverly than I was to make suggestions about the Duck.

Interestingly, some of the things that I had suggested, they had already gone through another half a draft by the time we got together, and they had already done those things. We did actually talk out one of the climactic scenes in the picture. I don't want to talk about it too much, because I don't want to give anything away. But, they were having a problem with the staging of it, and I had a couple of peculiar suggestions that they seemed to like. Oddly enough, a lot of the stuff that I've done in animation and comic books bore directly on the kind of stuff they were doing, and the kind of problem they were trying to solve, which was how to make something smaller, and more frightening at the same time. I don't know whether they used it, whether the scene is done the way we talked out, but I'll be real interested to see it.

Q: Howard and Beverly's relationship is toned down somewhat …. In the comic, we always got the impression that they were somewhat sexually involved ….

SG: You're the second or third person that's said that. I never made that explicit. Bill Mantlo did the only explicit sex scene I remember. I never did. I left that entirely up to people's imaginations, figuring that whatever they could imagine would be much filthier than anything I could even contemplate. There was nothing I could have come up with that could have been anywhere near as raunchy or revolting as what other people would dream up. I had no idea what the relationship was, beyond that they literally slept together. They slept in the same bed together, went to sleep together. Whether they did anything else in that bed is something I never contemplated. Willard and Gloria avoided the subject in an interesting way also, but also raised the possibility. Again, I think it's very true to what I did. I'm very pleased with it.

Q: Do you think that, on the technical side, Howard can be done in such a way that people will think of him as a real creature, and not a man in a Duck suit?

SG: Technically, it was very difficult, obviously. But I think they pulled it off. I've met the Duck and talked with him, and I thought he was a Duck. There was no way to relate to him as a human. It looked like a creature to me. If I met that thing walking down the street, I would be taken aback.

The design of the face is changed somewhat to accommodate the technology. Also, he's white instead of yellow, to accommodate the color photography. But, the design works, I think. It's not the Duck exactly as he was in the comic books, but it works.

Q: Do you think the public at large is going to respond to a three-foot tall, cigar smoking, wise-cracking Duck stuck in a world he didn't make?

SG: Ah, I feel exactly the way Willard and Gloria feel, actually. I know they don't want me quoting them, but I think someone else said it to them, and they found that they agreed with it too. This picture is either going to make a fortune beyond all reason, or it's going to go straight from release to cassette, by-passing theaters. It will become a $30 million cult classic, that they show at midnight at the Fifth Street Mission. I don't know which it will be, but it's going to be one or the other. Personally, I hope it's an enormous hit.

Q: Does Howard have a philosophy on life?

SG: Yeah. "I don't like stupid people, let me alone!" That's the entire philosophy. "Just, keep stupidity out of my way."

Q: Do you have anything you'd like to say about "Howard the Duck"?

SG: The one thing I really want to say is that I'm sorry I can't write the comic-book anymore. I would really very much like to be doing it. It bothers me that whatever egos are at play out there, possibly including mine, are such that they won't allow me to do that book the way it needs to be done in order to work. It's the one sour note in this whole experience. I am thrilled about this experience except for that.

Q: Howard is like the child of a divorced couple, when one parent won't let the other parent see it?

SG: We've fought the custody battle! They got custody, but boy, did I get visitation privileges!

THE JAMES BOND FILMS (1980-1989)

Nothing can stop James Bond—not megalomaniac villains, not middle age, and certainly not an identity crisis.

The coveted License to Kill has passed from Sean Connery to Roger Moore to Timothy Dalton (and more recently Pierce Brosnan), but there's no doubt James Bond will emerge victorious, unscathed by either the vicissitudes of the box office or the slings and arrows of critics.

It's been over 25 years since the first 007 movie, and now, after 17 films, 4 stars, and over $1 billion in revenues, people will still line up around the block for more. It is a success story "so far beyond the movie business dreams of glory as to be mind-boggling," wrote author Richard Condon.

James Bond has grown past the boundaries of mere popular entertainment to become a cultural artifact—not one relegated to history, but one that's still going strong.

"The elimination of James Bond, either by Her Majesty's enemies or by the disfavor of the movie public is not to be thought of," wrote novelist Anthony Burgess. "He goes on."

However, much of what audiences love about the James Bond films is the formula they all know so well. How much longer can the formula last before audiences get bored of it?

"We are in the same position as the members of the U.S. House of Representatives. Every two years they come up for reelection," says writer/producer Michael Wilson. "Every two years we come out with a new Bond film. People go to the box office and vote. We are either voted back in or we aren't."

"There's no reason the Bonds can't go on forever," said the late Richard Maibaum, who wrote or co-wrote 13 of the Bond films. "Some characters are immortal—Robin Hood, the Three Musketeers, Sherlock Holmes ... and now, James Bond."

THE NAME IS BOND. JAMES BOND AN OVERVIEW

The crush of tourists on Fisherman's Wharf encircle a tiny, dock-side corner of Tarantino's. A heavy-set man, wearing a grey "I Survived the Demon" sweatshirt, holds his Nikon to his face like a mask. He snaps picture after picture, ignoring his wife's insistent nudging.

"For God's sake, Frank, there are sights to see," she complains.

"Yeah," he replies, snapping away, "but this is *James Bond.*"

Roger Moore, smoking his cigar, is wandering restlessly in front of the crowd as the crew of the fourteenth 007 adventure, *A View to a Kill*, set up their next shot. Suddenly, a woman breaks from the crowd with her baby and whispers something to the 55-year-old actor. He smiles, nods affirmatively, and takes the baby from her hands. Planting herself beside Moore, she motions to her husband, who comes out and snaps a quick picture with his instamatic ... and then tells his wife to come over and take a picture of *him* with 007.

And through it all, Roger Moore grins.

James Bond is more than the most successful screen hero in motion picture history. Today, he's a bigger draw than the Golden Gate Bridge, where the second unit toils atop the towering spires shooting footage for the film's climactic finale—a battle that involves a blimp, a helicopter, and a vicious fist-fight on the cables.

Spectacular? It's all in a day's work for this tight-knit, seasoned crew. They've been doing it for 22 years.

But the cinematic adventures of James Bond had their beginnings even earlier—only nobody noticed.

They called him "cardsense Jimmy Bond" way back then, and he wasn't the suave, witty womanizer he is now. And he also wasn't one of the actors we've come to associate with the role.

The year was 1955, long before the adventures of 007 would explode on the silver screem, when Barry Nelson played James Bond in a live production of Ian Fleming's book *Casino Royale* on CBS' "Climax Theatre."

"No one *ever* stops me on the street and recognizes me as James Bond," jokes Nelson, who played the hotel manager in *The Shining*. "It's kind of a novelty for me to be the first one. I've never pretended to be anything more than 001!"

The kinescope, which featured Peter Lorre as the sadistic Le Chiffre, wasn't anything like the 007 stories moviegoers have spent $1 billion over the last two decades to see. Nelson's Bond was a rough American gambler, more of a thug than a spy. "I was very dissatisfied with the part. I thought they wrote it poorly," he recalls. "No charm or character or anything."

And while audiences are accustomed to Bond films beginning with an exhilarating stunt, *Casino Royale* (again filmed in 1967 as a comedy starring Woody Allen, David Niven and Peter Sellers) opened with a dull pop from a late-firing gun.

"My entrance in the picture was really, truly funny," he says, "and that's too bad, because it wasn't supposed to be."

"It certainly is a curiosity," he adds, "there being a James Bond film hardly anyone has ever seen."

But Kevin McClory, a struggling producer, saw some potential. He contacted Fleming and, with writer Jack Whittingham, they developed a screenplay entitled *Thunderball*. No one was interested. CBS expressed some interest in a TV series, to be called "Captain Jamaica," and even had Fleming write some episode outlines. That too fizzled, though Fleming used the outlines to develop *For Your Eyes Only*, a book of 007 short stories.

It wasn't until 1960, when producers Albert R. Broccoli and Harry Saltzman bought the screen rights from Fleming, that the cinematic 007 took shape. They contacted writer Richard Maibaum, whom they had worked with on several Alan Ladd films, to re-shape *Thunderball*.

Complications (legal and otherwise) shelved Maibaum's script and the producers selected another Ian Fleming novel, *Dr. No*, for their maiden effort.

The first thing they did was cast against type. Sean Connery was a virtual unknown and "was nothing like Fleming's concept of James Bond," says Maibaum. "If we had chosen somebody like David Niven, that was more like the way he wrote it."

"Sean was a rough, tough, Scottish soccer player, not a suave, cultured gentleman of the Cambridge/Whitehall type," explains Maibaum. "The fact we attributed to him such a high style epicure was part of the joke."

The big question was whether audiences would laugh with them or *at* them.

Maibaum believes that by casting Connery they inadvertently took a larger than life role and made it someone the average person could relate to. "It enabled the ordinary guy and girl to look at the screen and say 'That's me. I could do all those things.' It was a slight take off, not belabored or done consciously. But it came off as if it was planned and it was a great, great plus."

Dr. No was a modest success and became the blueprint for the entire series. Joseph Wiseman, who played the villainous doctor (originally offered to Christopher Lee), served as the mold from which future Bond foes were cast. Maibaum believes Wiseman's portrayal was responsible for "the elegance of many of the Bond villains."

One of Maibaum's favorite lines in the whole series is when Dr. No says to Bond "You disappoint me, Mr. Bond. You are nothing but a stupid policeman."

"That was a funny line, " he says, "but the way Joe read it was delightful."

However, the most remembered line from the film was far less creative. "When Sean, in the beginning of the picture, said 'The name is Bond. James Bond,' if you didn't believe it then there would have been no series, Now, of course, the line seems like the understatement of all time because of course this is James Bond, and everyone knows it. They just get a kick out of hearing it anyway."

From Russia with Love followed and, while that film is widely considered, as Maibaum says, "the most successful artistically" of the Bond films, the series really hit its stride with the next adventure, *Goldfinger*. The movie set the style for the Bonds that would come–the double entendres, the suggestive character names, the bizarre henchmen, the stylish deaths, the amazing stunts, the outlandish capers, the eccentric villain. And, above all, the Aston Martin.

The car was more than just another catchy gimmick; it was a spectacular vehicle driving on the treacherous road dividing comedy and drama. "We took into consideration the audience's growing sophistication," says Maibaum. "We dared to do something seldom done in action pictures. We mixed what was funny with what was serious."

Jack Lord was asked to recreate his *Dr. No* role as CIA agent Felix Leiter, Maibaum says, but he demanded co-star billing, a larger part in the film, "and a great deal of money. I've never liked another Leiter, and as time went on, they hired older and fatter men to play the part in order to make James Bond look younger and more handsome."

Shirley Bassey's rendition of the *Goldfinger* theme (Maibaum says the musicians called it *Moon Finger* because it sounded so much like "Moon River") and Maurice Binder's sensual title sequence featuring lithe, silhouetted nudes became two other Bond motifs continued in subsequent adventures.

The formula continued to work through *Thunderball* and *You Only Live Twice*, by which time the audiences so identified Connery with the role that the advertisements proclaimed in bold letters: "Sean Connery *is* James Bond."

So when Connery decided to quit, it's no wonder the producers thought the series was in dire peril. If they believed their own hype, there could be no new 007.

What they didn't see, and what they didn't discover until much later, was that their advertising was true, but in a completely different sense. George Lazenby, an Australian male model, understood it intuitively before they did and used it to his advantage.

"I think the most acting I did was to acquire the role in the first place," says Lazenby. "I walked in looking like James Bond and acting as if that's the way I was anyway. And they thought, 'all we have to do is keep this guy the way he is and we've got James Bond.'"

At first they decided to use the change of actors as a plot point. "We had this plastic surgeon idea," Maibaum says. "Bond had to have plastic surgery because he was being recognized by all his country's enemies. But, we thought that was awful and threw it out. Finally, I came up with that line, when the girl leaves him flat after she rescues her. Bond said 'This never happened to the other fellow.'"

When George Lazenby delivered the lament at the opening of *On Her Majesty's Secret Service*, it worked. The audience laughed.

"Because it was funny, the audience liked it. It said 'Look, you know it's not the same James Bond, so we're not going to kid you or do anything corny to excuse it. You'll just have to accept this isn't the same fellow."

What they had was a man imitating Sean Connery and, in *On Her Majesty's Secret Service* he did it poorly. But the producers finally realized what they unconsciously knew already. "When you cast James Bond, you're casting a leading actor, not a character actor," says Michael G. Wilson, Broccoli's stepson and co-writer and co-producer of *For Your Eyes Only*. "What that means is, the actors to a certain extent are playing themselves."

And Lazenby *was* himself, a man with no acting experience, a handsome model wearing someone else's clothes—Connery's clothes. What the producers needed wasn't someone who would step into Connery's shoes, but someone who would reshape Bond in his own image. They couldn't find that man in time for *Diamonds Are Forever*. They signed John Gavin but, at the last minute, they stalled the inevitable by luring Connery back one more time—in exchange for a $1 million donation to his favorite charity and financing for two films of his choice.

Maibaum's original *Diamonds Are Forever* script featured Goldfinger's twin brother in a scheme to blackmail the world. But it met with lukewarm response from the producers. "I was heartbroken when they rejected it."

Broccoli went looking for some young, new writer to rework Maibaum's script. United Artists' then-president David Picker recommended Tom Mankiewicz. Although he was a relatively unknown screenwriter, filmmaking was practically a family business. Tom is the son of famed writer/director Joseph Mankiewicz and nephew of screenwriter Herman Mankiewicz.

Maibaum's script was radically altered in the Mankiewicz rewrite. Goldfinger's brother was scrapped and Ernst Stavro Blofeld, the mastermind of SPECTRE, returned. And the ending became, as Maibaum describes it, "an interminable thing on an oil rig."

Sean Connery was back as Bond, but even as the cameras were rolling, the producers knew he was a temporary solution to a big problem. A new James Bond had to be found. Paul Newman, Patrick McGoohan, Burt Reynolds, John Gavin, and even Timothy Dalton were among the dozens of actors considered before the producers settled on Roger Moore.

Moore made his name in television playing quick-witted, debonair adventurers like smooth-talking gambler Beau Maverick, globe-trotting adventurer Simon Templar "The Saint," and notorious playboy Lord Brett Sinclair in *The Persuaders*. Somewhere along the line the roles, and the actor who plays them, became one. He seemed perfect.

When Moore replaced Sean Connery as James Bond, he didn't just continue the role as George Lazenby did. Moore *absorbed* it. James Bond became yet another extension of himself. Beginning with *Live and Let Die*, he imbued James Bond with the same playful, coy charm that typified his TV characters, radically transforming the style of the series and making 007 undeniably his own.

"I'm not Sean Connery. In *Live and Let Die*, I didn't do any of that tough stuff because that was what Sean would do. My personality is entirely different than his," Moore says, "I'm not that cold-blooded killer Sean can do so well, which is why I play it for laughs. The producers encourage me to impersonate myself." He believes the only difference between himself and James Bond is that he doesn't carry around a Walther PPK.

Maibaum was unavailable to write the script, so the assignment fell to Mankiewicz. "I would have liked a crack at the movie," says Maibaum. "I didn't particularly like what they did to it. It was about nothing, a lousy cooking-some-dope-somewhere-in-the-jungle movie. That's not Bond at all."

Perhaps his biggest reservation about *Live and Let Die* lies with Moore's portrayal of Bond. "In a strange way," Maibaum says, "some people like Roger better than Sean. I certainly don't. I think Roger does very well. He's suave, witty, and so forth, but as far as I am concerned, he has a dimension of disbelief. He does what I considered unforgivable—he spoofs himself and he spoofs the part. When you start doing that, the audience stops laughing.

"The most important thing in a Bond picture is a pretense of seriousness," he says. "If your leading man doesn't really appear to believe in what he is doing as an actor or as the character, that's bad."

Roger Moore makes everything "so arch, and is so coy about everything. We knew Roger was not a rough, tough guy like Sean was, so we deliberately gave him things to do that would make him tougher. But you see, he hasn't got it. You believed Sean could be pure steel if he wanted to."

Live and Let Die, besides being Moore's premiere outing, was also the first 007 film noticeably influenced by the competition. It was written when "blacksploitation" movies were the rage, thanks to the success of *Shaft* and *Supetfly*. So this time, the villains were black, the caper involved drugs, and ex–Beatle Paul McCartney was hired to give 007 a hot title tune.

The ploy backfired. By the time *Live and Let Die* came out in 1973, the blacksploitation craze was dead and the film, by trying so desperately to be trendy, came off looking tired and out-of-step. Only the song was a hit.

For Moore's second outing as 007, Mankiewicz was asked back to write *The Man with the Golden Gun*. Mankiewicz envisioned it as a *High Noon*-like confrontation between Jack Palance and Roger Moore. Director Guy Hamilton (*Goldfinger, Live and Let Die*) envisioned it differently. Mankiewicz was out, and Maibaum was in.

The Man with the Golden Gun was trounced by critics, who panned it as small-scale and unimaginative in comparison with early 007 films. It performed badly by Bond standards at the box office and took a critical drubbing. *Variety*, the bible of the entertainment industry, said the film was placid and Bond himself had become stale. "At this rate, the [next] film might be phoned in."

The James Bond phenomenon, it seemed, might finally be ebbing. Clearly, something had to be done. Producer Albert R. Broccoli bought out partner Harry Saltzman and took on the naysayers with a vengeance. *The Man with the Golden Gun* cost $7 million; for *The Spy Who Loved Me*, Broccoli doubled the budget. If *The Man with the Golden Gun* was small in scope than *The Spy Who Loved Me* would be gigantic.

And they went back to Maibaum to craft it. In his original script, the story opened with a group of terrorists, comprised of everyone from the Red Brigade to the Weathermen, breaking into an ultra-modern SPECTRE lair.

"They level the place, kick Blofeld out, and take over," explains Maibaum. "They're a bunch of young idealists and in the end, when Bond comes in and says 'All right, you're going to blow up the world. What do you want?' they say 'We don't want anything, we just want to start over—the world is lousy. We want to wipe it away and begin again. So, there's no way we can be bribed.'"

Broccoli didn't like it. Instead, Broccoli hired screenwriter Christopher Wood and turned to the most extravagant Bond film, *You Only Live Twice*, virtually lifted the entire plot, and embellished the whole thing with elaborate special effects and gadgetry. The future of 007 was riding on a steel-toothed villain named Jaws, a sports car-turned-submarine, and Roger Moore, who was heartily encouraged to run wild.

It worked. The *Spy Who Loved Me* made $78 million, twice as much as the *Man with the Golden Gun*, and the critics loved it.

"I think after *The Man with the Golden Gun* we started letting a little more of my humor creep in," says Moore. "The first two Bonds I did were a little experimental, but with *The Spy Who Loved Me*, I think we found the right ingredients, the right level of humor, the right approach."

By now George Lucas and Steven Spielberg were setting box-office records with *Star Wars* and *Close Encounters of the Third Kind*. Broccoli apparently felt threatened by the young upstarts, and the special-effects savvy audience they were creating. With *Moonraker*, it was as if he was trying to prove he could do it bigger and better than they could.

Moonraker was a special effects spectacular involving stolen space shuttles (which were still a few years away from being a reality) and climaxing with a laser battle at the villain's orbiting space colony. It cost $30 million, twice as much as *The Spy Who Loved Me*. And while it did out-of-this-world business, $87 million worth, it didn't wow the fans.

"I can understand a Bond purist saying 'God they ruined him,' but I think the Bond films have changed properly with the times," says Tom Mankiewicz, writer of *Live and Let Die*, and co-writer of *Diamonds Are Forever* and *The Man with the Golden Gun*.

"The moment that gadgetry appeared in *Goldfinger*, the audience went bananas," says Mankiewicz. "It was as if the producers were then under an obligation to make each picture bigger, a little more filled with gadgetry, until the audience came to expect that from Bond."

James Bond, 007 had changed all right. The hard-edged, quick-witted spy had become a caricature of himself. *Moonraker* left James Bond in outer space and, despite the film's financial success, producers Broccoli and Michael G. Wilson, his stepson, realized it was time to bring 007 back to earth.

"You try different ways to go and I think with *Moonraker* we went that direction about as far as we could," says Wilson.

They tried to reverse the trend by toughening Bond up in *For Your Eyes Only* and concentrating on the espionage rather than the special effects. But it didn't work artistically. "We tried to go back to the earlier films with *For Your Eyes Only*, but we didn't have Sean Connery to make it real," says Maibaum, who co-wrote the script with Wilson.

There were other problems, too.

"*For Your Eyes Only*, I suppose, was the most different in the villain respect and perhaps the film suffered for it," says Wilson. "The villain was not central enough to the story."

And some say, neither was James Bond. One critic wrote that Moore had been reduced to being "an occasional stand in for the stunt man."

"It's true. I don't think it's good. I think it's five times better when they have the stunts and a real James Bond, too, and there's no reason why we can't do it," says Maibaum. "I think we blew an opportunity to go back to the *From Russia with Love* Bond."

They tried, once again, to toughen Moore's portrayal of Bond. In the film, there's a scene in which a bad guy's car is precariously perched on the edge of a cliff. Bond gives the car a kick, sending the bad guy inside to his death.

Roger Moore took James Bond into outer space in *Moonraker*, to the dismay of many Bond fans, including screenwriter Richard Maibaum.

"Yeah, there was a big discussion about whether that was too brutal," Moore says, "not unlike the discussion we had in *Man with the Golden Gun* when I wrestled with Maud Adams and she said 'you're hurting my arm' and I said 'I'll break it.' Look, I play the role differently. I can't play the cold-blooded killer that Sean could."

Nor can he deliver the jokes as well, Maibaum says. The one-liners in *For Your Eyes Only* and other recent Bond films, weren't as sharp as they once were and Maibaum places the blame on Roger Moore. "My lines are 'red wine with fish, that should have told me something' and 'she had her kicks' (both from *From Russia with Love*). Those are my lines, the ones I claim and I enjoyed writing. Some of the stuff I think is awful, like 'something big is coming between us.' Roger insists on making some script changes and is very proud of them and tells everybody. And some of his improvements are just awful."

The next adventure was *Octopussy*, the Bond film Moore feels best exemplifies his approach to 007.

"I think we reached a peak with *Octopussy*, which was very outrageous," Moore says. "What we were saying to the audience was 'Look, you've been seeing these things for twenty-two years and they are intended to be fun and we want you to laugh with us, not at us.'

"The Bond situations to me are so ridiculous, so outrageous. I mean, this man is supposed to be a spy and yet everybody knows he's a spy," Moore adds. "Every bartender in the world offers him martinis that are shaken and not stirred. What kind of serious spy is recognized everywhere he goes? It's outrageous. So, I think you have to treat the humor outrageously as well."

Because *Octopussy* was so much a reflection of Roger Moore, it served as a strong counterpoint to Sean Connery's rival Bond film, *Never Say Never Again*. Connery's film was a remake of *Thunderball*, the exclusive rights to which Broccoli lost in a lengthy and complicated court battle with Kevin McClory.

McClory sold his share of *Thunderball*'s licensing rights to Fleming, who sold it to Broccoli and United Artists. When the rights reverted back to McClory ten years later, he announced the production of a remake entitled *Warhead*, which he co-wrote with Sean Connery, and novelist Len Deighton. Broccoli and United Artists took McClory to court, trying to stop the project on the grounds that they owned the James Bond character. They lost, but McClory failed to get the project off the ground despite his on-again, off-again announcements to the contrary.

At one point, Paramount Pictures was reportedly backing *Warhead*, with Orson Welles cast as Blofeld and Trevor

Howard as M. A frustrated McClory even threatened to turn James Bond into a television series if feature film backing didn't materialize soon.

Then along came entertainment attorney-turned-producer Jack Schwartzman, who cut through the legal red tape and convinced Warner Bros, to back the project, which Schwartzman had hired Lorenzo Semple, Jr., to rewrite.

"*Warhead* never got off the ground because McClory was supposedly a very difficult personality," says Semple. "I heard that as long as McClory wasn't actively connected with the picture it would get made. Schwartzman persuaded McClory to take the money and step into the background. In effect, he arranged for McClory to step out."

Never Say Never Again portrayed Bond as an elder agent, put out to pasture by a new regime running the secret service, but he was still as hard-edged as ever.

The actual competition between Connery and Moore, now no longer a philosophical issue but a real box-office battle, seemed to put the hotly debated question "who is the *real* Bond?" to rest. Audiences flocked to see both. And although *Octopussy* beat *Never Say Never Again* at the box office, they were *both* extremely successful.

Albert R. Broccoli emerged unscathed and ready for *A View to a Kill*, the fourteenth in the series. Roger Moore, as he has done every time since *Spy Who Loved Me*, told the press he was finished with the role—only this time he sounded half serious. While Maibaum and Wilson developed a treatment, Broccoli went looking for Moore's possible replacement.

The candidates in the widely publicized Bond hunt included Pierce Brosnan, Oliver Tobias, Lewis Collins, Tom Selleck, James Brolin, Mel Gibson, and Ian Ogilvy. Insiders felt Collins, the star of the British series "The Professionals" and the movie *The Final*

Option, had the best shot. However, MGM/UA had their hearts set on Moore and managed to coax him back for $3 million plus.

So Roger Moore packed his bags, strapped on his triple-draw holster, and headed for San Francisco for his seventh performance as James Bond 007.

"Actually, I'm playing James Bond again because I feel sorry for Cubby" (producer Albert R. Broccoli), Moore says, his playful grin never waning. "He'll have a terrible job finding anybody else who will work as cheap as I do. Actually, I enjoy the work. I'm glad people are still misguided enough to employ me."

The only time he regrets taking on the role "is when the explosions start" and says he's "encouraged to impersonate myself."

He approaches an interview like a performance at the Comedy Store. But that's his way of staying congenial in the face of the countless reporters and autograph-hungry fans who have assaulted him since he arrived in San Francisco. *A View to a Kill*, the fourteenth in the series, is the first Bond film to shoot in the United States since *Live and Let Die*.

"I can't say that Roger likes it," says producer/writer Michael G. Wilson, "but he's very easy-going about it."

Dealing with the hype and hoopla is "easier than saying dialogue," Moore quips. "Actually, I'm running for governor of California. Wait, I can't, I'm not American-born. I could become dictator …."

But, to die-hard 007 fans, he'll *never* become James Bond, at least not the James Bond that Sean Connery created.

"The comparisons between me and Sean stopped until *Never Say Never Again* and the British paper had the headline 'The Battle of the Bonds,' which was picked up everywhere," Moore says. "I never saw *Never Say Never Again*. We weren't having a battle, we're friends."

Moore was even approached to be in Connery's film.

"They had an idea I might walk through a scene. Sean would say to somebody that he was getting tired and didn't want to be a spy anymore and I'd walk past and wink at him. But, it was a rival production."

And, as far as fans are concerned, Connery and Moore are still rivals as regards the Bond role.

"Sure, people are going to still compare," Moore says. "Christ all mighty, though, 4,000 actors have played *Hamlet. Chacun à son goût.*"

Moore fights against efforts to toughen him up in Connery's likeness and prefers his own, light approach. "Basically, we have very little brutality in Bond," Moore says. "As Cubby once said, we are sadism for the family." He has no doubt Bond will continue if, and when, he leaves it. "And *that* actor will have his own interpretation."

Right now, though, the film is rolling on Roger Moore.

Two films crews work simultanously during the day. One crew is devoted to shooting the climactic battle on the Golden Gate Bridge involving a blimp, helicopter, and dozens of stunt men. The city refused to let them toss a dummy off the bridge—for fear it would inspire suicide attempts—and demanded a $4 million insurance policy to cover the shooting.

The other crew follows the actors around from locations at City Hall, Dunsmuir House, Fisherman's Wharf and the Richmond Harbor.

Another $100 million policy was taken out to cover accidents on the streets where a *third* crew labors from 8 p.m. to dawn. They're shooting a hook-and-ladder firetruck, driven by Moore's stunt double, as it roars down Market Street pursued by a fleet of police cars.

"It's a great chase," say director John Glen, who also helmed *For Your Eyes Only* and *Octopussy*.

Bond thwarts an attempt to bomb City Hall, is mistaken for the villain by police, and steals a firetruck to make his escape.

"If you look at that firetruck, you'll realize that it was made for filmmaking. The angles are fantastic. The vehicle is a big, heavy piece of machinery that swings around and has great character," Glen says. "The camera positions are ready-made. You can scramble all over it and find beautiful shots everywhere you look."

"This is certainly the hardest Bond film we've ever made," adds Glen. And at $30 million, it's also one of the most expensive.

"We don't cheat the public," says Glen, "We spend a lot of money and every penny of it is on the screen."

The Bond films have always been extravaganzas, and *A View to a Kill* is no exception. Evil computer genius Max Zorin (Christopher Walken, *The Dead Zone*), with the help of his assistant May Day (Grace Jones, *Conan*), plans to control the computer market by triggering an earthquake that will plunge California, and its "Silicon Valley," into the sea.

It's up to 007, aided by Patrick Macnee (*The Avengers*), Tanya Roberts (*Sheena*) and newcomer David Yip, known to British television audiences as the "Chinese Detective," to stop Zorin and claim a unique microchip that could change the balance of world power.

The plot sounds a bit familiar.

"Somebody told me this sounds like *Superman*," says Wilson, who cowrote the script with 007 veteran Richard Maibaum. "I didn't even remember it. I went back and saw it and yeah, the bad guy had a plot to sink California and turn Las Vegas into beachfront property. Our plot tends to be more realistic. This is something that could almost be done. In other words, once you see this picture, you'll see that it's a little frightening. Everything from a geological standpoint is absolutely true."

Grace Jones, starring as the villainous May Day, demonstrates her prowess as a bodyguard by overpowering a menacing KGB agent in *A View to a Kill*.

But the story is familiar in other ways, too. Once again, Bond is battling a megalomaniac bent on apocalyptic evil.

"They are all different, each story is different," says Moore. "There is a formula, you know, a white knight riding out to combat evil with evil in different shapes and in this one it's Max Zorin, played by Christopher Walken, and his aide May Day, played by Grace Jones. She's fun to work with if you keep out of the way of her feet and her handbag."

Moore doesn't see any way to get rid of the megalomaniac villains.

"How else could you do it differently? That *is* the formula.

"Bond has to combat something," Moore says. "The more evil the villains, are the better it is. The more the audience roots for 007."

Though, Moore admits that, "Yeah, I'd like to play the villain. They are the best parts."

Max Zorin is the product of steroid injections given to pregnant women by the Nazis, who were trying to create super-intellects. The offspring, Zorin included, turned out psychotic.

Sting and David Bowie were among the actors originally approached to play Zorin before producers settled with Walken.

"I think for an actor it's probably an interesting thing to do," Bowie told *Rolling Stone*, "but for somebody from rock, it's more of a clown performance. And I didn't want to spend five months watching my double fall off mountains."

He's not the only rock star the producers courted. They've had Grace Jones in mind to play a Bond villainess for some time.

"Grace Jones was first suggested to us by Barbara Bach [*Spy Who Loved Me*]," says Glen. "Grace has such an electric personality."

"We always thought she'd be a colorful character," says Wilson, "To some extent, the part in this film was written with her in mind. We were thinking of her for *Octopussy* but couldn't quite arrange it because she was performing on the road. We managed to see some of *Conan II* and were very impressed with her."

Wilson, Broccoli's stepson, left the legal profession to join the Bond team as assistant producer on *The Spy Who Loved Me*. He was upped to executive producer of *Moonraker*, which did well financially but was critically assailed for its campy approach and an outlandish plot that launched 007 into outer space.

The stunts, though, are still as abundant and wild as ever.

"There's nothing wrong with stunts as long as they arise naturally out of the story and are not just injected artificially," says Glen.

"I don't think a really, well done, honest-to-goodness stunt is ever bad," Wilson says. "We only have two or three that are really, really breathtaking."

The rest, he implies, are merely exciting.

"It's one thing to think the stunts up and another to think how to do them. I won't write anything unless I've already figured out how it can be done safely and not be a cheat," Wilson says. "Sometimes we've had stunts rattling in the back of our minds that we never got around to doing because they weren't suitable to the plot. The Eiffel Tower stunt in this film is a good example. It was originally in an early *Moonraker* script."

Bond meets a contact on the Eiffel Tower. Before the man can talk, he's killed by an assassin who makes her escape by parachuting off the tower.

By those standards, things are much tamer on the Fisherman's Wharf set. Crew members rush around, setting up the background "atmosphere." One guy barks orders into a walkie-talkie, preparing the choreographed movements of cable cars, taxi cabs, fishing boats and, ironically, dozens of actors hired to play tourists. A crew member tosses bits of fish into the air to attract seagulls.

"Action!" Glen yells. Fishing boats chortle out of the harbor. Seagulls ride the wind. Tourists bustle on the sidewalk. A cable car bulging with passengers comes to a stop.

This is the raw excitement of movie-making, an establishing shot that says "this is San Francisco."

"Cut," Glen says, "that's great."

Maud Adams, the star of *Octopussy*, slinks through the crowd of onlookers unnoticed and slips onto the set. She's come to watch her boyfriend, Beverly Hills doctor Steven Zax, do a cameo in the next scene. She's followed by Maurice Binder, the designer of the Bond title sequences, who is in town to plot out the sales campaign with MGM/UA execs.

In this scene, Bond meets CIA agent Chuck Lee at Tarantino's fish market. No gunshots, no car chases, just simple exposition.

For David Yip, the actor playing Lee, "This is like a holiday. No one recognizes me here and the work is great fun."

In England, Yip is TV's famed "Chinese Detective," "a metropolitan, plainclothes detective, an off-beat 'Columbo'-type figure." But to American audiences, he's an unknown. Well, not completely.

"I'm the fellow who gets shot right at the start of *Indiana Jones*," Yip says. "It was nice, I was the first corpse."

After playing opposite cult heroes like Indiana Jones and James Bond, Yip jokes "I can only go downhill from here. Unless there's a part for me with Superman."

Yip says there's nothing stereotypically Chinese about his character in *A View to a Kill*. "What I like about Chuck Lee is that you could have played him," he says, "He could have been anyone, not necessarily Chinese. That's nice. It's a challenge and I'm grateful for it. I mean, they brought me, a British actor, all the way over to America to play an American."

"We originally thought since we were in the United States, we would use Felix Leiter," Wilson says. "But then we thought, since we would be in San Francisco, in Chinatown, it would be a good idea to use a Chinese/American agent."

Besides, this CIA agent won't be celebrating any more birthdays.

"My character survives for quite awhile in this," Yip says, "but after my four-minute bit in *Indiana Jones*, nothing seems short anymore."

When writing on *A View to a Kill* began, the producers were faced with the possibility that Roger Moore wouldn't return. The uncertainty about who would play Bond didn't hamper the start of the screenwriting process.

"In the treatment stage, Bond is just a character," Wilson says. "But when we get down to writing the scenes, we tailor it to Roger. He has a particular personality and the scenes have to be written accordingly."

Wilson says they haven't thought about the next Bond film yet and dismisses the possibility that they are searching for Moore's replacement.

"There's lots of speculation about that but we're shooting on Roger Moore right now, not anybody else," Wilson says. "I think Roger is a good Bond."

But is he the only Bond?

"I think we could make a picture with a new Bond," Wilson says. "But he looks good. I don't know if Roger is ready give up the role yet."

Neither is Moore.

"I always say this is going to be the final one," Moore says. "Why should I change my dialogue now?"

THE LIVING DAYLIGHTS
MICHAEL WILSON INTERVIEW

Sean Connery *is* James Bond.

That's what the advertisements for the 007 adventure *You Only Live Twice* proclaimed back in 1967. But the statement was wrong.

True, to many moviegoers Sean Connery is the one and only James Bond. But that James Bond is dead. When Roger Moore portrayed James Bond, James Bond *became* Roger Moore. Alas, now Moore's 007 is dead, too.

So forget Sean. Forget Roger. Now Timothy Dalton *is* James Bond. Whether you like it or not.

"When you cast a James Bond, you're casting a leading actor. They aren't character actors," says Michael Wilson, producer and co-writer of *The Living Daylights*. "What that means is, the actors to a certain extent are playing themselves."

George Lazenby wasn't a leading man, he wasn't even an actor. He was a male model and, hence, his characterization in *On Her Majesty's Secret Service* wasn't so much a reflection of himself, but a pale reflection of Connery as Bond.

When Roger Moore played James Bond, he says he was "encouraged to impersonate myself." His Bond was different than Connery's Bond simply because, "my personality is entirely different than his. I can't play the cold-blooded killer that Sean can do so well, which is why I play it for laughs."

When Wilson, who co-wrote and produced the last three 007 films, and veteran Bond screenwriter Richard Maibaum wrote *The Living Daylights* script, they didn't know who would be James Bond—all they knew was that Roger Moore *wouldn't* be.

"Roger realized it was time for a change," says Wilson, "time to get off the treadmill." The producers—namely Wilson's stepfather, executive producer Albert R. "Cubby" Broccoli—didn't argue with him. Suspending disbelief is one thing, but it was getting pretty hard for audiences to swallow a 57-year-old 007. Besides, Moore's price tag was getting pretty steep—reportedly over $3 million a picture.

At first, the producers toyed with a radical reaction against the aged, tongue-in-cheek 007 Moore has come to represent. Wilson and Maibaum crafted a story that would take Bond back to his origins, to his very first adventure as a spy.

"We thought as long as we were changing Bond, why not go for a younger man that we traditionally think of for the role? Maybe do it as a period piece?" he says.

The writers wrote a treatment, and even screen-tested some younger actors, people under 30 years old that Wilson prefers not to name. Actors who don't cost anywhere near $3 million.

"We had some very good things in it," says co-writer Richard Maibaum. "But Broccoli felt the audience doesn't pay to see James Bond as an amateur. Naturally, if you tell that story, you have to show him making mistakes and how he learned his trade. It cuts out to many of the things the audience enjoys watching Bond do."

"It just didn't work. There's something about James Bond that makes you believe he wasn't ever an apprentice," says Wilson. Part of Bond's charm is the fact he is an expert, an expert in just about everything.

So the writers shelved that treatment ("we still may want to use the story some day") and began a new one, which eventually evolved into *The Living Daylights*. They still didn't know who would be Bond, but knowing it wasn't Roger Moore gave them some freedom.

"I think with Roger, the films were more of a romp; it was fun action/adventure," says Wilson. Moore admittedly couldn't play tough guy convincingly, so the writers had to take that into account. Now they didn't. They could get tough.

The producers have paid lip service to "toughening" Bond before, most notably after the outer space silliness of *Moonraker*, ironically the biggest grossing of the 007 films. And while *For Your Eyes Only* did bring Bond down to earth, it was still *Roger Moore's* Bond.

The last Bond film, *A View to a Kill*, was a cartoon, a big-budget, critically panned extravaganza that epitomized the Moore tenure as 007. Because it wasn't well received, "we did feel as a reaction to that we would go this direction," says Wilson. And now, they weren't bound by Roger Moore's self-professed limitations.

"Roger brought a certain style to the films, his style, and you have to write scenes a certain way to fit that style," says Wilson.

The Living Daylights script was completed without an actor in mind, although "we did know that, depending on who we got and how the words fit in his mouth, some adjustments would have to be made," he says. "By that I mean, you are generally dealing with dialogue changes and the way the scene is played rather than adding or subtracting scenes."

The producers originally wanted Timothy Dalton, whom they had tested in 1971 for *Diamonds Are Forever* and then later for *For Your Eyes Only*, but he was tied up indefinitely on the London Stage with *The Taming of the Shrew* for its run and "it put him out of the running."

Scores of actors came in, and were screen-tested acting out scenes (under John Glen's direction) from *On Her Majesty's Secret Service* and *From Russia with Love*. The producers finally narrowed it down to Pierce Brosnan and "one other serious contender," whom Wilson won't name. United Artists, which finances the 007 films and distributes them worldwide, was rallying for Pierce Brosnan, a marketable name thanks to his years as "Remington Steele" on NBC.

"We thought well, for someone who is available, he is okay. We could have a James Bond with Pierce Brosnan," says Wilson. "We did want him. We would have hired him at that point."

But NBC changed its mind about canceling "Remington Steele," and MTM Enterprises, which makes the show, held Brosnan to a contractual obligation to return.

MTM offered to delay production so Brosnan could be James Bond before returning to "Remington Steele." Naturally, it was in MTM's favor to do so. The publicity surrounding the Bond film, and the inevitable hoopla that would swirl around Brosnan as the new 007, could only stoke the popularity of "Remington

Steele." In the end, it was that possibility that nixed the deal. The 007 producers couldn't live with Brosnan juggling two major roles. "We didn't see how he could be two heroes in the audience's mind," Wilson says.

More importantly, they didn't want to see their big screen Bond as a small screen hero every week. If Brosnan could be seen roughly as "James Bond" every week, for *free*, on television, it could seriously undercut the popularity and box office viability of future 007 films.

"When this happened with Pierce, we stopped dead," says Wilson. Luckily, *The Taming of the Shrew* closed and Dalton was now available. That was that. Brosnan was out; Dalton was in.

And, as the producers expected, adjustments had to be made in the script. Dalton wanted his characterization to capture the flavor of Ian Fleming's literary Bond and be more of a human being than a suave superhero. For one thing, he did something few actors would ever do—he asked for his lines to be cut down.

"He said don't worry about giving me a lot of dialogue, I'd rather play it quietly," Wilson says. "He believes there's more menace and strength in a man of few words, a man of action. And for him, it works."

"If you remember in *Dr. No*, there was a scene where a tarantula crawled up Bond's arm. We saw him sweating and agonizing and, when it got to the pillow, he smashed it with a shoe. Then he ran in the bathroom and threw up." Wilson says. "Now, that scene works for some actors and for some it doesn't."

It wouldn't for Roger Moore. It does for Timothy Dalton. "I think that sort of human vulnerability has been a part of Bond, but with Roger's style it was less prominent. Roger was a fine Bond, he took us in a different direction than Sean or this fellow will. He created a very successful characterization."

Dalton knows he's inheriting a "Roger Moore audience" and is worried they may not accept his harder approach. Wilson isn't concerned. "I think people are naturally resistant to change. Certainly, the people that love Roger will need a period of adjustment," he says. "I think the people who hate Roger Moore, and there are such people, will need a bit of time to get used to it too. By the end of the film, they'll be completely sold on Timothy Dalton."

Dalton gives the movies a "new lease on life," according to Richard Maibaum, and Wilson agrees. "Absolutely. I think this takes us in a whole new direction."

In many ways. Virtually the entire cast has been changed (though Desmond Llewelyn is still Q, and Walter Gotel is still a KGB chief), and a new continuing character has been added—John Rhys Davis as the head of the KGB. And over a dozen children of veteran behind-the-scenes personnel—for instance, Broccoli's children, now producers, Michael Wilson and Barbara Broccoli—are taking on more responsibility with each film.

"We do have what you might say is an apprenticeship style of working," Wilson says. "Based on the people who have tried to imitate us, it doesn't seem to me we are missing anything by not going 'outside.' We will go outside when we feel we need to. I don't think changing for changing's sake is good."

Nor does Wilson entertain any serious notions of doing other film work. Why bother? "We seem to have the tiger by the tail with Bond." Besides, there just isn't time.

"We have an audience, and an expectation that every two years we will provide a film," Wilson says. "By the time we get one out, we start worrying about the next one. And before you know it, two years go by."

Disguised as an Afghan freedom fighter, James Bond 007 (Timothy Dalton) guards a military transport plane in *The Living Daylights*.

THE LIVING DAYLIGHTS
TIMOTHY DALTON INTERVIEW

The new secret agent is frightened, and he has good reason to be. He nervously lights yet another Benson and Hedges special filter and eyes his dozen adversaries warily.

Their weapons are poised to fire, and his future is on the line.

"Are you ready for the third-degree," asks one of the steely eyed interrogators, pointing his pen at him. And Timothy Dalton nods, taking a deep drag on his cigarette. "As ready as I'll ever be."

Thus begins, on the morning after the gala Royal Premiere of *The Living Daylights* in London, what promises to be months of grueling interviews with the world press. Dalton faces this daunting task in the same way any secret agent would—reveal as little as possible, and stick to the prepared speech.

Granted, Dalton isn't exactly trapped alone in some grimy cell in some evil villain's clutches—he's luxuriously ensconced in the plush Dorcester Hotel and protected by a cadre of smiling publicists. But the stakes are still life or death, in the service of Her Majesty.

At risk is Dalton's career, and the fate of a $1 billion industry so important to Britain, that Prince Charles and Princess Diana visited the set and hosted the premiere.

Dalton has accepted the coveted License to Kill, and as the new James Bond, he can't just play the role, he has to make it his own. If he succeeds, the 25-year-old series survives to make more millions for the movie-makers and the Royal coiffers—and he will become an international star able to command a stellar salary and major roles.

If Dalton fails, he may suffer the fate of George Lazenby, who was fired after his single stint as James Bond in *On Her Majesty's Secret Service* and has languished in obscurity playing limp 007 clones ever since.

Dalton is well aware of the precarious position he's in. "If I cock this up, it's going to put a full stop to my career for a year or two."

Which is why he is reluctantly facing the press. He doesn't like doing it, especially when they start asking questions about his personal life, but it has to be done. The people have to know the movie is there, and that it's good.

The big question, and the one he has best-armed himself to answer, is whether he can overcome the memories of Sean Connery and Roger Moore and, more importantly, whether he can bring something new to the role.

When Roger Moore became 007, he overcame the unwelcome comparisons to Sean Connery by completely reshaping the role to fit his own light-hearted personality.

And Dalton has a similar problem: he can't play the wise-cracking playboy Moore created. "I knew there was only one approach I could take."

Dalton knows he is inheriting an audience that thinks Roger Moore and James Bond are one and the same. Rather than tackle the issue head-on, Dalton has wisely chosen to side-step it completely by embracing a higher authority—Ian Fleming, author of the James Bond novels.

"The only way I can work as an actor is to find out what the man is I've got to play, in this instance its right there in the Ian Fleming books," says Dalton, in what has become his tireless refrain to reporters. His Bond is Fleming's Bond. It's almost as if he's invoking Ian Fleming's name to justify his hard, realistic portrayal to Moore audiences, as if to say "It was Moore who was doing it wrong, not me."

While Roger Moore says he was "encouraged to impersonate myself," Dalton says he tried to "capture the original essence and spirit of those books that were the springboard of this series. I don't think it's right to just make an abstraction, to just say 'how would I play Bond?' That, to me, is not the correct approach. The last thing I would ever aim to do would be to impersonate myself."

Actually, the Bond producers feel he must if he is to make the role truly his own. And, he probably has. But rather than have *his* Bond compete with *Moore's* Bond, he is letting *Fleming's* Bond take the heat. After all, Fleming is a far stronger, and better-known, personality to take on Moore than Dalton himself.

The James Bond character Dalton found in his pre-production crash course in Fleming literature is "a very real human being, not a superman at all. Fleming was always writing about how anxiety-ridden Bond was, how his guts were wrenching in fear, how frightened he was, how he'd take pills or drinks to get him through it. There's no doubt that Bond has tenacity and resolution, but he's an ordinary man beset with moral confusions. Bond often thought he had a very dirty, very nasty job."

Dalton takes the role seriously, something Roger Moore openly admitted he didn't. "That's the only way I could do it, because that's the way I think all work should taken," says Dalton. That's good news to fans of Connery's Bond, but Dalton is careful not to invite comparisons between himself and Connery, nor is he foolhardy enough to criticize Moore and risk the ire of his fans.

"I wouldn't say anything against Roger Moore whatsoever because, God knows, he made the movies a terrific success," says Dalton, on the verge of a shrewd discourse that once again downplays Moore's portrayal and dubs his own as more authentic. "Those films developed, they became rather fantastical films didn't they? They became very gimmicky films, they became very lighthearted films. Whether that was the writers moving towards Moore or Moore moving to the writers or just a good creative blending of the two, I don't know. But I don't think that was Fleming."

And guess what is? He would have us believe that *The Living Daylights* is pure Fleming, and that Timothy Dalton isn't a new James Bond, he's the *old* James Bond.

It's a pretty nifty strategy, and best of all, it works. Just when it seemed like the Bond series had finally become tired, *The Living Daylights* takes the character back to its roots, back to the wild espionage stories and back to the ruthless spy who takes his job very seriously.

While Dalton makes it seem as though he single-handedly turned Bond around, he does, under questioning, admit "the script was pretty well there. But you have to realize the script is a blueprint. There is a story there that has all the potential to be a very good film, but during the course of working there are some creative alterations."

The "creative alteration" of dialogue was where Dalton was allowed to reshape Bond so the character fit him—Timothy Dalton, not Ian Fleming. The biggest alteration was the cutting of as much dialogue as possible. "Film is a visual medium, if you can cut away anything that's unnecessary or superfluous, make your point more economically, so much the better. I mean we cut quite a lot, yes."

And the first thing to go were the jokes. "I cut most of those flippant lines. They had to go. I think there's real good humor in the movie, but it's not humor in the flip sense, it comes from the situation and from the believability of it. I think what we did was right, but there are still some terrific one liners, aren't there? Some big laughs."

Dalton's Bond may have cut back on his jokes but he regained his penchant for smoking—a vice abandoned late in the Connery era. It's not so much a return to Fleming's character but a reflection of Dalton's own pack-a-day habit.

But Bond's near-monogamy in *The Living Daylights* is neither a reflection of Fleming's character nor Dalton's morals, nor is it a statement about AIDS. "It's absolute baloney. James Bond is not defending the realm against AIDS," says Dalton. "It's nonsense. Bond can't get involved with women on a mission. It's too dangerous. He can't afford it. He has to be quite ruthless."

The Living Daylights is the culmination of a 15-year courtship between Dalton and the series producers, who first made a pass at him in 1971 when Connery finally left the series. Dalton had already won critical acclaim on the London stage in various plays and on the screen in *The Lion in Winter*, but he wasn't interested in having a License to Kill.

"You couldn't beat Connery, it would have been pretty damn stupid to try. I had a very good career going in movies as a young man, having done *Cromwell*, *Wuthering Heights* and *Mary, Queen of Scots* and trying to take over from Sean would have been stupid," he says. "But, a more objective and practical reason is, I was twenty-four or twenty-five years old and Bond can't be that young."

He went on to do such films as *Sextette*, *Agatha*, and *Flash Gordon* as well as various television and London stage work before he was, once again, wooed by the Bond folks for *For Your Eyes Only* when Roger Moore was making noises about quitting. But Moore didn't, and Dalton went on to star in the movie *Doctor and the Devils* and the mini-series *Jane Eyre* among other things.

After *A View to a Kill*, both Moore and the producers decided it was time for Moore to quit. Suspending disbelief is one thing, but it was getting pretty hard for audiences to swallow a 57-year-old 007. And it was getting even harder for the producers to swallow his salary demands, which were now in the $3 million range.

The producers popped the question to Dalton, who had to turn them down once again—he was tied up doing Shakespeare on the London stage. Pierce Brosnan, NBC's "Remington Steele," was eventually signed, but when he couldn't wiggle out of his TV contract, he was dropped.

"Then someone had the bright idea of asking if I was out of my play now. So they called up and I said, yes we are coming off next week, but I've just signed up to go to America and do *Brenda Starr*," says Dalton. "But, since I was only on that for four or five weeks they said fine, we can deal with that. They started shooting. When *Brenda Starr* finished, I left America on a Saturday, got to London on a Sunday, and started work on Bond on a Monday."

Although Dalton doesn't command a salary in the Connery or Moore range just yet, he does admit "I'm getting very handsomely paid but when you've been very fortunate to start in a film like *Lion in Winter* and to work in movies on and off for twenty years, you get very well paid. My salary in this represents an increase, a most significant increase, but I think that reflects the nature of my responsibility in this project and of course if its a very long schedule and that does add up. But, as a professional, I have a professional price."

He has two very basic criteria for choosing his projects, and he used that same criteria in weighing whether or not to play Bond—and accept all the responsibility (and press) that comes with it.

"There's my artistic criteria, which is do you like the story, is there something about it that appeals to you? Then there's the purely pragmatic one, do I need to earn some money? Life is always a blending of the two."

Like *Brenda Starr*, with Brooke Shields. In that, he gets to play "a man who has one eye and lives in the depths of the Amazon jungle, where he drinks the juice of black orchids to avoid going insane. I mean, certainly there's a curiosity to that. I've also always enjoyed working in America very much and here was another nice opportunity to work there."

One of the reasons he finally decided to do Bond was that the benefits outweighed both the risks and the downsides. "Anybody has qualms about any job they do. You've got to look at things objectively and rationally. What you have to believe is that you can overcome the problems."

"I had never done anything like it before. It was the first modern contemporary action role I'd ever done," he continues. "There is also the challenge of pulling off a major international picture, one of the few that offers a leading part of a British actor.

"I was very conscious of the problems of taking it on. There is a weight of responsibility. But if it's a success, it will increase my commercial viability. I think it should help my career. Films are a business, it's a commercial business and it's a ruthless business. If you are a successful, you get offered more roles. Already a lot more scripts have come through my door. If it increases choice, or if it increases my ability to get films that would normally not get made without some kind of backing, then that's terrific."

But whether Dalton, who is signed for four 007 adventures, will get to enjoy that "star" status is still yet to be seen. So he's grudgingly traveling around the world, talking to reporters, fending off questions about himself, and eschewing his party line.

As his publicists pull him away to yet another pack of quote-hungry reporters, Dalton snubs out his cigarette and lets a little pride sneak out.

"I hope the audiences get a cracking good piece of entertainment, a movie that I feel is a lot more believable, a lot more watchable, a lot more interesting, and a lot more realistic."

Take that, Roger.

LEE GOLDBERG, RANDY LOFFICIER, JEAN-MARC LOFFICIER, WILLIAM RABKIN

LICENSE TO KILL
INTERVIEW WITH MICHAEL WILSON

Few things age as badly as movie heroes. They are products of an era, and when that time is gone, they become dated, or worse, caricatures of what they once were. The cutting edge never stays sharp, and what was unique becomes ordinary.

Agent 007 is different—to a degree.

James Bond was born during the chilliest days of the Cold War and has weathered two af the most turbulent decades in American social and political history, countless imitators, several different stars, and the likes of Luke Skywalker, Rambo and Indiana Jones.

For 25 years, the producers of the 007 series have been performing a delicate balancing act, keeping James Bond both new and unchanged at the same time. For the most part, they've succeeded. But they have occasionally fallen by being too trendy too late, as with their embarrassing foray into blacksploitation (*Live and Let Die*), and by relying too much on formulaic elements (*A View to a Kill*). So far, those haven't been fatal mistakes. But the balancing act doesn't get any easier, only more perilous.

"You can't disappoint the audience, but you can't give them what they expect," explains Michael Wilson, co-writer (with Richard Maibaum) and producer of *License to Kill*.

Wilson concedes that he, and longtime 007 producer Albert R. Broccoli are "running scared," attempting to maintain the formula while also "being slightly ahead of our time." But how long can James Bond remain a cultural icon, and a money-making machine, and not become an anachronism? Wilson admits they "worry about it all the time."

Far one thing, they must keep a close eye on the international scene. In the post-Cold War thaw of Watergate, feminism, glasnost and AIDS, they must pick their villains and their stereotypes carefully.

"We have to be aware of the world situation and what people will accept as a 'loosely based on reality' sort of plot," Wilson says. The Red Threat just won't wash today, not with Gorby-mania in the headlines. "I guess people are more hopeful today than ever before and don't want someone undermining that hope." Today, the average moviegoer is less afraid of what Mikhail Gorbachev will do, than they are of the powerful drug lords working out of South America. And that, with a touch of "Miami Vice" for good measure, is where *License to Kill* finds its menace and its perspective going into the nineties.

This time, Bond's adversary is Franz Sanchez (Robert Davi), a powerful drug lord in a fictional South American country. "Actually, drug lords are very political. There are countries where legitimate institutions of democracy are undermined by the huge wealth and power of drug lords."

Americans don't have to look much further than General Noriega for the reality upon which this particular Bond opus, Timothy Dalton's second as 007, is based. The changing face of Bond, from Sean Connery to George Lazenby to Roger Moore to Dalton, has actually been a mixed blessing. With each actor comes the opportunity to tell the Bond stories in a different way, freshening the series while keeping it the same until, as with Moore, the freshness becomes stale.

That fact is born out financially as well as artistically. *The Living Daylights* outperformed the last Roger Moore, *A View to a Kill*, both domestically and internationally. Exit polls showed diehard Bond fans were "extremely satisfied" with Dalton, and that women, especially young women, found Dalton more appealing than Moore.

And *The Living Daylights* scored high marks with critics, who applauded the more serious tone and the realism that Dalton brought to the role, a fact not lost on the producers.

"Timothy gives us a different direction to go in," says Wilson. "I think the films with Roger emphasized his talents. For Timothy, a gritty, more reality-based piece is the way to go. Giving him one-liners won't play to his strong suit. He plays it fairly straight."

Dalton gives producers the chance to show a darker, more violent side to Bond who, in this film, "is thrown out of the service, and he has lost the objectivity he normally has, and that makes for a rather impassioned, exciting film."

And violent. Bond is best man at the wedding of his old friend, CIA Agent Felix Leiter (David Hedison). Hours later, Leiter is maimed, and his wife murdered, and Bond goes rogue, seeking vengeance. Bloody vengeance. The producers had to trim some of the more gruesome scenes from the final cut in order to maintain the series' standard "PG" rating, even in a day when most adventure hits are in solid "R" territory.

"This film's thrust is that Bond loses his professional objectivity because of his vendetta," Wilson says. "In a sense, it's the awakening in him of the realization that when he loses his objectivity, he begins to make things worse for himself."

Bond also lost a wife (*On Her Majesty's Secret Service*) and went looking for vengeance (*Diamonds Are Forever*), but those events aren't touched on in this film, which obviously tackles similar themes. "There is a reference, but very indirect, to Bond being married before, and it's sort of bittersweet," says Wilson. "We never really saw Bond go for revenge before. It wasn't a very developed idea in those films."

Although grittiness doesn't lend itself to the series' more cartoonish elements, the producers have compensated by emphasizing the stunts, some left over from other movies. "I have stunts

I haven't even unpacked yet," Wilson jokes. "The truck chase in this film is something [director] John Glen has wanted to do for years.

"We find our stunts where we can. Normally, we think the stunts up in house or go with a person we've worked with before. For instance, the stunt with Bond and the seaplane was done by Sparky Green, the fellow who directed our air unit in the last film. He gave me this stunt and it blended perfectly with the narrative, which was fortunate. Otherwise it would have gone on the back shelf."

The balancing act that keeps Bond alive depends, to a large degree, on the continuity behind-the-scenes. Albert R. Broccoli has been producing the films from the start, and Richard Maibaum has written (or rewritten) almost all of them. Wilson has been working, in one capacity or another, on the films since *The Spy Who Loved Me*. John Glen, now directing his fifth 007 film, served as an editor and shot second unit footage on many of the early Bonds. And so it goes, all the way down to the publicists.

This time, though, the Writers Guild strike drove a wedge between Wilson and Richard Maibaum during the film's writing. They worked together on the outline, which was turned in just before the strike. Wilson wrote the script alone, while Maibaum walked the picket line, although Maibaum shared the script credit. "I said to Dick that we've worked a long time together over the years, and I didn't feel I wanted to go through an arbitration, I told him I would be happy to share credit, and he said wonderful," Wilson says. "He was put in a difficult spot, and I wasn't prepared to make it more difficult." (Wilson maintains he did not violate any WGA rules by working during the strike. The WGA, through a spokesman, had no comment.)

The producers have bowed to the old Bond films by eschewing a pop band in favor of a "power ballad," in the tradition of

Shirley Bassey's *Goldfinger* and Tom Jones' *Thunderball* themes, by Gladys Knight. "We had gone with Duran Duran, which paid off handsomely, but A-Ha was a disappointment. We thought that we'd be better this time to go with a power ballad, a ballad with guts in it."

And the producers have also stuck with Desmond Llewelyn as Q, the only series regular not yet replaced. They turned to David Hedison to reprise his *Live and Let Die* role as Felix Leiter rather than rehire John Terry, the fresh face they used in *The Living Daylights*.

Ever since Jack Lord played Leiter in *Dr. No*, the producers have been looking for someone to replace him with no luck. "We've never found someone who was that solid a performer. This time, we were looking for someone whom we've seen as Felix, and whom the audience might have some association with. David Hedison fit the bill."

Wilson won't say whether Q will be back next time, though "people love him so much, we would like him to stay on." (Lois Maxwell had to be replaced as Miss Moneypenny because "it would have meant a change in the playing of the character, and we wanted to keep that relationship intact.") It's certain Timothy Dalton will play Bond again, but Wilson feels it's "not appropriate to discuss his contractual situation" beyond that, although there are no more Ian Fleming books or stories to plunder, there are several new 007 bestsellers written by John Gardner, though "we haven't seen anything in those books that are useful for films," Wilson says. Nevertheless, the books are "encumbered by us. No one can option those books to anyone but us for perpetuity."

That's optimism. *Diamonds Are Forever*, but is James Bond?

The character's immortality is assured, but the future of the most successful series in film history still rides on a movie ticket—and time.

LADYHAWKE (1985)

Ladyhawke had all the ingredients of a blockbuster—just a few years too late and a couple years too early.

Michelle Pfeiffer was several years away from super stardom, while the popularity of both Matthew Broderick (*Wargames*) and Rutger Hauer (*Blade Runner*) was beginning a slide that would continue into the nineties. And director Richard Donner, whose last hit was *Superman*, was still two years away from his *Lethal Weapon* resurgence.

Ladyhawke was an admirable attempt to straddle several genres—fantasy, romance, adventure and action—creating a schizophrenic movie that was not only hard to market, but even harder for audiences to peg. The confusion was exacerbated by Broderick's "urban" comic performance and an electronic score by Andrew Powell.

What makes the movie a milestone, however, is that it marks the first teaming, personally and professionally, of producer Lauren Schuler and Richard Donner, a marriage (literally) that would lead to such films as *Maverick, Scrooged, Radio Flyer* and *Free Willy*.

INTERVIEW WITH RICHARD DONNER

Etienne Navarre is a dashing knight and Isabeau of Anjou is his breathtakingly beautiful lover—and boy, do they have problems. She's cursed to be a hawk by day and he a wolf by night. The only time they ever see each other is during that split second of transformation at sunrise and at sunset.

It's putting a real strain on their relationship. It is also the kind of bizarre situation legends are made of—and movies. Director Richard Donner (*Superman*), ably assisted by Rutger Hauer (*Blade Runner*) and Michelle Pfeiffer (*Scarface*), has turned that "high concept" into *Ladyhawke*, a medieval fantasy he has championed through three years of rewriting, false starts, and casting snags.

In December, Donner was simultaneously supervising the final editing of *Ladyhawke* and hurriedly directing *The Goonies*, a secrecy-shrouded, children's adventure tale conceived by Steven Spielberg and written by Chris Columbus (*Gremlins*) and targeted for a May premiere.

"I'm utterly exhausted," Donner groans, clad in faded jeans, battered Nikes, and an American High sweatshirt. His office, Steven Spielberg's old digs at the Burbank Studios, is cluttered with kid stuff—toy race cars, a pinball machine, a Pluto clock, airplanes, balls, Superman dolls, and candy.

"I have never been so tired in my life," Donner combs his fingers hands through his greying hair, "but boy, I'm a happy son of a bitch."

While shooting *Ladyhawke*, he fell in love with the producer, Lauren Shuler (*Mr. Mom*), who "discovered" the *Ladyhawke* project and, Donner says, "didn't let up on me about the film, she persevered. And, six months into the making of *Ladyhawke*, instead of fighting with my producer I fell in love with her."

Over three years ago, Shuler and the Ladd Company sent Donner three scripts—two comedies and *Ladyhawke*, written by first-time Edward Khmara (who has since written *Enemy Mine*). Sean Connery and Dustin Hoffman were interested in the project, but progress had slowed. It needed work. And it needed a catalyst—a strong director to take it over.

"I didn't think it was a very good script but it was a good idea. There was a passage in it, when the monk explains the story of the cursed lovers. I started crying because it was the most beautiful story of unrequited love," Donner recalls. "So I got excited about it, called Laddy and I said yes, I'll do it, but it needs a major rewrite first."

The problem with the original script was that Donner didn't *believe* it. As a director, he can't do a film unless he can convince himself that, no matter how improbable the concept, that the story is *true*.

"The original script had lots of monsters in it. If you can believe your story, you can make your audience believe it. I didn't believe the story with all the monsters and things. I believed the impossible love angle. I mean the curse itself crosses the line of believability," Donner says. "I felt if you were really go to be moved by the story and caught up in it, you had to believe in it. Seeing the monsters and the horrible things that lived below the earth and everything, it crossed the line, it broke the word verisimilitude, which is a word I love. It means something that has the appearance of being true or real. *Superman* was made on the word verisimilitude and *Goonies* is being made on the word verisimilitude."

Donner hired David Peoples (*Blade Runner*) and Michael Thomas (*The Hunger*) to recraft Khmara's story, which chronicled the efforts of the lovers, teamed with a con-man, to punish the evil bishop who cast the curse upon them and, somehow, break it.

The Peoples/Thomas script was "a smashing job, a very good job," but not good enough. Peoples dropped out and Thomas crafted another version. Donner was still dissatisfied and coaxed

Tom Mankiewicz (*Diamonds Are Forever*), whom he had worked with polishing the scripts for *Superman* and *Superman II*, to take a shot at *Ladyhawke*.

"Tom is a dear friend and he snapped some of the story back where we got carried away. We had been too close to it. He also gave us the humor and enhanced the loving part of the relationship between Navarre and Isabeau," Donner says. "Then the Ladd Company decided not to make it. They were going through some bad problems at the time."

So Donner set the project aside and tackled *The Toy*, a comedy which starred Richard Pryor and Jackie Gleason, an experience "I did not enjoy," he says, "but I learned a valuable lesson: never give up final cut. The picture you see is not the picture I made. But, I'm glad it made money and everybody is happy."

The Toy behind him, he dusted off *Ladyhawke*.

"Laddy is a dear friend and he let the project fall back into our hands," Donner says. "We started working with Tom again and realized we had a good thing going. The script was falling into shape beautifully and we decided to shoot it in Italy."

The film they were going to shoot hardly resembled the screenplay Schuler had enticed him with several years before.

"It was totally different. I feel sorry for Ed Khmara. I think he's a good writer and he obviously came up with a wonderful idea. It's too bad somebody didn't go out and make his movie. But, if I was going to make a movie, that wasn't what I wanted to make," he says. "I'm sure he's not happy, I haven't heard from him, but I don't think he likes it. He's a good writer, he's going to be a major talent and I wish him a lot of luck. But, just the fact that we brought in other people to rewrite his material has got to hurt him."

Donner and Shuler, armed with a usable screenplay, began scouting for actors.

"Before I got involved Sean Connery and Dustin Hoffman were going to do this together. Sean would have been Navarre and Dustin wanted to play Phillipe, the conman. They would have been wonderful but there was no way I could get the two of them," Donner says. "It would have changed the budget profile tremendously. It's a small budget, but God, when you say $15 million is *small*, it kind of gets you sick to your stomach. Anyway, Connery was going to do that Bond thing [which Donner had declined because he didn't want to do a "big, major action piece"] and Dustin I couldn't get an answer from."

Hoffman had a hard time making up his mind whether he wanted to do the film or not and finally, "we were right down to the wire with him, talking day and night for weeks, when I finally just gave up," Donner says. "But, it ended up for the best. We cast Matthew Broderick (*Wargames*). I'm thrilled because I don't think anyone could have played it as well as Matthew.

"My sister was the first one to mention him to me," he continues." She said 'God, he's wonderful but too young.' Then I went to see him in New York in *Brighton Beach Memoirs*. He just destroyed me. I said he's going to change the whole story but it will make it so much richer, cleaner, fresher.

"He brought a very fresh, naive approach to it whereas Dustin would have played it probably a few steps back. He still would have been a hustler and street urchin but he would have been a man, his life would have been exposed to him already. With Matthew, he's very naive and it's very refreshing."

Rutger Hauer seemed to Donner a natural choice for the role of Navarre. "Think," Donner says, "how many actors are there around who could play that romantic macho ballsy hero riding a grey horse and carrying a sword—and make it believable?" Michelle Pfeiffer won the Isabeau part with some inspired cleverness during the screen test.

Michelle Pfeiffer and her lover-turned-wolf in *Ladyhawke*.

"I saw some film on Michelle, *Grease 2* or something. I thought she was very pretty and did a fairly good job. I don't think anybody gave her much support in doing that particular part. And so, I was back in Europe and we had a wonderful casting lady here and whenever she had anybody interesting she would tape them, not a reading, though. Talking. Interviewing. Rapping," Donner says. "To me, I can learn more about an actress or actor from just talking with them than having them doing a scene. So the casting lady sent a tape over and Michelle had prepared a little scene. And at the very end of this Michelle said 'By the way, this is my impression of *Ladyhawke*' and she had this little parakeet that she had brought in and they cut to a close-up of the bird," he continues. "She had us on the floor in hysterics. She had prepared; she did something interesting; she was energetic. So, we said terrific let's go with her. She's a wonderful little actress and breathtakingly beautiful. She has an unbelievable career ahead of her. She's a real Carol Lombard type."

Now that *Ladyhawke* is behind him, he's worried about how it will fare against the other new year releases. It's got a built-in failing, a weakness that doomed *Buckaroo Banzai* to a swift demise—it is a difficult film to classify and, therefore, a difficult film to create an advertising campaign for.

"Selling the picture is the biggest problem we're having," he says. "I don't know how to sell it, I really don't. It isn't sword and sorcery. It isn't comedy. It's a medieval, action adventure love story with humor. It encompasses so many things."

It's also predictable, from the opening frame to the closing titles. And Donner knows it.

"I always make predictable movies. I think a love is unpredictable if they die at the end and they don't get together and the hell with it, I don't want to make a movie like that," he says. "I like predictable movies. *Superman* is predictable. *Inside Moves* is predictable. *The Toy* is predictable. This is predictable. I get a tremendous charge out of the happiness at the end of a picture. For me, happiness at the end of picture is terribly predictable and I love it. I like to walk out of a movie being up and elated and a happy son of a bitch. I can't stand going to a movie and coming out depressed and annoyed and saying the picture didn't really have an ending or why did they have to kill them. I couldn't handle a movie like *Testament* where you come out of it and cry for two days."

Even *The Omen*, his first big-screen hit, had a happy ending.

"Sure, it had an up ending. There's that little funny face staring into the camera giving you a big smile. It's scary but it was up, it was up," he says. "That picture, when I first read it, had cloven-hoofed people and devil gods and I said oh fuck, let's treat this like it's real. Take somebody and all this terrible coincidence happens to them and it drives him insane and end on a note, where everybody dies and the little kid turns and looks into the camera.

"I love that little boy, he was the funniest little guy and he'd never acted before. So I did a second take and just before he turned I said look severe, look angry and DON'T YOU LAUGH," Donner continues." And he kept fighting the laugh and we ended up with this wonderful smile. I said that's it! And everybody said don't do that, you'll ruin the movie. He's laughing *at* the movie, they said. I said just try it. Everybody fought me. I felt what I thought he was saying was 'Is this all true? Has this been a big put on? Am I the Devil?' The first screening when he turned, they all gasped, because he was alive. And then he smiled, and they started screaming and cheering. It was perfect for me."

It must have been perfect for a lot of other people, too. *The Omen* was an enormous hit and led to him being hired for *Superman*. Both those films have inspired sequels, something Donner has mixed feelings about.

"If the sequels mean they like my work enough to copy it, I'm thrilled. I've never seen a good sequel to my films, but maybe that's ego. The only thing I saw good in any sequel was in *Superman II*, and that was the two-thirds of it that I did and not the bomb that Richard Lester made out of it, as far as I'm concerned," Donner says. "We made one and two at the same time. We did all the Hackman stuff. I would love to have finished it. *The Omens*, my partner made them, I wish had been made differently. But at that point, *The Omen* had turned my career around and I didn't want to go back and do another *Omen*."

And what about the possibility of a *Ladyhawke* sequel?

"If they wanted to make a sequel to *Ladyhawke*, I would probably want to executive produce it and find some super young director or something and bring something fresh to it. I dont think I could bring anything fresh to it and I don't think it would be a smart thing to do. Also for me, every picture is such an individual challenge because it becomes a part of your psyche and your personality and you run with it and start to put things in it that are you. Once its done, it's done. It's born. It's gone to college."

Donner got his movie-making education in television, working on shows like "Gilligan's Island."

"I reshot the pilot for them," Donner says without a hint of reticence. He also admits, minus the slightest trace of embarrassment, to directing many of the subsequent episodes.

"I'm not embarrassed about anything I ever did in my life except a girl I knew in Detroit once," he laughs. "They were wonderful shows when I was doing them. Every once in awhile, if you really sit there, and once in awhile I'll get stoned and sit in front of my TV, and analyze 'Gilligan's Island,' there's some interesting stuff going on behind them. There was a lot of sociology snuck into those shows. It was very profound in a very silly, stupid way. The producer could have been a great propagandist during the war." He continued in TV, directing such diverse fare as "Kojak" and *Portrait of a Teenage Alcoholic*. "I was very happy, I was thrilled I was working in TV. I was selling pilots like crazy, doing movies of the weeks and specials. I was one happy son of a bitch. I was amazed I was doing them. When the opportunity came along to do movies, I was in the position to capitalize on it."

He was applying the finishing touches to *Ladyhawke* when Spielberg called up and "said he had this wonderful story and would I please, please read it?"

"Well, I went home and read it. I was laying in bed laughing and I thought it was so cute, so charming, it's going to be really easy, too. Just a coupla kids, I can knock this off, have a wonderful time doing it, and relax," he says. "What I thought would be a snap has turned out to be, including *Superman*, the most difficult film I've ever been involved with. At times I just want to go through the roof. I can't tell you much about the plot, only that it's about a bunch of wonderful kids in a small town. There are a lot of wonderful *physical* effects, not opticals.

"This is also the best-designed picture I have ever worked on," he adds. "I'm working with a genius, a designer named Michael Riva."

Donner discovered Riva's work in *The Adventures of Buckaroo Banzai*, a film the director says he "absolutely loves."

"I saw Riva's work in *Buckaroo Banzai* and I said I want that guy. God, I loved that film. It was great!" Donner says. "I think that 20th Century–Fox shit on it. It should have gone through the roof. It should be playing in every theater in the country. I saw it in Westwood and I thought it would be the biggest picture of the year, I mean the kids will line up for this. It's a classic. I just don't think it was sold properly, I don't think it was introduced to the world in the right way. I *still* love it.

"I laughed, cheered, jumped. At first, I didn't know what I was seeing. It took me a few minutes to get into the film. It wasn't until Lizardo sucked electricity and remembered the past that I got caught up. I said those fucks, they've really taken me down the road, WOW!" he continues. "I started to cheer. I felt like I was on acid. I was just having the best time. I just loved it. W.D.

Richter is a wonderful director and writer. And anybody who could have conceived that story and execute it deserves all kinds of credits and kudos."

Donner's production staff includes another acknowledged genius, a guy who's turning out to be a handy second unit director—Steven Spielberg. Although Spielberg's presence is keenly felt, the two directors aren't clashing on the set.

"I like Steven. Sometimes I want to kick him in the ass but we have the kind of relationship that allows that. He loves *Goonies*. It was his idea that he gave to Chris Columbus to write," Donner says. "He's a very involved producer so every once in awhile he'll come over and I'll see him talking to one of the kids and I'll grab him by the seat of his pants and tell him: 'Don't fuck with my cast.' We start to laugh and have a ball.

"It's not only a good relationship; it's a relationship I need because I've brought him in now to shoot second unit for me because I'm tired," he adds. "Things that I can't shoot, where I would have to shoot into the night to continue, he'll go off and knock it out for me. It's been one of the better relationships I've had with anybody. I hope it continues."

It will. Donner has agreed to direct an episode of *Amazing Stories*, Spielberg's new NBC anthology series, and there's a good chance *The Goonies* will be back.

"I think just the fact that the kids are alive and well and living on the planet earth at the end leaves it open for a sequel," Donner says. "I assume there will be sequels. God-willing, if the picture is a success. I'd like to see it for the kids. I'd like to see it for Steven, and I'd like to see it for myself."

LAUREN SHULER INTERVIEW

Love makes people do funny things.

Although Etienne of Navarre turns into a wolf at night and Isabeau of Anjou is a hawk by day, they travel together. Although they never can ever be human at the same time, love keeps them together.

And it's love that brought their story to the screen. *Ladyhawke* is the culmination of producer Lauren Shuler's five-year love affair with the concept. To see the film made the way she wanted it, Shuler had to go through three studios, four writers, and "millions" of endings.

And in the end, she got the movie she wanted.

Ironically, Shuler came across *Ladyhawke* by accident.

"In 1980, I was looking for a writer for a project I was developing," Shuler says. "One executive thought Ed Khmara was right for the job and gave me a copy of his *Ladyhawke* script as a writing sample."

It was love at first sight.

"As soon as I saw the script, I said, 'I want to make this movie,'" Shuler says.

Some people in Shuler's position would have shied away from a film that promised to be as logistically difficult as *Ladyhawke*. This was, after all, Shuler's first feature.

Shuler started as an assistant film editor, then became a camerawoman. She quickly rose to associate producer status on ABC's "Wide World of Entertainment."

"I really wanted to crossover into production," Shuler says. "I was laid up for a while after a major car accident, and thought this was a good time to start writing. It turned out I was only an okay writer, but a great collaborator."

Shuler worked for a while at Motown Productions, then left to produce the TV movie *Amateur Night at the Dixie Bar and Grill*.

And in 1980, Shuler found *Ladyhawke*.

"*Ladyhawke* was the first property I optioned," Shuler says. "As soon as I read it, I thought 'this is it.' I thought it was the most interesting, original idea I'd ever come across."

Not everyone agreed.

"In 1980 when I optioned the script, people weren't doing this kind of movie," Shuler says. "The only movie around at that time that had people with swords in it was *Excalibur*. The film was a failure, but it had a big audience-opening weekend. That proved to me that audiences wanted that kind of film. *Excalibur*'s failure had nothing to do with genres; it failed on its own merits.

"People kept telling me I was crazy, and I should work other projects. But I was in love with this movie, this was the movie I was going to make."

Or almost the movie she was going to make. Neither Shuler nor the Ladd Company executives she was dealing with was entirely happy with Ed Khmara's script.

"The core of the story was the same in Ed's draft," Shuler says, "but it was too diffused. There were too many things going on at the same time, and the romance, which was the most important part for me, tended to get lost.

"One problem with the original script was that there wasn't one strong villain. In the original draft, in addition to the bishop, who is the primary villain in the film, and the commander of the guards, there was a monster that lived under the dungeons. The bishop fed people he didn't like to the monster."

Shuler didn't like the monster. She fed it to the garbage can.

"Monsters are very difficult to portray in movies," Shuler says. "They're always scarier in your mind than on screen. I wouldn't have minded if we could have done the monster the way they did it in *Alien*—only show it in bits and pieces. But there was a scene in which Phillipe climbs on the monster's back to kill it, and there was no way we could get away without showing the whole thing. I was afraid it would look like a man in a rat suit, so we killed the scene."

Khmara's script not only had too many villains, it also had too many lovers.

"Phillipe had a girlfriend in the dungeons he wanted to go back and rescue. The second love story undercut the romance between Navarre and Isabeau."

When the time came to rewrite *Ladyhawke*, Shuler chose not to bring Khmara back. "It was probably a mistake not to bring Ed back," Shuler says. "He's an incredibly imaginative writer and I've stayed in touch with him all along. But at the time, the studio wanted to take the script in a different direction from Ed's, and they thought someone else should do the rewrite. I agreed. What can I say? We were all young back then. It's certainly no reflection on Ed's talent."

Shuler started looking for a new writer. Her first choice was David Peoples (*Blade Runner*). But he was quickly ruled out for reasons that had nothing to do with his talent.

"We were about to start on the rewrite in 1981. I went to David Peoples in Los Angeles and talked to him about working on the film. But just as we started talking, the Writers' Guild went out on strike and he couldn't work on the project."

With the writers on strike, there wasn't a successful writer in Hollywood who could work on the project. Shuler didn't want to wait for the strike to end. She went to England. There she found *Ladyhawke*'s second-to-last writer, Michael Thomas (*The Hunger*).

At first glance, Thomas might seem like a strange choice, considering *The Hunger*'s script was universally panned when the film came out. But, Shuler explains, that film had nothing to do with her choice.

"I hired Michael on the basis of his unproduced screenplay, *Fire on the Mountain*. I thought it was terrific," Shuler says.

In Thomas' *Ladyhawke* script, Shuler saw the film she wanted to make take form.

"Michael's script was much more romantic than Ed's. It was much more about Navarre's journey to defeat the bishop, and Phillipe becoming an unlikely hero." Michael Thomas made one very important change in the concept of the film.

"In Ed's script, the wolf and the hawk were more almost like people; when Navarre and Isabeau changed, they retained most of their human personality. I felt that the curse was much worse if the animals were animals in spirit as well as in form," Shuler says.

The script now had its proper form. But the style wasn't quite right. Shuler brought in one last writer.

"Tom Mankiewicz, who wrote *Superman*, really streamlined the film and pulled it all together. The script was good before, but he really brought it to life.

"What Mank did most of all is bring the film its humor. In Michael's draft, Phillipe was already like the Artful Dodger, but it was Mankiewicz who gave him all those great lines and really brought him to life," Shuler says.

About the time Shuler was looking for the *Ladyhawke*'s first rewriter, she was also looking for a director. She had only one man in mind.

"Richard Donner," Shuler says firmly. "I wanted a director who filled a lot of shoes, who could direct adventure and action, and yet who had a heart and a sense of humor at the same time. Based on *The Omen, Superman*, and *Inside Moves*, I felt he embodied all those characteristics."

Back when Michael Thomas was laboring on the script, Shuler and Donner started working on two other crucial elements of the film: casting and location-scouting. Although casting the actors for a film like *Ladyhawke* is crucial, casting the locations can be even more important. And more difficult.

"Richard and I spent months scouting locations, first in Czechoslovakia, then in Italy. There are a lot of locations in the film, and each one has to be convincingly thirteenth century. We decided to shoot the film in Italy because there were more suitable locations there."

Ladyhawke's script called for a very specific location. "For the city of Aquila we need a walled city with a castle cathedral on a mountain surrounded by a beautiful landscape and no hint of modern civilization," Shuler says.

Unfortunately, the *Ladyhawke* crew put in their order for such an unspoiled palace about two hundred years too late.

"If we found a city that came near our specifications, there was inevitably something wrong with it. Usually there were too many signs of civilization around. Maybe not twentieth century civilization, but maybe seventeenth or eighteenth century."

Shuler's answer was to use pieces of different cities for different parts of Aquila.

"The bishop's castle is actually three different locations: The tower of the castle is at Castle Arquato, the interior of the castle is at Torrechiara, and the interior of the city is at Soncino Castle," Shuler says. "For the interior of the cathedral, we built a set."

To convince the audience that these pieces of cities were all one, Shuler needed a long shot of Aquila. After a long and fruitless search, Shuler turned to special effects.

"I considered using a matte painting or a miniature for the long shot of Aquila," Shuler says. "We were at the stage when we were starting to consider just who should do the painting. We had someone design a miniature and he started to build it. But finally we found an actual location for the shot. It looks incredible, but it's real."

At the same time they were looking at castles, Shuler and Donner were looking at actors. For the lead roles of the knight Navarre and the thief Phillipe, they considered—and decided against—one of the most exciting and bankable combinations imaginable: Sean Connery and Dustin Hoffman.

"When I first optioned Ed's script, I heard rumors that Hoffman was interested. Further down the road, we very seriously considered him. But we felt he wasn't going to work out for the film. If we'd cast him, there would have been a long delay while we had to make changes in the script for him. I'd already waited three years to make this film, and I didn't want to wait any longer."

With Hoffman out of the running, Shuler decided to "go younger overall on the casting. I had always wanted Connery. We'd always needed someone foreboding, strong, and ruggedly good looking like him for Navarre. But we felt we needed someone younger. Don't get me wrong, he's certainly not too old to be James Bond, and I think he's terrific. But our film was going in a different direction."

The Dutch actor Rutger Hauer, whom Shuler had loved as the villainous replicant in *Blade Runner* fit Navarre perfectly. Now there were only two important roles to be filled: Navarre's lover Isabeau, and Phillipe. Isabeau was a breeze. Shuler got her first choice.

"I knew about Michelle Pfeiffer from *Grease 2*," Shuler says. "She seemed to fill all our requirements: she was breathtakingly beautiful, and at the same time she had spunk, strength, and a sense of humor. It was her sense of humor that won us over completely."

At first, Pfeiffer wasn't interested.

"When we first went to Michelle, she was involved in doing *Scarface* and wasn't interested in thinking about her next project," Shuler says. "We looked all around and didn't find anyone we liked as much. We went back to Michelle, and by this time she had finished *Scarface* and was wondering what to do next. She read the script and accepted."

There was only one bit of casting left: the lead. Although Richard Donner claims that Matthew Broderick (*Wargames*) was brought in just before shooting, Shuler had had the young actor in mind for a long time.

"Matthew Broderick was *not* a last minute choice for me," Shuler says. "But casting is the director's decision. Richard likes to make the best choice possible, and he delayed the final casting to make sure. I had hounded Richard a long time to cast Matthew before he finally did."

Broderick had the quality Shuler most wanted for Phillipe.

"Matthew can be both wise and innocent at the same time. And he's always intriguing to watch."

Although the part might open up a new range of roles to Broderick, there were probably times he would have preferred that Dustin Hoffman got the part.

"Poor Matthew," Shuler says. "He was always getting dumped in water or rained on. He was terrific about it, though. He always had lots of enthusiasm. He's a professional."

With the script, cast, and locations finally set, Shuler got the go-ahead to start shooting. And three years after the first option on the script Shuler loved, the *Ladyhawke* team started production.

At least, most of the *Ladyhawke* team. The Ladd Company, which had bankrolled much of the preproduction, was feeling the beginnings of its financial problems and had to drop out.

"I was disappointed at seeing the Ladd Company leave the project," Shuler says. "They were with us for years. I was disappointed for them, but I was more disappointed for us. I knew the project would be picked up by another studio—it was too good not to—but there's a scary moment before you can set it up again when you wonder if it will all fall apart."

Ladyhawke wasn't picked up by another studio. It was picked up by *two* studios.

"When the Ladd Company dropped out, we went over to Fox. They were immediately interested. Then Warners, who had first refusal rights to Ladd's films, said they wanted to read the script. After they read it, they said they wanted it. Fox suggested the two studios share the project."

As any producer will tell you, there are always problems when you work with one studio. Working with two studios could have doubled the problems.

"We were aware of the potential problems of working with two studios. It's always a little more difficult with yet another voice coming in. To make things easier, we asked the executives to select one studio for us to answer to. They decided on Warners."

Ladyhawke started shooting in Italy three years after Shuler fell in love with the script. It was, as Shuler says, a "tough shoot."

"We were scheduled for four months of shooting," Shuler says. "There was a lot to film. Of course, when you have a lot of action scenes, that slows things down. We were working with an Italian, so there was a lot of miscommunication. We had a large unit to move all around the country. Our cinematographer Vittorio Storaro (*Apocalypse Now*) is a slow lighter and a slow shooter. And then, of course, there were the animals."

Oh, yes. The animals.

Since Isabeau spends most of her time in the film in the form of a hawk, and Navarre spends a good deal of his screen time as a wolf, the animals played a very important part in the shooting.

"The animals were easier to work with than some stories I'd heard," Shuler says, "but there were problems. We used four Siberian wolves in all, and the wolves were difficult in that wolves are difficult. Wolves don't always do what you want them to do, and they don't always hit their mark. They tend to be nervous. If you want them to attack a man, they might do it, but they get distracted very easily. If they hear a noise at the wrong time, they get nervous and decide not to do it."

Matthew Broderick comes across a grisly sight in *Ladyhawke*.

One scene the wolves were decidedly opposed to was the one in which Phillipe rescues the wolf Navarre from drowning in ice water.

"Most of that was done on a soundstage in warm water. It would have been impossible to keep anyone in the real ice water as long as we needed. Still, the wolf objected to going in the water. We got him used to it as much as possible, and did it as fast as we could in short intervals. We had extra cameras on the scene to cut down the number of takes. But the wolf was definitely not happy about the whole thing."

The hawks were slightly easier to work with, if only because a hawk doesn't stand six feet tall on its hind legs.

"We didn't have any major problems with the hawks. They were pretty good overall, but they were noisy. Sometimes they'd destroy a shot by opening a wing into Rutger's face or flying off in the wrong direction. There was one time a hawk was supposed to take off and land on Rutger's arm. Instead, it landed on the boom mike."

The last of the animal stars was the black beauty playing Navarre's horse.

"It's a big beautiful animal like a circus horse. The woman who owns him rides him for show. He was trained for shows, not for movies. It was difficult enough simply because the horse was made nervous by all the activity. To add to the problems, the horse was trained to rise up, dance, or prance by the reins—if you pull the reins one way, he'll rise up; if you pull them another way, he'll prance. When Rutger, who is a very good horseman, pulled reins the way he's used to doing, the horse would start dancing around."

Not all the difficult moments of the shoot were the fault of the animals. The low point, Shuler says, was shooting the scene in which Phillipe escapes the bishop's dungeons by swimming through the castle's sewers.

"We shot that scene in the real sewers underneath Rome. They're huge, ancient sewers that are now used as mushroom farms. We filled the sewers with water, and it looked great because there were natural stalagmites there and we didn't have to build anything. But it was horrible down there. There was a terrible stench. We just wanted that part to be over. At times like that, you just have to keep reminding yourself how much you love the project."

There was one other time on the shoot Shuler had to remind herself just why she was putting herself through all this.

"We had just shot the snow scenes in Cordina. It was lovely and sunny there. Everyone was happy. Then we left and went to a town called Petouse. It rained the whole time we were there, and there was no heat or hot water. It was miserable," Shuler sighs. "That's show biz."

There was one major question that had to be answered before shooting was completed: How to end the film?

"We went through millions of endings on the film," Shuler says. "Well, at least five or ten. When we were shooting, we had a scene where you saw Isabeau and Navarre walking out of the cathedral where their final conflict with the bishop takes place. As they walked out, you saw that Leo McKern had become the bishop. Navarre and Isabeau walked out among the cheering crowd, then rode off together into the sunset on his horse. We dropped that because it seemed redundant. Once you've seen the lovers united, that's the end. That's what you've been waiting for."

But in order to come to this simple ending, Shuler and Donner went through a lot of more complex ones.

"Many drafts ago, we had an ending in which Imperius turns the bishop into a rat, then turns himself into an owl. I think there was one in which the bishop blows up. That had something to do with his ring.

"It's true that the ending we have now seems like the most natural thing in the world. I guess it's always that way; you have to try other avenues in order to see that the right one is right."

Once the film was done shooting, the music was the only major element to be added. Shuler knew from the very beginning she wanted a new kind of score for her film.

"We wanted music that was in keeping with movie, and yet had a certain contemporary sound. We wanted a new fresh sound instead of old movie music, we wanted to experiment a little," Shuler says.

The composer they decided on will come as a surprise to those who can't think of the Middle Ages without hearing a Miklos Rozsa fanfare. Shuler's final choice was Andrew Powell of the electronic rock group the Alan Parsons Project.

"When we had our first meeting at Fox, one of the first questions Alan Hirschfield asked us was who we had in mind for the score. He suggested someone like the Parsons Project. We familiarized ourselves with their music and discovered we agreed with Hirschfield. We started looking for a composer who'd give us a sound like the Parsons Project. Then we went directly to the group itself. Andrew, the group's composer, agreed to write the music, and the group performed it."

The film Shuler worked on for five years out of love for the project is finally done. Shuler has a new love now, Richard Donner.

"Richard and I are involved," she says. "It came towards the middle of filming. After we had worked together for so long on business, a relationship came together."

Meanwhile, Shuler's first love is being released this month. She has little doubt that it will be a success.

"*Ladyhawke* is different from other films. It's not sword and sorcery. It's a romance," Shuler says. "I love this movie."

INTERVIEW WITH RUTGER HAUER

Director Richard Donner was looking for "the personification of the pure hero," an actor who could ride into a scene on a white horse and, without saying a word, be instantly accepted by the audience as *Ladyhawke*'s heroic knight.

Sean Connery was the first choice. Problem was, his license to kill had been renewed and he was in the Bahamas, chasing SPECTRE agents in *Never Say Never Again*. He was also too old.

Two weeks before shooting, Donner settled on Kurt Russell—a strong actor, but not your knight-in-shining-armor type. And Donner knew it.

So he called Rutger Hauer.

"Earlier Dick had offered me the role of a bad guy, the captain of the guards," Hauer recalls. "I said 'forget it. I want to play the hero.' He wanted someone younger. So I said why would you consider young people for this role? There is more to this than just a teen picture. If you want to tell a story about someone who is about strength, endurance and love you need an actor with balls. I act from my guts and I know I have the balls. I know I can do it. Dick wasn't convinced."

"I always considered Rutger as a heavy son of a bitch," Donner says. "I couldn't see him as a real macho hero, the whole 'make my day' kind of thing."

Hauer grins. "So, a year later he calls me up in Holland. He asked me to come to Italy in one week. I asked for what role? And he said Navarre. I was there in twenty-four hours."

Why was Hauer so enthusiastic about the role? Because he sees in it a strong shot at stardom.

"I think *Ladyhawke* will do a lot of good for me in America," Hauer says. "I loved the script and I felt it was a film that could attract a huge audience. It never hurts to succeed, you know."

But it's going to be a hard film to sell. *Ladyhawke* doesn't fit easily into any of the genres it tries to encompass: romance, comedy and medieval fantasy.

"*Ladyhawke* is very hard to pin down. It's a tale of love, I guess. It starts out as a tale of vengeance and half way it shifts into a lighter level," Hauer says. "It's daring to put this on the screen. But once you get into it's fun and I think it will be a hit for me."

He was once Holland's cinematic prince, the lead in such popular international hits as director Paul Verhoeven's *Turkish Delight* and *Spetters*. When Hauer tried to translate his appeal to American film, he failed. His noble efforts—*Nighthawks* with Sylvester Stallone; *The Osterman Weekend*, an adaptation of a Robert Ludlum bestseller and directed by Sam Peckinpah; Nicolas Roeg's *Eureka* and Ridley Scott's SF adventure *Blade Runner*, starring Harrison Ford—were all commercial disasters.

"I'm not sure why they all did poorly. Maybe I didn't make the right films. I don't know a lot about what makes a film *go*. I do know that I am very happy with *Ladyhawke* because I feel confident about my performance. I want to be in a good film, not because it will be a box office success, but because it's good," Hauer says. "I'm not out to be *Mr. Uno* and stand out. I understand the allure of being a big shot. It pleases your ego, but I don't need it. I want to do a couple of good films and so far I've done a couple of really nice tries. I feel this is the one. If I am wrong, I will admit it, but for me I think this will score."

He also thought he was the perfect choice for Navarre, the knight who is cursed by an evil bishop to become a wolf at night while his lover (Michelle Pfeiffer), who is a hawk by day, becomes a woman.

Michelle Pfeiffer and Rutger Hauer find true love in *Ladyhawke*.

"I feel very comfortable with larger-than-life stuff because I think I know what it is," Hauer says. "If you can bring it off, it feels great. It's the best hero you can play. There's a lot of substance I thought I could bring to it. I know there are very few actors who can do what I have done with Navarre, and that feels good."

But it wasn't easy.

"What screws you up is you've got a sword poking you in the ass, there are these saddlebags and crossbows sticking the horse in the ass, and there's this hawk sitting on your arm. So, you're out of control. You have to just hope the horse is feeling okay."

Not to mention the hawks.

"Their claws are very sharp. I noticed that right away. Their egos became very important. There were four hawks, actually. One was very sweet, two were so-so and the fourth was, ah, aggressive," Hauer says. "None of them hurt me but when we first started shooting, the trainers warned me that if you stare at the hawks they get uncomfortable and might go crazy. So for the first couple of days I was really worried every time I caught the bird looking at me.

"They see everything all the time. They sit there with this amazing concentration," he continues. "You can't ignore them. Besides, he was my co-star, I *had* to watch him. If they stare at you while you're playing a scene you have to relate to it otherwise you are denying the presence of the bird, and the bird is an integral character in the story. I think there were maybe ten times where I would have loved for the bird to look at me so we'd have a moment and once the bird did and it worked. We had a marvelous moment."

Doesn't he feel strange saying he had "a marvelous moment" with a bird?

"Well, it's a strange film, right?"

Besides relating to animals, Hauer had to brush up on his medieval combat skills.

"I lost twenty pounds doing the final fight scene in the church. We shot it at the beginning. It's the final act and, once you've done that, it tells you what the film is. It helps when you do the rest of the film. I have been fencing since I was fourteen and I'm very good at it but the floor of the church was cobblestone and one day I threw my ankle out," Hauer says. "It's the hardest floor you can think of to fight on because each stone sits in a different position. My boots were not boots that give support. They looked great but boy are they lousy when you have to fight."

Hauer is a seasoned veteran at playing knights. The 41-year-old actor was the star of the Dutch television series "Floris," the 23 episode, black-and-white story of a "Dutch Ivanhoe" which was directed by Verhoeven, who would later give Hauer the film roles that caught Hollywood's attention. Now Hauer has re-teamed with Verhoeven on yet another knightly adventure, *Flesh and Blood*, an upcoming Columbia release.

"*Flesh and Blood* was shot in Spain and it's the other side of *Ladyhawke*. This is in the air and that film is all in the mud," Hauer says. "It deals with the day-to-day problems of medieval man. Death was the big thing, and not from hacking each other up with swords but from all these crazy diseases. The Black Plague was killing everyone off. I loved doing the movie after *Ladyhawke*. It breaks up the image a little bit."

As much as he likes Verhoeven, he's going to try and stay away from him for awhile. "I have done five films with him now and I think that's basically it."

It's also unlikely that Hauer will be doing any more Dutch films.

"I'm getting into this market, why would I go back? Once you get into a certain level, it is very hard to go back," he says.

"Level doesn't only mean money it also means quality. Holland is not a very big country and the movie industry is not very big. I decided to make myself available to this market and this market is picking up for me. You know as well as I do you have to shape your career a little bit."

He tried hard once to make sure his career *wouldn't* be acting. Both his parents were actors but he thought "it would be better to be more down to earth, have some fun and get on with it," he says. "Finally, after trying a number of jobs, I still didn't know what to do. I wasn't very good in school. I was much happier with the girls."

At age 15, he decided to follow in the footsteps of his great-grandfather, who was the captain of a tea schooner in the Caribbean. Hauer lied about his age and became a merchant seaman on a freighter.

"I worked very hard, I was the maid of the ship, I had to clean everything. I loved it. I sailed for a year. I saw New York, Chicago, lots of places. It was wonderful," he recalls. "Traveling is so nice because, first of all, it's new. You've never seen these places before and you meet people who are totally different. It makes you see that there's more to life than your horizon. After that, I went back to Holland and tried high school at night. It was really hard for me."

So hard that he shrugged off education for the army. He did well in the military and was even offered a commission, which he turned down in order to try mountain climbing in the Alps. Later, he toiled as a stagehand and heating engineer at a Swiss theater before returning to Amsterdam and, at age 23, enrolling in drama school. For the following five years he worked in theater before copping the role in "Floris." His first film, *Turkish Delight*, was nominated for an Oscar as Best Foreign Language film. Six years later he starred in *Soldier of Orange*, another Verhoeven film, which was also nominated for an Oscar and won the Los Angeles film critic's Best Foreign Film award.

Hauer, who now speaks fluent French, German, and English, doesn't have a nagging urge to return to his theatrical roots.

"The stage scares the shit out of me," he admits. "It doesn't turn me on knowing there's a bunch of people sitting there in the darkness. I don't think I perform well in front of people," he says. "There's such a big difference between acting in film and acting in theater. In theater, you make it bigger and in films you downplay. I feel theater is very dishonest, it slows you down."

His career seems to be picking up momentum. Some people say he's one of a handful of actors tagged as a possible replacement for Roger Moore as 007.

"I heard those rumors, too. I don't know about Bond, but they asked me three times to play Bond's bad guy. At one point, I said I think it would be interesting if you really threaten Bond and what is the way to do that? Have a bad guy who has the same spirit, the same sense of humor and the same skill and let Bond face this guy and really be endangered," Hauer says. "But the villains are sidekicks, they aren't really strong. They wouldn't change it for me."

And he won't take on a role unless he can change it.

"When I play a character, I will do something different with it. I like to tease my audience," he says. "I like to surprise them a little bit every time I do a film. And, I think, I do."

THE LOST BOYS (1987)

Although only a moderate hit, *Lost Boys* was the perfect incarnation of studio thinking in the mid-eighties. It was a sexy vampire movie, a hot subject ever since Tony Scott's *The Hunger* put vampire lovers Catherine Deneuve and Susan Sarandon in bed together; it starred beautiful teenagers (Jason Patric, Jami Gertz, Kiefer Sutherland); it was shot in an MTV-style, and featured a soundtrack full of rock songs. And while the advertising was directed straight at the MTV audience (Sleep all day, party all night—it's fun to be a vampire), the film had elements designed to appeal to every demographic group: Corey Feldman's comic book reading boy vampire hunter was aimed at younger children, the romance between Dianne Wiest and Edward Herrmann at the older crowd.

A sequel was put into development after the success of the first film, but as of this writing has not been announced for production.

LOST BOYS SET VISIT

You can hear the screams all the way down the beach. You can hear the old man shout and hear the crash of bodies smashing into walls.

It's just another typical argument in Santa Cruz, California. In this city built on bean sprouts and granola, you have to expect fights over lifestyle between an aging hippie and his daughter's yupped-out boyfriend.

But there's one difference between today's battle and one that gets played out here every day of the week: This yupped-out boyfriend has blazing cat-eyes and two inch fangs. And the aging hippie is doing his arguing with a six-foot wooden stake.

Welcome to the Burbank Studios version of Santa Cruz, home of the new Richard Donner production, *The Lost Boys*. A horror comedy about a bunch of hip vampires preying on teen runaways in Northern California, *The Lost Boys* is Warner Bros.' big summer release of 1987, and Donner's shot at having two hits in one year after the cop thriller *Lethal Weapon*.

But in the middle of this cross-cultural conflict, no one is thinking about what a hit *The Lost Boys* is going to be. They're thinking about how long they've been on the endless production. And how they can't wait to finish.

"I feel like I should write a composition on what I did on my summer vacation," says "aging hippie" Bernard Hughes (*Mr. Merlin*). "I feel like I've been on this picture forever."

No one feels it quite like Ed Herrmann (*The Purple Rose of Cairo*), who is currently writhing in a gigantic fireplace, a fencepost sticking out of his chest. He's not having a lot of fun right now—and the large economy size stake-through-the-heart is the least of his worries. It's the vampire eyes that are getting to him.

"I can wear these lenses for up to about twenty-five minutes," says Herrmann. "But yesterday I was in and out of them about five times. By the end of the day, the surface of the eye is really tender."

Herrmann has had to wear his lenses for only a small part of the shooting. Most of the time he wears nothing more exotic than some flashy, hip clothing. But since Herrmann usually gets to wear hip clothes in a movie about as often as he wears vampire lenses, that's part of the fun of the movie for him.

"That's one of the reasons I chose to do the part: I wanted to get out of suits," says Herrmann, who has made a career of playing Franklin Delano Roosevelt—and millionaires who dress like him. "Or at least get out of three-piece suits and get into hip ones."

Herrmann's other reasons for doing the film were slightly more esoteric.

"We're really in a Mannerist period," Herrmann says. "The great Renaissance of our century took place in the twenties and thirties. After the Italian Renaissance, after Leonardo and Michelangelo and Raphael, painting began to get a little weird. Because all the ideals became a little poisoned. Like Shakespeare a hundred years later in England would reflect boundless hope for human potential, and then everything went sour in the Jacobean period. So now we're living in the souring of America, despite Reagan's seemingly pumping air into the dead body.

"There's a lot of hope, but there are a lot of people dying. It's been a long time since Gary Cooper and Cary Grant were the archetypes for young boys. For those of us who were born during the Second World War, we still had those guys in our minds. Now the archetype is Mick Jagger, and they've gone far beyond Jagger. When kids want to look cool, they don't want to look like the quiet, decent, moral fellow Cooper looked like. Or like me in a lot of my parts.

"Kids are not stupid. They're trying to make the best of a crazy time. Corporate immorality is reflected by immorality in the streets, so why not a vampire movie? It's fun. And at least this one isn't gratuitously ugly. There are some very attractive people here."

Kiefer Sutherland finds out that being a vampire isn't all fun.

Right now, most of those attractive people are being used to mop up the floor. Bam! There goes Corey Feldman (*Stand by Me*) flying across the room. Boom! Watch Jason Patric (*Solar Babies*) smash into a wall. Ouch! Jami Gertz (*Crossroads*) slides into a pile of furniture.

"It's been tough, physically," says Gertz, who plays the teen vampire chick who seduces innocent Michael (Patric) into the world of the *Lost Boys*. "It's been a long haul. I did stunts yesterday, and my whole neck hurts, my arm hurts. Ed Herrmann's character is going crazy and he's throwing everybody all over the room, so I'm being thrown to the ground. This is a tough life. I deserve to go to Hawaii."

But being thrown to the ground by kindly Ed Herrmann is hardly the worst Gertz has suffered on this production.

"Running through real caves with no shoes. Riding on the back of a motorcycle with Kiefer Sutherland driving. I love Kiefer—he's an animal. When he's driving, be careful. 'Don't worry, don't worry,' he says, then he pops a wheelie and breaks his hand. If I'd been on back, I would have been dead.

"We've been doing some scary stuff. We had to go down these stairs down a cliff with water running down them. Those stairs weren't very sturdy, and the water made them slippery. We were running up and down them all night."

And then there was the cave.

"The cave was absolutely incredible," Gertz gushes. "It's this old hotel that has fallen into the ground, and it looks great. But when designers design sets, they put a ramp here and a staircase there, and they never consider you have to walk on this ramp or up those stairs. It can get difficult. They had to carry half of us up the stairs.

"But I'm in a great mood. I haven't worked all day. I've been in makeup since seven this morning. I'm happy."

She's not as happy as the man with the ponytail who keeps shouting for *more smoke*. Director Joel Schumacher (*St. Elmo's Fire*) looks downright delighted to be directing this picture. And there's no reason he shouldn't be—it seems practically like a matter of luck that he ended up with the project.

Certainly, he wasn't anyone's first choice to direct *The Lost Boys*. Richard Franklin was, back in the days when the picture was still considered "Peter Pan with Vampires" (*that's why they never grew up!*). But after some conceptual reshuffling and a rewrite by Jeff Boam (*The Dead Zone*), Franklin was replaced by Richard Donner (*The Goonies*). And then Donner discovered Shane Black's *Lethal Weapon* script and decided to direct that instead.

Donner stayed attached to *Lost Boys* as producer and went looking for another director. He approached Schumacher, who was bogged down in studio bureaucracy over a proposed film of Jay McInerny's yuppie bestseller *Bright Lights, Big City*. Seeing that project going nowhere—it's now in the hands of Joyce Chopra (*Smooth Talk*)—Schumacher signed on with *Lost Boys*. Shortly after shooting on *Bright Lights, Big City* began, Chopra was fired and replaced by James Bridges (*The China Syndrome*). But after all the shuffling, the film, which starred sitcom-star-turned-serious-actor Michael J. Fox, bombed).

Schumacher might seem like a strange choice to helm a big budget fantasy film—his only previous genre offering was the Lily Tomlin vehicle *The Incredible Shrinking Woman*, and Schumacher himself says "I prefer to forget about that one, too." But if you ask Donner's long-time producing partner Harvey Bernhard about the choice, he merely smiles enigmatically and says "Joel thinks in color."

Right now, the color Schumacher is thinking in is *more*. More smoke. More snarling. More death. This is, after all, the end of the picture. It has got to be big. And it's got to be … exciting.

"Vampires are sexy, as opposed to other monsters," Schumacher says. "They're beautifully dressed, they come into your bedroom. I actually think that in Victorian times, vampires were created so people could express oral sex. Think of those Victorian ladies who used to swoon all the time in their musty old houses. They dreamed of old men sucking the life out of them, and of themselves being so totally under their spell that they were unable to resist.

"We're not going for a very classic vampire, not as you've seen them so many times. They don't sleep in coffins; there's no neckbiting; they're not dressed in white tie and tails or capes. But they're beautiful. Vampire legends are etched so indelibly in everybody's mind that you don't have to cover ground that's been covered before."

That's appropriate for Schumacher, who is essentially covering ground he's never covered before, all through *Lost Boys*.

"There were effects in *The Incredible Shrinking Woman*, but nothing like we have here," the director says. "The effects in *Shrinking Woman* were to show the ordinariness of life turned into madness for the heroine by her turning small. Here we're using effects to make people fly, kill, and maim. We have fun things here.

"This has been the hardest job I've ever had in my life, but it's also been the most fun and rewarding at same time. I think sometimes now that we're finally finishing the movie, that if I had known at the start how hard this was going to be, I wouldn't have done it. It's sort of like having your first baby—by the time you know how hard it is, it's too late. Between the special effects, the flying, the kids, the motorcycles on the beach, and the dogs, all of which are difficult to deal with, the cave set, which was hard to work in, everything's been quite a challenge."

Schumacher turns back to his physical effects crew. "More smoke," he bellows, and once again the vampire starts writhing.

Meanwhile, in a trailer across the lot, the vampire's killer is reclining comfortably with a book. Veteran actor Barnard Hughes plays the father of divorced Dianne Wiest, whose family is jeopardized by the arrival of the lost boys.

"I keep wondering why they keep giving me these old duffers to play," Hughes says. "I suppose there's a good reason for it."

Like so many of his "old duffers," Hughes' *Lost Boys* character is strong-willed and good-natured.

"Although there's not much seen in the picture, the history of the family is that he was a rather uptight, conservative man with a daughter who was a hippie type," Hughes explains. "Because of the difference in values, she left home. She got married and had two children and divorced and went back. Now she's a rather conservative wage earner and the old man has become something of a hippie. I don't think it's really exploited in the film, but at least that's the spine of our relationship. There's enough going on in the picture without introducing a subplot that can hardly be explored, but it's comforting to me to know where I came from and where I'm going."

Hughes doesn't need much comforting—he knows exactly where he's going.

"We're finally about to shut down and move on. I'm going back to New York. I keep coming and going, but this time it's for good. I left here almost six weeks ago and came back to find they've almost totally destroyed my house. And I finish up destroying what's left of it this afternoon."

If they finish up this afternoon. Back on the stage, Schumacher has finally got the right amount of smoke, and now he's calling "No more!" But smoke keeps pouring into the living room. Harvey Bernhard, dressed completely in black, stands to one side and watches patiently. After the problems of *Ladyhawke* and *The Goonies*, the problems of *The Lost Boys* haven't seemed so bad.

"I've made three tech films in a row, and now I'm looking for something simple," Bernhard says. "Something about people sitting around the table talking.

"This been very smooth, but it's a very tough picture. You can only do a little bit at a time. There are no clumps of dialogue where you can shoot three pages. It's an eighth of a page and an eighth of a page and an eighth of a page. It takes a long time."

And taking longer all the time. Sometimes it seems like it will never end. And no one will ever get to go home.

On the set, Schumacher throws up his hands. The smoke has gotten completely out of control.

"No more! No more!" an assistant director screams through a megaphone as the smoke continues to pour in. "Which word didn't you understand?"

JAMI GERTZ INTERVIEW

Sure, it's got vampires. It's got hip music. It's got cool clothes. But that's not why Jami Gertz likes *The Lost Boys*.

Jami Gertz likes *The Lost Boys* because it's one of the few times she's ever gotten to *do* anything in a movie.

"I save the whole group," Gertz says. "I save everyone from destruction. A girl does."

That may not sound like a reason to rush out and see the movie. But for Gertz, whose parts in movies like *Crossroads* and *Quicksilver* have amounted to little more than glorified wallpaper, it's a major step forward.

"Most of the parts I've played have been passive, girls who are just sort of *there*," Gertz says. "I have trouble with that because A: I'm not like that and B: being passive gets you in big trouble personally. It's not what girls should be looking up to personally."

Unfortunately, it *is* what Hollywood producers think audiences want to look *at*.

"There are a lot of passive women's roles in the movies," the actress says. "The ones that aren't are either bad or are snatched up by one of the *big* actresses."

Or they're like the female lead in *The Lost Boys*—they don't have the range that will bring Meryl Streep pounding on a producer's door, but they're a step above the "nice girlfriend"—the one whose sole purpose is to give the male lead a "human" side.

Jami Gertz and Jason Patric find love ... and vampirism ... together in *The Lost Boys*.

Actually, Gertz's *Lost Boys* role couldn't be more the opposite than the standard "nice girlfriend." As a teenage runaway turned bloodsucker she actually takes away star Jason Patric's human side by turning him into a demi-vampire.

"It's fun to play a vampire," Gertz says. "It's a stretch. For one thing, I'm nice, which is a switch after all the tough characters I've played. *My* vampire's a sweet vampire. I'm sent out to kill Jason Patric. But instead of killing him I fall in love with him. By saving me at the end after I tell him what's going on, he turns into a partial vampire himself. We're partial vampires, we're not totally vamped out because we haven't made a kill yet. If we were to kill, we'd be big bad vampires like some of the other characters."

And while a sexy young vampirette is not the kind of part that garners Academy Award nominations, Gertz feels there's some humanity to her role.

"I think she got mixed up with the wrong group," the actress explains, "enticed by the way they looked, the way they lived, and how free it was. And once she was in it she saw it wasn't the way she really wanted to live her life, but like many people, she got stuck in a situation she can't get out of."

That's not likely to happen to Jami Gertz. The daughter of a successful Chicago contractor who always encouraged her ambitions, Gertz has been a professional actress since she was sixteen—she was discovered in high school by Norman Lear's company and hired to play the regular role of snobby Muffy Tupperman on the CBS' short-lived sitcom *Square Pegs*—and she places the emphasis on *professional*.

"I can't afford to stay loaded on the set and stagger out of the trailer when I feel like it," Gertz says. "Not when there's ten to twenty million bucks riding on whether you're feeling up to working that day."

Of course, that money isn't riding completely on Gertz's feelings. Movies like *Crossroads* and the disastrous science fiction adventure *Solarbabies* have managed to lose plenty of money even with Gertz giving her professional all. Take *Crossroads*, for example. Walter Hill's (*The Warriors*) fantasy about playing the blues with Satan featured a great performance by Joe Seneca (*Amazing Stories*) as an old blues master, a Focus Awardwinning screenplay, and a brilliant Ry Cooder score. But even though it got some good reviews, the film disappeared after three weeks.

"I thought *Crossroads* was going to do tremendous business," Gertz says. "I think it couldn't find its audience. It got a bum rap when it got an R-rating. I don't think it deserved that by any means."

Which isn't the case with Gertz's previous genre film, the Brooksfilm production of *Solarbabies*, which the actress describes as a "triangle between *E.T., Mad Max*, and *Rollerball*." Originally slated for a early summer '86 release, the film was finally dumped into theaters at Christmas. The reviews were abominable, the grosses were worse, and by New Year's Day, everyone had forgotten the film existed.

"*Solarbabies* was a difficult movie to film," recalls Gertz, who took the job because she wanted to work with people like co-stars Charles Durning and Richard Jordan and executive producer Mel Brooks. "We were in Spain for four months and I hurt myself doing a stunt. I was in a cast for a month. As I get farther and farther away from doing it, it seems like I remember the bad instead of the good."

Most people who saw the film feel the same way. But one good thing did come out of the *Solarbabies* experience for Gertz—she met co-star Jason Patric, who has since starred with her in the play *Out of Gas on Lovers' Leap* and *The Lost Boys*.

"It's all a coincidence that we keep getting cast together," Gertz says. "We're hardly at a point in our careers where we can tell producers 'If you want me, you have to hire that other person.' But it's nice working together. We're like brother and sister. My family knows him, I know his family."

But Gertz doesn't know if or when she'll work with her new-found "brother" again. Next up for the rising actress is the movie adaptation of *Less Than Zero*, Brett Easton Ellis' novel about wasted rich teens in Los Angeles. And if she has to go back to the wallpaper roles again after that, at least she'll have her *Lost Boys* experience to remind her that, once in a while, there's a movie where she can actually do something.

"This is a real quality picture we're working on here," she says. "I think anyone would like to see this picture. It's like going to see *The Fly* or *Aliens*. It's got gory stuff. It has great elements. It has comedy, which is very important because one needs to laugh. It's got vampires. That's always immediately a hit for me. It has motorcycles and kids and everything. It's a whole mish-mash of stuff that makes it fun and exciting."

COREY FELDMAN INTERVIEW

Stand back, Rambo. Move aside, Arnold. Give it up, Chuck. This summer there's a new action hero in town, and he's tougher than all of you. He's Edgar Frog, boy vampire-killer—and he's *mean*.

At least until the shooting starts.

"He's a Rambo kind of character," says Corey Feldman, who plays the heroic lad in Joel Schumacher's teen vampire thriller *The Lost Boys*. "He's a tough guy who kills all the vampires, completely deadpan, serious, the kind of guy you wouldn't want to mess with. But then when things really start happening, he falls apart and goes crazy. Just freaks out."

That's the difference between Edgar Frog and the young actor who portrays him. Corey Feldman has proven that he can stay tough even when things really start happening. A professional actor since he was three years old, Feldman has faced Jason in *Friday the 13th: The Final Chapter*, fought dimwit Facca Brutos in *The Goonies*, and even suffered through Barth Gimble's crippling sarcasm on the satirical talk show *American 2-Night*.

But nothing quite compares to the teen vampires Feldman fights in *The Lost Boys*. They're not only thoroughly vicious, totally evil, but they're also incredibly good-looking. In other words, Brat Pack Bad Guys.

"This is a real teenager kind of film," Feldman says. "It's the kind of movie that will make teenagers *want* to go out and get scared. It's like *Friday the 13th* without the gore."

You may wonder what's left if you take the gore out of *Friday the 13th*, but *The Lost Boys* has found replacements for explicit bloodletting. For one, there's the hot soundtrack. For another, there's the hot clothes. But for the most part, Feldman says, there's the *comedy*—which came as a tough assignment for the actor.

"Comedy is a lot harder than drama," Feldman says. "Drama is so easy it just comes out. You don't need timing, you don't need anything, you just come out and say the line. Comedy you have to at least have your wits about you, because you have to be thinking about when you're going to come in with the line and how you're going to react, how your eyes are going to go. Comedy takes so much more than drama."

And Feldman should know, since the last film he did before *The Lost Boys* was his most intense drama yet—Rob Reiner's nostalgic Stephen King adaptation, *Stand by Me*.

"*Stand by Me* is the best movie I've done so far," Feldman says. "It was a lot of fun, because it was three months in the fifties. All three of us were in the fifties for the summer, and for me it was real neat."

Real neat—and real different. Because by the time Feldman was born, the fifties existed only in *Happy Days*.

"The fifties ended *quite* a few years before I was born," Feldman says. "Rob [Reiner] helped us through it a lot. He'd tell us what he did when he was that age. We just read the script and did the parts. When you have a full setting around you with everything fifties, it just kind of falls into place."

The one part of the film for which Reiner didn't have to coach his young actors, Feldman, River Phoenix (*Explorers*), Corey Haim, and Will Wheaton, was the intense camaraderie of the characters.

"We spent all our time together," Feldman says. "That's all we did, just be with each other until we finished. We're still friends, just not as close because we don't spend every minute together."

But the time they did spend together translated into a convincing portrayal of friendship on the screen. And that translated into great success for the film—well over $50 million at the box office and a nomination for the best adapted screenplay Oscar.

"I knew *Stand by Me* would be the kind of movie that would be nominated for Academy Awards, that critics would love it," Feldman says. "But I never expected it would get the box-office draw it has."

Feldman also didn't expect the box-office draw of his last picture, *The Goonies*—he thought it would be much bigger. At least he did until he saw it.

"I didn't love *Goonies* myself," Feldman says. "I thought it could have been done a lot better. They took a great script and turned it into a good film, while in fact it could have been a great movie.

"They should have made the bad guys meaner, more of a threat, and they should have made it not so silly—more suspenseful, more *Indiana Jones* kind of thing. If they'd done that and played it right, I think it could have turned out better."

Hopefully, that won't be the case with Feldman's new film. But the actor isn't making any guesses.

"I think *The Lost Boys* will do reasonably well," Feldman says. "You can never predict. With *The Goonies* we were saying it was going to be the biggest movie ever made. Then it turned out to be just another film. You hope for the best."

And while you're hoping, you just do the best work you can do. And if you're lucky, you have a good time doing it. That, at least, is Feldman's approach.

"I'm not a method actor," Feldman says. "I don't sit there for half an hour before each shot and become that person and treat everybody horribly because that person treats everybody horribly. I just get up there, joke around, and when they say action, I start."

But now, Feldman is going to *stop*. After doing *The Goonies*, *Stand by Me* and *The Lost Boys* in close sequence, Feldman feels a need for some time off. He hopes when he starts acting again, he'll be able to keep up the same ratio of "serious" movies like *Stand by Me* to lighter pieces like *The Lost Boys*.

"I'm going to go pretty much back and forth from now on," Feldman says. "Maybe two adventurous movies a year and one dramatic movie. I think that's a good way to go—one that's real down to earth, two that are just fun. The serious one keeps you sharp, keeps your wits about you; it lets you know what's real and what isn't. But I also like just having fun with movies—getting carried away and doing any old thing."

A NIGHTMARE ON ELM STREET (1984)

On the surface, *A Nightmare on Elm Street* was just another low-budget slasher movie, albeit a clever one, about a psychokiller who attacks you in your dreams.

But, like *Friday the 13th* before it, *A Nightmare on Elm Street* was a surprise sensation, one that changed the lives of many of the people associated with it.

For one, the unexpected success of the film, and the blockbuster theatrical series and merchandizing bonanza it sparked, transformed Robert Shaye's New Line Cinema from a struggling independent to a major force in Hollywood, one that would turn out such arty fare as *The Player* and pop blasts like *Teenage Mutant Ninja Turtles* and *House Party*.

The movie also made Johnny Depp, an unknown face, into a star capable of landing the lead in "21 Jump Street," which turned him into a teen sensation and a leading man.

It gave character actor Robert Englund an annuity as Freddy Krueger, the psychokiller everyone loves to hate—a role he played not only on the screen, but in a short-lived, syndicated TV series.

And it made low-budget, horror director Wes Craven into a marketable name in film. Unfortunately, Craven never anticipated the success of his little horror movie, and wasn't able to reap the financial rewards one might expect for the creator of a theatrical and marketing phenomenon like *A Nightmare on Elm Street*.

Ever since, Craven has tried to recapture the success, after first spurning horror in a seeming attempt to "mainstream" himself with Disney movies and television shows. But he inevitably kept returning to his roots in horror, with mediocre fare like *Serpent and the Rainbow*, *Shocker* and *Deadly Friend*.

It almost seems as if, for Craven, *A Nightmare on Elm Street* is as much a blessing as it is a curse—it made him into a brand name but, at the same time, was a film that is both difficult to live down, or to top. Its success has, in many ways, trapped Craven in a particular genre, one in which it will be difficult, if not impossible, to surpass what he has done before.

Nancy Thompson (Heather Langenkamp), and friend Glen Lantz (Johnny Depp) in parental confrontation with Nancy's dad, Lt. Thompson (John Saxon), in *A Nightmare on Elm Street*.

The question facing Craven in the nineties is whether he can reinvent himself, and in doing so, finally leave the ghost of Freddy Krueger behind him.

ON THE SET OF *A NIGHTMARE ON ELM STREET*

One two—
Freddie's coming for you!
Three four—
Better lock your door!
Five six—
Get your crucifix!
Seven eight—
Gonna stay up late!
Nine ten—
Never sleep again!

On Elm Street, a good night's sleep can kill you.

Take 16-year-old Glen, for instance. He's lying on top of his bed, with earphones on his head and a television set propped on his lap, when he lapses into sleep. Suddenly two claws rip out of his mattress and pull him, and everything he frantically grabs, down *into the bed.*

All is quiet. Then rivers of blood seep out of the mattress, streaming onto the floor and riding *up* the walls in crimson streaks.

"Great stuff, huh?" grins Johnny Depp, the first-time actor who portrays Glen in Director Wes Craven's (*The Hills Have Eyes*) *A Nightmare on Elm Street*, a New Line Cinema release that was being hurriedly completed in July for an October premiere. "It's literally being edited as it's being shot," says producer Bob Shaye.

The soundstage is a bustle of activity as the crew prepares for Glen's death scene, to take place in a rotating room, and for the filming of a pivotal expository scene with lead actress Heather Langenkamp and star Ronee Blakely (*Nashville*), as her mother.

Strewn throughout the soundstage are bits and pieces of this gruesome tale. In one corner, a blackened, bloody corpse is propped against the wall with a sign around its neck reading "CHARRED REMAINS, DO NOT TOUCH." On a makeshift, plywood table, the ravaged, clawed foam rubber torso of a nubile teenage girl is splayed beside someone's half-eaten cheeseburger and an abandoned Diet Coke can. A hallway of a suburban house is splashed with blood, hinting at the horror that occurred there.

Standing amidst it all, munching on a handful of Nacho Cheese Doritos at the snack table, is affable Craven, looking more like an Ivy League English professor than one of cinema horror's leading artisans.

"But this isn't horror, really," he says. "It's more of a fantasy, an impressionistic thriller. It's really a departure for me. I really feel this will be a landmark film for me, my watershed film. It's not an ordinary, run-of-the-mill little film. There's really something quite extraordinary about it. It's going to be a nice piece of work."

It is certainly the closest he has ever come to a film of mainstream appeal. *A Nightmare on Elm Street* is a low-budget cross between *Dreamscape* and *Poltergeist*. It's the story of a dead, psychopathic pedophile who stalks the dreams of teenagers and brutally kills them in a frenzy of inventive special effects. Written by Craven, and shot on a $3 million budget, it could make a tidy profit if moviegoers aren't satiated by the spate of killer-stalking-teenagers movies.

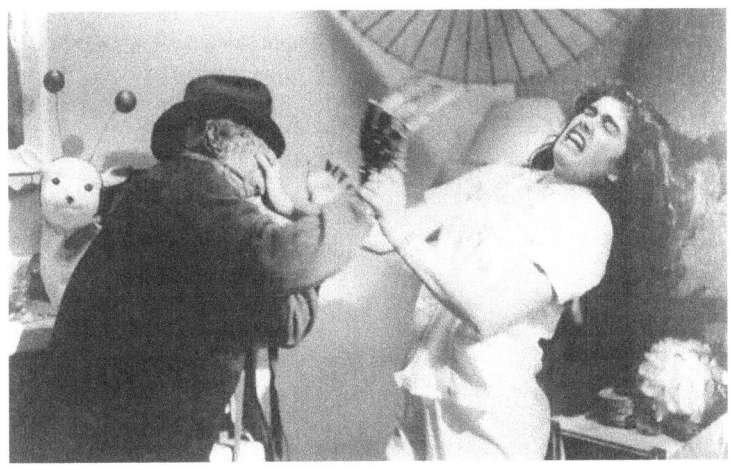

Nancy Thompson (Heather Langenkamp) struggles with the ghoulish Freddy Krueger (Robert Englund) in *A Nightmare on Elm Street*.

Producer Shaye doesn't think that will be a problem. "This is *not* a killer on the loose film," he says, "It's an archtypical monster in a dream who happens to have the ability to keep you from waking up while he gets you. There's none of the that slasher gore-for-gore's sake effects in this. This has some very unique fantasy, thriller moments."

Actor Robert Englund agrees. He's sitting on a folding chair on the edge of the set. The shadows obscure his charred face, but an occasional gleam of light reflects off the cold steel of the five fishing knives protruding from the fingers of the garden gloves on his hands.

"You're looking at essential evil, here," he says, referring to himself. "I'm the killer."

He thinks it's "unfortunate to refer to this as the typical slash and splatter thing. It's more more psychologically neurotic. That's not to say there isn't gore and a lot of effects, but it's all dream effects of visual cunning, reality and illusion."

Englund, the veteran of 18 movies, is perhaps best known as the friendly alien in *V*, though "it's hard to recognize me in this movie under eight pounds of make-up."

The role of vicious killer Fred Krueger "is a perfect contrast to my sympathetic, cuddly character in *V*. Krueger relishes the chase, the torture, and the predicament. The actor in me wants to talk a lot more intellectually about the part, but what it really comes down to is, I just wanted to be a monster. I mean, I've done my western, my space movie [*Galaxy of Terror*], my youth movie, my Vietnam movie, and this is my monster movie."

It's also the realization of Craven's fascination with the premise of doing a movie "where the line between what is real and what isn't is blurred," the director explains.

"It's a premise which has interested me for a long, long time. In some of my earlier films, I played with dream sequences where you weren't sure whether the person was dreaming or not. I found that the idea intrigued me so much I wanted to do a whole film around it," he says. "It was the first thing I wrote that I wasn't commissioned to write. It was a departure for me.

"This movie is not based on everyday reality," Craven continues. "It has a prosaic quality. I'm standing conventional scenes on their heads. A lot of scenes start off normally and then, all of a sudden, you don't know what the hell to expect next. It takes place as much in dreams as it does in reality. It's about a girl, Heather, who learns, in order to save her life, she must go into the dreamworld and confront the monster in its own cage."

The film, like many horror and fantasy works, has its sense of logic. For instance, Craven says the killer "can hurt you if you're dreaming. The flipside is, you can hurt him if you can get him into your reality." In the horror genre, that principle makes perfect sense.

"That's what I like about horror," he says. "It's an area much less hampered by rules and conventions. And in this, which is about dreams, there's very little limitation on what I can do."

Although he stresses that this movie is *not* horror, that doesn't mean he's forsaking the genre that made his reputation. "I don't think of it as dragging myself away from horror. This is firmly rooted in what I do best but it's different in kind. It's more entertaining than a film that assaults you. This is more of a rollercoaster ride than a graphic horror film."

"The question throughout the movie is what is nightmare and what is reality at any given moment?" says Englund. "It has sort of a *Twilight Zone* ending."

Special effects supervisor Jim Doyle thinks it's "brilliant the way Wes has written the story. He starts giving you indications of what is real and what is not then twists those around on you and makes you very uncertain."

Doyle is responsible for making the nightmarish world come to life. A veteran of effects work on *One from the Heart, Wargames*, and *Sword and the Sorcerer*, he is coordinating the five major special visual effects in the movie.

"In one scene, Heather falls asleep in the bathtub and Krueger's clawed hand creeps out of the water. Then the mother knocks on the door and wakes her up. The hand disappears and you see bubbles," he says. "She falls asleep again a few moments later and WHAM, she's hauled underwater as if the bathtub is bottomless. We plan to shoot the interior of that shot from the bottom of a swimming pool looking up."

Another teenager is strangled to death by his own bedsheet, while still another is bounced off the walls of a bedroom.

"We're having a good time," grins one crew member, "we really are."

A set decorator sprays cobwebs onto the cellar set while another adjusts a dim lightbulb that hangs beside the boiler where Heather and Ronee Blakely are a squatting, ready for the scene to begin.

The stagehands clear the set. Craven says "Action!"

"You want to know who Fred Krueger was?" Blakely rasps. "He was a filthy child killer who got at least twenty kids, kids from the area, kids we all knew …."

The production crew and lingering cast members watch in silent, rapt attention as the scene progresses.

" … the lawyers got fat and the judge got famous, but somone forgot to sign the search warrant in the right place and Krueger was free, just like that." Blakely continues, describing later how a vigilante group of parents set Krueger aflame. Screaming like a banshee, Krueger vowed to get them all by killing their children.

"He's dead, Nancy, he can't get you," she whispers, "Mommy killed him."

Mommy is wrong.

"I come back and manifest myself in their dreams," Englund says. "And I almost get them all."

Across the soundstage, up a ladder, is the room where Krueger will rip apart poor Glen. Mounted on one wall are the Datsun B-210 seats Craven and the camera man will be strapped into while the room does its spin, making the 110 gallons of blood pumped through the bed look as though it's defying gravity to crawl the walls. In the TV version, the bed will spit out a skeleton that smashes into the ceiling.

"I love this stuff," Depp says, surveying the room as technicians ready it for Glen's death. "The kid falls asleep and it's all over, he's sucked right into the bed and spit out as blood. His bloody body rises straight out and then topples over, too.

I heard somebody talk about having a dummy shot out of the bed but I said, 'Hey, I want to do this! It'll be fun! Lemme do it!'"

Call it newcomer's enthusiasm. Depp, a struggling musician, has never acted before.

"I always thought it would be real cool to act and I was always intrigued by it. My friend Nicolas Cage (*Racing with the Moon*) tried to talk me into it, but I said 'Nah,'" he recalls. "Finally, I was walking down Melrose looking for a job with a friend and we ran into Nick and his agent. Three days later I met Wes and got the part."

With the exception of veteran actors Blakely and John Saxon (*Black Christmas*), as her ex-husband the LAPD cop, the cast is primarily made-up of newcomers.

"They are all young and fresh. I'll tell you, frankly, I've never worked with such a talented group," Craven says. "My leading lady, Heather, is an incredible gal. She was in *Rumblefish* but her part was cut. She's just marvelous."

And she may be back battling Krueger again. Although Craven isn't contemplating a sequel, "we've left the door open." He shrugs. "We'd be foolish not to."

INTERVIEW WITH WES CRAVEN

Wes Craven has seen a lot of bare breasts and decapitated heads in his day. And if you've seen his movies, which include *Last House on the Left* and *The Hills Have Eyes*, so have you. Now he's working for Walt Disney. And he doesn't plan to kill, rape or torture a single talking mouse or flying elephant.

Craven is changing his image. He's becoming ... *nice*. Since the success of his last slash-those-nubile-teens epic *A Nightmare on Elm Street*, he's decided to leave horror behind—though not too far behind—and try anything that you'd least expect him to do. Before he could, though, he had to prove he could do it. The *Twilight Zone* revival gave him that chance. The six segments he's directed have shown a range and skill that's never been seen—or appreciated—in his low-budget, sometimes low-brow, filmwork. It's *the* year for Craven—and he's revelling in it.

Q: How did you get started in films?

WES CRAVEN: I wasn't allowed to see movies when I was a child. It was against the religion I was raised in, fundamentalist Baptist. I didn't go into a commercial movie house until I was a senior in college, and that was on the sly. It wasn't until I was in graduate school that I immersed myself in films. Then, I went to see all the films by Bergman, Fellini, etc.

The first film I made was when I was teaching. Some students came to me and said, "We see you have a camera, would you be our faculty advisor on a movie we want to make? You can shoot it." I said, "Sure," and got all of these free rolls of film from the drama department, and we went out and made a forty-five minute "Mission: Impossible" spoof. We taught ourselves how to edit just by doing it. We didn't have any sort of editing machine, so we did it on a school projector. Splices were Scotch-taped, and then glued for the final version. We couldn't figure out how to put sound with the movie. We knew that there was some film that had sound stripes along one side, but then we couldn't figure out how to do any sound overlap, or put music on there. So we did all our sound on a quarter-inch tape, and then ran it at the same time with the projector, and we had a rheostat so we could slow it down a little bit or speed it up to keep it roughly at the same pace.

Nancy Thompson (Heather Langenkamp) in the middle of conversation as the phone comes alive in her hand in *A Nightmare on Elm Street*.

We showed the picture at the local school auditorium. Well, we were smart enough to put everybody at the school, and everybody in the town that was of any significance, in the movie. So we had this huge turnout, and we made more than the cost of the movie in the first night! The next weekend, we showed it at the college that shared the town, and had another sellout crowd. Then, we showed it at another college, that was fifteen miles down, and they all came to see it. So we made a lot of money. We had this great cast and crew party afterwards, and we spent it all on that!

From this, I got the bug. I wasn't happy teaching. I was enjoying the teaching, but not the grades. The students would come and say, "I'm going to be drafted if you don't give me an A." The department chairman wanted me to get a Ph.D. on Elizabethan Lutes in the Time of Chaucer, or something that obscure. So I quit my job, I went to New York, and I looked that summer for a job in film, but I wasn't able to find anything.

I went back to upstate New York, and I taught a year of high school at a terrible school. At the end of that summer, I was talking to a student friend of mine, and he said he had a brother who was a film editor. That was Harry Chapin, who had once won an Oscar for, I believe, the editing of *Legendary Champions*, a short film on the great champion boxers.

So, I sat down with Harry, and he was very kind. He was working on a Steinbeck. He showed me how a film was put together. I sat with him for about a week, just watching him cut. He explained to me why he was cutting, pacing, and a great deal of things which stuck with me to this day. At about the end of that week, a man whose offices we were renting the room in, fired his messenger and said, "If you know anyone who wants a job as a messenger, I'm looking for one." I was thirty years old, had a master's degree in philosophy, two kids, and took the job as a messenger! That's how I got into film!

It was a film post-production house and, within ten months, I was assistant manager! Then, I quit that job for an assistant editing job. During that time, I crammed myself on film. I would work at night, synching up rushes or documentaries all over town, and got to know the young documentary film crowd in New York.

After that job, I drove a cab in New York for about three months, looking for a job in actually making a film. I finally got a chance on this small film that was being done by a twenty-seven year old named Sean Cunningham. It was a small, homemade film, and I got the job of synching up rushes determined on the system editing, and it turned into a full-time editing job, and even some directing, because he was having a falling out with the filmmaker that was working with him. We ended up finishing this film together.

The film came out, and made around $7 million. It had cost about $70,000. It was called *Together*, and very few people have heard of it, but it played all over the country for a summer. It was sort of like a sensitivity-training course for couples. It had a little nudity here and there. We all called it "Reader's Digest Sex." It was Marilyn Chambers' first film. She did a nude diving scene in it. But it had nothing beyond that. It talked about how to be more attuned to your husband's or wife's needs.

The releasers of this film, a small company called Vanguard, offered us $50,000 to make a horror film. Sean said to me, "Why don't you write it, direct it and cut it, and I'll produce it. We'll do it for $40,000 and pocket the $10,000. We'll do it in three weeks." So, I went out and wrote the script for *Last House on the Left*, and the reaction to it was so strong because it was just a crazy, wild script! Our agreement was that we would just hold nothing back. We would do the most outrageous things we could think of. So I wrote this crazy sort of ribald comedy, horror thing. And we couldn't get it out of the mimeograph place! That was the first sign that we had something special: they were all passing around the mimeographs to read!

We went out and we made the film. We went over-budget, and Vanguard had to give us another $40,000, so we ended up doing it for $90,000 after all. When it came out, it was immediately a big hit, and it's still playing. It was a sort of phenomenon, and I've been directing ever since—or trying to direct.

Q: Why was it also called *KRUG & CO.* on some prints?

WC: It's an interesting story about how an advertising campaign and a title can influence a film. Originally, the working title of *Last House on the Left* was *Night of Vengeance*. When it came out, we didn't like that, so we did a big contest among all the friends and relatives, and we came up with three titles: *Sex Crimes of the Century*, which is part of the conversation Sadie and Krug have in the car at the beginning, when Sadie concludes that the greatest sex criminal of the century was Freud, because he made everybody self-conscious about sex. We also came up with *KRUG & CO.*, because Krug was the main villain. Finally, *Last House on the Left* was a title suggested by an ad man, whom we all thought was terribly off the wall for suggesting such a title, which had nothing much to do with the film.

They opened it up in three towns simultaneously, all with the same demographic profiles, but using different ad campaigns. What an ad campaign determines is who comes out those first, crucial two nights to get the word-of-mouth going. The first two nights in the towns with *Sex Crimes* and *Krug*, nobody came. And in the town where they had the *Last House on the Left* title and the ad campaign that said "Keep repeating, 'It's Only a Movie!'" a crowd came out. And the next night, there was double the crowd, and it just took off. So it was a very dramatic example of how a title change and an ad campaign can work. To this day, there are people who still remember the ad campaign. You can hear the audience repeating, "It's Only a Movie!"

Q: Had you had any ideas for scripts before?

WC: As I said, they gave us money specifically to do a crazy horror film. Before that time, when I graduated from college with a bachelor's in English, I was sort of undetermined between a musical career—I was playing guitar in some of the cabarets in Chicago—and I also had been writing short story and poetry. I received a full scholarship to John Hopkins' writing seminars under a poet named Coleman, so I decided to do that. So I studied writing and philosophy at Hopkins, and got my master's degree.

Then, when I got out, I didn't know what I could do for a living. So, after someone suggested I teach, I did just that. I was very fortunate. I put in an application at a place and there were no openings, so I started a job selling rare coins in Baltimore. But then, some English professor in Pennsylvania dropped dead of a heart attack the day before the classes started! I got this telephone call, and they said, "If you come out right away, you can have this job!" It's the story of my life! So I jumped in an airplane and ended up in Pennsylvania teaching college.

Q: Other than for the fact that it got you in films, do you feel that *Last House on the Left* was a worthwhile experience?

WC: Absolutely! It's funny because I would never have thought of going out and doing a horror film, but now, I can see through whatever set of circumstances and luck that I was well-suited to doing that. The horror film is a typical way for a young filmmaker to gain entry into the filmmaking world. It is a kind of film that can be made on a low budget, and that can make a great deal of money.

As I look back over my entire life, I can see that I always enjoyed spooky stories, and I always enjoyed doing outrageous things. So I was indeed suited to doing that kind of film, although it would have never occurred to me, at that time, to actually do a horror movie on my own. I was trying to write very artistic stories and poetry. I was going in totally different directions, and not getting very far, and all of a sudden, somebody gave me a chance to do something that I never would have allowed myself to think about doing. Because I was totally anonymous at the time—I was living in New York on a shoestring—I figured I would do this picture and nobody would ever know I did it, or even go see it! So I just went crazy and did this really bizarre movie. And then, everybody knew that I had done it, and I became notorious for doing that kind of movie. It's kind of ironic how it all happened!

Q: Did you have fun making *Last House on the Left*?

WC: Yes, we had a LOT of fun making it! It was all friends that did it. Sean Cunningham and I were friends by that time, and we shot most of it in the homes of either his mother or his own backyard. We used friends of ours as actors, so it was a very homemade fun family movie, in a weird sort of way. Compared to some other shoots that I've had since, it was relatively trouble-free. I believe the original was shot in three weeks, then we went back for a fourth.

At the time, I didn't know about storyboards. I was sort of feeling my way as a director. So, I did weird things, like drawing lines in the script, like "this shot is sort of smilar to that shot on this page," and I would draw lines until it was such a mess I couldn't follow any of it! I really didn't know what the established procedures were for organizing a film. We had it budgeted, and we knew we had a certain amount for props and costumes, but beyond that, there was very little organization.

I didn't have much of an idea about what a director actually did, beyond shouting "Action!" and "Cut!" My orientation was more in documentaries, because that was the type of films I had worked on during that first year in New York. So I covered a lot of *Last House on the Left* as a documentary filmmaker would cover an event. The scene in the woods, for example, where the girls are first taken in the woods, I covered three times continuously, never stopping the action. Just played the entire scene as an event, and I had the camera stand in three separate places in general, and follow the action, and then planned to cut it together later. That scene had a real spontaneous feel, so we would rehearse it before hand, and then just do it.

As a result, the editing of *Last House on the Left* took nine months because it was such a mess. I didn't know what a master was. I didn't know how a master and reading a close-up could be used together. All of these things, I learned by either shooting a lot of material and then, finding out later that I should have done something else, or by finding from experience what worked and what didn't. But somehow, in the end, it all turned out OK.

Q: Did you have to do a lot of trimming down on *Last House on the Left* because of the violence?

WC: We had requests from sub-distributors, people in other sections of the country, who said that this film was too wild to play. They were getting audiences, but the audiences were tearing up the theaters! We had reports of people fainting, threats of lawsuits, fist-fights and near-riots. We had a case of people trying to get in the projection booth and the projectionist had to barricade himself in! [laughter] Wait! We had a case of half an audience leaving and cowering in the lobby!

We had lots of cases of projectionists and theater managers editing the prints themselves with scissors. We would get the prints back in pieces in the cans. So we voluntarily took out several scenes, two of which I don't really miss because they were so outrageously painful to watch, and one of which I think really hurt the film.

In the murder of Phyllis, the first of the girls to die, my whole intention was to show murder in a film that was as I would imagine it to be, rather than as it was depicted in films normally at that time. That is, the person delivered the killing blow, and the victim died, maybe with a few gasps, but not always. They would never fight a protracted fight, and would suffer clearly in front of the camera. So I did that with Phyllis, and I carried it through all the way, and the people that were killing her then went into a sort of psycho-sexual frenzy, where clearly they were going beyond what they even thought they were going to do, and it ended with them realizing that they had partially disemboweled her, and reaching down and pulling out a loop of her intestine. That was the point where a lot of people fainted ....

But that, to me, was the REALITY of murder, because at that point, their whole character changed, and they were suddenly sober and horrified by what they had done, and we had to cut that out. To me, now, that murder, as it stands, loses the whole climactic rhythm of that sudden realization. I think it gave the film a truth that was very painful to watch, but also very real.

Q: Was there anything about *Last House on the Left* that you didn't like?

WC: Oh, yes! The comedy scenes. I think the cliches of the stupid rural sheriff and his assistant did not work. All of us, for years, were under the influence of *In the Heat of the Night* and the stupid Southern sheriff. Some of the sound is also terrible: the scene in the old Cadillac where Krug and the others are riding along and do the bit about the Sex Crime of the Century, was one of my favorite scenes in the script, but you can't hear it, because we didn't know how to mike people, and how to make any post-production dubbing either!

Q: Did you feel able, after *Last House on the Left*, to go out and be a director?

WC: Yes, but the phone never rang! It was quite a period of time. Because *Last House on the Left* was so upsetting to the Establishment, I think I had only one call in two years, even though commercially the film was a big hit. That was from the producers of *Let's Scare Jessica to Death*, a horror film of about the same period. But Sean and I went out and wrote scripts for quite a while after that. We wrote comedies, we wrote a script on Vietnam, we tried to get serious, but nobody would take us seriously. So, I ended up accepting an offer from a friend of mine to do *The Hills Have Eyes*. By the time, *The Hills Have Eyes* was out, people saw that there was not only this wildman, but somebody who knew how to sit and direct. From that, I got on a television show, and from there to some more wide acceptance.

Q: Why are you so eager to escape your horror background?

WC: I had really grown tired, very limited by it and wanted to do other sorts of things. I'm out to educate the world that I'm not just an assault and slash guru of gore. I felt really restricted by that. It's easy to make a persona of yourself as one of the leaders of terrifying movies and I enjoy that but I do not enjoy being perceived as only being able too do that.

Q: But you're still doing horror movies.

WC: In the next year or so I will do films that are not scary and are certainly not violent. I'm trying very had to expand my horizons. There are some projects I have in development that will be horror, but I plan to expand beyond that narrow genre. It will take awhile for people to realize they will have good rides from Wes Craven but not necessarily horrendously violent ones. I've reached the point where I've established a firm foundation and am now able to move up to the next level.

Q: Can you thank *Nightmare on Elm Street* for that?

WC: Yes. *Nightmare on Elm Street* did that for me. I think it was widely perceived as not just a successful film but a film of great craft and imagination. A very original film that gave me the chance to be perceived in a new way. That was the springboard that led to *Twilight Zone*.

Q: Were you offered the *Nightmare on Elm Street* sequel?

WC: Yes. I turned it down because I didn't have time to write it and I told them if they came up with a script I found intriguing I would consider it. But the script has certain problems and I felt was not in my interest to direct, which is not to say it's a bad film.

Q: Are you happy there's a sequel to *Nightmare?* Would you have done one if you were in charge of New Line?

WC: Absolutely. If I were Bob Shaye, I would. He obviously had a moneymaker and it would be stupid not to exploit it to the hilt.

Q: Were you surprised by the success of *Elm Street?*

WC: It's never a surprise when a film does well. When you work hard on a film, you always assume or hope it will be a hit. It's always a surprise if it doesn't do well. When it does do well, you are enormously satisfied.

Q: Why do you think *Nightmare on Elm Street* worked?

WC: I think *Nightmare on Elm Street* opened up a whole new type of horror film the same way *Friday the 13th* did and spawned enormous imitations. I think *Nightmare* will spawn a type of horror directing that will expand the envelope of what reality and illusion is. That hasn't been explored much in horror before.

Q: What makes you think it will be explored now? I mean, is there any evidence this is the new wave of horror film?

WC: I just had lunch with Sean Cunningham, who has finished *House* for New World. It's very much in the ballpark of *Nightmare on Elm Street*. I think it's the new direction of horror films, hallucinatory horror films that are not restricted by day to day reality as, say, *Last House on the Left* was. Even in *Texas Chainsaw Massacre*, the only sort of expansion of reality was in the madness of the antagonists. The new horror film will be expanding the boundary of reality in the minds of protagonists, which is very different.

Q: Will your new films, like *Flowers in the Attic*, be in this new horror genre?

WC: No, I would not classify *Flowers in the Attic* as a horror film. Its a good old fashioned escape story, *Hansel and Gretel* on a big scale, children with mean parents who have to follow their own resources and gain freedom. It's a broader based, bigger audience kind of film that's based on an enormously best-selling novel. *Frankenstein*, which I've written and Roger Corman will direct, is a futuristic horror story and it's a very bizarre examination of the barriors between organic life and machine life. It's a movie where I go off in whole new direction again. It's very much about the frontiers of human evolutionary barriers.

Q: The two TV movies you directed this season, *Invitation to Hell* with Robert Urich and Joanna Cassidy and *Chiller* with Michael Beck, sure sound like horror to me. Aren't they just the same old thing for you, perhaps a step backwards?

WC: *Invitation to Hell* is about a country club that really is an organization of satanic powers and an entrance to hell. *Chiller* is about a man frozen cryogenically ten years ago and now is brought back to life and he is entirely restored except he has no soul. They are genre films but not horror in the sense that there's a maniac with a knife stalking people. Both involve families and humanistic dramatics and top-notch actors, like *Twilight Zone*.

Q: What are your other film projects?

WC: I'm doing *Artificial Intelligence* with Warner Bros. It's a bizarre love story based on the book *Friend*, which will be released by Bantam. It's the story of a fourteen-year-old genius who falls in love with the girl next door who is murdered by her father and the love story continues. It is a very compelling script written by Bruce Rubin, who wrote the initial story for *Brainstorm* I have two other films in development. One is *Haunted*, which is a love triangle I didn't write where the twist is that one person is dead by someone else. It first came across my desk four years ago and I've just gotten backing for it from Media Home Entertainment. I'll direct it. The other one is *Old Fears*, which I'll direct for Highgate Productions. It's another film that creates a new genre of horror. It's about a town where each person's worst childhood fear comes true.

Q: You are still doing supernatural-themed films, even with this change of heart you've had about horror.

WC: Two reasons. One is that many of these were deals put together quite awhile ago while I was still firmly in that genre before *Nightmare on Elm Street* took off and I was able to break out of it. The other reason is yes, they are within genre but they are not about people with knives coming after each other. All I can say is that things were put in motion before I had a chance to change the course of my career. In long haul, that will be last of that sort that I do.

Q: What happened to *Hills Have Eyes 2*?

WC: I have heard from the producer that it is already in regional release. My general feeling about it is that it was released before it was finished. I'm not happy with it so I avoid talking about it. We ran out of time and money on initial shoot so the producers' general approach was we must stop now but we will raise enough money to shoot another few days of footage later. That was fine with me, because that's how we did the first one. But when the footage was cut together they went straight to answer print. As a filmmaker, I feel they did an end run on me, They are my friends, I'm not terribly angry at them, and I got paid for it, but I don't believe it is complete. The whole story is there, but the whole thing needs work. Shots are missing, some scenes aren't right.

Q: What is the status of *Flowers in the Attic?*

WC: It has simply been a victim of New World Pictures not getting money from their public offering of stock as quickly as they thought they would. Seems now they are getting the money. I've heard in the last few days that they want to shoot the film in early 1986. It's simply a matter of whether they do get the money and if I am available. I want to do it, but I have to keep doing other films until they do or don't get money.

Q: What happened to *Circus Gang*, about circus kids who solves crimes?

WC: It's still bobbing around in the back of my head and I haven't had the chance to write it. With *The Goonies* out, the idea is on back shelf for another five years anyway. It's one of those ideas that perversely refuses to get into script form. I haven't been able to write a script for awhile because I've been working so hard.

Q: It seems like you've been working non-stop since *Nightmare on Elm Street*. Do you still recognize your wife?

WC: I've been working in town mostly, so it's not that horrendous. But I am working all the time.

Q: All the time? Geez, do you have loan sharks after you or something? An expensive drug habit? Who's blackmailing you?

WC: We went through a long period of my not working, It was terrifying. Now that the work is here, I'm happy I can be busy paying old debts—not that I have any loan sharks after me. It's been a hard time for us just to catch up on the long dry period between *Swamp Thing* and *Hills Have Eyes 2*. When hard times come, you get real broke real quick.

Q: The hard times seem to be long gone. From the looks of things, this is your year.

WC: It is. It's the year for Wes Craven to expand into new directions. It's the year for me to change.

Q: So many films are being done now with unusual events happening in suburbia. Do you think that's the modern arena for horror?

WC: I think it is, in a way. I think our appetite for the exotic sort of gets filled up. Certainly it's been filled up with gothic castles and things like that, then, Indiana Jones filled us to the brim with jungles and strange, archeological type places. To me, the most poignant and powerful area of our memory is childhood, and that, almost exclusively, takes place in regular, residential houses. In fact, for the first five years of our lives, we don't get away very much from the house and the yard at all. That's where you encounter most of the really primal events of your experience, and that's why you're afraid of the attic, the basement, the dark, and everything else. So, films that are set in those locations are able to evoke those memories more easily than films that are set in a castle, where we don't have personal memories, or even outer space. In fact, *Alien* had to create a type of rocket ship in order for it to really evoke the memories. And, the horrific place they had to go into where they find the alien, was very much like a human body. They had to go to things that had a familiarity to them.

It's my theory that familiar locations are not in and of themselves, horrific, but they contain the nodes of memory where horrific things take place when we're children.

SOMETHING WICKED THIS WAY COMES (1983)

"First of all, it was October...." Thus starts *Something Wicked This Way Comes*, perhaps Ray Bradbury's most famous novel after *Fahrenheit 451*. The book, first published in 1962, is universally acknowledged as a classic of American children's literature.

Bradbury originally conceived the *Something Wicked* story (the title is derived from the over-the-cauldron mutterings of Macbeth's witches) at the age of 25, in 1948, under the title of *Black Ferris*, a short story that he sold to the magazine *WEIRD TALES*.

Something Wicked is the story of Will Halloway and Jim Nightshade, two boys growing up in the small town of Green Town, and of Will's father, who wants to be young again. It is also the tale of good, ordinary people who are confronted with an evil as ancient as history.

One autumn night, Will and Jim witness the arrival of "Cooger and Dark's Pandemonium Shadow Show," a mysterious carnival that creeps out of the night with the eerie whine of a calliope. Immediately, the two boys perceive the hidden, evil nature of the carnival, and of its owner, the mysterious "illustrated man," Mr. Dark.

"Cooger and Dark's Pandemonium Shadow Show," as Ray Bradbury puts it, "gorges on fear and pain." Its inhabitants are the "Autumn People," who sense the wants, needs and desires of the dissatisfied, and come to offer supposed happiness—at a price.

"The stuff of nightmare is their plain bread" and, indeed, the citizens of Green Town, one after another, fall prey to the evil spells of the carnival. Among the victims are the local schoolmistress, who suddenly becomes a little girl, a rosy-cheeked boy who is turned into a wizened Methuselah and—almost—Will's father.

Something Wicked presents an enchanting version of the eternal confrontation between Good and Evil. More, it is also the tale of a rite of passage from innocent childhood into adolescence.

The sinister Mr. Dark (Jonathan Pryce) leads a parade through Green Town in search of two young boys who have discovered the carnival's terrible secret in *Something Wicked This Way Comes*.

Both Will, the more staid and conservative boy, and Jim, who has a dark, mercurial side and a love of adventure stories, embody childhood. The experiences that they share, and what they face within themselves, helps them to take another step on the path to adulthood.

Mr. Halloway, the aging librarian, haunted by the fears of his own mortality, also faces his devil. He, too, comes to realize that the carnival's promises are ultimately empty. "We are like the dumb dog who dropped his bone to go after the reflection of the bone in the pond." By the end of the story, he is no longer afraid of death, and understands that age is in the heart more than the body.

Twenty-five years passed between the writing of *Black Ferris* and *Something Wicked*. The quick success of the story, and Bradbury's Hollywood connections, ensured that *Something Wicked* would receive immediate attention. The book was first optioned by producers Chartoff and Winkler (*Rocky*), who took it to 20th Century–Fox. Sam Peckinpah, then Mark Rydell (*On Golden Pond*), were considered to direct, with Bradbury scripting. Coincidentally, at one time, Jason Robards was even pegged for the role of … Mr. Dark!

Bradbury had sent a copy of his original script to director Jack Clayton, but it wasn't until years later that the two men finally were able to work on the film together. In the mid-1970s, the project found a new home, this time at Paramount Pictures. Together with Clayton, Bradbury reworked his original script and, for a while, it looked like the film was going to get made. Unfortunately, the departure of the studio head caused the project to, once again, be abandoned.

Over the ensuing years, several directors successively considered *Something Wicked*. Steven Spielberg announced that he was going to direct it after *Close Encounters of the Third Kind*, but never followed up. John Carpenter and Jonathan Demme's names were also mentioned.

Finally, in the summer of 1980, Peter Vincent Douglas took the project to Walt Disney Productions, where new studio head Tom Wilhite was eager to change Disney's image and break into new areas of filmmaking. A preliminary agreement was reached, and a $10 million budget was allocated to *Something Wicked*.

Several directors were considered for the project. Among those were Tony Scott (*The Hunger*), David Lynch (*Elephant Man*), and Carroll Ballard (*The Black Stallion*). But it was finally Jack Clayton who was asked to direct. In the course of a meeting, he managed to overcome some of Disney's executives initial reticence, and found himself, for the second time, in charge of *Something Wicked This Way Comes*.

But Clayton wanted some changes, and brought in British writer John Mortimer (*The Innocents*) to help him polish Bradbury's script. But before the film was over—and even after it was wrapped—there would be changes, deletions and reshootings.

Scenes trimmed from the final print include a sequence in which Will and Jim run to the sheriff's office and attempt to convince him of the danger. In an effort to streamline the story, Disney cut a scene where Will and Jim try and convince the sheriff that the town is in danger and a dream sequence where Will and Jim see themselves in two small yellow coffins, pulled by the dwarves and the donkeys in the carnival's parade.

The ending of the film was also streamlined. In his script, Bradbury shows the village residents restored to their normal state, and the carnival's train leaving town, puffing off in the distance, not completely defeated. An ominous sticker proclaiming "Returning Soon by Popular Demand" is seen glued over Mr. Dark's carnival posters.

More important, Disney deleted a crucial conversation between Mr. Halloway and Will. In this scene, Will goes up his "escape route" and invites his dad to do so as well ("I don't want to ditch you"). Mr. Halloway then tries to go up the ladder, but cannot succeed until Will helps him. ("A smile is the best answer to everything.") This is the first meaningful father/son contact in the story. The deletion of this scene angered Clayton and Bradbury, but their objections were ignored.

Lastly, the beginning and the ending of the film were framed by an off-screen narration by Arthur Hill, as a grown-up Will. These were written by Bradbury and included only after some arguments with Disney.

Somehow, though, the magic of Bradbury's prose did not make the translation to the screen. And, despite some strong performances by Price and Robards, audiences were unimpressed and so were the critics. Even Bradbury himself was disappointed. Still, it ranks as one of Disney's first adult features and broke ground for a slate of more mainstream films that pushed Disney once again into the forefront of motion pictures in the late eighties.

SOMETHING WICKED THIS WAY COMES INTERVIEW WITH RAY BRADBURY

It is an undisputed fact that Ray Bradbury is one of the most prolific and famous living science fiction authors. He has, to date, published three novels, five collections of poetry, twelve screenplays, and over one thousand short stories. Even those who do not consider themselves to be lovers of the genre know his name. In many cases, when a science fiction fan is asked to recommend a first choice for an uninitiated reader, it is Bradbury's *The Martian Chronicles* that is suggested.

Ray Bradbury was born in 1920 in Waukegan, Illinois. This small town background played an important role in the author's writing. Indeed, the Green Town of *Something Wicked This Way Comes* is only a slightly mutated version of Bradbury's own home town.

When he was 14, Bradbury and his family moved to Los Angeles, California, where he spent part of his adolescence selling newspapers. When he was 21, he sold his first story, *Pendulum*, to Super Science Stories. After that sale, his name was frequently seen in science fiction magazines of the day. It was also seen on a story called *Lorelei of the Red Planet*, published in Planet Stories, which Bradbury had written with Leigh Brackett.

The red planet was to become further associated with the Bradbury name, as in 1950 his collection of stories, *The Martian Chronicles*, was published. The early fifties also marked the beginning of Bradbury's association with Hollywood. Although, according to the author, he was already an avid film-goer as a young boy. He says that by age ten he was seeing a dozen movies a week, and that Lon Chaney was his favorite performer.

"I've been movie-struck since I was two," says Bradbury. "I'm a child of the movies, and I've seen just about every film ever made, my favorites thirty or forty times." In fact, the author states that his middle-name, Douglas, is owed to actor Douglas Fairbanks.

In 1952, Bradbury was asked to rewrite the script for *The Beast from 20,000 Fathoms*, which was the beginning of a long friendship with Ray Harryhausen. The same year, he wrote a screen treatment called *The Meteor* (and later several other titles) for Jack Arnold, which eventually became the classic *It Came from Outer Space*.

In 1953, Bradbury published *Fahrenheit 451*, which was filmed by François Truffault in 1966. Three years later, he wrote the script of *Moby Dick* for John Huston. By then, the name of Bradbury had become famous, and his work started to be more widely adapted. Al Feldstein drew several of his short stories for the *E.C. Comics*. Alfred Hitchcock bought eight Bradbury scripts for his television series, "Alfred Hitchcock Presents."

Rod Serling acknowledged Bradbury's influence on him, and in fact, gave his name to characters in several of his early scripts. "Twilight Zone" produced "I Sing the Body Electric" in 1962, and purchased two other scripts, "Here There Be Tygers" and "Miracle of a Rare Device," which, unfortunately, were never produced. "I Sing the Body Electric" was remade for NBC in 1982 as "The Electric Grandmother," and drew much praise, including the author's.

Other adaptations of Bradbury's work such as the 1969 *Illustrated Man*, and the 1980 *Martian Chronicles*, have not been as well received by Bradbury. However, he expresses pleasure with the way that *Something Wicked This Way Comes* has turned out.

Q: Where did you first get the idea for *Something Wicked*?

RAY BRADBURY: I've been madly in love with carnivals, circuses and magicians since I was a kid. I learned in high school to begin to word associate, and out of that came ideas and stories. No one told me this, it sort of grew. Then, through my twenties, I learned to go to my typewriter everyday and put down everything that came to my head. I made a list of nouns such as, "the night," "the basement," "the closet," "what's in the closet," "the skeleton," "the old woman," "the witch," etc …. Then I said, "Why don't I write a story about each one of those nouns?" So, somewhere along the line, I made notes about carnivals, magicians and locomotives passing late at night.

When I was seven years old, one of my cousins died, way out in the farm country. At three in the morning, I'd wake up and hear a locomotive passing by. For me, that was like the sound of the dead going by in the night. I never forgot that. When I think of it even today, it still chills me. So, in my late twenties, all this came together in a short story I wrote, entitled *The Black Ferris*.

Q: How did *Something Wicked This Way Comes* come to be the title of the novel?

RB: I think it was one of those fabulous accidents. It went through four or five other titles. First, it was *The Black Ferris*, then it was called *Dark Carnival*. I was going through *Macbeth* one night, rereading the witch's scene, when, all of a sudden, I just looked at that line and thought, "My God! Of course, this is it!"

Q: Do you perceive Mr. Dark as being inherently evil, or someone that lives a life that is perceived by others as evil?

RB: *Something Wicked* is a novel about life, period! Everyone in it plays some role which is a part of life itself. Mr. Dark, for instance, isn't truly a character. He is those things in life that tempt us to destroy, or hurt ourselves or others. The two boys are me. The father is a combination of my father and myself. Mr. Dark, too, is me, moving in a direction I hope I never move in. Everyone in the book is me, at twelve, at thirty at forty, at sixty. They are all some part of my subconscious acting out the temptations that come at each age. Like when you're very old and you think "Somewhere up ahead, I'm going to die!" That's when Mr. Dark comes to you.

Dark is indeed evil, because he's offering to make you younger. He shouldn't be making you that offer, and you shouldn't even be thinking about it. But we're all tempted to be fools, by our sexuality, by our rampant murderousness, which occurs inside our head and which, if we're not careful, gets out in the open ....

Q: Are Mr. Dark and *The Illustrated Man* the same person?

RB: No they're two different people. In the original short story, *The Illustrated Man* had all kinds of problems, brought on by his bad marriage. Then, he finally kills his wife. Both were inspired by a real Mr. Electrico that I met when I was twelve years old, He worked in a carnival, Dill Brothers Greater Combined Shows—combined out of what, I never found out! Mr. Electrico was very kind to me, and I've repayed him by making him the villain in my novel all these years later!

Q: Do you see *Something Wicked* as a story with a message?

RB: *Something Wicked* turned out to be a metaphor for the total experience of being born, growing up, growing afraid, getting sick, growing old and dying. I didn't know that when I wrote it. Thank God I didn't know it, because that's why the book works.

I wrote the novel without knowing what I was doing. That's really the only way to write anything. You should just have a blind intuitive emotion about something. Of course, you should also have a direction, such as wanting to scare yourself, or an idea that is special. For example, you could start with, "Open the trap door, climb up in the attic, and go in to see what's in there." You could give that to a class of students and you'd get some very interesting stories, because we each have our own idea of what's waiting up there. Maybe nothing, maybe something horrible, maybe something beautiful, who knows?

I learned a long time ago not to care where I was going, as long as I had an idea. For instance, I wrote a short story recently called *The Banshee*. I've been thinking about it for twenty-nine years. It started with John Huston trying to scare the hell out of me, when I lived in Ireland writing *Moby Dick* for him. We were in this lonely old country house out beyond Dublin. Sometimes, we'd be there alone, and we'd sit around the fire at one o'clock in the morning and drink. Suddenly, there'd be a sound outside the house. John would say, [imitating John Huston's voice] "Ray, hear that, kid! You know what that was? That's the banshee, Ray! That's the voice of the dead predicting a death in the house sometime in the next twenty-four hours!" I'd say, "Oh, come on John!" And he'd answer, "Oh, no, Ray. It's real! Don't go outside, whatever you do!" Now, the story has all this dialogue in it from Huston.

Q: Hadn't you originally conceived *Something Wicked* as a screenplay before you turned it into a novel?

RB: Yes. I did it for Gene Kelly. I'd always admired his work. Twenty-four years ago, he started to direct. One night, I went to a screening for *Invitation to the Dance* at MGM. When I came out, I was in tears. I get these frustrating feelings of wanting to work with certain directors. I made a list of five people like David Lean, Gene Kelly, John Huston, Carol Reed and Billy Wilder. My list is very small because there are not that many directors in the world that I've wanted to work with. I've been lucky to work with two of those over the years.

Anyway, I went home and went through my files and found *The Black Ferris*. I did a seventy-page screen treatment of it and took it over to Kelly. He thought it was great and said he wanted to direct it. I told him it was his. He could take it and come back when he had some money, and we would make a deal. He went to Europe and rummaged around, but he never could get any money to make the film. So, he brought it back to me and said he was sorry. I figured, what the heck, and wrote the novel.

It took me two years and was published in 1962. Then, not much happened for eight or nine years. I guess the final product we have here is the result of twenty-five years of believing in something. I guess that's true for a lot of films.

Q: When you decided that you wanted to sell the rights to the novel for film, did you always want to adapt it yourself?

RB: Yes, I always made that a part of the contract. It's too precious to me .... I spent too many years on it not to have that kind of control.

Q: Before you started to work on the script with Jack Clayton at Paramount, didn't you do a version for 20th Century–Fox?

RB: I did a version for Chartoff-Winkler who, at that time, were at Fox. I don't know if they were going to try and do it there or not. It was ten or twelve years ago. We also talked to Spielberg, Sam Peckinpah and Mark Rydell. They were all interested at one time or another, then for whatever reasons, time passed and they all disappeared.

Jack became involved in *Something Wicked* because I had showed him a copy of the original novel when it came out. So he's known the genesis of this whole thing. Funnily enough, at the time, I had also sent a copy to Walt Disney. I have a letter in my office saying how much he liked the book, but he felt that it wasn't quite the sort of material that his studio could use!

Q: What happened at Paramount, and how did you come to do *Something Wicked* at Disney?

RB: It's a long story. We had David Picker as our producer at Paramount. He was wonderful, and a very nice gentleman. He stayed away and let me get the screenplay finished. Every afternoon, I'd hand in five pages of script to Jack Clayton. We'd sit and talk about it, have a couple of brandy and waters. When the day was finished, I'd go back and do more for the next day. I finished the screenplay in four or five months. It was a very happy relationship.

But then, we got caught in a political gunfight between David and Barry Diller, who was the head of the studio. I don't know Mr. Diller, so I can't have an opinion on him personally. All I know is that we got shot down. Anything one liked, the other wouldn't. So what do you do in a situation like that? You leave. That's what we did.

It took us many years to get reorganized. In the meantime, Jack had gone back to England. Finally, about two years ago, the

Disney people showed up in our lives and said they were looking for something unusual. I said, "Great!" because I've always wanted to work at Disney since I was a kid. I think Walt Disney is one of the greatest men of our century, on many levels. That's all cliche opinion, but nevertheless, over and above the cliche, I still think it's true."

Q: When and where did you meet Peter Douglas and get involved with him?

RB: I met Peter when he was a kid, at his parents' house. His father at one time owned "The Martian Chronicles" for a TV series. Then, at various times over the years, we met briefly for a few hours, maybe once in five years. Then, all of a sudden, the boy is grown and we pass in the street when he's nineteen. Out of that collision, we start talking about directors, and we both name Jack Clayton. So, he calls Jack, and Jack without being given his lines says, "There's a book I've always wanted to do, it's *Something Wicked This Way Comes*." So there was a wonderful collision of taste!

Q: Why do you think it's taken so long to get this film made?

RB: Look at the history of fantasy and science fiction films. How come more good SF films weren't made earlier? The film *2001* was really the big breakthrough. If you go back in time, great horror films, too, are sparse. Certain ones are a lot of fun, *The Cat and the Canary, Phantom of the Opera*, and what have you. But that's all.

This is because the role of fantasy has been totally misunderstood by teachers, by librarians, by professional intellectuals, who are all afraid of it. I don't know how many times in my life I've had people say to me, "Fantasy is bad for you. Imagining things is bad for you." How can it be bad? The inability to imagine things seems to be the lot of many people who don't know what the function of the imagination is. Since they don't understand it, they're afraid of it. And when you're afraid of something, you don't make a film about it!

That's true for science fiction too. Science fiction has always been looked upon as a toy-oriented, ridiculous nonentity. But it's really the center of all of mankind's activities, from the cave to here. All our toys have been created in the caves, have come out of the caves, and been turned into big machines. First, we have the war machines, and out of the war machines come the peace machines.

So you have this wonderful symbiotic relationship between progress, war and creativity, which we must all accept as part of our history. Refusing to realize that *Buck Rogers* and *Flash Gordon* are part of this dreaming ourselves into being and becoming, has caused the lack of trying to make good science fiction films.

So, thank God for the young producers and directors that have come along in the last decade and said, "I don't care what anyone else says, I care about these toys, and all the people I know do too." They are going to dominate the film industry, which is all to the good. In fact, they already dominate it. They have become their own producers and they're having fun! I hope they take the whole thing over, because then we're all going to have fun for the rest of our lives.

Q: Do you think that, aside from it being fantasy, one of the reasons that it took so long to clinch a deal for the film has to do with the poetic nature of the book?

RB: Years ago, one of the great days of my life, Gerald Hurt, the philosopher and writer, introduced me to Aldous Huxley. This was in November of 1952. I was terrified. I'd read everything of his. One of the first things that Mr. Huxley said to me was, "Do you know what you are? You're a poet. Gerald, bring the book over, let's read something for Mr. Bradbury." So he brought *The*

Martian Chronicles over and Mr. Huxley read me a paragraph of my own book and said, "My dear young man, that's poetry." What a dear thing to do!

So what you've said is true. I've always been in love with the great poets, and it shows in my work. Shakespeare's with me every week of my life. There isn't a week that passes where I don't read at least one page of *Hamlet*, or a scene from *Richard III*, or go back to Alexander Pope.

But poetry and movie scripts are identical. The more I've written for the screen, the more I've realized that my knowledge of poetry has been very helpful. Poetry is compact metaphor, image, and that's what screen is. Poetry and movies are closer together than any other art forms, except painting and advertising art.

Q: Are there many changes now between the book and the film, and was it hard for you to cut certain things?

RB: Well, some things are missing that I would still like to have in, like I wish we had more of the Dust Witch. But I suddenly realized that my book was very long, and that I couldn't possibly cram everything in the film. Although, on occasion, I've been very hard-nosed, I've also understood that you have to help your director, or he has to help you, to say good-bye to certain things that just could never be in the film.

Let me give you an example of what I'm talking about. Eugene O'Neill is a very difficult author to do, not only on the stage, but almost impossible on the screen. If you do *Mourning Becomes Electra*, for instance, you've got murder, suicides, incest, abortions, etc. It's like a carnival! On the stage it works because stage is fantasy. But on the screen, which is a realistic medium, with all that drama, you'd start laughing because it'd seem funny. With O'Neill, if you're not careful, tragedy turns into farce. You have to find ways of compacting him down so the audience doesn't have time to think of how ridiculous this is.

That's the same reason why it's so hard to do fantasy or science fiction well on the screen. It has to be perfect. When a rocket ship lands, you can't let down the platform on some ropes. When you do monsters, the more you put them in the shadow, the better they work. If you start bringing them out, they've got to be ten times better.

That's one of the problems I've faced in *Something Wicked*. The novel is so rich in detail. In fact, some of my friends said I put in too much. You can't put it all on the screen, because you don't have enough room. And, even if you do, after a while, people are going to start laughing at you. There are two points now in the film where you're allowed to laugh. I'm trying to make sure that they stay in, so that the audience gets a chance to relax for a second, and they won't start laughing on their own elsewhere.

Jack made me boil the script down from 240 pages to 120. That was really a very intense experience. That was difficult to do, but great fun. It was like an adventure because it took so much time to cut it down to the essence.

Q: How do you feel about the "spider" scene being used in place of the scene in the book where the Dust Witch flies overhead in the balloon?

RB: Part of it is still there. You still have the sense of the Dust Witch flying over in a balloon. In fact, the cloud sort of looks like one. I would still like to have experimented with a balloon. But, now that the scene's in place, I think it works. The spiders are wonderful and frightening. You really get the same effect. As long as you get the same result, then you haven't hurt the film in any way.

Jack Clayton said to me about that scene, six years ago, "I don't think I can make that work. I'm so afraid people are going to laugh for the wrong reason." I told him I could accept his opinion because he's the director. I just had a feeling about my

Dust Witch because I love her. But that doesn't mean I believe it would have worked. I think it's very important to make that clear when I discuss the missing witch. Either of us could be wrong and either of us could be right. But when you're in doubt, you'd better leave it out. You don't want to destroy your film.

Outside of that, there's very little that I can really say I'm sad about missing. There are quiet, philosophical things in the novel that I wish we could have put in if we had time. But, I'm not sure they're cinematic. Past a certain point you certainly cannot do them.

Q: Other than the script, what other controls did you have? Were you involved in casting?

RB: Only indirectly. I talked to Jason Robards ten years ago, when I was discussing the film with Peckinpah. He was always my choice. It's so great to wind up with one of your heroes. Jonathan Pryce, of course, is wonderful. I just hope that, a year from now, he'll get some sort of recognition for his role as Mr. Dark. The scene in the library is one of the best scenes by any actor I've ever seen in my life. And it hasn't a thing to do with the fact that it's my film!

Q: Did you go on the set often when they were shooting?

RB: I've never visited a set so often in my life. I was there two or three times a week because I felt I was home. I loved to sneak out there at sunset on my own, just stand up in the band cupola and be sentimental and, I suppose, soapy. But it was just great to be surrounded by this small town.

Q: Did you have any input while they were shooting or did you keep your own counsel?

RB: Once a film gets started, it's no longer the writer's. First of all, once you pick the director, that's it. If you have the chance to select a director, then you shut your mouth. You either trust him or you don't. If something goes terribly wrong, of course you should speak up. But as with Carol Reed and Truffault, you've finally got to trust them. They've got to know what they're doing and they've got to make their own mistakes.

My relationship with Jack Clayton has been very good. We see eye to eye. I'm sure that we have diverged here and there, ten percent of the time. That's not a bad percentage though. What's important is what the film really means. If he comes up with a better way to tell things, then I'm always very open.

Q: How do you feel about the addition of special effects, and all the gore they use in films today?

RB: As far as the effects are concerned, everything I've seen is excellent, so I don't mind at all. You get trepidations about these things. The scene in the library is the best example. When I heard they were going to "enhance" it, I really was afraid. But I have to admit I was totally wrong. It's so subtle and beautiful that the whole thing is given an extra five to ten percent.

For the gore, we learned from the past that the greatest movies have had implied violence and implied blood, and because of this, they were even more terrifying. You really don't need all that. We had a scene in the film with a little blood. We all looked at it and realized that we didn't need it, so we took it out. It was on the screen for seven seconds and we left one second.

Q: Do you think it's hard to satisfy an audience that's looking at a film that is made from something that they remember and love?

RB: Sure! You're working uphill! If you're dealing with a book where a million people either bought it or borrowed it from somebody, that's a hefty number of people to satisfy. And there are always people who have memorized portions of it. If that portion is missing, you're in big trouble.

But I can't afford to be concerned about it. You can't afford to worry about anything when you write a play, a book a screenplay or make a film. You can't afford to think about it or you go crazy. As long as Jack and I generally see eye to eye and the studio agrees, that's what's important.

Q: How does *Something Wicked* compare with your other film writing experiences?

RB: I haven't made that many films. I think that, in the case of *Something Wicked*, there's a huge step up. I did a film called *Picasso Summer*, fourteen years ago, for Campbell, Silver, Cosby and Serge Bourguignon, the French director. It was so bad it was never released. They didn't follow the script at all. They just tore it up every day and ad-libbed it.

I've also had films like *The Illustrated Man*, which are kind of just half there. The photography is lovely, the music is great, casting is very fine. But the final product can be summed up in the words of a little boy who staggered up to me following the first night opening, and said, "Mr. Bradbury, what happened?" That boy was right. Something had happened during the making of the film. He was smart enough to see it, and the studio wasn't.

The Martian Chronicles, on the other hand, was mainly boring! I liked the scenes with the priest on Mars, the fire balloons and the appearance of Christ in the church late at night. It was too long and needed cutting, but the metaphor is so beautiful. When I wrote the original short story, I was so touched at the idea. I wanted to evoke in the readers the feeling of this young priest who had always wanted to meet Christ. He joined the church so he could be ready for the Second Coming. Wouldn't you like to be there if He ever does show up again? Of course you would.

Then, I loved the scene at the very end where the Martian and Wilder speak on the edge of the dead city, and they each see a different thing. That's lovely. If the whole film had been that good! That's what drives you mad. All of a sudden it goes into focus and you want them to keep doing it, but then, it doesn't. Then you want to kill everyone.

Lately, I've had some good luck on television, with Maureen Stapleton in *The Electric Grandmother* and Fred Gwynn in *Any Friend of Nicholas Nickleby Is a Friend of Mine*, and *All Summer and a Day*, directed by Ed Kaplan.

In the case of *Something Wicked*, I think we're well on the path, and I'm very optimistic, which is very unusual for me.

Q: How was working on *Fahrenheit 451* with Truffault?

RB: I didn't really work with him. I trusted him which, as I said, is the best thing you can do. Truffault offered me the screenplay of *Fahrenheit 451*, seventeen years ago. I said, "There's no way for me to do it." He asked why not, and I said, "Because I've just done a play version of it, which didn't work. I just think I'd be a danger to my own book. I'm too close to it right now. Give me five years, and I could come back and do it, Right now, I need a rest. I don't want to see my characters for a while. I trust you. You write the screenplay."

So I trusted him and it turned out well. It's a great romance about a man falling in love with books. A very unusual theme and, I think, one that is mostly successful. A touching, haunting film. That's the best way to describe it.

Q: Do you find it depressing to work hard on something, then by the time it gets on the screen, to find that it is not at all your project because other people interfered with your story.

RB: Yes, because I know what to do, you see. I've been around film for so many years. I'm sorry to sound so certain of myself, but I've seen everything, and I know how things can be made to work.

For *The Martian Chronicles*, for example, if the director had only asked me, I would have said "Set your camera up here; do this. Cut the cackle—don't talk too much. Use the metaphor.

Rebuild those rocket ships. They're all ugly; they all look like flying phalluses." Embarrassing. They looked like scenes out of *Buck Rogers* in 1934.

But then, you have different experiences with different people. My experience with *Moby Dick*, for example, was excellent. Working with my hero, John Huston. Working with my literary hero, Herman Melville. The film turned out very well. It's still around and it looks like it's going to be playing forever.

Twenty-five years ago, I also worked with Sir Carol Reed, who made one of the greatest films of all time, *The Third Man*. My relationship with him was a real love affair. Every afternoon, I'd turn in four or five pages of script, which he would read. He'd call me every night and say, "Ray, oh Ray, continue!" Well, you know, you'd kill for a man like that.

Q: Do you prefer adapting your own material or somebody else's?

RB: I'd like to try to do mainly my own work from now on. It takes a full year, unless you're lucky, of living with someone else's book. Then, after you know their book, you have to rewrite it to turn it into a screenplay. So you not only have to read the original novel, you also have to write your own novel based on it. Then, you have to adapt your novel and put it on the screen. Why should I do another writer this favor?

JACK CLAYTON INTERVIEW

Jack Clayton's office at the Disney Studios is far from glamorous. The shelves under the windows are filled with a haphazard collection of books and scripts. There are a few left-over Christmas cards, and an electric kettle to aid in the preparation of instant coffee, Clayton's substitute for the cigarettes that he gave up five years ago. On the corkboard over the desk is a striking, black and white watercolor created by *Something Wicked* set designer, Richard MacDonald. On either side of it are pictures of each of Clayton's two stars, Jason Robards and Jonathan Pryce.

Looking at a photograph of Jack Clayton, one imagines him to be small and rather frail. In fact, he is at least six feet in height and solid enough to defend himself in any situation that might arise. Dressed in jeans and a blue, turtleneck that almost matched the color of his slightly down-slanted eyes, Clayton appeared to fit comfortably in the California lifestyle.

Always hospitable, he was genuinely apologetic for the interruptions that occurred several times during the interview. One of these, however, provided an interesting insight into Clayton's gentle personality. Pam Grier (the Dust Witch in *Something Wicked*) stopped in to say hello. The two hugged and shared an animated conversation about their mutual hobby ... growing orchids!

Born in England in 1921, Jack Clayton has been involved in some aspect or other of film production since 1948. His early experience included serving as associate producer on several of John Huston's films, including *Moulin Rouge* (1953), and Henry Cornelius' *I Am a Camera* (1955). That year, he also directed his first medium-length feature, *The Bespoke Overcoat*, which won a prize at the Venice Film Festival.

Clayton's first full-length feature, *Room at the Top*, directed in 1958, introduced a new style to the treatment of social issues.

He followed it with *The Innocents* in 1961. This film is today considered by many as a classic of fantasy. Its mysterious atmosphere is often used as an example of the ambiance that can be created without the use of extravagant special effects.

The scheduling of Clayton's next films, *The Pumpkin Eater*, 1964; *Our Mother's House*, 1967; and *The Great Gatsby*, 1974, are a testament to his viewpoint on filmmaking. He likes to concentrate on one film at a time, and it must be a quality project to interest him.

In this respect, his long-standing involvement with *Something Wicked This Way Comes* is no different. Clayton has devoted all of his heart and talent to bringing to the screen Ray Bradbury's classic tale of fantasy. Considering the fame of the book, and the fact that it has deeply marked several generations of young adults, this has proven to be a colossal task. Yet, as he himself expresses it, Clayton is an "artisan," and it becomes apparent in this interview that he has indeed brought to the film the love and the care of an antique craftsman.

Q: When did you first get involved with *Something Wicked*, and had you read the book before getting involved in the film?

JACK CLAYTON: Too long to tell you! Almost ten years ago I was first asked by Ray Bradbury and 20th Century–Fox if I would make it. I had not read the book before, but I knew Ray's material, it never came to anything, though.

About two years later, I think, I wrote a script with Ray for Paramount. David Picker was running the production for them. Unfortunately, it didn't get made at that time, only because of the feud that was going on between Picker and Barry Diller, Paramount's chairman. Therefore, because it was David's idea to do it, it got thrown away, as most development deals do in this town!

I started again about eighteen months ago. Peter Douglas, and the Kirk Douglas family, owned it. They were very successful in selling it to Disney. At the time, I was working on another film which could only be made in the summer. By the time we completed the script, summer wasn't there any more. So Kirk, whom I love, and Peter, whom I also love, most kindly asked me to do it again.

Q: After being away from the project for such a long time, did you have any hesitancy about getting involved again?

JC: Ray and I totally rewrote the script. After seven years, that's necessary unless you're a dullard! So it was like a new project, I always loved the story. The reason that I really started with it was because I've never done any fantasy. The nearest that I've got was *The Innocents*. But this is real fantasy-fantasy. My pattern of direction is trying new things out. My first film, *Room at the Top*, created a kind of furor in England, because it was the first "kitchen-sink" film. After that, I spent two years refusing exactly the same subjects, because I don't like to do the same thing twice.

Q: You haven't made a great many films, but the ones that you've made seem to all be things that you have a special feeling for. Am I right?

JC: Yes, I don't make a film unless I've got a special feeling for it. Nobody understands that type of thing in this town. Every director is expected to produce at least one film a year. My record, which I'm not proud of, is about one every three years since I've started directing. The longest gap was between *Gatsby* and this film, which was seven years. I'm only unusual in that I'm not in it for money; I'm in it for my soul!

Q: Is it difficult then for you to think of another project while you are working on a film?

JC: That's always been one of my problems. Most directors, and very wisely for them, have at least three scripts in development with different studios. That is impossible for me, because I can't think of anything else but the film that I'm on. I'm in a strange position that I'm being asked now about a lot of other films that I'd like to make and, even after eighteen months, I don't know if I want to make them.

Q: Coming back to *Something Wicked*, I had heard that, when Barry Diller turned down your script at Paramount, you broke three windows. Could you comment about this "incident"?

JC: Well, it's old times now. It's been so many years. I have a violent temper on occasions, and know how to look after myself physically. Yes, I did break a few windows with my hands, both of them were cut and bleeding after that ... but I like that kind of stuff! I've mellowed since then. I only break one window now!

Q: When did you meet Ray Bradbury?

JC: Ages ago. I've worked for John Huston as an associate producer on two lovely films, my favorite films that I've ever worked on, not for the results, but for the doing of them. After that, John made *Moby Dick*. I was supposed to produce it, but I couldn't because I was under contract to the Wolf brothers. Ray wrote the script on that. That's how I met him for the first time. We both liked and respected each other very much from the start.

Q: Were there any problems in turning the book into a script? It is written in such beautiful, flowing language, that it's hard to imagine it being put on film.

JC: It's impossible, of course, and that's the answer! The only thing you can do, if you attempt that kind of thing, is to keep the fantasy going without the absurdities in the book. When I saw the absurdities, I mean the Dust Witch arriving in a balloon and Will shooting her down with a bow and arrow, for example—that kind of stuff is fairy tales and I wasn't interested in making a fairy story. It's total Disney. They should have done it when Walt was alive and made something beautiful out of it, like one of their classic cartoons.

I approached it in a totally different way. I wanted the fantasy, but to have fantasy—this is my theory and we'll see if I'm right or wrong—you have to dig the roots of the story deeply into reality at the start. The film starts as an ordinary little town in the midwest, and certain strange things keep happening. Although I do have the Dust Witch in the film, for example, she comes up in a series of different disguises, and other than one flash of her face, where you're not sure if you saw it or not, she's beautiful. I think it's much more interesting to have a beautiful witch. Why not? Beautiful women, and beautiful witches, can create much more havoc in the world than ugly witches or women!

Q: How many changes did you finally go through with the script, before getting to the version that we'll finally see on the screen?

JC: I can't even tell you! I think Ray said in one interview that, at the start, the script was about 265 pages! I try to use charm with every artist. He proudly showed me the results and I said he should come back the next day to discuss it. We then agreed to take ten pages out, and the next day we would take another ten pages out. Anyway, it went through an enormous process, because his first script was almost the same as the book.

Q: Obviously you have a creative ego, or you wouldn't be directing. Is it ever a problem when the writer has his own opinion about what his script should be?

JC: No, I always get along extremely well with writers. I gave Harold Pinter his first screenplay and he offered to give me a co-writer credit. But I'm not interested in being anything but a director, and I feel it's part of a director's job to not only guide, but make-up scenes. I've worked with Truman Capote and John Mortimer, all of which I'm deeply friendly with.

Q: Are there things that you threw out and that, looking back, you wish you had kept?

JC: Not that I can remember. There are many things that I shot and whose absence I regret in the him, but it had nothing to do with the script. They were little subtleties, nothing major. I think audiences are underestimated today. They can pick up subtleties as well as anybody else.

Q: Did you prefer to keep the film more realistic and have the audience think of the happenings as being possibly imaginary in the minds of the boys and of the townspeople?

JC: The townspeople are not involved really, other than that they are all caught in the net of the carnival—or a few of them are. I suppose you could say it's really through the eyes of the boys. But, normally, when you stick to that kind of device, which I didn't, it seems as though what's happening is not real. So, in the end, it's also seen through the eyes of Mr. Halloway. To be really seen through the eyes of the boys, the film shouldn't contain a scene that the boys are not in, and there are many scenes towards the end that are seen by Halloway.

Q: What kind of concepts did you toy with for the look of the film?

JC: One of my new ideas, when we came here, was that I suddenly realized that the things the boys went through wouldn't be possible today because of TV. Therefore, I put the film back to the thirties. That was really because, in my opinion, the children today are not as bright as the children of the past, and they would be sitting in front of TV instead of going out to see the carnival. It's sort of a voyage of discovery that they make which I think would be impossible with kids of today.

Q: Why did you decide that you would build the sets instead of trying to find a location that looked the way you imagined Green Town to be?

JC: Basically, because it gave us much more control, although we didn't realize it at the time since we didn't have any special effects to control. I think they also wanted it on the backlot for their future films and TV things. It's paid for itself almost three times. It's the best set on any lot in Hollywood. We shot the carnival on the Disney ranch, and the outsides and interiors of the boys houses on stage. I think it was a wise decision in the end. I think the original place was in Texas and, when we started shooting, it was just on the border of the rainy season. This way, the film was shot exactly on schedule.

I can't say enough about Richard MacDonald as a set designer. I'd heard of him, obviously, for he's extremely well known, and I'd always wanted to meet him. It was sort of love at first sight. Strangely enough, we're both English and I can't understand one word that he says! He's so English, English, English! It became a joke! But he's a great artist.

Q: In general, if you had to choose between shooting on location or on a built set, which would you prefer?

JC: It depends on the film. For this, shooting on the set. For other things, on location, I'm fifty-fifty location and studio.

Q: What did you do to try to transform to film Mr. Dark's evil nature and the evil nature of the carnival?

JC: I was blessed by a brilliant young actor, who will soon be a star, Jonathan Pryce. I saw him for the first time, three years ago, playing Hamlet on the stage. He was my perfect Mr. Dark. I hope when you see the film that you will agree. He's got such power! The enormous power that Mr. Dark exudes is very difficult for somebody like Jason Robards, who plays Mr. Halloway. At the same time that he's being weak, he has the same strength that Dark has, but in a different way. The weak man's way. There's a ten-minute scene in the library between the two of them and, thanks to their being the best in the world for the parts, it is magnificent. Actually that's the only scene from the book that's in the script in its entirety.

The wonderful thing about these two actors—and you must understand that I'm one of the directors that love my actors and have never worked with an actor I didn't love—that they were perfect for their roles.

Q: When you chose the casting, did you have Robards and Pryce in mind from the beginning?

JC: Yes, Jason was obvious and my first choice, Jonathan was also my first choice. Fortunately, I had no problem with Disney over either of them, although they hadn't even seen Jonathan Pryce. All the rest I selected from casting lists and interviews because, not being American, I don't know that much about the smaller parts. But I'm very happy about everybody that I chose.

Q: Was it hard to find boys that were right for the parts of Jim and Will?

JC: Absolutely. I must have some kind of masochistic streak in me, because I've made three films with children! I don't know if you saw *Our Mother's House*, that has seven children in it. It was lost here, but was an enormous success in France and in England, and there was also *The Innocents* .... I think I get along well with children.

Other than comedy, which I would adore to attempt, but would never do because I think it's too difficult for me, I think the next best for a director is to direct children. I almost always choose children who haven't done anything before. Therefore, they mimic me. It's quite exciting. *Our Mother's House* took about twelve weeks, and it wasn't until the third week—junked the first two—that they suddenly got into their parts. They were no longer mimicking me, and suddenly one of them would be a natural actor and take off on her or his own.

The kick that you get out of directing children is quite extraordinary. You feel that you've trained the children, and you have in a way. Ninety percent of what you get is your interpretation of the lines which they say back to you. But the odd ten percent is like a miracle, when they suddenly become actors on their own.

Q: What was the first thing you did when you started working on the film?

JC: Get Richard MacDonald, find a cameraman, find a crew. You must remember, that other than Richard, because he's English and I knew him from the past, I had no guidelines to go on. I had to take people's word on who was good and who wasn't, then interview them and rely on my instinct. In most cases, it was right.

Q: When did you start shooting and how long did it take?

JC: We started in September 1981. The actual shooting took sixty-three days. It was very, very short. You have to remember that the boys are in almost every shot, and you can only work them for four hours a day. It's very frustrating because you line up a complicated tracking shot after lunch for instance. You know you've got them until maybe four, and everything goes wrong! The lamps break, the camera breaks down and, by four o'clock, you haven't got the shot.

You send them off to be taught at every opportunity that you can. But a complicated shot could take two hours, including all of the setting up time. We had a delightful teacher, and I admire her for protecting the children and not allowing me to go over with them, but it is very frustrating to lose those two hours because where do you go from there? You have to break up that set, all the tracks, all the lighting, and go on to something else with grown-ups. Sixty-three days is too fast I think. Particularly for special effects.

Q: Did you have many rehearsals?

JC: We spent two weeks at rehearsal. With children it's absolutely essential. Without it you're lost.

Q: How did the shoot go in general, and did you feel there is a difference between working in Hollywood and in England?

JC: Yes, it was an interesting experience for me because I never worked in Hollywood before. Besides, I have a way of winning a crew over within two weeks. Even if I sound conceited, it is true. So, I think it was fine.

As regards the differences, strangely enough, I would compare New York and California. I shot half of *Gatsby* in Newport, Rhode Island. The film was basically a British film, so I had an English camera crew, assistant director and somebody else. But we were serviced from New York. Now, to compare the crew there and the crew here is quite extraordinary. They're much quicker in New York. Of course, you're talking to an Englishman who hasn't worked in any other studio except Disney, so maybe it's Disney that is slow …. In any event, I would say that we're even slower in England.

Q: Were there any amusing or interesting incidents that happened while you were filming, that you can remember off hand?

JC: I'm totally the wrong person of whom to ask this! I'm so obsessional, and although I love jokes on the set, and I love a warm happy feeling, I find it very difficult to remember jokes or any things that were funny. It takes me even longer than a woman takes to give birth; it takes me about two years to get the film out of my system. After that, you could ask me questions about any of my films and I would look at you as though I didn't know what you were talking about.

Q: Do you have a particular shooting order that you like to work with, or does it depend on the story?

JC: That is really dictated by the budget. It's a question of stage space. If you're shooting outside, you have to take the weather into consideration. Ideally, every director would like to shoot from scene one to the end, but I don't think anyone has ever done it. It is a very difficult part of filmmaking because it's only in the director's head. You shoot a film as basically the budget dictates it.

Q: How was shooting here at Disney? Were they much concerned about staying in budget, and did this affect the filming?

JC: They didn't worry me, because I was always within budget. The only department that caused me problems was Richard's. That was only because, being an artist, he insists on building everything to last. That part of the budget went way over. Otherwise, nobody can tell a director who keeps on schedule and within budget anything. Quite apart from the fact that I have total artistic rights.

The filming was not affected, at least not more than on any other film. You're always in a hurry, because you always think you're behind, or if you have a good A.D., he makes you think you're behind!

Q: Did Ray Bradbury come on the set much during shooting?

JC: He came along often with students and all sorts of people. I made it always very clear that I never wanted a writer on the set, but you can come on the set just to watch. He was very good, kissing me all the time, being very lovable, but as far as the shooting was concerned he had nothing to do with it.

Q: How was the spider scene to shoot, and didn't you find the idea of working in a roomful of spiders rather terrifying?

JC: It was my idea, because we had a scene in the original script which, due to misfortunes, didn't work. It was an enormous arm that comes across the window. As I said, due to serious misfortunes it never worked, and it looked too phony for words. We had one moment where the boys had an enormous spider on their hands, and they run screaming out. That seemed to work extremely well. So it was my suggestion to have the 500 spiders. I think it works very well in the film. We did have a few problems, with the spider dust for instance. Poor little Sean, who plays Jim, was very allergic to whatever they give off and came up with welts all over his face. So did many of the crew. But we made it work.

Actually I love all animals. I started it because the boys were interested in them the first time we shot in the caravan. I asked the wrangler—I love that expression!—if I could have it on my hand. I believe in teaching children what is dangerous and what is not. They loved it. Sean actually was more in love and asked me to give him two spiders. Then he came up with these welts, poor boy. But it was nothing frightening to them. I wouldn't do it if it was. I'm like a father to any children that I have on the set.

Q: Did you keep a spider yourself?

JC: No. But only because I keep a number of birds, plants, everything else, and there's no room for a spider!

Q: Were there any other pitfalls that you tried to avoid in adapting the story?

JC: I had a great problem when I started, because I came here thinking about Disney Studios and special effects, and openly declared that I was a director that knew nothing about special effects. I just deal in human beings, atmosphere, story, love and hate between the collection of them. I was promised at the time, and I asked at the time, for them to give me the best people that they could.

Unfortunately, and it's no blame on Disney because they were doing *Tron* at the time and they were very full of that, I was given three old men, dating back to Disney's fairy era. Every week a test came through, and it was always wrong. This is the reason why the film has taken so long. Only after a pre-dub did they realize it. After the team from *Tron* became available, and only then, did I get the special effects that the film deserves.

Q: Did that upset you?

JC: At the time, honestly, I didn't realize it, because like all directors, I'm so obsessional. Therefore, I am always concerned with the acting, the story, changing words, and "Why don't we do this or that?" I expected somebody to be looking after the special effects, in which I probably am at fault. I didn't realize what was happening until half-way through the film. Then I immediately started to bleat and cry, and almost break a window!

I was allowed to go out for certain special effects to outside the studio. But anyway, it's been rectified now, and I'm very happy with the results. The film would have been out six months ago if things had been done from the beginning.

Q: Was it a revelation for you to be working with all those special effects, especially after not having had any experience before?

JC: It's a difficult thing to answer. To be frank, there's an awful lot of overkill in special effects. Whereas my idea of special effects is a very minimum and very, very subtle thing. I hate to say it about my own film, but *The Innocents* is considered today a classic and yet, there are no special effects in it. It's all done with the audience's imagination. That's my idea of how to make a special effects film.

Q: Don't you think it's a problem with the sophisticated audiences of today, who have been raised on *Star Wars* and may not be willing to use their imaginations without seeing it on the screen?

JC: I loved *Star Wars*, but I think it's a totally different kind of media. There's nothing subtle in it. I tried to make some subtleties in this story, but whether it comes off or not I don't know.

Q: What do you think of some of the special effects footage that has been done?

JC: Because I shot them, and because they're originally my idea, I should say that I like them, but I won't. The nature of the special effects department is to make something, then tomorrow make a thousand more effects that are bigger and better. It's always trying to overkill.

Q: Do you think it's possible today to convince a studio to do any kind of fantasy without having special effects?

JC: I would say no! If you ask me that question now, I would definitely have to say no. Maybe in two or three years time, it will become possible again. Everything in film goes in phases. Look at *Tron*. I admire enormously the special effects in it but, as a film, I hate it. For me, a film has to have a story and characters. Special effects is like shrubbery around the garden. It doesn't make a film.

Now, *E.T.* is so simple. The special effects there are basically simple. But why is it such a big success? It should have been made by Disney. It's like *Old Yeller*, a boy and a dog. It's typically Disney in the right way.

Q: Having worked on a film with effects, and seeing what has happened with *Something Wicked*, would you like to make another film and start the effects from the beginning?

JC: Absolutely yes, but not for about another two pictures. I think I've told you that I always try to make something different. Something that I've never tried before. *Something Wicked* is a fantasy, I would like now to do either a love story or a thriller, or who knows. After that, I certainly would welcome with open arms a film with a lot of special effects, especially now that I know so much about them!

Q: How did you come to James Horner for your choice to do the score, and did you get involved with the scoring?

JC: He's young, and I had heard one of his scores. I just hope he'll be good. In the past I've always worked with George Delerue.

Communicating between a director and a composer, if the director doesn't know anything about music at all, but has specific ideas how it should go, can be a problem. What I usually do, and have done on this, is to substitute the mood of the music for certain sections of the film, before bringing him in. It's very helpful. I think I've done it on all my films. It's very difficult to talk to a composer. I like music, but I don't know much about it. It's very difficult for me to put into words the flavor that I want, the mood that I want. But it's easy if you can find a piece of music from Schubert, Brahms, Richard Strauss, that kind of stuff, not to give any kind of indication of the type of music, but just the atmosphere and the mood.

Q: Looking at the film in retrospect, how do you feel about it?

JC: I'll tell you after the audience has reacted to it!

Q: Does the audience's reaction affect you, and how do you feel about test screenings?

JC: Critics no, absolutely not. They love putting down anything possible because it's the easiest thing to do. I do listen to an audience. I listen, and if you can hear a pin drop, then you know that you've got them.

As regards test screenings, I think they're absolute rubbish! Sixty percent of people filling in a card are showing off to their girlfriend. Then, there is in-depth questioning, which is a hundred telephone calls at random. They ask them specific questions. I guarantee that, if you gave me a film, I could produce totally different marketing replies from those hundred people, just by the way I put the questions to them.

Q: Do you think that doing an adaptation of a book is difficult, as far as pleasing an audience that has preconceived notions?

JC: It's always difficult to do anything that is considered a classic. I personally would much prefer to have the author's okay on my film, than the audience's.

I've never been through any experience with an audience. I've had a very bad experience with the critics on *The Great Gatsby*. It's not an excuse, but Paramount thought it was the end of the world as a film, and hyped it up to such an extent that there were six pages in *Time* and four in *Newsweek*. Things like Frank

Yablans saying, "This is the final jewel in our crown!"; quotes from Bob Evans and Charlie Bluthorn. Everything that would irritate a critic. I don't blame them for slamming it. But, you see, time is a great healer, and now when it's shown on TV, I guarantee that if you went around to the same critics and asked them to have a look at it, they would write a totally different review. I had a telegram from the daughter of Scott Fitzgerald saying, "My father and I loved your film of *The Great Gatsby*." I was very touched by that.

Q: Do you like the fantasy genre in general or does it depend on the film?

JC: It depends on the film. I loved *Star Wars*, I'm getting a bit bored with the constant remakes of it. I loved *E.T.* because it was original, or Disneyish original. I hate things which are done just for the sake of frightening people. I love to frighten people, I intended to frighten people over *The Innocents*, but in an imaginative way. For instance, I didn't like *Poltergeist* because I wasn't thrilled, I wasn't frightened. I was just quite disgusted with the effects they used such as when the mother was in that pool with the skeletons. I don't think that this was necessary.

Q: If you were going to start *Something Wicked* tomorrow, instead of being finished with it, are there things that you would do differently?

JC: There always are. You always see things that you did wrong, that other people did wrong, a line here, a line there. To be truthful, I've never been satisfied with any film I've made. I've been satisfied with odd bits of them, but never the whole. I know many directors who would say the total opposite of what I'm saying. I call myself, not an artist but an artisan. No artist or artisan can ever be fully satisfied with their work. Anybody else that says they're happy with it, they're not an artist.

THE EFFECTS OF
SOMETHING WICKED THIS WAY COMES.

Something Wicked This Way Comes was originally budgeted at $16 million when Disney Productions gave the go ahead to producer Peter Vincent Douglas and director Jack Clayton. Ultimately, after some extensive reworking, the film ended up costing over $23 million.

Prior to the hiring of the cast, and the start of the shoot, which began in the fall of 1981, Clayton called in production designer Richard MacDonald to build the sets of Green Town and Mr. Dark's Pandemonium carnival. MacDonald's credits include such films as *Day of the Locust, Marathon Man, Cannery Row, Altered States* and *Supergirl*. Originally, the studio had scouted for locations in Texas and other places, but it was eventually decided to build Green Town on the Disney backlot. It took 200 men three months to build the small fictional Illinois town, following MacDonald's specifications, for a total cost of $2 million.

The carnival itself was built at Disney's Golden Oak ranch, in Newhall, California. Strangely enough, its centerpiece—the magic carousel—was not built at all. Instead, the production tracked down and renovated an authentic, 70-year-old carousel that had been in operation.

Clayton then chose cinematographer Stephen Burum, whose credits include working for Francis Ford Coppola on *Apocalypse Now* and *The Outsiders*. Burum was reportedly dissatisfied at having been hired after the sets had been built, which made his task more difficult.

Lastly, Clayton went looking for a special effects house able to manufacture the sophisticated effects required by the script (most of Disney's effects technicians were, at the time, involved in either *TRON* or EPCOT).

Reportedly, the director talked with Douglas Trumbull's E.E.G. company, but did not hire them. Clayton later said that he could not understand their language, or obtain simple answers to simple questions. This can probably be attributed to the high degree of technical knowledge necessary not only to explain how to achieve certain effects (and how much it will cost), but also to convey precisely, and to the angle, what a scene requires in terms of effects.

Finally, Clayton decided to work with what he had, and hired Alan Hall, whose credits include *Popeye* and *Cat People*, to do a number of mechanical effects on camera. Hall also ran into some conflicts, in particular with the head of Disney's mechanical effects department, Tony Lee. Lee was later replaced by Ron Tantin, which improved relations between Hall and Disney.

Something Wicked's principal photography ended in December 1981. At Clayton's request, an original score was composed by George Delerue, and a first cut was edited by Argyle Nelson. Somewhat concerned over the finished product, which did not seem to live up to their expectations, Disney decided to organize a test screening in July 1982 in the Los Angeles area.

The spectators' comments confirmed Disney's worst fears, and convinced them, rightly or wrongly, that the film could not be released as it stood. Drastic steps were to be taken if the company was to recoup its investment.

It is difficult to estimate whether the results obtained at the July 1982 test screening were indeed valid, and whether they were enough to justify major surgery on the film. Clayton disputes this, and Bradbury was reportedly happy with the first cut as well.

It would seem that the conflict centered around different expectations. Clayton's original cut certainly did not contain the big scares or multi-million dollar potential that Disney wanted.

On the other hand, it was a moodier, deeper, more sensitive treatment of Bradbury's difficult book. Whether it would have been more, or less, successful than the final version will never be known.

In any event, Disney called in special effects man Lee Dyer who, after careful consideration, proposed to add no less than two hundred optical effects, to delete entire scenes, to reshoot others, and to rescore and reedit the film. As could be expected, convincing Clayton was not an easy task, but the director finally gave up and joined the collaborative effort.

Dyer started his career at Disney at age nineteen and had worked on the studio's character animation staff for 12 years, from *The 101 Dalmatians* through *The Jungle Book*. He then left Disney to work for Hanna-Barbera and Ralph Bakshi, but eventually returned to work on *TRON*, where he had been supervisor of effects animation.

"I'd talked with Clayton around three months before the end of *TRON*," remembers Dyer, "and he'd said that he wanted me to work on *Something Wicked* because it needed effects. About one week before *TRON* was finished, I had the opportunity to see *Something Wicked*. I'd read the script and I was very excited about it, but I hadn't read the book yet. Later on, when I read the book, I thought that the adaptation was very good, because Bradbury is not the easiest thing to adapt on screen .... So I went into the movie with a couple of my assistants, and I couldn't believe this film. In my opinion, it was in an incredibly bad shape. I came out of that theater with a cloud over my head like you couldn't believe!"

Studio executive Tom Wilhite asked Dyer to write down what he thought was wrong with *Something Wicked*. "Frankly, we had a director who had done *The Innocents*, which is an absolutely beautiful film, that holds up very well, even today, but the problem was that today's movie-going audience was more 'sophisticated,'" explains Dyer. "By this, I mean that they want to see that head being chopped off, or they want to see on the screen what you're talking about, rather than implied effects. On the other hand, we were still dealing with a Disney film, so rather than using the word 'horror,' which I couldn't use, we used words like 'terrifying,' 'mysterious,' 'magical' and so forth.

"After I saw the film, I wrote Tom five pages of what I thought should be done with the movie, purely in terms of effects. I then went on a week's vacation. During that time, Jack Clayton was brought in and showed my suggestions. I understand that, at the beginning, he was opposed to what I had suggested. But by the time I got back, he'd agreed to go along with seventy percent of them. As it turned out now, he's gone along with a hundred percent of them."

Among the scenes that were deleted in a desire to liven up the film were most of Alan Hall's work, not because it was not good, but because the Disney executives felt that it was not dramatic enough.

This included the mirror maze scene, where Jack Halloway, Robards' character, is confronted by his own mortality. It had originally been done with transparent glass, laid in front of black velvet background. Behind this glass, a number of old extras, dressed like Robards, marched towards the actor. Dyer decided to replace this sequence with an entirely new scene, including many opticals. A new mirror maze was built for the occasion, and new footage was shot, including Robards, Dano, Pam Grier and the two children.

"The mirror maze scene was really bad," explains Dyer. "They didn't use any mirrors to speak of. They used safety glass with charges. They had twenty old men going towards Jason Robards from behind the glasses, then they would detonate the charges and the mirrors would just crumble. It was all very abstract. You couldn't understand it. To correct it, I had pieces of mirror made into triangular shapes and I rebuilt the whole maze. We called back the actors and reshot it entirely. We put a layer of dry ice on the bottom, so that you couldn't see the floor. The picture takes place in the 1930s, so we had to be careful in designing the look of this thing. We had to stay in period, and not become abstract or disco. So when the characters walk in the maze, the fog will give a high-pitched humming sound, so you won't hear footsteps and other noises.

"We needed to widen that maze and make it look larger. The first time, when Halloway walks in, I decided that I would put each mirror in an oval, so that when you're inside the maze, it looks like an abstract forest of black ovals, creating the likeness of tree trunks. With the fog on the ground, it was very effective. Then, we took the ovals off the mirrors, so that we would have a whole new area of the maze, with rectangular or square mirrors. Then, we had a long runway, and we could take one section off and put a fifty-fifty mirror with the camera behind it and get an infinity-like effect. We had all kinds of options and opportunities to get very strange illusions inside this maze.

"When Halloway stumbles in, you hear Dark's voice-over welcoming him. Dark then introduces the Mirror of Lust, which shows Croscetti dancing with the women. Then, something else catches Halloway's attention; it's the various townspeople waving at him .... You hear Dark saying, 'Now see yourself grow old,' and the audience will see Jason as he is, but his reflection will grow old. We'll do that through animation."

The most controversial change brought by Dyer was the addition of opticals in the "library scene." There, Dark tempts Halloway in a scene that was deemed too good to be tampered with. In that scene, Dark takes one of Halloway's diaries and tears the pages, saying "I can make you thirty again!" As he tears the pages one by one, Dyer added an interactive light on Dark's face so that, in those few frames of film, he could be seen as a demonic figure. Then, an interactive light was added to the library background, created by this page tearing. Finally, as the pages are torn out by Dark, they are seared on the edge and fall to the ground, where they once again become normal pages.

"Now, it's a very dramatic sequence, probably the best one in the picture," explains Dyer. "But I'll admit that I was afraid to touch it at first. However, I felt strongly enough about this specific effect. Done subtly enough, realistically, I should say, I thought it would just heighten the sequence. At first, Bradbury absolutely refused to let me touch it. Jack Clayton didn't like the idea either, although he did say, 'I don't like it, but I'll wait to see the first scene or two that you do before I make up my mind.' We were well into the sequence when Bradbury saw it. He went absolutely crazy. He came up to me and said, 'I told you months ago that we couldn't do this, but I think you've done just a marvelous job with it.' He was absolutely sold on it. Jack felt the same way. I think it really adds to it. When the sound effects are added, the music and so forth, it will be a terrific sequence."

Michael Wolf, effects animation supervisor, was one of the effects animator who worked on *TRON* under Dyer's supervision. He and Clint Colver, composite supervisor, were acutely aware of Jack Clayton's reservations about this latter-day addition of effects. Wolf comments, "I think Jack felt we were taking his nice, little picture, the way he had envisioned it, and doing a Hollywood treatment on it. The original list of effects was a pretty long one, and we were going to do all sorts of crazy things to it. That scared him off. When we actually sat down and started showing him effects that we were really seriously considering, he had reservations about some, because he felt that we were being given too much of a free hand over his objections, but others, he was genuinely excited about. So there's been a compromise along the way. Some of the things to which he was opposed, we've dropped, but we've won him over to some other things.

"He was having a problem earlier with not having any special effects people on *Something Wicked*, and trying to muddle his way through without the benefit of professional advice. So, in one sense, he was glad that we were coming on the picture, because now he was going to get people who knew what they were doing to enhance what he wanted to enhance. That made the group of us feel more comfortable. It wasn't so much like we were shoving this down his throat."

The library sequence was one of these scenes where Clayton had expressed strong reservations, concerned that the adding of optical effects would in some way damage or overshadow the fine performances of actors Jason Robards and Jonathan Pryce. "The studio overruled him," explains Colver, "but when he actually saw the stuff on film, then he liked it."

"I had reservations myself about doing this," comments Wolf. "I was familiar with Jack Clayton's work as a director, having studied some of his films in film school. So I thought, 'here's a classic director, and who are we to come running in here and saying we can do a better job on this film than what he's been doing.' I felt a little like we were trampling on his picture. But he's been very gracious about including us in all the discussions about how we were going to be fixing the film. He had delivered his cut, but I don't think he had been really happy with the effects part of it. The effects that they had done were just accepted because that's all he could get at the time."

For the effects team, coming in on a film that had already been shot, instead of working on it from the beginning, created its own set of problems. "It was a big inconvenience," explains

Colver. "A lot of things could have been done differently to begin with. Shots could have been done with specific effects in mind. Normally, this type of stuff should be designed in the film from the beginning, and not be attached as an afterthought. That's one of the reasons we ended up having to shoot so much new material."

Two such scenes which had to be reshot to allow the addition of optical effects were the sequence where Tom Fury, the lightning rod salesman, was being tortured by Mr. Dark, which was originally accomplished with a Tesla coil and live electricity, and the death scenes of Mr. Dark who, in Clayton's first version, ended up caught under one the carousel horses' hooves and aged to death.

"They had gone to the extent of trying to make a tinfoil dummy of Tom Fury," remembers Colver, "then, they had real electric arcs flying over that, and had tried to capture it on film. It ended up looking less realistic than what we've done with animated effects, because what we did was a lot more controllable. For the death of Mr. Dark, we had a situation there where a storm, that is the force of good, has come in to help destroy the evil character. The carousel has the power to make people older, or younger. When the lightning hits the carousel, it makes it go crazy, and Dark, who is stuck on the carousel, starts rapidly aging, while all this lightning effect is playing around him.

"Among other things, we had to figure out which shots we wanted to put lightning in, or electric arc types of effects, and figure out color and motion choreography as well. Since there are a number of these sequences back-to-back, we didn't want it to get too repetitive. Figuring out the motion was a big part of it. The rest involved the color wedging on the optical printer, and coming up with the final combined look."

The scene of the destruction of the carnival, which had originally been done on stage with mechanical effects engineered by Hall, was another that was completely redone in order to enliven the "new" version of *Something Wicked*. For this sequence, Dyer enlisted the help of Harrison Ellenshaw and Ron Tantin, who supervised the building of a miniature 20 × 24 (or a scale of 1/12th) carnival.

Harrison Ellenshaw is the son of Peter Ellenshaw, undoubtedly one of Hollywood's best matte artists (he worked on *Treasure Island, 20,000 Leagues Under the Sea, Darby O'Gill and the Little People, Mary Poppins* and *The Black Hole*). Harrison, who was also involved in *The Black Hole*, has also worked as a matte artist on *The Man Who Fell to Earth* and *Star Wars*, for which he painted the Death Star power trench matte.

The French-born Tantin started his special effects career at MGM in 1965, where he worked under the legendary A.D. Flowers. Tantin then worked in television (his credits include "The Wild, Wild West" and "The Man from U.N.C.L.E."), was nominated for an Academy Award for his work on *Ice Station Zebra*, and finally won an Oscar for *Tora! Tora! Tora!* Tantin joined Disney in 1969, and eventually became head of the prop department.

"My first involvement with *Something Wicked* was after the principal photography had been completed," says Tantin, "which was in October or November of 1982. I was approached by the production office and we had preliminary discussions on what needed to be done."

"We came up with an idea that I think works fairly well," adds Ellenshaw, "which was to convey the feeling that the carnival wasn't simply destroyed, but literally taken away by the storm, and therefore goes up into the clouds. To do that, the intricate miniature was mounted upside down, about twenty-five or thirty feet off the ground, and the camera was also put upside down, so that when we dropped the miniature piece by piece from what was in reality the roof, it looked like it was going up into the air, it was being sucked up into the clouds. We first released the miniature components one at a time for the close-ups and isolation shots. Then we backed the cameras up to get a wide master shot and we dropped everything at once."

"Rather than go for the conventional materials for the models," explains Tantin, "we went for a very light material. We used foam core, which is a styrofoam sheet, surrounded by paper on each side. We used that for the facades and all the walls. All our wood was balsa wood, because even though we wanted gravity to play to our favor, we didn't want the units to be so heavy that they would fall straight. We wanted to be able to use wind machines to direct their fall and give us a swirling motion.

Handpainting all those miniatures—some of the facades were very intricate—would have been unfeasible from a financial standpoint. Instead, we took some stills of the originals, had them blown up to the size we wanted them to be, and proceeded to cut and paste them onto the miniatures. It saved a lot of time.

"The most difficult part was to get the ground to look realistic enough to allow the cameras to close in, without the shot screaming 'miniature!' The completed shot wasn't as rough as I thought it would be, because of these stills we used on the carnival. We didn't go three-dimensional too much because of the low light that we had. It was shot in very low key, and the fact that we had a lot of debris and dust, and swirling, non-descript, chaotic pieces falling through the screen was very forgiving to us."

"We had the typical problem that you always have with miniatures," adds Ellenshaw. "That is, you have to hold focus, you have to recreate reality on a smaller scale, you have to light the miniature correctly, which is very difficult. We have the advantage that the scene took place at night. But it's also a disadvantage because at night there's no light, so you have to add light and make it look like it's natural.

"When you're working with a miniature, you also have a big problem with the depth of field because, in this case, you crank the camera at five times normal speed so everything slows down and has more scale and mass to it. When you do that, you need more light because you have to hold focus. If something is out of focus that in correct scale would be twenty feet away, then it looks phony because it would never be out of focus with a real camera."

"From the very beginning to the last drop, the destruction of the carnival took three months," comments Tantin. "It took us a month to build it, four days to shoot it right side up for the computer animation sequence that was later taken out of the final print, another five days to invert it, then we spent another week shooting that. So the actual work was really about a month to a month and a half."

Tantin also oversaw the cloud tank effects that were used to simulate the whirling storm clouds and *Wizard of Oz*–like tornado that bring an end to Mr. Dark's evil.

"The tornado effect in the cloud tank was created with fresh cold water in the tank," explains Tantin. "At first, we tried an impeller, but it agitated the water too much, and wasn't giving us what we wanted, as far as giving the outside water a slower revolution than the actual vortex. We finally decided to go with a quick draining system. Basically, what we had was a cylinder in the center of the tank, attached to the bottom drainage, and tied in line with powerful pumps. What we did was start the water circulating in motion. Once the water was turning, suction from the central system caused it to vortex in the middle, while still retaining the slower motion we were looking for at the outside.

It took maybe thirty seconds for the first vortex to appear. We could alter the shape of the vortex by altering the suction system. What we've used is a six-inch outlet, but we could have gone as far as two feet, if the pipes could have handled it."

Tantin describes the process for forming clouds. "We're working on the principle of two buoyancies, two liquids that will not separate. Since we want clarity, both liquids have to be water. The way to arrive at two waters that will not separate is that we increase the salinity of the bottom layer, making it salt water, and we also keep it cold. The top layer is fresh water, heated. The optimum temperature is a forty-degree difference. We lay our salt water down, half-way up the tank, or whatever height we want the inversion layer to be. We then stop the salt water and inject the fresh, hot water on top. You have to be careful to have a slow feed over a piece of polyethylene so that you don't disturb the layer. Then, you fill the rest up with that, and slowly pull out the plastic sheet, and it keeps the two waters perfectly separated. In fact, if you look at it through the side, if the two waters are perfectly still, it's as if somebody had put a sheet of glass right across the whole tank. They won't mix as long as you don't disturb the layer by churning it up.

"The secret of getting clouds with a different look lies in the type of injection that you do. When I say type, I also mean the pressure and the size of the orifice, which are very important. Among the chemicals we've injected in the tank are tempera paints, silver nitrates, potassium permanganate, for purple clouds, evaporated milk and liquid latex. We've gotten some beautiful results with latex, which you can color any which way you want. Each one of these materials will give you a cloud of different texture. The most successful for thick, billowing clouds was the tempera. The most successful as far as being realistic-looking was the evaporated milk.

"Because you're operating the system from the top of the tank, with the lighting, you can't really see the camera view, so we set up TV monitors on the side to help us determine the right amount of material that we had to pour into the tank, because if you have too much, it can destroy the whole look you're striving to achieve. Then, by altering the direction of the injector, we can control the direction, the speed, and to some extent, the shape of the cloud. For instance, we can have them adopt a forced perspective, coming from a very small point on the horizon and going all the way across the screen."

The water used inside the cloud tank was carefully filtered so that the resulting photography did not look like it had been shot through water. "We have a high efficiency, dual filter system," says Tantin. "We can actually get tap water from the sink and change it to crystal clear in less than two hours. We also have an external filter that we can throw into the tank itself and that can recycle the water that's in there, if we do pollute it by accident, so we don't waste a whole tankful of water. We also have two storage tanks of water, with already filtered water, so that if the need arises for some more, we'll have some ready."

Special effects such as the cloud tank require special photography. "We've been using a high speed camera to slow down the action," explains Tantin. "Because your cloud, when you inject it, especially at the beginning, really bellows at a high rate of speed. So, in order to slow it down and give you a more natural effect, we shoot it up at 120 frames per second. Actually, the speed depends on what effect you're after. Afterwards, it took two hours to clean the tank, and an hour to set it up again. So for the vortex, we needed a crew of five men to physically form it, and we had a back-up crew of three plumbers, and a craft service person to clean up the tank after we were done."

Ellenshaw confirms the cloud tank scene went like clockwork. "It worked sooner than we expected, so we're under schedule and therefore under budget. Frankly, we thought we'd have to play around with it for two weeks before we got any footage that was any good, but it worked just like people said it would! Those who had used cloud tanks before said we abused it, in the sense that we weren't all that careful. The first time we filled it, we were very careful to put the water in very slowly to maintain the inversion layer. After the fifth day, we were just dumping the water in, we weren't even putting the polyethylene film in between the layers and pulling it out. We just threw it in there and it worked just as well. Everybody was a little scared at first, but now there are twenty-five people on the crew, and everybody is an expert in cloud tanks!"

Another modified sequence was the scene where the Dust Witch, after having tracked the two boys home, unsuccessfully attempts to invade Jim's room. For this scene, Hall had built an eight-foot long clawed arm, which was scrapped and replaced by a scene involving 250 tarantulas attacking the film's two young heroes. Working with Tantin on the miniatures was Isidoro Raponi, who was particularly instrumental in conceiving and executing that sequence.

The Italian-born Raponi has worked in the field of miniatures and props for over twenty years. His first film was John Huston's *The Bible* in 1963, where he collaborated on scenes such as the Birth of the Universe, the Flood and Noah's Ark. Other films Raponi worked on include *The Pink Panther, Barbarella, Modesty Blaise, What's New, Pussycat* and *Andy Warhol's Frankenstein* and *Dracula*. Raponi came to the United States in 1976 to work with Carlo Rambaldi on *King Kong*. He remained there, working on *Close Encounters of the Third Kind, Nightwing, Looker* and *The Black Hole*.

"I had designed the mechanism we used for the spiders for the movie *The Hand*," explains Raponi. "The only thing I had to change was the size. I made 250 spiders in total, but only six were mechanically equiped. All the others were non-moving. For the mechanical ones, I had to make joints for the legs for the movement. The mechanism is very small, but everything was built in one week. We tried different kinds of materials, but velvet was the closest to the shiny effect of real spiders. We put some yellow-orange fur over to give the effect of the color of real spiders."

Since that scene was shot much later in the post-production schedule, Shawn Carson and Vidal Peterson had to be called back for a reshoot. An observant spectator might notice that the two boys indeed look older during the sequence.

Not all changes worked as well. For example, Dyer arranged for a sequence of computer animation to show the magical building and assembling of the carnival, to be executed by MAGI. "In Jack's version," remembers Dyer, "we had a puff of smoke that dissipated, and suddenly the circus was there. I thought that wasn't magical enough. So, at first, we were going to animate the circus and have it erect itself without human beings. Tom [Wilhite] then suggested that we go into computer simulation on this, which we did. We came up with the concept of the whole circus 'rezzing up,' like in *TRON*. The camera seems to ride on the wings of the wind. The ground undulates and forms tents. You follow the camera up in the air. As you get up, you look down on the tents, and it's like looking through spider webs. The camera drops through the webs and, on the other side, is the 'Wheel of Fortune,' spinning. When it stops, it stops on the sign of the spider!

"You then drift over through an animal cage. You see something. At first, you're not aware of it, but then you see something in the corner of the cage, with these burning red eyes. It comes lunging at you, but you never see what it is. It gives a screech instead of a howl, and comes out of the cage. The camera quickly comes through the bars, and the thing dissipates and turns back into ectoplasm. It forms back around a tree. The camera goes one and a half times around the tree, and gets up to the top. The top of the tree starts forming a ferris wheel. As that happens, we start to pull back and see the whole circus, formed. We continue to pull back and it's the kid's point of view. That is something that I understand Jack had in mind, but was not able to accomplish."

As it turned out, neither was Dyer. The entire MAGI computer-animated sequences were ultimately pulled out of the film, two weeks before its release, because their stylized look was deemed to clash too much with that of the rest of the picture. Instead, a scene using the model of the carnival built by Tantin and Raponi, and showing it fully formed in an impossible period of time, was eventually used.

Additional scenes included new footage shot in Vermont, to establish the local "color." These were completed by matte paintings of rural scenery, and were used to highlight Tom Fury's arrival in Green Town. Some of this footage involved using a double for Jason Robards. "In the first version, there were only three matte shots which had been done by the studio artist," explains matte artist Jesse Silver, another *TRON* alumni (he was background painting supervisor). "Due to the extensive changes that were being planned, and the fact that we wanted to get some location stuff on the film to open it up, it made it a whole new ball game. So the mattes which had been created for that version were replaced by the ones I did with Michael Lloyd. We've gone from three to, I think, about fifteen mattes."

Silver explains the painstaking process. "When we're doing a painting that requires rear projection, the action plate that we've taken on location, or on stage, is run from the projector and projected on the back side of a sheet of glass. We have this translucent material that acts like a projection screen, which goes over it. The painting is done in the front, and is photographed by the camera. It goes one frame at a time, and the whole thing is synched up.

"The camera is a motion control camera. It allows us to make moves on the paintings, which also help kill the stigma of it being a painting. Something standing still is a pretty good indication that it's a painting. So, if we have some action going on, as with this shot of a fellow walking down the road, we can move in on that, and that also helps sell that this is real. In this case, the computer allows us to repeat our motion, so if we were doing something that had three or four elements combined, with a painting in between to join them together, and we needed one move for that end shot, we could repeat it however many times we needed.

"With our system here—we use YCM's—there are black-and-white records of the original color negative, which are split into various color separation records. That allows us to do very nice balancing and rebalancing to get just the kind of color balance that we want. Then, I paint to that, we shoot it, we rebalance the end product, which then goes to Technicolor for finishing.

"We did have a problem with the Vermont shot, that required a little creative thought. As the camera began to move in on the painting, we found that we were getting a cone of light effect from the projector. What happened was that we had a hot spot in the center of that. And that angle of light for the hot spot changed. The result was that we were beginning to get a slightly darker edge on the background plate, so the painting appeared first in the shadows, and then, as the camera moved in, it seemed to get lighter. In fact, what was really happening was that the background plate was getting darker because the exposure is constant on the painting. What we ended up doing was writing the exposure, frame by frame, throughout the whole move, so that the whole thing is balanced beautifully. In effect, it is a very minute fade, but you never realize it."

Another of the talented craftsmen who worked on *Something Wicked* was make-up artist Bob Schiffer, who was one of the most respected professionals in Hollywood (he was often personally requested by Lana Turner, Marlene Dietrich, Burt Lancaster and Rita Hayworth) worked on a number of films including *The Birdman of Alcatraz*, *The Wizard of Oz*, *The Picture of Dorian Gray* (the 1945 version) and *The Lady of Shanghai*. Schiffer is generally acknowledged as having created the so-called "forties look" of red lips and thin eyebrows.

"After reading the script, I did numerous sketches and presentations of the characters," says Schiffer. "First, we discussed the Dust Witch. I gave Clayton every possible Dust Witch you could imagine. We went round and round about what she should look like. First, he wanted the face to look like a walnut shell, which I managed to do by taking a real walnut shell and sculpting a face out of it. We went back and forth for a long time. After all this work trying to come up with a proper Dust Witch, the irony is that they're now using my original design, which was the one I liked best."

Schiffer also designed the scene where Mr. Dark crushes Jack Halloway's hands. For this sequence, a prop arm was used. A fake bone of dental material was made to perforate a pre-cut section of fake skin. "We took an impression of Jason Robards' hand," Schiffer explains, "and then built a mechanical contraption that went down the arm. We got some chicken bones, put stabilizer in them and shattered the ends. Then, we built the hand with breakaway flesh on top of it. When you squeezed, the bone pushed right through. It was pretty impressive." According to Schiffer, the scene caused the test screening audience to gasp and, much to his dismay, was subsequently trimmed lightly for the final version of the film.

Mr. Dark's death was another of Schiffer's accomplishments. The artist worked first on Jonathan Pryce himself, then on four mechanical heads, sculpted by Stan Winston. "We did that with different appliances. Then, after the last shot of Jonathan Pryce, with all the appliances on, we took that last stage and duplicated all that on one of Stan's puppet heads, so that the audience wouldn't visually jump. The transition is perfect. From then on, we worked with these puppet heads. I did a set of storyboards and took them up to the director, hoping that he would go along with it, because I had already sculpted and made all the heads just that way.

"I asked for a week to shoot it, because that's almost the minimum time needed to get it done. Unfortunately, as it sometimes happen, the filming was over, the cameraman and the crew had left, etc. So they said no. Then, later, they changed their minds and decided to shoot the disintegration scene after all, and suddenly we had only a few days! It was the most important part of the film for me, and they only gave me three days to do it! Once we started, they got quite excited about it. I don't think the director had ever believed that the audience would ever accept a puppet head as a human, until he saw it work on the set. So it did work out in the end, but it could have worked better from my standpoint.

"What I wanted to do, and it's never been done before, was to take the skull and coat it with an impression material, which sort of cracks when it dries. I was going to mix that with clay, and then put a heating element inside the skull. Then, with stop action, photograph it with the heat element on, as the skin would start to dry, then crinkle, then fall away to reveal the skull. But they didn't want to do it."

In the end, the new, enhanced version of *Something Wicked This Way Comes* came out, to mixed critical reviews and definitely downbeat commercial results. Dyer acknowledges that making so many changes in a film after it had already been completed was far from an ideal situation, but declares himself satisfied. "It was very hard," he says. "If you're brought in at the beginning, working on a film that you know is going to rely on special effects, then as the special effects director, you should be there for the shooting, so that you can stage it in a certain way. You can't expect a live action director to realize these things. Jack was the first one to realize this, and really wanted someone from the beginning.

"I looked at this job as a real challenge. It's been a lot of fun and I'm happy with what we've done. But I don't know if I'd like to do it again. I really feel, in all honesty, that we've got a good movie that we can be real proud of."

Milton Keynes UK
Ingram Content Group UK Ltd.
UKHW010139030124
435363UK00009B/684